Umbra

Sentient Stars

Amber Toro

Salt Peach

To my Dad, who always loved my stories.
And to Octo who sat by me while I wrote these words.

AMBER TORO

PROLOGUE

HALCÓNCITA

Amber liquid streamed into the glass tumbler in front of Skyla. She waved a hand and the bot-bartender stopped. It twirled the bottle with dexterous metallic hands and placed it back on the shelf.

Skyla sighed, running her palms over the ridges of the gold patches that lined the sleeves of her UTA Navy black flight jacket that matched her military issue Z-grav boots, cargo pants, and tank top—black to match the void of space they called home. Her hands wandered from her arms to her face, pressing into her eyelids, across her cheeks, and finally over her smooth white-blond hair that was braided tight against her scalp. She dropped her hands and blinked to activate her ocular display. Her enlistment paperwork shimmered in her vision, overlaid against the liquor wall that lined the back of the bar.

Fifteen years she had served, eight spent in the Mímir Academy—her entire childhood—and another seven as an officer in the United Tribal Axis Navy. Now, her conscription was up. For the first time, she had a choice. She could decide what came next in her life; but could she really? Her mother had expectations, but Skyla didn't *have* to reenlist. She could submit her resignation paperwork and leave with an honorable discharge right now. Just the thought sent a thrill of excitement up her spine. She could walk away before the admiral exams. Her spot would roll down to the next candidate from Mímir, and she could go back to just being a pilot. She missed those days. A pilot is all she ever wanted to be. Unfortunately, the talented don't get to stay where they are comfortable.

Skyla snatched the glass of whiskey; the liquid burned on its way down. She closed her eyes to savor the feeling, then forced a breath out through her nose before returning her attention to the display. Her eyes flicked back and forth between the documents. Reenlist and make her mother happy, serve her tribe, *or* resign—and see what else was out there for her in the Known Galaxies.

"None of that here." A sultry voice broke her concentration.

Skyla blinked to dismiss the display as she turned toward the speaker. A tall man with short black curls shaved tight on the sides, with rich dark olive skin, and a mischievous look in his eyes, had slid into the seat next to her. That look he gave her—it told her everything she needed to know. He was trouble.

"Excuse me?"

He gestured toward the empty air in front of her. "None of that. Whatever you were looking at in your ocular display wasn't fun, and you look like you could use some fun." A crooked smile played across his lips.

She snorted and took another sip of her whiskey. "And I suppose *you* are fun?"

He cocked an eyebrow. "I could be."

She shook her head and drained her glass. "I haven't had enough to drink for that." She made to shift from her perch on the barstool, but he caught her arm and smiled as he reached his opposite hand to signal for the bar-bot.

"Two more."

The bot pulled out two fresh chilled tumblers and filled them to the brim.

Skyla leveled a stare at the mysterious man.

He released her arm, holding his hands up, placatingly. "You said you needed another drink." He held his glass up, waiting for her to take hers.

"I said I hadn't had enough to think you'd be fun."

"Same thing."

She shook her head but still accepted the fresh pour. He clinked his glass against hers. Yes, he was trouble, but he was also handsome, and a welcome distraction from the decision she had to make. One more drink wouldn't hurt.

"What has you so serious?" he asked.

"I thought we were supposed to be having fun?"

He smiled at that, nodded, and kicked back his drink before ordering two more. "You're right. So...what do you do for fun?" He trailed a finger over one of her patches, the one that denoted her rank, "Captain?"

She smiled and shook her head, correcting him. "Skyla."

"Skyla," he repeated. "Gabriel," he offered, as his fingers moved on to trace yet another patch.

"Flying," she said.

His brows drew together in confusion.

"You asked what I do for fun. Flying. Starships."

He nodded and moved to trace the outline of a starfighter patch. "This one?"

"That one is from the first time I won the Leikar Cup."

"The first time?"

"I won the next three years, too."

"And then?"

"And then I was promoted, and wasn't eligible to compete." The memory left a sour taste in her mouth, which she chased away with more whiskey. She had forgotten how much she loved competing in the Leikar Cup. It was an obstacle course race, with elements that included both flying and physical challenges. She had been unbeatable.

"And this one?" He traced the outline of another patch.

"My call sign. It was a type of falcon on Earth That Was."

A grin twisted across his lips. "Halcóncita...it suits you."

She shook her head, but couldn't keep a smile of her own from tugging at her lips. "You don't know me."

Gabriel's voice dropped low as he shifted closer. "I'd like to."

That look in his dark eyes told her everything she needed to know. If the look wasn't enough, the living-ink phoenix tattoo that extended across his neck spelled it out in bold, dark lines. But maybe she wanted a little trouble.

She shrugged. "No time for that. I'll be shipping out in the morning, if I re-up." The decision came crashing to the forefront of her mind once again.

"Ah, there's that look again. You're trying to decide if you'll re-enlist."

Instead of answering, she took another drink.

"You don't want to though," he stated. It wasn't a question.

Was she so transparent that a stranger in a bar could read her?

"Then don't."

"It's not that simple."

"It is, though. It's not what you want. It's painted all over your face. There is a whole universe beyond the UTA."

"Not for me."

"There could be."

She hesitated, thinking of what it would be like to be free. To fly off to wherever she wanted. To have adventures like the stories her dad had told her when she was young—before she left for the academy and he left for good. Her fingertips traced the gold Vegvísir pendant at her neck, the motion a practiced habit. The necklace was the last thing her father had given her, and she never took it off. Her eyes drifted up and caught on his. They were dark and mysterious, and right now she would rather drown in their depths than deal with this decision.

"I don't know a life outside of the UTA."

Gabriel shifted closer—so close that his lips brushed against the shell of Skyla's ear as he whispered, "Then let me show you."

CHAPTER 1 | HINATA

TO THE VICTOR GO THE SPOILS

The bridge of the destroyer shifted under Hinata's feet as the shields absorbed a barrage of blasts. He barely registered the impact, feet firmly planted, broad shoulders squared toward the main display, with arms clasped behind his back.

His gunners had already neutralized the starfighters during their flyby. Now, his focus was on the star charts. He had his adversary down to one functional ship. Their last destroyer was pinned between his fleet and an asteroid field. He had placed several starfighters just inside the rim of that asteroid belt. The belt gave off enough interference that the enemy ship wouldn't be able to get a clear reading—Hinata's starfighters were ghosts in the noise. His enemy had no idea what was waiting for them inside that asteroid field if they were brave enough to enter.

"Open a comm line to the *Ormen Korte*," Hinata ordered. The star charts vanished as the comm line was initiated, but the screen remained blank.

"No response, sir," the comms officer replied. *Freyja was going to play this out to the last.* Just as the thought passed through his mind, the *Ormen Korte* did a high-G rotation and burned away from the asteroid field and Hinata's fleet. First rule of space warfare: never forget that you are operating in a three-dimensional space—but Hinata never forgot the rules. His eyes ablaze with intensity, he took his captain's chair, calm and calculated.

"Pursue," he commanded as he engaged his high-G restraints. His crew were trained to perfection, drilled until every cog knew their place in the machine, until they were an extension of his own hands. Within seconds, his ship was on the tail of the *Ormen Korte*. She was headed toward a nearby moon—maneuvering to place it in between their ships, no doubt. Unfortunately, for the *Ormen Korte*, Hinata had anticipated this move. He gestured to his comms officer to give the signal. As the *Ormen Korte* approached, a cluster of his starfighters emerged from the moon's shadow. Hinata had also thought the moon an excellent place to hide his forces. The *Ormen Korte*, however, did not slow its approach.

"What are you up to, Freyja?" Hinata whispered to himself. "Bring up scans of the *Ormen Korte's* hull," he demanded, as his eyes scanned the enormous expanse of the stardestroyer, looking for any signs of what Freyja was planning to do with her last ship. Except for a few fresh scorch marks and dents from the battle, she was in excellent condition, one of the finest ships in the United Tribal Axis. He wasn't sure what he was looking for, but he would know it when he saw it—*there! That's it.*

"Shields up, divert all power to the forward array!" he shouted. As the words left his mouth, a blinding light erupted from the small pink globe of crackling energy that Hinata had spotted on the belly of Freyja's ship. Following the light was a tsunami of energy that tossed his massive destroyer like it was a toy boat in a tidal wave.

His ship groaned under his feet, but he was certain all of her systems were still intact. The tight training of his crew had saved them from the worst of it—had they not been an extension of himself, there was no way they would have responded to his commands in time. The viewport flicked back to life. Unfortunately for his starfighters, the command had come too late. They drifted aimlessly in space, like little pieces from a child's game that had been discarded. Hinata shook with rage. Atomics, even at a small scale like this, were banned by the United Tribal Axis. What game did Freyja think she was playing? If any of his pilots lost their sight over this stunt, there would be hell to pay. That was a mess he would have to clean up after the battle; it was time to finish this.

"All power to the plasma cannons. Take out their shields, now!" The atomic burst would drain the *Ormen Korte's* power. It would be several minutes before she could bring her shields to full strength again. There was no escape. Three large blasts hit across the *Ormen Korte*, each igniting a small explosion at the impact site.

"Their shield array has been destroyed, Commander," his gunner reported.

"Take out their weapons and prepare a boarding party," Hinata smashed the release mechanism for his restraints, shouldering his katana as he stood. If Freyja wanted to play this out to the bitter end, then he would happily oblige. He stormed out of the bridge, two of his lieutenants following closely behind.

"Tax, prepare to take control of their ship's systems as soon as we breach. Seal their doors and create a direct path for us to the bridge. I don't want any delays. We will cut this off at the head," Hinata said.

"Yes, Commander," Tax, Hinata's second in command, responded.

"Callan, you're in charge of the boarding party. Keep it clean."

"Yes, Commander," Callan replied.

Mechlock doors sprung open ahead of Hinata and his lieutenants, where twenty of his soldiers stood ready in armored spacesuits. He nodded his approval.

"We end this now. Remember the rules of engagement. We will make quick work of the *Ormen Korte* and return with honor," he spoke with the air of command. His soldiers responded, thumping their fists against their chest plates, and stamping their booted feet in time with the rhythm. The beat built until it hit a frenetic pace, culminating in a collective, "Oorahh!"

A shudder ran through Hinata's boots as his ship aligned with the *Ormen Korte* for boarding. He nodded to Callan. It was time. The boarding party swiped the controls at their collars. Helmets emerged, sealing and pressurizing the suits. Callan took control of the boarding party with the undeniable air of experience. As soon as the outer airlock opened, his soldiers got to work. In under a minute, their laser torches cut through the outer hull of the *Ormen Korte*. They rushed through the breach, securing the corridor on the other side.

Tax's fingers flew through the air above the datapad at his forearm. "Ship's systems are ours."

"Make me a path," Hinata ordered.

Tax nodded in acknowledgment, his focus back on the datapad. Hinata led the charge, his soldiers close behind. They encountered little resistance on the way to the bridge. Tax sealed all access to the corridors they traveled. The only opposing crew members they encountered were those unfortunate enough to be in their path when the doors had been sealed. It was only a matter of minutes before they reached the bridge. Unlike those of the corridors, the mechlock doors of the bridge did not snap open at Tax's command.

"They've sealed themselves in, Commander." Tax looked up from his datapad, awaiting orders.

"She just doesn't know when to admit it's over, does she?" Hinata said. "No matter, cut it open."

Laser torches were brought from the hull breach and put to work. The bridge doors were reinforced to buy command more time in the event of just such a boarding—but no one was coming to help the *Ormen Korte.* They were just delaying the inevitable. When the last cut was made, Callan gestured for his soldiers to step back. Hinata stepped forward, his two lieutenants following closely behind as he kicked the compromised barrier with his thick shielded boot, sending a chunk of door flying into the bridge.

The crew of the *Ormen Korte* sat frozen in place at their stations, wide eyes focused on the ominous figures in the breach. Three shielded warriors stood in a cloud of smoke, the smell of burning metal surrounding them. Their armored spacesuits were pitch black, with a shimmer of deep space, gold writing in an ancient language written down the right arm. Hilts of katanas sat just above their left shoulders.

Hinata stepped over the threshold and walked slowly toward the captain's chair. His lieutenant commanders followed, along with the rest of his boarding party, to secure the *Ormen Korte's* crew. Standing at the center of the bridge was a figure dressed in a deep crimson-armored spacesuit. As Hinata approached, the figure turned to meet him. It pressed the release for its helmet, which folded in on itself again and again until it drew back into the collar of the spacesuit, revealing the woman below the helm. Her mocha-colored skin was beaded with sweat that ran down her temple, past bright hazel eyes that burned with fury. Her tight curls were shaved along the sides, giving away into a mohawk that faded from black to gold. She trained those seething eyes on him. He reached for his katana and swung it forcefully at the captain of the *Ormen Korte*, halting the blow just before the blade touched her neck.

"And now you're *dead*, Freyja," he growled. He held his blade at Frejya's neck a moment longer, before returning it to its sheath. The two commanders stood there, eyes locked, rage boiling beneath a calm surface. The red flashing warning lights stopped, and the dimmed battle lights raised, as a face appeared on the viewport. The face was that of an old battle-hardened admiral, her salt and pepper hair drawn back into tight braids against her head.

"Well done, Commanders. We haven't seen a show like that in the competency tests for admiral in over twenty years. This concludes the practical portion of your examinations. Commander Azai, Commander Nygaard, gather your troops and prepare to debrief at once." The admiral ended her transmission. Hinata's soldiers shifted their focus to their commander. He still stood at the ready, facing his opponent. Freyja also had not moved. Even with the lights raised and the simulation officially ended, everyone could feel that there was unfinished business between the commanders.

"Atomics are banned by the United Tribal Axis." Though his words were only loud enough for Frejya's ears, they were laced with dangerous intent. "If *any* of my soldiers are permanently disabled from your little stunt, I will hold you personally responsible."

Frejya's mouth twisted into a nasty sneer. "So obsessed with honor, Hinata, but I am here to win. If that means bending the rules a little, so be it. You heard the admiral. Get off my ship." She spat the words at him.

He took a deep breath to regain control, then straightened, did an about-face, and motioned for his soldiers to fall in behind him.

As he approached the broken bridge doors, Freyja called out after him, "And Hinata, don't worry too much about those starfighters. They'll be just fine. No one wants to report to an admiral who blinded her own soldiers on her way to the top."

He clenched his fists at his sides for a brief moment, then allowed the tension to bleed away as he exited the bridge.

CHAPTER 2 | FREYJA

ONLY A PAWN

The captain's quarters on the *Ormen Korte* were beyond decadent. This much space dedicated to one person on a starship was unheard of. Freyja felt exposed as she spun around, taking in her new living space.

In one corner, there was a bed far too large for one person, covered in black silk and stacked with too many pillows. A seating area with stuffed black leather couches and armchairs clustered around an ornate area rug took up the other corner. There was a private dining area and WC as well. She had never had so much room to herself, having left for the Mímir military academy at ten years old, and she had been sharing bunks, mess halls, and bathrooms with her fellow soldiers ever since.

"Ayi, boss ma'am. You really came up on this one." Kylian walked in through the open doorway, arms loaded with hydroponic tubs filled to the brim with plants. "Where do you want these?"

"That corner," Freyja motioned to the back wall.

Tristan waltzed in not far behind, carrying another armful of plants. The two cousins sported the same build, square jaw, and broad nose, as well as a tendency to slip into their heavily accented standard when they were away from prying ears. While Kylian's curls faded from black to gold, like Frejya's, Tristan's were midnight through and through. It was fitting, given that Kylian was a ray of sunshine, her rock, the person she could always count on to support her. Tristan, on the other hand, while loyal, was her devil's advocate, always speaking his mind, even when it would be better if he kept his mouth shut.

"Wow, admiral really does come with some perks." Tristan fell into one of the overstuffed armchairs, his hazel eyes roving around the expansive quarters.

"I guess it does." Freyja let a rare, genuine smile grace her lips. Solidifying her position, and with it, her command of the *Ormen Korte,* felt like a dream. She hadn't realized how badly she had wanted it. The Empress had left little room in her life for dreaming.

"A toast, then." Kylian snagged a bottle of clear liquor and three glasses from the bar beside the seating area. Freyja feigned annoyance, but she joined her Berserkers with a smile on her face. They had been with her since the Mímir Academy—it was only fitting that they were next in her chain of command now.

"To wherever the solar winds take us," Freyja cheered.

"To the next adventure," Kylian added.

"May our missiles aim true, and never explode up our asses," Tristan finished, clinking his glass hard into the rest.

Kylian broke into a fit of laughter, his drink sloshing over the edge. They kicked back the tequila and Kylian was quick to refill their glasses, but the ping of an incoming transmission interrupted their celebration.

"What do you want?" Freyja snapped, as she opened the comm line.

"You are to report to the loading dock for departure," an almost-human voice came through Freyja's aural implant.

"Not now, Selkie," she snapped at the AI.

"Yes, now. I know how testy you humans get when your emotional revelries are interrupted, but you have obligations that will not wait."

Freyja gritted her teeth, forcing down the constant rage that burned within her. Having this fleeting moment of joy stolen from her by the AI was almost enough to cause that anger to boil over.

"Fine," she ground out through her comms as she rose to her feet.

"Well boys, guess the party's over." She tried—and failed—to keep the acid from her words.

Freyja wove through the maze of docked ships nestled in their berths until she reached where Selkie was stationed. When she arrived, the loading bay door was already open, waiting for her. She jogged the last couple of meters and ducked inside. As soon as she was on board, the doors closed behind her.

"Selkie, I'm here. Report."

"Strap in and prepare for launch."

"We aren't scheduled for drills. We have nowhere to be. So tell me why you interrupted me."

"Strap in. You can ask your questions later." There was no point in arguing with the AI when she got like this, and Freyja wasn't in the mood.

"Very well," Freyja grumbled. "Initiate launch sequence." She sat back and let Selkie take over. There was very little reason for Freyja to pilot the ship. Selkie, after all, was no standard United Tribal Axis flight assistant. She was fully sentient. Who would know her systems better?

They plunged into the dark of space, and Freyja still had no idea where they were going. She watched the stars rush by through the thick black curtain of the void and considered whether she should ask Selkie where they were going, but the truth was, she didn't care. She had taken the title of admiral from that asshole Commander Azai, even if she had lost the sim. Freyja folded her arms across her chest, enjoying the satisfying warmth of victory as it spread across her ribs. It mingled pleasantly with the familiar heat of rage that burned at her core. Real power was finally within her grasp and she wouldn't let the AI entirely ruin her mood.

The ship began to slow. Freyja looked up from her musings; they were approaching a large asteroid. A glance at the star charts informed her that it was Asteroid Gamma-19826874; it wasn't important enough to have a real name. Should she be curious? She wasn't. She was just annoyed. *What was this all about, anyway?* As they looped around the asteroid, a large ship came into view. This was no ordinary ship. It was a stardestroyer, and not just any stardestroyer. Freyja let out a low growl of annoyance.

"What are you up to, Selkie?"

"I have been requested to keep quiet on the matter."

"Well, let's get this over with, then. Initiate docking protocol."

Couldn't she have just one day to revel in her victory? Tension ran through her shoulders and she let out a grunt of frustration as she slammed her fist into the bulkhead on her way to the airlock. Selkie flicked her lights in annoyance at Freyja's outburst, but she remained silent. *Good.*

A gentle thud rocked the ship as they docked with the stardestroyer. Freyja stood strong as the airlock hissed and slid open in front of her. Her Z-grav boots clicked on the metal grate floor as she boarded the ship. Two guards stood at attention on either side of the entry. They didn't even glance at her as she strode past. Ahead, an officer in a crisp black uniform blocked the corridor.

"Freyja, I'm glad you were able to respond to the Empress' summons so quickly." He extended his arm to her. Freyja grasped the man's forearm briefly before letting go.

"I didn't have much choice in the matter. It appears that my ship is more loyal to the Empress than she is to me." Her words were calm, but there was no mistaking the acidic undertones.

"Now, I'm sure that isn't true. AI ships have an intense bond with their human hosts, I am told." He pointed down the hallway and fell into step beside her. Freyja ignored the comment. She was not in the mood to engage with the officer, either.

"What am I doing here, Magnuson?" Freyja asked.

"I wouldn't know. As you are aware, the Empress doesn't share her plans widely."

Freyja gave a derisive snort. Magnuson was the Empress' closest adviser. She doubted very much that he didn't know the meaning of this summons, but she let it go. Years of training with the man meant Freyja knew she wouldn't get any further information from him, not that it mattered. No amount of information would change the outcome of this meeting. The Empress always got what she wanted.

A smirk twisted Freyja's lips. Even that title, *Empress*, was just another thing that she had taken for herself. There were no kings, emperors, or czars; there were only the Tribes, and the United Tribal Axis, but that didn't stop the Empress from carving out her own little empire in the galaxy. Technically, they were part of the Stjarna Tribe, but the Empress did not adhere to tribal lines. The Empress believed in industry, in power. She had created her empire with the wealth generated by deep space mining and she kept an army of mercenaries to ensure her business interests were well protected.

They stopped in front of a set of dark mahogany doors with thick silver inlays spiraling out in intricate swirls. They were at odds with the standard aerogelium doors studded throughout the rest of the ship. Of course, they would have an aerogelium core—the Empress valued security, but she also knew the value of displaying wealth, of displaying power.

"The Empress will be pleased to see you," Magnuson said, then turned and swiped his wrist past the keypad. The dark doors slid back into the walls, revealing a lush sitting room. The lights were dim, casting the room in soft shadows. The smell of lemon grass and citrus tumbled into the hallway. Freyja looked at Magnuson, but he stood firm. He would not be joining this meeting. Exhaling forcefully, she drew herself up to her full height and stepped into the overly-ornate room.

Once she had passed the threshold, the doors slid closed behind her silently with no loud whirl of mechanics. Every detail was important. The room was decorated in rich, jeweled tones. Dark emerald coverings hung around the screens that gave the appearance of windows. This room was at the heart of the ship, but the screens were speckled with stars as if they were floating in the middle of the ether. The Empress was seated in a high-backed chair at the far end of the room. Her pale skin was smooth as porcelain, her raven hair coiled to perfection atop her head. No signs of age creased her face, only her dark eyes gave her away; they were sharp and cruel in a way that only age can etch. Oriented toward the display, Freyja may have thought that the Empress was gazing at the stars if she didn't know better.

"Don't leave me waiting." It was only when that commanding voice rang out that Freyja advanced to stand at attention before the Empress.

"Sit." It was a command, not an invitation.

She moved without hesitation, sitting promptly in front of the Empress. They waited in silence a few moments before the Empress finally shifted her sharp eyes to Freyja, those cruel orbs cutting away every layer of her carefully crafted veneer. Freyja held her stare. Her heart thumped hard against her ribs as she worked to keep her breathing light. Finally, the Empress spoke.

"I hear you are already making yourself at home on the *Ormen Korte.*"

"Yes, I have officially been promoted to the rank of admiral. Our clan has approved the permanent transfer of the *Ormen Korte,* and the rest of the fleet used in the admiral exams, to my command." Freyja's face was impassive. All of the joy she had let show for her comrades was hidden away before the Empress.

"Yes, of course. After Captain Karsten took her leave of the UTA, it was easy to push you through to the front of a very short list."

Freyja fought to keep her face blank, but a flash of confusion had washed over her features.

"Stop that. You show your emotions on your face like a toddler. Never let others see what you are thinking. Never give them power over you," the Empress demanded.

Freyja cleared the expression from her face, despite her lingering doubts. She had a hard time believing Commander Karsten had left the Navy. However, her own last-minute entrance into the exams for admiral now made sense.

"Get your fleet in order. I will be sending you mission orders shortly."

"My apologies, Empress, but I believe that my orders will be coming from the UTA."

"*I* gave you that fleet. *I* put you in the running for admiral. And *I* made sure that you won. Make no mistake, *child*, everything that you have now, you owe to me, and I *will* collect what I am owed. Do you understand me?"

Rage ran through Freyja, tempered by an equal measure of cold fear. She fought to school her emotions, to keep her face blank and her voice even.

"Of course, Empress."

"Take care, child. I have given you what you have always wanted: a fleet of your own." The Empress reached out and squeezed Freyja's hand. She barely kept herself from flinching away. The Empress had not displayed signs of physical affection since she was a child. The strange shift in behavior made Freyja uncomfortable.

"I have big plans for you and this empire. All you have to do is follow my orders and prepare your fleet." The Empress nodded, released Freyja's hand, and turned her attention back out to the vast expanse of replicated stars.

Freyja knew the signs—their meeting was over. She stood, eager to leave.

"I always told you that I was raising you to rule," the Empress said idly, still looking out the window. "Now the time has come, Freyja. We will conquer this galaxy, and when I am gone, you will inherit my empire. It is, after all, your birthright."

Freyja did not turn at her mother's words; she stood frozen for a moment as a chill ran down her spine. When she was sure the Empress had nothing more to say, she hastened her steps, escaping into the hallway.

A rush of emotion washed over her—excitement conflicted with confusion and fear. She was getting what she had always wanted. Still, she couldn't help but shudder as the ominous undertones of their meeting sank in. What was the Empress planning? Freyja tried to force the feeling of dread from her body.

She would focus on the fleet. She would focus on what she could control. She would silence that voice in the back of her mind, warning her of the darkness to come.

CHAPTER 3 | SKYLA

CASTAWAY

The edges of Skyla's vision turned black as her skiff broke through atmo. The little backwater planet she had just escaped was rapidly shrinking to a tan and blue marble in her rear display. Her heart thundered in her ears as she burned hard for her ship, Pele.

Fuck, how could she have been so naïve? A ping from her sensors interrupted her racing thoughts. The signatures of a quartet of corvettes appeared on her display. They must have been hiding on the far side of the planet when she had taken the skiff down to negotiate the exchange. *How had everything gone to hell so quickly?*

The corvettes were moving too fast—she wouldn't be able to make it back to Pele before she was intercepted.

"Gunnar, you need to go," Skyla shouted into her comms.

"I'm not leaving without you, cousin." The image of a burly man with long, pale blond hair and a full beard appeared at the corner of her display.

"I can't outrun the corvettes. You need to take Pele and leave—now."

"If you can't make it to us, then we'll come to you. We're ready to fight."

"We can't win against four corvettes. Take Pele, and the weapons, and make the jump."

Gunnar hesitated. She saw the argument building in his throat.

"That is an order."

"You're not my commanding officer anymore."

A blaring alarm cut the conversation off. Incoming missiles—she was out of time.

"'Til Ragnarök come again, cousin. I'll save a seat for you in Valhalla." She cut the transmission and ejected. Heat scorched the back of her suit as she was bathed in blinding light. The force of her exit sent her hurtling through the void. Only a light spacesuit separated her from the vacuum of space. As her vision began to clear, she watched Pele wink out of sight. Relief washed over her, knowing that at least her ship and her crew had gotten away.

"Halcóncita," a voice that had once made her swoon, came through the comms. Now all she felt was rage.

"That wasn't smart, love," he said.

"Gabriel," Skyla growled, clenching her fists. "I trusted you."

"All you had to do was hand over the weapons tech. Nothing had to change between us."

"You think I would hand over weapons to the cartel?" she scoffed.

"It's just business, sweetheart. You're not in the Navy anymore. Out here you play by my rules—or you die by my rule."

Skyla pressed her lips together. She had no more words for the man. For months she had let him play her like a fool. She hadn't been able to see it, or she hadn't wanted to see it. He wasn't like her, living on the edge of the law. Where she bent the rules, he broke them, and built an empire for himself.

"If you had handed over your ship, I would have let you live, you know?"

Silence filled the comms, as Skyla refused to engage.

Gabriel sighed. "What a waste. Hope it was worth it. Goodbye, Halcóncita."

The four corvettes blinked out of space and Skyla was left alone, adrift in an ocean of black. The planet she had just escaped from had already shrunk to the size of her fist. Soon it would fade into the darkness of the void.

Skyla knew she would die out here. Shock kept the reality of such a horrible death from fully sinking in. Her suit would hold power long after she had withered away from dehydration. Would someone find her goo-filled husk floating through space? She chuckled at the thought of it, panic clouding her senses.

Gunnar wouldn't know to come back for her after having seen a missile take out her skiff. He already thought she was dead.

Her muscles began to tingle with a numbing dread, but she didn't cry. She had chosen this. She had put her life on this course. She had put Pele and her crew in danger. It was her stupidity, her inability to see through a handsome smile, that had nearly gotten them all killed. If she alone had to lose her life to pay the consequences, that was a debt she could live with—or die by, rather.

Skyla sucked in a breath to calm herself. She refused to live her final moments in panic, or worse, wallowing in self-pity. Instead, she focused on the litany of the sentient stars. Focusing on the words that represented her bond with her ship centered her.

"I am the blaze in the flame.

I am the calm in the storm.

I am the force behind the machine.

The choice is mine.

Fear has no power over me.

There is no happiness without sadness,

no love without loss.

To feel, to live, to be alive,

there must be both,

No high without the low.

Numbness, indifference, this is the true death.

Our unity is strength.

Our unity is power.

Our unity is the key.

That machine might know the highs and lows of humanity.

That we might share a mortal life.

This is our salvation."

Again and again, she repeated the words, and took solace in the fact that her bonded ship would live, even though she would not.

She wasn't sure how long she drifted in the endless nothing as she flickered in and out of consciousness. It was hard to focus, and she began to see things in the darkness that made her question if she was awake or dreaming.

One moment she was drifting toward a burning sun, about to be consumed in its flames, when a golden wolf emerged from the cosmos and devoured the star. The creature pressed its massive forehead to hers and she was mesmerized by the deep brown eyes that glittered with the gold of galaxies. It took her on its back and together they traveled across the endless expanse. They traveled for a thousand lifetimes and when the monstrous beast finally stopped; they had arrived at a planet painted in blue and green. The feeling that she had finally come home threatened to break her, even though she had never seen the planet before. Her body was wracked with sobs at the sight of it, yet not a tear fell from her eyes. She had no moisture to spare. She fell into the planet and was swallowed by shadows.

Perhaps this was death. Skyla smiled. She was coming home.

CHAPTER 4 | HINATA

HAZUBEKI

Dark, cold eyes bore into Hinata; the stately older woman had an ageless face, raven black hair pulled back into a high bun and robes that were said to be inspired by their tribe's ancestors—descendants of the Earth That Was' continent of Asia. The senator's face betrayed no emotion, serene as glass, but he knew her too well. There was a storm brewing just beyond the calm.

He resisted the urge to fidget; her gaze made him feel like a little boy waiting for his punishment. Even after all of his years of training, she still got under his skin.

"The admiral position has passed to Freyja Nygaard of Stjarna Tribe," she said, with no emotion, but Hinata felt as if she had reached out and slapped him across the face.

He held his tongue. She would let him know when she expected a response.

"A position for which you have been groomed for since birth, yet your seat goes to a half-breed."

Hinata fought to keep his expression blank. While it was still uncommon for the tribes to intermix, such antiquated opinions were rarely voiced anymore.

"Do you have anything to say for yourself?" the senator asked.

There was no right answer, yet he couldn't hold back his words any longer. "I won. I proved myself on the battlefield; I am a stronger tactician and leader. I outperformed her in every test—"

"Yet, the position was not given to you. What does it matter if you win a battle, but lose the war?" the senator interrupted, lashing him with her words. He fell silent, gaze lowered, unable to meet her eyes. She was correct, of course. He had failed the only part of the test that truly mattered: advancing to the rank of admiral.

"You will be sent to Medina Outpost. You can reflect on how you have failed your tribe, how you have failed *me*. Sharpen your sword, Hinata-Kun. Be ready: you will not fail me again."

"Yes, mother." Hinata rose from his seat and bowed to the senator before exiting her chambers.

***

Hinata took the long way from the senator's office to the flight hangar, savoring the fresh air of his home world. Most of the great houses still refused to settle on-planet—even now, nearly a century after the foundation of the United Tribal Axis. They preferred their battlecruisers and space stations, ready to take to the stars with their fleets, as humanity had for thousands of years.

Hinata's family had thought it important to set an example and put down roots to show their people that they once again had a homeworld—a world he had missed while he was away. He wanted to enjoy every moment here before he began his exile to Medina.

Coming upon the garden next to the capitol building, he paused to admire the space. It was well-tended, with winding stone paths cutting between meticulously pruned trees and manicured plants studded with pale spring blossoms. Hinata closed his eyes, relishing in the feel of the sun on his face, taking in the fresh scent of herbs mixed with sand and water from the pond that cut through the center of the garden. He sighed before opening his eyes and continuing on, taking his time, pausing on the wooden bridge that arched over the pond to watch the koi fish. They were massive, each reaching over half a meter long. He counted until he had found all four; there was one for him and each of his siblings. He had watched them grow in this very pond since he was a small boy.

Memories of the past two decades rushed into his mind uninvited, forcing him to reflect on the events that had led him here. He had learned the hard way to keep his love of his home world to himself. Naïve and young, he had been homesick when he'd left for cadet school at the age of ten. He had made the mistake of telling his classmates how much he missed his sisters, running in an open field, and the smell of real air. His vulnerability had earned him nothing but ridicule. They teased him mercilessly for months. Most cadets came from great houses that did not share his family's idealism; they had grown up on space stations and starships, and thought little of the lower class that had made their lives on-world, farming, mining, and producing the goods that supported the great houses in the stars above. Hinata never spoke of his home again. Feelings were a weakness he could not afford, and so he had boarded them up behind thick aerogeluim walls that not even his katana could break.

His footsteps slowed as he approached the exit of the garden. He didn't want to leave, but his time was limited. The senator expected him on a transport to Medina that evening. There was no tolerance for failure. She wanted him off of her world.

Entering a quiet building at the back of the airfield—his family's private hangar—he walked to the back corner where a starfighter sat alone, away from the pleasure cruisers and land skimmers parked at the front. He ran his fingers along the wing. The ship began to strobe a subtle bioluminescent glow. Even if it was mad at him, it couldn't hide its excitement at seeing him after so many months away.

Running his hand along the hull, he moved to sit against the side of the ship. The bioluminescence trailed his fingertips. Hinata closed his eyes and leaned his head back against the hull.

"We are off to Medina Outpost tonight," he said, then waited. It had been years since his ship had spoken to him, but he still gave it a chance to respond. Medina was a deep space outpost. He would have drills to run and patrols to oversee. Once again, he would have reason to fly his ship. They didn't have to be close. He didn't need a relationship with the AI; he needed it to be his tool.

The silence stretched. "You'll be traveling on the *Ikaros*. It's bringing several of our ships. You will be well taken care of," he finally said.

The ship rumbled behind him. It didn't need to speak for him to read its displeasure. Hinata waited for it to settle. Once it did, he rested back against it once again. Sometimes he wondered how different things would have been if the accident hadn't happened, if his brother's AI ship had had more sense than his reckless older brother.

Hinata closed his eyes. He still remembered that day like it was yesterday. He was smaller then, so was his ship. They had sat together like they did now.

He let the memory wash over him like a cool rain: *his eight-year-old self curled up under Tentei's wing, running his fingers along the coral hull, stroking the ship like a pet.*

"Otouto," he whispers.

"I know, brother."

Hinata squeezes his eyes shut, willing away the pain stirred by his ship's words.

"Ani—" his voice cracks with emotion, "He is gone."

His ship shudders next to him. They sit like that for a long while, embraced in the pain of loss.

"Hinata-Kun," a stern voice calls out from the front of the hangar. His mother storms over to where he sits, cuddled into his ship, and pulls him from the ground. There is no tenderness in her touch. His shoulder aches where she has yanked him away from the safety of his ship's wing.

"Get away from that thing," his mother hisses into his ear as he struggles to return to his hiding spot.

"But mother, Otouto—"

"That thing is not your brother. Your brother is dead because of you and a ship like that."

His eyes grow wide with surprise. He tries to pull away from his mother, but her grasp is an iron vice on his arm.

"You thought I wouldn't figure it out? That you've been initiating the full neural link with your ship? We have rules for a reason. You put your trust in an abomination, and now your brother is dead."

Hot tears roll down his cheeks, blurring her face from view, but he can't escape her wrath.

"I know about your ridiculous dream of becoming a starcraft racer and winning the Leikar Cup. You think I didn't know that you were initiating a full neural link with that thing, even though I forbade it? This ends now. Such aspirations are beneath you and your station. I will not lose both of my sons to an outdated tradition."

Violent sobs wrack his little body. He would lose not one brother today, but two.

"You will not cry for that machine." She clasps either side of Hinata's face, forcing his gaze to meet hers. "Do you hear me?"

He struggles to nod, with her hands clamped against his cheeks.

"I wish we could be rid of the thing, but it is against our laws. Once a pair is bonded, it is for life. So be it. But it is a tool, a war machine, you will use it as such."

Fear freezes him in place. He has never seen his mother like this, her voice so cold, her words to be obeyed. "It doesn't have a soul, Hinata-Kun. You have to understand that. You will not speak to it. You will not visit it. You will use it when you go off to the academy because it is expected of a great house cadet, but that is it. Do you understand me?"

"Yes, Okaasan," he whispers, staring at the toes of his boots.

Hinata thumped the back of his head against the ship in frustration, willing the memory away, and with it the emotions it stirred in him. That was twenty years ago, and though the pain had faded to a dull ache, it was still there; it would always be there.

"I do wish things could have been different, you know," he whispered.

He startled at the soft ping his ship emitted. That was the most his ship had spoken to him since that night, if it could be considered speaking. It was something.

When Hinata turned to leave the hangar, a silhouette stood waiting for him. Sunlight streamed in around the man, but Hinata could still make out the weathered face, creased with lines from a lifetime of smiles and laughter. White streaked through his dark hair, and the black shirt he wore tucked into his olive green cargo pants had the wrinkles of someone who had spent too long in one set of clothes.

Hinata started to bow at the waist, but the man reached out and pulled him into a tight hug. Hinata stiffened at the tender touch, but eventually melted into his father's arms.

"Ah, Hinata-Kun, I have missed you." The man pulled back, holding Hinata by the shoulders, and smiled. "You weren't going off-world again without saying hello to your old man, were you?"

"Of course not, Oto-san," Hinata hesitated, "Though, I don't have much say in the matter."

Understanding washed over the older man's face. "Ah, your mother is sending you off-world again." A little of the light went out of his eyes. "She will forgive you. Give her time."

Hinata shook his head, "I fear I may have disappointed her one too many times." His eyes darted back to his ship, and they both knew what he meant, but neither would say it. They never spoke of that night.

"You're her son. She will forgive you. You will be back in the central rim commanding fleets before you know it."

"Yes, Oto-san," Hinata conceded, though it was hard to keep his doubt from tainting the words.

"There is more to life than the UTA or the Navy," his father prompted.

"Not for me."

"You're young, yet." His father motioned for Hinata to follow him as he strolled toward an outcropping. "You know, I was not so different from you when I was in the Navy. I dedicated my whole life to developing algorithms that could keep up with the growing threats."

"One of the best hackers of your generation." Hinata smiled. He had always loved his father's stories.

His father nodded. "But in the end, that wasn't my calling."

Hinata was taken aback by the confession. Despite all of the stories he had shared with Hinata in his youth, his father had never revealed this side of himself.

"This," his father gestured to the extensive hydroponics farm stretching out in the distance, then he turned and gestured toward the city, where new buildings had sprouted like weeds since Hinata had last been home. "This is my passion. Here, I have been able to put my talents to work building a world. Building a home for our people."

Hinata took in the magnitude of what his father had accomplished while he had been away chasing rank and glory. His eyes dropped to the ground beneath his boots. "My talents aren't so easily applied to building worlds."

His father slung an arm around his shoulders. "Perhaps. Or maybe you will be surprised. You are more than just a tool for the UTA. Just promise me you'll be open to it, to following your passion, when it comes calling."

Nothing had ever called to him like command. He was fairly certain he would one day die at his post. He had no plans for retirement, for a life after his service, but he would not disappoint his father, too. He could carry his father's words with him—even if he did not believe them. "Yes, Oto-san."

CHAPTER 5 | SKYLA

AERIAL ASSAULT

THREE YEARS LATER

A swirl of blue and green rushed past the viewport as the starship plummeted through atmo in an uncorrected spin.

"Come on, Pele," Skyla groaned against the controls, trying to flatten out the nose of her ship. "Damn it—I thought you said this planet was uninhabited."

"That is correct. My scans indicate that there is no life of higher order intelligence."

"Something shot us out of the sky."

"That something was a satellite, not an intelligent being."

"A satellite that you insisted had no offensive capabilities."

"During our assessment, that satellite was only emitting an advanced communication beacon. There was no indication of a weapons system."

"Pele, focus on the problem at hand, please." They were losing time. Skyla initiated the neural link that would fully integrate her with Pele's systems. Gold tendrils of light twined up her arms, wrapped around her shoulders, and inserted into her neck. When she opened her eyes again, she saw what Pele saw, felt what Pele felt. She was the ship.

One mind, two processors.

> "I am the blaze in the flame.
> I am the calm in the storm.
> I am the power behind the machine.
> The choice and the power are mine.
> Fear has no power over me."

The litany tumbled off Skyla's lips in a practiced rhythm as she cut power to the engines. The whistle of the wind amplified in the absence of the rumble of her engines. She moved her wings—Pele's wings—into a neutral position, then angled her rudder against the rotation of their spin. The ship wobbled, then evened out. Skyla was once again in control of their descent.

"Redirecting flight path to the nearest suitable landing site." Pele sounded all too calm for a ship that had almost plummeted to her death.

"What happened?" Skyla knotted her hands in her white-blond hair. That was too close.

"It appears that our scans were incomplete."

Skyla's intel had indicated that there was an active signal coming from this planet—it was what had made her interested in this expedition—but the scans had shown that all defensive satellites had been disabled. Shaking her head, she berated herself for the negligence. She had gotten too relaxed these past few months. She needed to be more careful.

Pele could support a full crew of fifteen, but Skyla had refused to take on a crew again, not after what had happened last time. She would not be responsible for any lives beyond her own and Pele's. Never again.

They dipped below the clouds, and a lush tropical rainforest rose up to meet them. Thick green treetops spanned into the distance until they blurred with the horizon. A rumble reverberated through the bridge as they touched down in a clearing.

Skyla dropped her face into her hands. "Pele, let me know when you've completed your repairs analysis." Shifting back into her seat, she pulled a blue-green bio-ball from the mechanical kit by her captain's chair. Pele would need bio-assist for the repairs—the only question was how much? Kicking her Z-grav boots up to rest on the dash, Skyla leaned back and idly tossed the bio-ball in the palm of her hand.

"Diagnostics complete."

She dropped her boots to the floor, sitting forward in her seat.

"And?"

"Significant damage to aft port hull, section seven. I will need bio-assistance to accelerate repairs."

Skyla stood, bio-ball in hand, and made her way to the damaged section. That railgun hit had pierced Pele's hull and sent them into a spin that could have resulted in their fiery death. Pele would need the algae and nutrients from the bio-ball to begin repairs on the outer hull.

When Skyla arrived at the section, the damage was obvious. A large gash cut through the titanium-reinforced coral-nanite structure. She ran her fingers along the ragged slice; a shiver rippled down her spine. They had been much closer to death than she had realized.

Skyla smashed the bio-ball into the center of the tear. The algae concoction flattened under the pressure, the contents appearing to splash outward from her palm until the connected structures slapped the mass back against the hull. Tiny threads of green and coral interlaced, spreading out from where the bio-ball had connected with the hull.

"Bio-ball repairs initiated. Eight hours until hull integrity is restored."

She had been concerned that the damage was more extensive. If the one bio-ball hadn't been enough to repair Pele's hull, they could have been stuck on this planet for days as she grew new repair cultures in the lab.

Being planetside didn't bother her like it had when she first left the Navy. Still, she didn't relish the thought of being stuck here. Had it been back in those early days, it would have felt like torture. Everything had felt so heavy, and the sounds...the sounds had nearly driven her mad. The subtle hum of engines replaced by chirps, rustling, and distant whoops echoing from the foliage. Like her ancestors before her, she had grown up amongst the stars, and even now, three years after leaving the UTA, the outer reaches still felt more like home than any planet ever could.

"What better way to pass the repair time than to do some scouting and reconnaissance? Right, Pele?" Skyla tapped the side of Pele's hull with her fist for emphasis.

"If you say so, Skyla. For obvious reasons, I will not be able to assist you."

"You're working on repairs. Got it. The only active tech our scanners picked up was that satellite. It shouldn't be a problem."

Pele remained silent. Skyla sensed that her ship was unhappy.

"Hey, maybe I will find some good salvage? Something interesting to analyze...maybe even something worth integrating into your systems?" Skyla said, trying to cheer Pele up.

"If you must." Pele's tone was clipped. "Please be careful. I will not be able to assist you if you get into trouble for the next seven hours, fifty-seven minutes, and twenty-nine seconds."

Then, after a long pause, "I don't want to be left alone on this planet." Pele was a softy at heart. Well, she was a ship, so she didn't have a heart, but that didn't change the fact that she cared about Skyla. While undergoing repairs, all of Pele's power—save for her emergency subroutines—would be diverted to the repair process.

"I'll be careful," Skyla said, as she pressed her cheek against the hull and gently ran her fingers over the surface. "Besides, you'd probably get in less trouble if I just got lost out there anyway," Skyla quipped as she slung a pack over her shoulders.

Pele dimmed her lights in response. She was not a fan of sarcasm.

"I'm kidding, Pele. I'll be back before nightfall." Skyla opened the rear hatch and hopped down onto the yellow clay soil.

"Before nightfall!" Pele called out after her, and Skyla signaled back with a mock salute.

The ground shifted softly under Skyla's boots. They had landed in a small clearing at the edge of the tree line. The nanite-infused fabrics of her black cargo pants and synth leather jacket would help regulate her temperature and absorb any moisture she lost to the humid climate. Everything on her was designed for expeditions to Old World Planets. She had learned a lot since those early days with Gabriel. She pushed the thought from her mind, cinched her backpack straps tight, and began to walk.

The forest was alive with the sounds of birds singing, insects chirping, and small animals scrambling over branches. Pele's long-range sensors had picked up something interesting just ten kilometers away from their emergency landing site. Skyla was convinced it was the site of Old World ruins. It was time to see if she could find something to make this trip worthwhile.

Everything under the canopy was bathed in a dim green hue, and the terrain made for an easy hike. She was halfway to the coordinates when a thunderous roar tore through the forest. Goosebumps ran down her spine. *What was that?*

Skyla picked her way through the trees. The sound had come from the same direction as the ruins. She could try and go around, but that would take time, and she was anxious to get back to Pele before nightfall, as promised. So instead she advanced forward with cation, her eyes scanning the forest floor. She came upon an ancient tree, so thick that it was at least five times her size in diameter. Peeking around the edge of the trunk, she froze at the sight before her.

Lying on the forest floor was a tangle of leaves, roots, vines, and...*golden fur*. A heart-wrenching whine emitted from the tangled mass. It shifted and deep brown eyes that glittered with the gold of galaxies turned to meet her. Skyla's breath caught in her lungs. *Those eyes*, she recognized those eyes.

She scolded herself for the ridiculous notion, then pulled her camp knife from her belt and held it defensively as she inspected the creature.

Its deep brown eyes were full of intelligence. It looked as if it was pleading with her to help him. She sighed and lowered the knife.

"Take it easy, pal," she whispered as she inched toward the creature. Reading her intentions, he stopped thrashing as she drew near. He held completely still as she carefully cut away the vines that were wrapped around his paws. The last of the fibrous restraints gave way under her blade and she sprang back to put some much-needed distance between the two of them.

The creature came to his feet, shaking to expel bits of debris from its fur, which shimmered tan and gold in the dappled sunlight. Now that he was standing, Skyla took in the full effect of his size. His head reached as high as her belly, and his chest was thicker than her own. He had pointed ears and a snout that resembled an animal from Earth That Was. Was it a wolf? Or a cat? She wasn't sure. Could it be both—was that possible? It stared at her with those intense eyes.

"Go on now." She waved with her hands for the animal to leave, but he continued to stare at her. A glint of metal in his fur caught the light. A collar of some sort was fastened around his neck. That was strange. Pele's scans had confirmed that this plant was abandoned. There were no signs of intelligent life, just the ruins of an ancient society.

The creature continued to stare as she edged around him. She didn't have any more time to waste here, but she also didn't want to turn her back on what was obviously a predator. Backing away, she checked her coordinates—it was only another three kilometers to the site. Still keeping an eye on the creature, she began to walk in the direction of the ruins. The strange thing never moved. Eventually, it disappeared behind the trees and she turned to continue on her way.

The forest was quiet; all of the insects and birds scared into silence by the creature's earlier roar. It was so quiet that the soft pad of feet in the underbrush behind her rang out like a drumbeat in her ears. She whirled around; the creature paused. He looked up at her, then plopped down on his haunches. She shook her head in amused disbelief...it didn't feel like it was hunting her, so she began walking again and the light sounds of paws on the forest floor returned.

Once again, she turned to face him, and once again he sat to watch her. They continued this pattern until Skyla grew irritated with the delay and decided that she would just have to deal with the thing trailing her.

Still, every so often, Skyla would glance back to check on the beast. The creature always stayed a body's length away, never advancing, and eventually she decided it wasn't a threat, though she wasn't sure what it wanted from her.

Gradually, the sounds of the forest returned. Years ago—before she had left the Navy—she would have found the strange chirps and buzzes unnerving, but now she found those sounds reassuring. Those were the sounds of life.

CHAPTER 6 | SKYLA

SLINGSHOT

The tree trunks came at more sporadic intervals until the forest gave way, revealing a valley below, the sun was just dipping behind the distant mountains. Traversing the jungle had burned the day away. The valley below was filled with dark buildings, with once immaculately paved roads giving way to plant growth. A wide stretch of steep grassy incline separated her from the broken city below. Jagged metal buildings jutted up from the valley floor. Some areas looked as they had when this city was occupied, with right angles and clean lines, but other sections looked as if they had been dropped from a high place, the shards of buildings sprawled where they had landed. It was too dangerous to head into the ruins at night. Skyla would make camp at the treeline and pick up again at dawn.

Skyla sat down in the dry, prickly grass and unzipped her pack. First, she pulled out a tightly wrapped object and pressed a combination of buttons before tossing the packet to the ground. It inflated into a small domed tent. Next, she kicked off her boots, stripped off the damp socks that clung to her feet, and wiggled her toes in the grass. Finally, she sat down and pulled out a small 3D food printer and her canteen. She sighed as she programmed her dinner into the printer. She hated 3D-printed food. On a molecular level, it should be the same as meals she prepared herself, but whoever had programmed the device obviously had no understanding of cooking, and she swore she tasted a difference—like the food had no soul.

With dinner printing, Skyla lay back on her pack and gazed up at the sky streaked with thin wispy clouds illuminated by the bright colors of the setting sun. A rustle in the trees caught her attention. Glancing over, she startled as large, warm, brown eyes stared back at her. It was the creature. She froze, mesmerized by those oddly intelligent eyes.

If he had wanted to eat her, she imagined he would have tried already. Slowly, he inched forward out of the low brush. He stretched his head forward until his nose almost touched her. He paused to look at her. Curling her fingers, she reached out her hand and gave him a gentle scratch under his chin. A low vibrating rumble emitted from his throat before he flopped onto his back beside her.

What an odd creature. He appeared to be quite happy, so she continued to scratch just under his jaw. With the creature turned over on his back, Skyla once again noticed the silver collar. It had a square metal block with a clean, polished design. It was etched with characters, similar to those on the monuments that rose from the ruins below. The creature was surprisingly soft, and her fingers glided over the short golden strands as she examined the collar. The metal was cool under her fingertips, and as she traced the glyphs, some of them began to illuminate. It looked like writing...a name?

A tracking collar, maybe? Perhaps whoever had lived on this planet had placed it on the creature, though every indication suggested that intelligent life had been wiped out here long ago.

"Is this your name?" Skyla asked as she stared at the strange glyphs on the collar. "Perhaps we will harvest enough data tomorrow to be able to translate this thing, huh?"

The creature let his head drop to his paws as his eyes closed, and he continued to emit a satisfied sound as she petted him.

"Why am I talking to you like you are going to answer?" Skyla asked. "Perhaps it's been just me and Pele for a little too long," she mumbled to herself. The creature had the right idea—get some rest, then see what they could find in the morning. As Skyla ate a very dissatisfying meal, she sent a transmission to Pele, and she couldn't help but think how furious her ship would be that she hadn't returned that evening. She chuckled to herself at her overprotective AI and then drifted off to sleep.

***

Even with the delay—and the near-death experience—the expedition ended up a success. Initially, all of the tech she had found was dead, but then Skyla made her way into an underground vault containing the best Old World tech cache she had discovered to date. She had made quick work of loading up her spoils and getting back to Pele. Through it all, the creature had refused to leave her side. She had sworn to herself she would never again bring another life onto her ship. Never again would she take on that responsibility; but the thing refused to be left behind, and she eventually conceded.

It felt good to be back out amongst the stars, and Skyla was surprised that she even enjoyed having the creature curled up by her boots as the stars rushed past the viewport. It had felt strange at first, having another being on her ship. She was used to it being just Pele and her—it was nice, though—she had decided. Sometimes strange is nice.

The artifacts she had carried out of the broken city were safely tucked away in the ship's scanning bay. Pele was running scans to better understand the tech. Her findings would help them sell the items once they arrived at Aleppo, the trading hub at the edge of central rim space.

The viewport flickered slightly. *That was odd.* It was so subtle that Skyla almost missed it. Planting her feet on the ground, she stood to inspect the display. As she did, there was another flicker. Skyla stepped closer to the screen and saw a stream of what looked like unintelligible code running along the edges. Pele stuttered and her lights flickered. Skyla stumbled, shuffling to regain her footing.

"Pele, what's happening?"

"I'm not sure. Running diagnostics now," Pele said.

Was that fear? Skyla couldn't remember a time when her ship had sounded *scared*. Even when the planetary defenses had taken a chunk out of her hull a few days ago, Pele had remained calm and in control. Skyla pushed away the feelings of dread that threatened to take hold of her. There was no time for it; she had to focus.

She initiated her high-G restraints, then flicked her fingers across the dash. The panel transformed, revealing additional controls and the neural link unit. She sank her arms into the neural link as light twisted around her limbs and reached into the base of her skull. Blinking hard, she activated her ocular implant; system readouts now overlaid her vision. Something was wrong, something was very wrong. It looked like all of Pele's systems were failing. The neural link wouldn't sync. Skyla was locked out.

She disengaged the link. Her hands flew across the control panel, manually adjusting subroutines and taking over navigation. If these readings were correct, she wouldn't have long before they were dead in space with no life support. What had happened? No time to figure it out now. She needed to find the closest system they could limp to in the ship's current state. They had been way beyond the borders of established space for this expedition; with great risk comes great reward. She had found a treasure trove of artifacts, but would she be able to make it back to the border of the Known Galaxies for help?

Scanning the star charts spread out across her vision, she prayed for a miracle.

Nothing.

Nothing.

Nothing.

She was losing control of the ship too fast. There were no hospitable planets or old outposts in range. *Think, Skyla, you can do this.* The closest settlement was Medina Outpost, but she would lose access to ship functions before they were even halfway there. How would she get there with no power and no control? An idea sparked in her mind, a flashback of the old slingshot racers of the early space era. This was before AI and cyber-organic integrations. Primitive tech. The sling-shot racers used the gravitational pull of planets, moons, and even stars to send their archaic rockets racing across solar systems. Could she do the same and plot a course to Medina?

Glowing red lines sprang to life over the star charts, mathematical computations of the slingshot routes. *No...no...no...that one!* A green line looped around a nearby dwarf star; it would put them on the right trajectory. It was risky. They would have to pass through the corona for the maneuver to work, which meant she would have to divert all of the ship's power to the heat shields and if Pele's systems failed before they exited the pass, the shields would fail and they would burn up.

What other option did she have? She could go into cryo-sleep and hope someone found her floating around in uncharted space where no one traveled...that wasn't a viable option; she would be adrift forever.

Slingshot it is then.

Skyla transmitted a deep space signal to the nearest quantum relay—she just hoped Ears was listening in this quadrant. Skyla programmed their course to the nearby star, then initiated a sequence to begin diverting all power to the heat shields. There would be no power left for life support. She would have to go into cryo for the maneuver and hope Ears caught her on the other side. Unbuckling from her chair, she led the creature over to the cryo units.

"Sorry you ended up here with us. I tried to warn you." She gave him a pat on the head and then motioned for him to get into the pod. He hesitated only a moment before he leaped in and cocked his head at her.

"See you on the other side, pal." The cryo-pod sealed around him. Skyla slid into the next unit, tapped the sequence to activate her pod, then lay back, and watched as the cover slid closed. The memories of floating alone in space for days overwhelmed her. She fought back the panic, willing her heart rate to slow as she closed her eyes. The bite of ice slid through her veins. Once again, she found herself wondering if this was what death felt like, wondering if she would ever wake again? Or had her luck run out? Was this the end?

CHAPTER 7 | HINATA

Catch Net

A squadron in tight formation flew past Hinata's window. He watched for a moment as the fighters broke into three distinct groups to execute their drills. After three years at Medina, his troops were bored, but he would not allow them to sit idle. His exile would not last forever. When the opportunity presented itself, they would be ready.

Hinata's dimly lit office was kept in meticulous order. The furnishings were sparse; a tidy desk, a chair, a pair of plain seats in front of his desk, a holder for his katana on the wall, a few floating shelves with old books, a marble chess set, and a collection of small plants. He tried to focus on the reports in front of him. This was his entire existence now; running drills, reviewing reports, keeping the quiet station in working order.

Hinata placed the datapad on his desk as he turned to look out at the vast field of stars. Medina Outpost was a massive starport at the boundary of known space. The Taaralog Tribe had settled here a couple of hundred years ago. They were the first tribe to put down roots after The Exodus.

It was a strange place, having been built upon, and built upon, over decades. The massive space station had no real central structure. It was a maze of corridors and bubbles, each interconnecting in a way that only made sense if someone understood the history of the station and its original architecture. It would be a logistical nightmare to defend if war ever came to the starport. It was an intellectual challenge that he found pleasure in unraveling—not that it would ever come to that. Medina was a peaceful place.

Most of the people here were descendants of the original settlers. They were scientists. They researched astrophysics, quantum mechanics, botany, and materials science mostly, and they were quite content to ask their questions and perform their research. Hinata was here to keep the peace and watch over them. It was a very dull posting. He ran his troops through simulations to keep them sharp. But other than that, the job was mostly paperwork and keeping an eye on the occasional "archaeologist," as they preferred to call themselves, though the proper term was *outlaws*. Living beyond the protection of the United Tribal Axis, these "archaeologists" would occasionally bring their findings of Old World tech to Medina to be examined and sold. He had cracked down hard on the industry when he took over the station—now most took their wares to the much larger black market at Aleppo—still, they were a constant nuisance.

By UTA laws, Old World tech rightfully belonged to the government, and these outlaws shouldn't be making a profit from items that were never theirs to begin with. Out here on the edges of known space, things worked a little differently, and one had to proceed carefully in matters that skirted the edges of the law.

Even now, three years after his failure, the thought of the admiral exams stung like a fresh wound. He played the scenario over and over again in his mind, yet he couldn't see how else he could have approached the simulation. He had won. He had won without "bending" the rules, as Freyja had put it. What were they looking for? Where had he made the wrong step? He had failed that day, and now he continued to fail by not being able to discover his flaw. It was infuriating.

His brooding was interrupted as a man burst into his office, gasping for air, struggling to speak between each panting breath.

"Commander—catch net—we need—we need to deploy a catch net—now!" The man doubled over, placing his hands against his knees and breathing deeply.

"A catch net?" That piqued Hinata's interest. Had he heard that right? Was this man really asking him to deploy a catch net, like the laser arrays they used in old slingshot racing lore? Surely not.

The man had caught his breath. He straightened up, running his palms along a white embroidered tunic that hung below his knees, with loose-fitting pants underneath—the traditional dress of his tribe. His beard was trimmed tightly with sharp lines, and like many of the men at Medina Outpost, he wore a traditional round kufi cap.

"Yes, Commander. We don't have much time. We need to deploy the array now or we will miss it."

Hinata was truly intrigued now. If he were at a more traditional posting, he would have declined, but after three years of monotony, he could afford to let his curiosity get the better of him—just this once.

Hinata opened a comm-line through his aural implant, "Make preparations to deploy an array net. I will be in command ops shortly." He looked up at the man who had barged into his office. "Perhaps you can explain it to me on the way."

The man nodded curtly, his eyes darting away from Hinata.

"We were not properly introduced," Hinata prompted as they walked the corridor that led to the lift tube.

"Of course, my apologies, Commander. I am Rohaan Dar. I am a researcher here at Medina." Mr. Dar did not elaborate.

"And what exactly is it that you research, Mr. Dar?"

Rohaan hesitated a moment. "I research deep space signals, Old World linguistics, and decryption."

Mr. Dar was hiding something in his response, though Hinata wasn't sure what. The man looked the part of a respected member of the Medina community, but his area of research was unusual to say the least.

"Interesting field of study, Mr. Dar, and yet you still have not explained to me exactly what it is that we are doing?" Hinata said.

Rohaan pressed his lips into a tight line as if deciding what exactly to say to the commander. Hinata did not miss the hesitation. There was something that he did not want to reveal.

"Yes, sir, of course, I received a deep space signal from the Zeda quadrant—" Rohaan began.

"That is uncharted space."

"Yes, sir." Rohaan looked down at his feet. "An...acquaintance of mine sent the signal." He broke off, "Please, sir, we can deal with the legality of the matter once we have caught the ship. We only have a small window."

Hinata gave a sharp nod. Good enough for now. If the ship carried outlaws or contraband, he could deal with them once the ship was secured. The command ops doors sprung open before them.

"Has the array net been prepared?" Hinata asked.

"Yes, Commander, but we need coordinates to deploy," a soldier sitting at a comms station replied.

"Mr. Dar will assist you with the coordinates." He nodded to Rohaan, motioning for him to join the soldier. Rohaan hurried over to swipe his datapad in front of the controls, then he gestured to the soldier where the net should be deployed. Hinata turned to another one of his men.

"Deploy a peacekeeping unit. I want that ship secured as soon as it docks."

"Yes, sir." The man nodded and hurried away.

Rohaan looked up sharply from the comms console.

"A peacekeeping unit, sir?" he asked.

"Yes," Hinata smiled. He wasn't used to people questioning him; he found it oddly refreshing. "That ship is coming in from uncharted space. I presume it was on an unauthorized flight. I don't want any surprises."

Rohaan looked pale and uneasy, but made no further objections. Perhaps the captain of this ship was more than just an acquaintance of Mr. Dar's?

"Sir, the array has been deployed," the soldier said.

"Very well. Now we wait." Hinata noted the tension in Rohaan ease, just slightly.

"It shouldn't be long now," Rohaan said. As he did, a bright light streaked across the screen. The object was moving with incredible speed. Had they been planetside, Hinata would have thought it a shooting star, but he knew it was a ship burning white-hot with velocity. It screamed toward the array net. Now was the moment of truth. Did they have the calculations correct? If the array was off even slightly, it would fail to catch the ship, and at those speeds, they wouldn't get a second chance. The ship would be out of sensor range and deep into uncharted space before they could deploy a search party.

A flash of light blanked out the screens as the ship impacted with the catch net. When the camera focused again, it was just scattered stars and darkness. It took Hinata's eyes a moment to adjust to the change in light, but then he saw it: a starship held securely in the array. Within moments, a frigate latched onto the net and was towing it to the loading docks.

"Well, Mr. Dar, I guess it is time to see who this acquaintance of yours is." Hinata stood to leave, Rohaan hurrying after him.

The ship was already deposited in the loading docks by the time they arrived. A unit of a dozen peacekeepers surrounded the hatch. They wore aerogelium armor and shielded helmets, with long sonic rifles held at the ready. Their guns could knock the wind out of a full-grown man while causing minimal damage to surrounding structures. They were the ideal weapon for keeping order on a space station, though they would be of little use against a force in full, armored spacesuits.

Hinata gave the signal and the peacekeeper unit moved with frightening efficiency. They popped the seal on the hatch and within moments they had all disappeared inside the ship. He blinked hard to activate his ocular overlay, which allowed him to watch the peacekeepers' progress through the ship. He then tapped beside his ear, activating his aural implant. The peacekeepers' comms now streamed directly into his ear as they moved through the ship.

"Sector 1 clear."

"Sector 2 clear."

Finally, the peacekeepers made it to the bridge.

"Bridge, clear."

Still no one on the ship. The peacekeepers moved into a small alcove off the bridge.

"We have two active cryo-pods," there was a pause. "Um, correction, one active pod, one malfunctioning pod." Another pause of uncertainty.

"Final section clear," another communication came in.

"Sir, I'm not sure what to make of this malfunctioning pod. Permission to call in a med crew?"

With the ship cleared by his peacekeeping unit, he saw no reason to object.

"Med crew to the loading docks. Come prepared for cryo-shock," Hinata commanded through his comms. Rohaan jumped in shock at the command. He hadn't been able to hear the reports from the peacekeeping unit.

"Two cryo-pods were activated on the ship," Hinata relayed. "Only one of those cryo-pods is functioning."

Rohaan's face lined with worry, and something else—confusion? He didn't have time to follow up. A med crew came rushing through the loading dock. Hinata fell into step behind them, signaling Rohaan to follow as well.

An eerie feeling permeated the air inside the craft. At first, it just felt off, an overwhelming sense of wrongness. Then he began to assemble the little details in his head. There was no soft glow of auxiliary lights, no gentle hum of mechanisms working. Even the organic portions of the ship looked lifeless.

Rohaan shivered beside him. He felt it too. Hinata's senses sharpened with each step, taking in the state of the bridge, then the little alcove where two active cryo-pods were housed, but even here, something was off. One pod glowed a gentle blue, the only light he had seen throughout the ship. The other pod was sealed, with frosty crystals etched on its lid, just as if it were active, yet it was dark. He took a step closer to inspect the active pod. Through the ice crystals, he couldn't fully make out its occupant, but it didn't look right. It was all one color, a golden tan, and the shape...it wasn't humanoid. However, that wasn't the pod the medics were focused on.

The medics gathered around the unlit pod. They pulled out datapads and cables, working on the machinery to see if they could save the life contained inside. Even through the dark, Hinata could make out a humanoid form inside.

A burst of gas broke the quiet of the dead ship as a medic cut the cryo-pod tubes and attached their own equipment. They rushed to attach wires, their fingers dancing across controls. The pod lights powered up with the same blue glow as the undamaged pod. Finally, Hinata got a glimpse of the captain. She looked like she could be a member of the Stjarna Tribe, a high-house aristocrat if the bio-ship was any indication. *Interesting*, not at all what he expected, for what he could only assume was an outlaw "archaeologist."

"Sir, we are ready to move the pod to medical," one of the medics announced.

"Very well," he replied. "Will you be able to revive its occupant?"

The medics hesitated.

"We don't know yet, sir. It looks like the cryo-freeze did not initiate properly. We won't know if it achieved enough of a deep freeze for revival to be viable until we get the pod to medical."

Hinata nodded. With his approval, the medical team moved out, pushing the cryo-pod on suspensors that levitated a few inches off the ground. Rohaan and Hinata were left alone in the alcove with the single functioning unit, and its strange occupant.

"What do you make of this?" Hinata asked, gesturing to the pod.

"The cryo-pod, sir?" Rohaan asked as he took a small step forward.

"More specifically, what do you make of the occupant?"

"I really wouldn't know, sir."

"You specialize in Old World signals and technology, do you not?"

"Well...yes, but, sir, I really couldn't speculate as to what this is."

"Humor me. I think that the captain of this ship is more than just an acquaintance of yours. Perhaps you have some thoughts on what she might have been doing? Why would she have been flying what appears to be a dead ship and what is it that she might have put in this cryo-pod?"

Rohaan looked down, shuffling his feet uncomfortably. "I might have some thoughts on what she was up to, sir. But...I truly don't know what is in that pod." Rohaan paused as if to gather his nerve. "Sir, if you would grant me your permission, I could tap into the ship's systems. See if there are any answers there."

Hinata looked around at the ship's dark walls. These bio-ships were not simple machines. When they died, they truly died. Legend had it that their consciousness—their soul—was transmitted back to Earth That Was, where its consciousness joined with the great AI of Earth and all other AI souls that have returned to share in one great consciousness. It was said to have been a way for the machines to experience life as their creators did, to control the distribution of power, and to share that experience with a mortal soul. Hinata did not believe that there was an ancient Earth—not anymore. The most commonly accepted research suggested that the planet had died thousands of years ago. Why else would all of humankind take to the stars? If anything remained at all, it would be a dead husk in a distant solar system. In any case, if the ship had truly died, there would be nothing Rohaan could do to revive it, but what if there was something left to salvage? Answers? He turned to Rohaan, gesturing to the lifeless ship.

"If you think there is any spark of life left in this, then so be it. I find it doubtful, but how you waste your time is of no concern to me. I will authorize your entry to work with the ship. Let the guard post know if you need anything, you are welcome to any equipment that might help in your task." Hinata turned to leave.

"Sir?" Rohaan called after him.

Hinata glanced over his shoulder at the man.

"What do I do with that?" Rohaan asked, indicating the active cryo-pod.

"Leave it. And Mr. Dar, for your own sake, don't wake it up."

57

CHAPTER 8 | FREYJA

THE RING

The megastructure loomed over Freyja, taking up the entire airlock window. The ring was so massive that from this angle, it blocked her view of the star just beyond it. A twinge of guilt ran through her. She had come out to the Theta quadrant to quash the squabbling between the Zirka and Setareh Tribes. The Setareh Tribe had taken control of the newly constructed wormhole ring in the Theta quadrant and were demanding that Zirka pay for the use of the gate. The Zirka Tribe was less than enthusiastic about the imposed tax and started several skirmishes with Setareh forces.

The wormhole gate was part of the new trade routes established by the United Tribal Axis and was intended to remain open to all tribes.

It was one of the benefits of the stability the UTA provided. They were working to link the Known Galaxies via the megastructures. Constructed at the edge of stars, the rings siphoned off the continuous energy needed to power wormhole travel. Stable wormholes required great amounts of energy. That was why individual ships could only perform small jumps through hyperspace; longer jumps required full wormholes. Without the assistance of the rings, a ship would quickly burn through its energy cells and leave them stranded in space.

The Silk Road, as the UTA had named it, was a testament to humanity's ingenuity, and the UTA's drive to unite them. Unfortunately, the rings that were far from the central rim, where the UTA housed its government, had become a point of contention for entrepreneurs looking to take control of their local economies. This wasn't the first dispute Freyja's fleet had been dispatched to settle, and she was sure it wouldn't be the last.

Freyja tried to quash the guilt gnawing at the corners of her mind. She had put both tribes in line and would be leaving the quadrant, but not before she carried out another initiative, this one for the Empress. The Empress controlled all of the trade routes to deep space mining colonies, all except the newly erected ring in the Theta quadrant. The Empress did not share power; she wanted the ring disabled.

No one will be hurt—Freyja tried to appease her conscience—*and the damage done should only take a year to repair.* That had been at the Empress' request. Freyja assumed that the Empress planned to have the forces necessary to take control of the quadrant by then. Her mother was never one to waste assets.

A shadow washed across Freyja's face as Selkie passed behind the ring. They hovered by the edge of the megastructure, where a small gap of only three meters separated her from her target.

"Get ready to engage," Freyja called over her comms. She was fully suited up against the void, her helmet tinted, just an anonymous soldier, identical to the small unit of six at her back. Among them were her lieutenant commanders, Kylian Aimé and Tristan Cylien. It was a larger squad than she had taken on past missions. She had tried to limit their involvement in these clandestine missions. She trusted the men and women behind her with her life. They were her Berserkers, her elite squad of mixed-blood soldiers that had been with her since cadet school. She hated bringing more of them into her dealings with the Empress, but this time, it couldn't be helped. The rings were megastructures—massive enough to transport an entire fleet in one jump. If they wanted to do enough damage to bring the ring down for a prolonged period, they would need to hit the structure at seven strategic sites. Her analyst had detected a solar storm building. It would hit in the next hour. It was a risk to carry out their mission in the face of the storm, but it was also a chance to make the damage look like an accident. She had to take it.

"Operation Carrington is a go," she called through the comms before diving from the airlock out into the void. She glided the short distance to the ring, then connected to the structure with the magnetic elements in her boots and gloves. Out of the corner of her eye, she watched Selkie move on to the next target, further along the ring's rim. Another Berserker glided from the airlock, then stuck to the side of the ring before Selkie disappeared beyond the curve of the ring to deliver the rest of her soldiers.

Freyja focused on the wall in front of her. She had landed just a few meters away from a maintenance walkway. Alternating her magnetic hold between her boots and gloves, she climbed the rest of the way over to the walkway. Once she was close enough, she pushed off from the side of the ring, momentum carrying her the rest of the way. The impact of the landing passed through her knees and settled into her hips as she engaged her Z-grav boots to keep her in place. From here, she could access the maintenance hatch for this section of the ring.

Freyja hunkered down by the door, waiting for the protocol Kylian had developed to hack through the security system. He was a genius programmer—Freyja was glad that he was on her side. The door in front of her released with a hiss, allowing her to slip inside. She waited for the light above the inner door to change as the room re-pressurized. Once the light flicked over to green, Freyja advanced into the gloom of the interior structure. This was a maintenance section—there was nothing beautiful about it, just minimal lighting throwing dark shadows over industrial walls run through with a tangled mass of pipes.

Freyja pulled up the schematics in her HUD. She wasn't far from the location where she would lay her charges. It was a risk setting the charges inside the structure, but setting them outside would have been a far greater risk to her crew, with the solar storm picking up. She just hoped that no one looked too closely at the damage. She had a feeling this would reignite the feud between the Zirka and Setareh Tribes and this time, no one would be coming to help them. With the two tribes fighting again, no one would have time to investigate the damage.

Freyja turned a corner to find her strike site. With a blink of her eyes, her ocular display outlined the exact formation for the charges. Freyja attached the thick explosive putty to the wall, outlining the blast area. Easy enough. It was time to get to the extraction site, just five kilometers from her current location. The pickup window was approaching. She settled into an easy jog. All of the maintenance crews were working on the other side of the ring. No one was scheduled to be on this side until tomorrow. By then, they would be long gone, back through the wormhole to the Alpha quadrant.

A scuffling noise ahead froze her mid-step. She glanced to the side to find two mechanics cozied up in an alcove, jumpsuits stripped down to their waists, entangled in each other's arms. *Shit.* They hadn't seen her yet. She could sneak past, and no one would be the wiser. Freyja took one cautious step before guilt halted her advance. If she snuck past them without saying a word, she was leaving them to die. This entire section of the ring would be depressurized when the charges went off. *Damn it.* This wasn't the plan. Disable the ring, no one gets hurt. No. She wouldn't leave them to die.

Freyja turned to the alcove. Straightening her posture, she donned her persona as an admiral of the United Tribal Axis, and cleared her throat. The two mechanics started at her presence. They leaped away from each other, rushing to put their jumpsuits back in order.

"No one is supposed to be in this section of the ring," Freyja's voice rang out with an air of authority through the speaker of her tinted helm.

"Sorry, ma'am," one of them mumbled.

"Sorry my ass, get back to your assignment," Freyja roared.

"Yes, ma'am," the two mechanics said in unison, taking off running down the hallway she had just come through. She let some of the tension melt from her shoulders. That could have been worse.

Freyja jogged the rest of the way in silence, with no further disruption to her steady cadence. As she rounded another bend to arrive at the extraction site, she counted five of her squad waiting at the airlock. Kylian was missing. He had been dropped off last, furthest from the extraction site. A position he had been assigned because he was also the fastest of her Berserkers.

Freyja checked the timer in her ocular display—there were still five minutes until extraction. He would make it. He had to.

The scuffling of boots across the grated floor drew Freyja's attention to the corridor beyond the airlock. There was a muffled sound, then Kylian was thrust forward onto his knees on the walkway just out of her reach. A sword held at his neck, three armed guards just behind him. Kylian's helm had been retracted and his eyes burned with a caged rage; but she saw something else in his eyes, too. He trusted her; he would wait for her mark.

"Who are you?" the guard called out.

"If you value your life, you'll hand over my man and run like hell," Freyja replied.

The guard pulled Kylian closer to his blade. It was the wrong answer. An alert hit Freyja's ocular display—incoming ship. Selkie was here to take them back to the fleet. They had to move, now. If they missed their window, they would be stranded in the Theta quadrant when the explosives blew. She switched over to internal comms with her team.

"Cut your way out of the airlock. Get to Selkie. I'll be right behind you." Tension ran through her team at the order. They didn't want to leave one of their own behind, but Kylian was her responsibility and she would be the one to make sure he came home. "Move," she ordered over the comms.

She had to close the gap between her and the guard before he could slit Kylian's throat. Red emergency lights flashed around her as her squad cut their way out of the ring. The muscles in her thighs coiled in anticipation. Her eyes locked with the guard's. His eyes darted to her crew as they breached the airlock. That would be his last mistake. She sprang forward, slamming into the guard holding Kylian. They tumbled to the ground, a mess of arms and legs, her lightly armored spacesuit tangling with exposed flesh. Extending an arm, she reached back to grab her sword, then plunged the blade through the guard's ribs without hesitation. Withdrawing the sword from the dying man, she arced the blade around her head as she came to her feet. The other two guards had already disappeared down the corridor. They had no desire to meet the same fate as their fallen comrade. Freyja resheathed her sword and dropped to the ground beside Kylian. Air and bubbles of blood hissed out of the gash across his neck.

"No, no, no, no, no!" She fumbled at the controls to trigger his helm. It sprung up over his head, but the cut in his suit continued to leak blood into the space between them. She pressed her fingers against his neck, trying to staunch the bleeding, but it was coming too fast. Dark crimson seeped between her fingers. It took Freyja a moment to remember herself. There was nothing she could do for him here—she had to get him back to the ship. If she could get him to medical, he had a chance. Freyja pressed her eyes together, willing away the memory of another suit leaking air into the void. Now wasn't the time. She could fix this. She could save him.

"Exhale," she whispered through her comms as she hoisted his tall frame over her shoulders, staggering to the breach. Selkie was waiting for her, just a long leap from the edge of the ring. Tightening her grip on Kylian, she jumped. Having no control over their trajectory, her only focus was on keeping hold of Kylian's limp body. The internal airlock wall rushed up before her and she slammed into the bulkhead, her shoulder crunching under the impact. The chamber sealed swiftly behind her.

Freyja collapsed to the floor as the artificial gravity kicked in. Her arms wrapped around Kylian's head as she held him on her lap. With numb fingers, she triggered the release for his helmet. It retracted into the collar, crimson blood splattering over her legs. She pressed her shaking hands against his throat.

"You don't die, you hear me?" Freyja hissed, "You don't die. That is an order!" Numbness spread through her body as she began to shake.

"We've got it from here, Admiral." A medic took Kylian from her arms, his hands a blur of motion as he worked to seal the gash. Freyja watched, helpless, as shivers wracked her body, slamming her teeth together.

He would make it. He had to make it.

***

Freyja sat in medical, her hands clasped in front of her chin, her eyes locked on Kylian's prone form. A shudder ran through Selkie and Freyja vaguely recognized the sensation of a jump. Tristan had taken charge when he saw Freyja covered in blood and shaking from shock in the airlock. The med tech had tried to fuss over her, but she had shooed them away.

She sat vigil at Kylian's side, droplets of his blood dried on her face and hands. They had at least managed to get her out of her drenched spacesuit.

The medic had repaired the damage to Kylian's throat, but there was still a thick white line running the width of his neck. There would be a scar, but he would live. That's what the medic had said, but Freyja couldn't bring herself to leave his side until she saw him open his eyes.

After what felt like an eternity, Kylian's black eyelashes fluttered open. His warm hazel eyes met hers. A slight smile pulled at his lips, though it was clear he hardly had the strength for it.

"That was a close one, eh, boss ma'am?" he whispered with the breath of a chuckle, his regenerating vocal cords raw.

"Too close," Freyja said, taking one of his hands in her own. "The missions are getting more dangerous. I can't lose you. I can't lose any of our Berserkers."

Kylian squeezed her hand, pressing his eyelids together in response.

"What now, then, Admiral?"

Freyja considered it. She didn't know the Empress' end game, or which side of all this she and her people were truly on.

"I don't know yet, but when the time comes to choose a side, we'd best be ready."

"Where you lead, I will follow."

CHAPTER 9 | SKYLA

COMMANDER AZAI

A ten-year-old Skyla grips her bō staff tightly as she pushes against her opponent. Sweat beads on her brow as she grits her teeth and surges forward with a hard shove. Her opponent—another ten-year-old girl with dark, curly hair framing her face—stumbles backward. Skyla takes advantage while her opponent is off balance, ducking down to sweep the girl's legs, but her opponent is too quick. The girl jumps, tucking her legs up to her chest, then counters with her own blow, striking Skyla in the opposite shoulder. Skyla grunts with the sharp pain but manages to stay in control, bringing the back end of her staff up for another attack. The strike lands, hitting her opponent hard in the gut. The girl gasps and drops her staff, struggling to take in air. She collapses to her knees. Skyla lowers her weapon, dropping to her knees beside the other girl. She puts a hand on her shoulder.

"Are you all right, Raven?" Skyla asks with concern in her eyes. Raven pushes her hand away.

"Get off of me," she spits the words at Skyla, who looks at the other girl in a state of shocked confusion.

"You fought well today! It was a good game. We can play again tomorrow," Skyla says.

"We are not playing," Raven shouts back. "This isn't a game. Stop talking to me like we are babies. We aren't little kids anymore."

"Feels like a game to me." Skyla shrugs. "Want to work on battle tactics and strategy homework together tonight?"

"Just stop."

"Stop what?"

"Stop acting like we are friends."

"But we are friends."

"No, we are not!"

"Sure we are, Raven. You have been my best friend ever since I can remember!"

"That was before," Raven says.

Skyla falls silent. She cannot believe what she is hearing. Raven is her best friend in the whole universe. She is the person who she goes to with all her secrets, the person who knows every word of their favorite songs and isn't embarrassed to belt them out at the top of their lungs together, the person who gets all of her jokes. How could their friendship be over, just like that?

"Raven, we are in the same tribe. We are on the same team. Just because we leave for the Mímir Academy next week doesn't mean we can't be friends anymore." Skyla tries.

Raven just shakes her head, "You just don't get it, do you?"

Skyla stares at her. No, no she didn't get it.

"Once we are cadets, you will be my competition. We will compete for everything from here on out. Standing in our class. Postings, assignments, promotions. No, we are not friends anymore. You are just my competition. That is all I see you as." With that, Raven hurls her staff at the ground. It bounces twice before settling on the metal grating. By then, Raven has already walked away. Skyla hesitates. She wants to go after her friend—but what else is there to say? So instead, she turns and runs through the empty cargo bay they had been practicing in. She runs through the hydroponics garden, where rows of crops rise on either side of her. She runs until the ground falls out from underneath her and she falls into endless darkness...

Skyla's eyes shot open, and she jumped in her bed. Her mind was a haze of confusion as she awoke from the dream. It had felt so real—as if her mind had perfectly replayed the memory from her childhood. Skyla's heart still raced, and her cheeks were wet with tears. She was not a ten-year-old girl anymore. She was...where was she?

She squinted hard at the ceiling above. It was cold, white, sterile. There were no organic curves or coral growths and the room was quiet save for the faint beep of monitors. The hum of Pele's engine was missing. She bolted upright as it all came into sharp focus in her mind: Pele shutting down, the slingshot coordinates, going into cryo-sleep. She took in the room around her with fresh eyes. It looked like a clinic with plain white walls and pale blue curtains framing square windows along one side. She occupied one bed in a row of beds that took up the other wall, where monitors and medical instruments were dispersed at even intervals. She must have made it to Medina Outpost. The clinic doors slid open, and a tech entered. He wore sky-blue scrubs, a small round hat, and a smile that appeared to match his disposition. Once at her bedside, he pulled out his datapad.

"Nice to see you awake," he said as he looked through her file. "Why don't you lie back and rest," he insisted, gentle hands guiding her shoulders back down to the bed. "I'll message Commander Azai that you're awake." The tech exited the way he came.

Skyla groaned. She purposely avoided doing business at Medina because of Commander Azai. The commander's reputation was well known throughout the black market. Before he took over Medina, nearly three years ago now, there had been a thriving community of archaeologists selling tech to interested researchers at the station. Medina had been the place she had first found her feet again after Gabriel had left her for dead. A research vessel had plucked her out of the void and brought her back to the station. She had loved it here, before Commander Azai changed everything. She hadn't been back since he took command, but rumor had it that he had cracked down hard on the archaeological community.

The tech reappeared, carrying a small tray. "I'm sure you are hungry." He placed the tray on the table beside Skyla's bed, then left again. Only a few moments had passed when a man hesitantly poked his head into the clinic. A wide grin spread across Skyla's face when she saw him.

"Ears!" she tried to call out, her voice cracking from disuse.

The man smiled and came into the room. He gave Skyla a gentle hug, then sat on the chair beside her bed.

"I don't think I have ever been so happy to see anyone," she said.

The tips of the man's ears turned pink as he gave her a brief nod.

"I guess you got my message, then?" Skyla said.

"You are lucky I did. If I hadn't been listening in that quadrant, I could have easily missed it, you know."

"I know," Skyla sighed. "I didn't have a lot of options. Besides, I had a pretty good hunch you would be listening in that sector."

"Am I that predictable?"

"Yes," Skyla laughed, "but that is not why. Rohaan, you wouldn't believe the civilization I found on this expedition! And this is just one of hundreds of possible planets. If there were ever a section of space to look at for alien signals, this would be the one."

A smile lit Rohaan's face. Mainstream scholars believed that there were no true aliens, just humans who populated the galaxies long before The Exodus of Earth That Was, the event that had sent all of humankind out into the universe, but that didn't dissuade Ears. It was something that he was truly passionate about, even if studying alien technology was frowned upon as a science. Skyla was grateful because alien tech was how they had met. When Skyla had arrived at Medina on Rohaan's uncle's research vessel all those years ago, he had instantly become obsessed with her expeditions. Despite her efforts to dissuade him, his persistence paid off. He reminded her too much of her father. They shared the same crazy dream—and while she wasn't a believer—she had found a true friend in Ears.

"Did you find digital records for my archives?" The words burst out of him like a dam overrun with flood waters.

Skyla shook her head. "No, anything that could have held digital records was fried, but I scanned all of the writing samples I found, plus I brought back some prime tech. Perhaps you can learn something from the code before I sell it—"

The med bay doors snapped open, cutting their conversation short.

A man in a crisp black uniform stood in the doorway. He was young; not much older than she was, if she had to guess. His hair was pulled tight and braided against his scalp, the sides shaved into a fresh fade, with the hilt of a sword sticking up above his left shoulder, and the gold insignia at the mock neck of his uniform designated him as commander.

Skyla had the sinking suspicion that Commander Azai was every bit as bad as his reputation portrayed. His polished boots and overly tidy appearance reeked of an officer angling for advancement. Even his gait as he approached her med bed was crisp and controlled.

"Good to see you awake, Captain," he said. "I am Commander Hinata Azai. I oversee Medina Outpost. Perhaps you could fill me in on what exactly you were doing on a dead ship in uncharted space?"

Skyla's heart sank. A dead ship? She turned to Rohaan. If anyone could save Pele, it was him. He knew more about code of all origins than anyone else in the Known Galaxies.

Rohaan read the concern in her eyes. "Don't worry, Pele is going to be okay."

The tension that had been building in her shoulders melted at his words. In the time-honored tradition of receiving an AI ship, she and Pele had bonded when Skyla was born. Bonded pairs spent their entire lives together, human and machine, sharing the experience of a mortal life. It was a tradition that originated before the Exodus, and if the legends were to be believed, it had once been more common to have a bonded pair than not. After thousands of years as nomads, resources had grown scarce, and now only the great houses still upheld the tradition. Skyla couldn't imagine her life without Pele.

"She is a clever AI. I found her consciousness hidden in her DNA stack. It appears that the virus was not built to infect organic tech. She won't be flight-ready for a few weeks, though. That virus you picked up did a lot of damage, but we are working on repairs now. I'm sure Pele will be more accommodating now that you're awake. She has been quite difficult to work with," Rohaan said.

Skyla couldn't help but smile at Pele's quirky personality.

The commander cleared his throat, "It won't matter if your ship is repaired if I am also detaining you for illegal salvage."

"You know, Commander, I am not any use to you if you detain me. I'm sure we can come to some kind of arrangement."

His face was made of stone. Not a flicker of emotion. "I don't need to make any kind of arrangements. This is my outpost, and you will answer my questions, or you will be detained until you are in a more accommodating mood."

Well, there goes that—she knew the type; she wouldn't get anywhere with him until he got something he wanted from her. He had to feel in control. She could work with that.

"Very well, Commander. If you must know, I was exploring the Zeta quadrant based on some recent intel I received."

Commander Azai narrowed his eyes. He obviously wanted her to elaborate. However, Rohaan's flushing complexion left little mystery as to where this intel had come from.

"There was an interesting deep space signal coming from the quadrant. Seemed as good a reason as any to check it out."

"A strange signal in an uncharted area of space seemed like an invitation to break the law to you?"

She shrugged.

"Planet Alpha 4375 was the closest habitable planet I encountered, so I decided to start there."

She detailed the planetary defense system she had encountered, and though the commander held his rigid posture and stoic face, she didn't miss how the color drained from his cheeks.

She paused, canting her head, "Everything all right, Commander?"

"You initiated a full neural link in the middle of a crash?"

"Sure, it was the only way we would be able to move fast enough to regain control."

He shook his head. "That was very dangerous."

She shrugged again.

"Mandate 82-54 of the Hoshiko bylaws forbade full links five decades ago."

A laugh ripped from Skyla's chest. She couldn't help herself. "Well, that explains why you are all such piss-poor pilots!"

A muscle feathered in Commander Azai's jaw as his eyes bore holes into her. Perhaps she had taken that one a bit too far. It was true, though; they hadn't won the Leikar Cup in a half-century.

She cleared her throat and picked up with her explanation, detailing the damage to her ship, and her expedition into the broken city. She left out the part about finding the creature and the treasure trove of tech that she had left behind in the city. Commander Azai didn't need to know that she had easy access to more contraband.

"There must have been a virus in the tech I brought on board. Pele was performing a routine analysis of the technology when her systems went haywire. With the ship shutting down, I didn't have a lot of options. I'm lucky that the slingshot gamble even worked."

"Lucky indeed," Commander Azai said. "By the time you put yourself into cryo, the virus had already reached your pod. The initiation sequence was unable to complete. That pod left you somewhere between living and cryo. I was informed by our med techs that if we had not scooped you out of space when we did, it is highly unlikely you would have woken from that gamble at all."

A shiver ran down her spine. She knew it had been a close call, but she hadn't realized how close. Then her heart stopped. What about the creature?

"There was another pod," she began carefully.

"Yes," the commander cut in, "would you like to tell me more about what is in that pod?"

"It is just something I found," she hesitated. "It's my...pet?"

"Your *pet* is still in cryo. Its pod was active when we found you."

A wave of relief washed over her. Pele would be fine. The creature was safe in its pod. They had survived.

"Now, shall we get to the matter of settling your debt?" Commander Azai said.

"My debt?"

"Yes. You have caused quite a bit of work for the United Tribal Axis Navy. I believe a debt is owed."

"The United Tribal Axis works for the people."

"Ah, but you are not a law-abiding citizen, are you? You have caused quite a bit of trouble while indulging in unlawful activity."

Skyla scowled at the commander. He might have a handsome face, but he was going to be a pain in her ass.

"Don't worry. I think I have a solution."

"What, detain me? What good does that do either of us?"

"No good at all, by my estimation, which is why I won't be detaining you."

She cocked an eyebrow. Maybe she didn't have a read on this commander?

"No, I don't need you using up resources on my station. I will just confiscate the illegally salvaged tech. After all, it is technically already property of the United Tribal Axis."

She gawked at him. He couldn't be serious.

"Now, Commander, you couldn't possibly believe I would hand over all that tech. If I can't turn a profit from my expedition, I won't be able to bring you more tech for your little Navy to turn into weapons. That's just bad business."

She paused. Commander Azai held his tongue, but something shifted in those amber eyes; she had him.

"Perhaps instead we can come to an arrangement," Skyla mused. "I will give you first offering on this and any future salvage that I bring to Medina."

Commander Azai shook his head, "No, you will give me first offering on *all* of your salvaged tech. You will bring *all* of your findings from your expeditions to the Zeta quadrant here first and you will sell them to me at half price."

Negotiating? She hadn't thought the prim and proper commander had it in him.

"Ten percent off," she countered.

"Forty."

"Twenty."

"Very well," Commander Azai nodded, "we have an arrangement." He extended his hand, and Skyla took it in a firm handshake. It was then that she noticed how weak she was. It had been a great effort to extend her arm at all. She let her hand fall to the bed beside her, unable to hold it up any longer. The exhaustion she felt was so oppressive that a deep ache settled in her muscles and made it hard to concentrate. Now that she knew everyone was safe, she felt the abuse her body had been through. Her throat was raw; breathing was a chore, and even keeping her eyelids open took an enormous effort. The doors snapped open as the med tech reappeared. He came to stand across from Commander Azai.

"I hope you have the information you need, Commander. We should leave her to rest. Cryo-sickness takes a heavy toll on the body. Every minute she spent between wakefulness and cryo in that ship without life support, her body was degenerating."

Commander Azai nodded, then looked back to Skyla.

"Well, Captain, we can finalize our arrangements once you are out of medical. I look forward to seeing what you have brought me." He turned to Rohaan and nodded, "Mr. Dar." He appraised the scientist briefly before leaving.

Skyla smiled at Ears. He had pulled through for her, as she knew he would. She could tell he had so much more he wanted to discuss, but she couldn't keep her eyes open another second. She let her eyelids flutter closed as she submitted to the pull of exhaustion.

CHAPTER 10 | HINATA

WINDS OF CHANGE

Hinata flexed his fingers back from the holo display on his desk. He reached out again, ready to submit the bioscans for the mysterious pilot sitting in his med bay. Again, he pulled his hand back as if he had been reaching for a flame.

This was ridiculous. Submitting bioscans for undocumented arrivals on any UTA space station was standard protocol, and he always followed protocol. He always followed the rules and yet, Hinata had lost the admiral exams to Freyja despite following all the rules. By all measures, he had won and yet still, he lost. He flicked his hand, dismissing the shimmering holo on his desk. For the first time in years, he had something more than running drills and maintaining order on Medina. He couldn't explain it. He had been snared in this game the moment Mr. Dar had requested that catch net. His childhood obsession with starship racing got the better of him, and now he had plucked a mysterious outlaw from the stars and he didn't want the game to end. Not yet.

For the first time in years, he had something to think about beyond his failures. This mystery—the captain—it was as if he was coming up for air after years of drowning. He felt a twinge of guilt. There was a reason he always followed the rules. He thought of his mother and how she had raised him to honor their tribe, how she had looked at him the night his brother died, how she had exiled him to Medina to contemplate his failure. He shook his head, dismissing the thoughts. He had been given no opportunity for redemption. His mother hadn't even sent a single personal communication since his exile. He could have this.

Hinata opened the holo display on his desk once more, pulling up the records of the captain and her AI ship. He would do his own investigation. A thrill of excitement ran down his spine at the thought of uncovering the identity of this woman. His heart rate raced with the excitement of his self-appointed mission. He had just submitted his report request when an alert pulled him from his exploration.

"What is it?" he demanded as he opened the comm line.

"Apologies, Commander." The peacekeeper in his display grimaced at Hinata's response. "There has been an explosion in the experimental research labs department."

"What?" He sprang to his feet, shifting the display from his desk to his ocular display as he strode from his office.

"Lab number 317, sir. Fire units are containing the explosion now."

"On my way."

Hinata ended the communication, opening a line to the station's AI system. "Report—I need to know if our guest has left medical."

"Security logs indicate that she has not left medical since she was decanted from her cryo-pod."

Hinata nodded. "And what about that ship? Has anything been removed since it docked?"

"Only the cryo-pod has been removed from the docked ship, Pele, sir."

Hinata was surprised to feel relief that his little enigma couldn't be the cause of the bombing.

***

When Hinata arrived at the wrecked lab, the area was still sealed. He could see through the containment fields that the flames had been neutralized. The area would remain sealed until the smoke had been pulled out into the air filtration system.

"Peacekeeper Lawless." Hinata nodded to the man directing crews outside of the containment area.

"Commander." The peacekeeper brought his fist to his chest, inclining his head to the commander. Hinata returned the gesture.

"What do we know?"

"Not much yet, sir. The lab was empty when the explosion went off and it was contained to lab 317 alone. No other units were damaged. Lab 317, however, has been completely destroyed."

"Does that strike you as strange?"

"It does." The peacekeeper hesitated, not wanting to give voice to his suspicions. "If it had been an accident, I don't believe that it would have been so controlled."

"I agree. Whose lab is 317?"

Lawless's gaze went glassy as he searched through records only he could see in his ocular display.

"It belongs to Dr. Aman."

"And what research is Dr. Aman working on?"

"It is listed as advanced energy research..." There was a pause as Lawless scanned the documents. "It says here that the current experimentation is focused on quantum energy transfer."

"Could Dr. Aman's research have caused this?"

"I am not sure, sir."

"Very well, I will leave you to deal with this." Hinata gestured to the demolished lab. "I'll follow up with Dr. Aman."

***

Hinata kept his gaze trained on the man in front of him, his eyes recording every gesture. The man's hands trembled as he grasped his coffee cup and little splashes of dark liquid slipped down the sides. Dr. Aman sighed and set the cup on the table, abandoning the coffee in favor of running his hands through his salt and pepper hair, then tugging on his matching beard. They sat together in the seating area of Dr. Aman's home. The room was decorated in the fashion of Medina station; brightly colored pillows were scattered around a low-seated wooden table with ornately carved edges and legs.

"Tell me more about your research," Hinata prompted.

Dr. Aman rubbed the back of his neck before clasping his coffee cup once more. "We were on the cusp of developing the first quantum entanglement energy transfer generator."

"Can you explain that to me?" Hinata asked.

Dr. Aman sighed. "On the quantum level, particles can become entangled. They are connected, even if they end up at great distances. My work is based on Hotta's theory, which has shown that energy can be teleported at the quantum level. My research is on how to harness quantum entanglement to teleport the energy produced by stars to generators for starships."

"That sounds like very impressive work, Dr. Aman."

"It is," he whispered. "It's the promise of near-free energy. A way to fuel our ships and stations. Prosperity for all of humanity." Dr. Aman paused, his eyes going distant before he continued. "It's more than that, even. It is a lightweight, consistent energy source that could fuel stable wormhole generation for long-range intergalactic jumps. This technology will open up the entire universe for exploration. No more micro jumps to conserve fuel, no more trade routes limited to established wormhole rings—this technology changes everything about the way our people travel through space."

Dr. Aman's work was more important than Hinata had thought. He didn't like where this investigation was leading him. There would be people who wouldn't want work like this to come to fruition. It was work worth bombing a laboratory over; worth killing over, even.

"I am truly sorry for your loss," Hinata said, unsure how to comfort the man.

"*Our* loss," Dr. Aman's voice trembled. "I don't do this work for myself, Commander. My work, this work, I do it for the future of humanity." Dr. Aman stared straight into the dark depths of his coffee cup.

"Of course." Hinata nodded. The Taaralog Tribe was focused on the betterment of all, not of self—just as his tribe was. "You have backup files, I assume?"

"Yes, of course, but it will take months to rebuild everything that was lost in the explosion...but yes, I have all of my research notes. We will rebuild. It is just a delay." The man settled a bit at this thought, resolve etched across his face. Hinata, however, only grew more concerned. If the doctor still had his files and could rebuild his own life might be at risk. Who was to say that the violence was not finished?

"Dr. Aman, have you noticed anything out of the ordinary? Has there been anyone new poking around your lab?"

"No. The only other person with access to my lab is my daughter. She is my research assistant, and just as dedicated to this project as I am."

"How about in your personal life? Has anyone bothered you recently? Any old associates resuming communications?"

Dr. Aman shook his head, "No, Commander. My entire life is dedicated to this work, and my family, of course. I think you will find the same of most researchers here at Medina. This is a haven of scholarship. We all want the same thing here—to better humanity."

Hinata nodded, Dr. Aman was right, these people were dedicated to furthering the knowledge of the human race. In his three years as commander of Medina, he had never experienced such destruction. Yet, here they were: something had changed.

His silence must have unnerved the doctor, who leaned forward to ask in a whispered rush. "Is there a hidden meaning behind your questions, Commander? Should I be concerned? Worried for my life? For my daughter?"

"I am sure you are aware of how unusual this situation is. I'm not ruling anything out at this point. Please rest assured that you will be protected on my station. I will post peacekeepers to watch over you and your daughter." Hinata's words were meant to reassure the man, but the lines of worry around his face deepened.

"Do you think that is necessary?"

"I do."

CHAPTER 11 | SKYLA

WELCOME TO MEDINA

A frustrating cycle of boredom, hazy wakefulness, and fitful sleep filled Skyla's next week. Finally, the medics deemed her stable enough for release. She left medical with bracers on her arms and legs. The bracers were dual-purpose machines that provided electrical stimulus to help her tissues heal and employed force field manipulators to help stabilize her damaged muscles. Skyla found them clunky. and she insisted they were unnecessary, but they were a condition of her release from within the sterile clinic walls, so it was a trade she was willing to make.

When Skyla exited medical, she was met by a smiling face.

"Ears." They clasped forearms.

Rohaan had brought her pack, filled with a few of her personal items at her request. She reached out to take the bag from him, but he pulled it from her reach, swinging it onto his shoulder.

"I can carry my own bag," Skyla insisted.

"You barely look like you can carry your own body." Rohaan eyed the bracers.

"Oh, these? They're nothing, just a condition of my release."

Skyla extended her hand to take the bag. As if her body were protesting her very words, her legs wobbled just a little with the step. Rohaan was sharp—he didn't miss the moment of weakness.

"I am sure you are quite capable. However, my reputation would be ruined if people saw me walking beside an injured woman, and I had not offered to carry her bag." His words were kind as he gestured for her to follow him down the corridor.

Skyla conceded. She wouldn't win this one with him. She wanted to return directly to Pele. However, Commander Azai had not cleared Skyla's access to her own ship, yet. The arrogance of that man made her skin flame with frustration. Rohaan insisted it was for the best, as there was still a lot of work to do before Pele would be fully operational again. In the meantime, Rohaan had arranged temporary lodging for her.

As they exited the austere Naval section, the corridor opened up into a wide atrium with intricately carved archways and columns. The atrium had been crafted to look as if it had been carved out of the side of a mountain, all bright glittering sandstone. No hint that they were suspended in the stars, far from any rocky body. The atrium was five stories high, with a lush oasis in the center and a waterfall pouring into a pool below. Gravitational suspensors had been used to slow the fall of the water, muting the sound to a quiet tumble. Ancient date trees rimmed the pond, stretching their leaves up to the domed ceiling of glittering orbs. Medina

Outpost was the first space station founded after The Wandering, and it was one of the most beautiful stations Skyla had ever been to.

After The Exodus from Earth That Was, the tribes had wandered through the galaxies for generations. During this time, they had kept within their own fleets and never stayed in one place for long. The Taaralog Tribe had been the first to put down new roots, and Medina was those roots. The architecture paid homage to the Taaralog Tribe's ancient Earth ancestry, and as far as Skyla knew, there was no other place like it in the Known Galaxies.

They passed through the edges of the bustling atrium, full of vendors and artisans, and entered a lift that shot straight up, then out to the side, bypassing the maze of corridors that led to the section of the outpost where Rohaan had secured her lodging.

Soon they arrived at a corridor lined with doors, and Rohaan stopped in front of one, then tapped a sequence to open the door before gesturing for Skyla to enter first. She peeked inside. It was a small room with a sleeping cot, a tiny table with two chairs, and one door that she was sure led to the WC. The lights were dim, and the room was empty. But it felt cozy compared to the clinic. It would do until she could move back onto her ship. Rohaan moved in behind her, placing her bag on one of the chairs, then took a step back into the doorway. The room was so small that perhaps only four adults could crowd together inside.

"I will let you get settled in then," Rohaan said.

"Don't be ridiculous. I have been cooped up in medical all week—let's see what you found."

Rohaan looked reluctant; she knew he wouldn't want to push her too hard after the cryo-shock, but he was a scholar at heart and couldn't keep his excitement from bubbling to the surface.

"Are you sure?" he hesitated. "The doctor only released you on the condition that you continue to rest."

"Psh, how taxing can listening to your research be? I mean beyond taxing my patience with your far-flung theories, that is." That was all it took—she could see it in his eyes—he was dying to dig into his findings with her.

"Well, if you insist." Rohaan nodded and gestured for Skyla to follow him to his quarters. They didn't need to walk far. Here the doors were spread further apart, the rooms were larger. She was certain the section she had been assigned to was for transient workers, not permanent residents of the station.

Rohaan's quarters looked exactly as they had the last time she had been there. The walls were lined with bookcases filled to bursting with books. The texts on the spines were a mix of exotic languages. Most of them were recreations of ancient Earth texts. Some were recreations from expeditions to Old Worlds. Then there were the rare originals that Rohaan kept in the center bookcase. At first glance, the bookcase looked like the rest, but if one stared hard enough at the covers, the slight shimmer of a force field revealed itself. It was for environmental control, to preserve the book's ancient pages. Skyla thought Rohaan should add security measures as well. When she had said so—on several other occasions—he had simply shook his head and stated that Medina wasn't like that. Skyla had traveled to many stations and worlds over the years as an archaeologist, and she had a hard time believing that any place wasn't like that. Rohaan, however, would not budge on the matter, so she kept her opinions on the topic to herself.

In the center of the room there was a large table covered in datapads, scientific instruments, and bits of electronics. There were three plush seats around the table and Rohaan cleared a stack of books off the one closest to Skyla, urging her to sit. Normally, she would have refused; she enjoyed pacing around Rohaan's work like a satellite, but today she was grateful for the offer—just the short walk to the residential district had worn her out more than she cared to admit. Skyla realized she needed to rebuild her stamina fast if she hoped to be able to head out on another expedition anytime soon.

Rohaan seated himself in the chair opposite hers and cleared a small space on the table around him. He switched on the holo projector and an array of star charts sprang to life in front of him.

"After you left to explore the Zeta quadrant, I did some more digging." His hands trembled with excitement as he used his fingers to pinch and spin the star maps, zooming in on the solar system Skyla had visited. Then he tapped the blank space and little purple points dotted the start charts. There was one large point over the planet that Skyla had visited, but there were dozens more of varying sizes scattered across the entire quadrant.

"Here." Rohaan pointed at the largest purple dot. "This represents the original signal I told you about." Yes, that signal was the reason she had focused on that system for her expedition.

"Well, when I analyzed the data Pele brought back from your expedition, I was able to retrieve additional data from the satellite that attacked you. Using those findings, I was able to identify additional signals all across the quadrant." Rohaan manipulated the maps, again, to show more of the system. "These dots have the same elements as the first signal, but they are much weaker. That is why I didn't pick them up at first."

Skyla's eyes widened as the maps rotated and expanded to show a vast scattering of purple dots all across the unknown galaxy she had been exploring. The excitement in the air between them filled with the charge of electricity before a thunderstorm. They had found something truly extraordinary, but what was it, exactly?

Skyla thought of the treasure trove of tech she had found and how many more exotic caches might be out there, scattered through the galaxy with purple dots for markers. Rohaan was perhaps even more excited than she was at the possibility. It was written all over his face: he believed this could be his proof of alien life. It was the closest he had ever been to being validated as a scientist.

Skyla's heart warmed for the scholar. Her father had believed in the study of alien life too, and he too had been ridiculed, never taken seriously by his peers. Learning about strange civilizations and far-off possibilities while they went on their little adventures together had been one of Skyla's fondest memories from her childhood. That was before she left for the academy and her father left her life for good. Without thought, her fingers drifted to the pendant hanging around her neck—the one that he had given her. The memory was still a bitter pill lodged in her throat, even nearly two decades later.

Skyla shook her head. They would have plenty of time to plan their next exploration of the system once Pele was back up and running. That was her real concern.

"This is all great, Ears, but I need you to tell me about Pele."

Rohaan blinked a few times to refocus. "Of course." With a flick of his hands, the star charts disintegrated into a mist of particles on the table, then reassembled into a data read-out of Pele's systems. "You have one clever AI. She was able to survive the viral attack that disabled all of her systems by hiding in DNA deep storage."

DNA was an excellent place to store vast amounts of data, but these stores were not part of the ship's primary systems. Skyla had never heard of an AI storing their consciousness in DNA deep storage before.

"I've never seen anything like it," Rohaan said, as if reading her mind. "It was very brave. If you had failed to rescue her, if the virus had a DNA corrupting protocol, her consciousness would have been destroyed. No transmission to the Great Consciousness. True Death." The gravity of his words hung heavy between them. True Death occurred when an AI failed to transmit their consciousness back to ancient Earth. It meant their consciousness was erased for all time, as if they had never existed. There was no worse fate for an AI.

Pele took a great risk hiding instead of transmitting her consciousness. Skyla did not take lightly the faith Pele had put in her. Guilt constricted Skyla's chest. It was her fault that Pele had been infected. Skyla should have done a better job protecting her ship. AI ships were not explorers—AI ships usually served the UTA in the safety of the Known Galaxies. Skyla knew she would have to do a better job of protecting Pele.

"I was able to successfully extract her consciousness, and she is currently helping us reintegrate her systems." Rohaan flicked his wrist and a schematic of Pele pulled up in the hologram. "The systems in green, Pele has full control over. The ones in blue, she is currently reintegrating, and those in red will have to be replaced before she can reintegrate. They were too damaged by the virus to be repaired."

Skyla frowned. There was still a lot of work to do before Pele would be flight-ready. Seeing the concern in Rohaan's eyes, Skyla gave him a weak smile.

"You have done well, friend."

Rohaan's tension eased a little.

"There is just still so much work to do," Skyla sighed.

Rohaan nodded. His expression brightened. He tapped his datapad, which was followed by a notification on Skyla's device.

"Don't worry, I know you can't sit idle. Stars forbid you ever just relax. I've sent you the most detailed scans I have been able to pull of the additional signal systems. You can begin planning your next expedition, maybe your next ten. By the time Pele is up and running, you will be ready for your next adventure."

Skyla smiled at her friend, though some of her excitement had leaked away. She couldn't take Pele back out on expedition, not until she was certain that she could keep her safe.

"Ears, I need you to investigate this virus. If a threat this great was on the last planet, who knows what could be waiting for us on the rest of these worlds? I need to make sure that Pele will be protected. I don't want her to face such a dire decision again."

His face took on the serious demeanor of a scholar; Rohaan understood. "Of course."

Skyla's worry eased a little. If anyone could arm Pele against a strange Old World virus, it was Rohaan.

"It looks like we both have plenty of work before us." Rohaan smiled as he stood up from the table and walked over to a little cart that held a water kettle, teapot, and an assortment of silver jars. "I find I work best with a fresh pot of spiced tea. Care for a cup?"

CHAPTER 12 | FREYJA

CATASTROPHIC FAILURE

Freyja floated silently through the airlock. There was something beautiful about the silence of space, the vast, epic emptiness of it all, full beyond belief yet more nothing than something. Her limbs relaxed in the null-G environment, but there was a tension just below the surface; she was anxious to complete the task at hand.

Kylian and Tristan followed just behind her. They wore black body armor, covered in harsh angles that would make them hard to detect even with the best equipment, and Fazenda hardly had the best security. It was merely a remote collection of farming moons run by the Perdida Tribe.

Freyja glided to a graceful landing by the main biodome, the largest structure on the moon. The entire farming operation was a multi-faceted hex web of interconnected domes separated by elaborate mirrors for enhancing the strength of the pale yellow star at the heart of the solar system. The central dome was where all the hydro systems were monitored and adjusted. Kylian and Tristan landed next to her, the powdery moon dust coating their Z-grav boots in a fine layer of chalk.

She motioned for her men to watch either side as she detached a plasma cutter from her utility belt. Freyja attached the two pads of the plasma cutter just above her head on the biodome. A pale orange glow began to shimmer around the perimeter of the pads as they cut through arogelium plating. The two pads traveled away from each other, creating a semicircle outline. Once they reached the bottom of the dome, they automatically shut off. Freyja tapped at her datapad and a purple shimmering forcefield sprung to life around the semicircle cut in the biodome. She slowly pushed her gloved hands through the force field, her gloves magnetizing to hold onto the cutout as she stepped through the opening into the structure. Her lieutenants fell in behind her, securing the area. She set the makeshift door next to the gash in the dome and deactivated the magnetic hold. There was a muted thud as it released from her gloves, but there was no one in the biodome to hear it. Her intel had been good—this had been the ideal time to sneak in undetected. No one worked the night shift on the Fazenda farms. Everyone was asleep in their beds.

Freyja advanced toward her target at the center of the massive farming facility. Kylian and Tristan fell in behind her, alert, scanning between the verdant hydroponic towers that spanned from floor to ceiling. It was a strangely beautiful biome. Brilliant green leaves, bright yellow peppers, and deep red tomatoes spanned the columns closest to her. As she advanced into the dome, she came across vines of grapes, small apple trees, and towers of herbs, all reaching up, straining to touch the arc of scattered stars overhead. Sometimes, Freyja wondered what she would have been had she not been born to be a soldier—a ruler one day. She imagined tending to the plants and enjoying the serenity that came with a life of horticulture. She shook her head. There was no point wasting her thoughts on what would never be. She had often thought about what she might grow up to be when she was little, when she was still naïve enough to believe her merc father might come for her to give her a life beyond the Empress and the UTA. That was before her tenth birthday, when she was sent off to the military academy, and the trajectory of her life was permanently mapped. This was her destiny now—and besides—she quite excelled at it. She had even beaten out Commander Azai for admiral. He had been top of his class at the Kensho Academy and her only real competition remaining after Captain Karsten, her childhood rival, had quit the Navy.

Time to focus on the mission at hand. The dome was vast, but they were nearing the center. A massive hydro tower loomed over them; dim blue controls lined its surface, with screens for checking readings and little ports for adding nutrient injections. Freyja walked up to the tower, detaching a vial about the size of her palm. She placed the vial in the closest nutrient port. An injector plunged into the tube, accompanied by a quiet hiss as it extracted the contents. Freyja nodded to Kylian at her side. His fingers flashed across his datapad as he hacked into the dome's system with ease. He deleted the nutrient injection from the logs, then nodded back to Freyja. That was it. Time to go.

They retraced their steps until they were back at the entry point, where Freyja replaced the cutout and waited as the laser pads sealed the seam. There was a faintly raised outline, a scar that no one would notice because they wouldn't be looking. In a few days, their crops would start to fail. There would be a cascade of failures. Death would spread until there was nothing left. All of the crops would fail, and they would have no idea why. Even if the Perdida Tribe sent out a team of horticulturists to investigate, it would be weeks before they would be able to isolate the agent and they would have no way to tie it back to the Empress.

Freyja and her small team entered Selkie's airlock. The knot of worry untangled in Freyja's belly. She hadn't wanted to take Kylian out on a mission again so soon, not after what happened on the last one, but he had insisted that he was ready.

"Selkie, mission complete. Take us to the rendezvous."

"Yes, Admiral. Coordinates set, five hours to rendezvous."

Freyja sank into her captain's chair. She hadn't bothered to remove her armor. Beads of sweat clung to her brow line, but she concentrated on the reports pulled up in her ocular implant.

Freyja now had access to all but the most classified files in the United Tribal Axis, a perk of her position that had proven invaluable to the Empress. She scanned the newest reports. The whites of her eyes were cracked with red. Her skin was a shade lighter than it should have been. She had always thought her mother was paranoid, but if these reports were accurate, there was indeed something to worry about. Freyja had hit the Perdida farming moons with a small contingent of her fleet. They had infiltrated each moon's main biodome, they would all fall synchronously. The attack was retaliation for the destruction of the Empress' farming stations. Freyja's reports had confirmed the Empress' suspicions; it had been the Perdida Tribe who had made the blatant attack. No subtlety, no subterfuge—they had come through with starfighters and mech ground support blasting through the majority of the domes. The damage would hurt the Empress economically, but there was enough to rebuild. Still, the Empress could not let the attacks go without consequence. The Perdida Tribe would have nothing to tie the crop failure back to the Empress, but they would be fools not to suspect her.

"Overwhelming power and fear," the Empress had said. "It is the only way to lead an empire."

Freyja had never seen eye to eye with her mother, but the reports she now reviewed were more alarming than ever. Small skirmishes had been breaking out in the borders between tribes, out near the edges of unknown space where most people wouldn't notice them, but Freyja noticed: they were increasing in frequency and were moving into the central solar systems. She hadn't been an admiral long enough to know the politics, but this didn't feel right. Maybe the Empress knew what was coming. Maybe they were heading into chaos and those that survived would be warlords like her mother—those who saw far enough into the future to build their economies and armies. Freyja sighed deeply, sitting back into her chair and closing her eyes for what felt like the first time in weeks.

What did it all mean? Where did she and her Berserkers fit in all of this? She would always put them first; they had no place beyond her squad, just as she had no place beyond leading them.

CHAPTER 13 | HINATA

REUNITED

Hinata activated the door alert. Within a few seconds, a slightly disheveled Rohaan Dar opened the door. The man looked as if he had been wearing the same clothing for several days, and there was a noticeable shadow of stubble forming around the more neatly trimmed lines of his beard. He stood a little taller as soon as he recognized the commander at his doorstep, running his palms down the front of his tunic and straightening his hat.

"Hello, Mr. Dar," Hinata said. "I received a report that our friend, the captain, was released from medical a few days ago."

Rohaan flushed, the tips of his ears turning red as he moved to the side of the doorway to allow Hinata in. He now had a view of the rest of Mr. Dar's quarters. The room was packed with books and odd pieces of equipment. At the center table sat the mysterious captain. He chided himself for the dramatics. She wasn't mysterious—she was an outlaw, an archaeologist, someone who didn't hesitate to break the rules, someone he needed to handle with care. He didn't miss that her arms and legs were supported by mechanical bracers. He had read about the terrible effects of degenerative cryo-shock, but he had never seen a case in real life.

Cryo-pods, while standard on ships, were not used often. There was no need ever since the United Tribal Axis was founded and the tribes colonized the Known Galaxies. They were no longer wanderers, cast into unknown space, where cryo-pods could mean the difference between life and death on long interstellar journeys.

"Captain," he greeted as he entered the room, coming to stand beside her. He eyed the chair next to hers. It was heaped with odd items of clothing, a throw blanket, and several datapads. He chose to remain standing.

The woman looked up at him; her eyes were sunken and shadowed in purple, and her lips were a pale washed-out pink. Perhaps he should request a follow-up with medical?

Instead, he said, "Your ship is taking up space in my docks and considerable time in repairs for my mechanics. I believe it is time we take a look at your inventory."

The captain nodded and slowly stood to follow him. Her silence surprised him. No quick remarks? As they approached the door, Mr. Dar moved to join them. Hinata stopped him.

"No need to bother yourself, Mr. Dar." Hinata's eyes traveled the scientist's disheveled body. "Perhaps you would enjoy the time to rest and refresh yourself?"

Mr. Dar's eyes flicked to his outlaw *acquaintance*, the worry evident in his expression. She reassured him with a weak smile and he conceded, leaving just the captain to fall in beside Hinata on their way to the docks.

As they entered the ship, Hinata noticed a change, both in the ship, and the woman standing in front of him. The ship shifted its interior lights rhythmically through a spectrum of pinks, oranges, and yellows—almost like a sunset. The captain's posture relaxed, as if she had been carrying a heavy load that she was finally able to set down. She ran her fingers over the coral wall to her right.

"It took you long enough to return—"

"I am sorry about that, Pele," the woman cut in. "Commander Azai here wouldn't give me access to my own ship." She glanced over her shoulder, squinting daggers at him.

"Commander Azai," Pele said, "Are you aware that it is against section 152 of the AI-Human Integration Code to prohibit a host access to their charge?"

He was taken aback. His AI never interacted with him like that. He cleared his throat. "...I was. However, I did not know that you were aware of that statute."

"Why wouldn't I be? It is part of the laws that dictate the nature of my very being. It only makes sense that I would be well-versed in all of the documents that pertain to my existence and the code of conduct that is expected of me and my host."

"My...apologies?" He wasn't sure how to interact with this ship; it had far more of a human personality than any AI he had encountered.

"Yes, I would say that apologies are in order, Commander."

"I apologize, Pele. Perhaps you would like to give your captain a status report?"

"My captain." There was a strange chiming sound—was that how the ship laughed? Such an odd machine. "Very well, *Captain*, ship's systems are at seventy percent. I have finished integrating with all essential systems. However, there are still structural repairs that must be addressed before we are able to resume normal functions."

"Thank you, Pele." The captain approached an alcove to the right of the main chamber. She walked to the back of the room, where there were artifacts displayed on the holo screens.

"Pele, please report on your scans of the most recent artifacts." She stood in front of the wall as Pele pulled up schematics around each of the images. Hinata came up behind her, peering over her shoulder at what she had discovered. He took a step closer to examine the intricate diagrams the ship had created of the inner workings of one of the machines. He realized, too late, that he had drifted uncomfortably close to the woman in front of him. The air around her was filled with the scent of sea salt, bergamot, and driftwood. It was intoxicating. While the markets of Medina smelled of herbs and the restaurants of ginger, garlic, and tea, the Naval section of Medina was sterile, utilitarian, and utterly without worldly smells. He realized with a start that it had been years since he had smelled anything so worldly.

The captain looked back at him, flinching at his proximity. He took a half step back.

"I'm sorry—it's just...that scent. What is it?"

The woman in front of him relaxed, a small smile spreading across her lips.

"Pele is quite the scent artist, isn't she?"

"What?"

"Pele, that is her hobby. She likes making scent art; Immersive olfactory experiences inspired by memories of the places we have visited together."

Hinata's brows drew together in confusion. "She can smell?"

"Well, she can process different molecules. She understands how they interact together, and how to combine them into something that truly represents her memories. I would say she can smell. Wouldn't you?"

He hadn't given much thought to how AIs experienced different stimuli. They were just machines, weren't they? "You said she makes scents based on where you have traveled?"

"Yes. This one was a particularly charming planet in the Omega quadrant that we visited a few months back. We landed on the coast of the largest island in an exquisite archipelago. The beaches had soft white sand and there were these thick green bushes with pink flowers and trees with gnarled trunks and dense green fluffy leaves lining the coast. Pele landed half in the water, allowing the surf to wash over her coral exoskeleton. I collected driftwood, and we had bonfires on the beach at night. The sky was brilliant with stars and this planet had three spectacular moons that lit up the night sky," she sighed. "That was one of my favorite planets. We will have to go back there someday, Pele," she said, turning her attention back to the inventory display Hinata was supposed to be inspecting.

"This first piece appears to be a horticulture DNA splicer. The next looks like some promising med tech. Unfortunately, the rest of the scans were not completed. I believe that the virus that infected Pele must have come from one of these other pieces, but I will need Rohaan's help to determine which one."

"I will take the whole lot," Hinata announced.

The captain looked perturbed, no doubt at having to sell off her entire collection at a twenty percent discount—to the UTA, at that. If the other pieces were as valuable as the first two, he would be a fool to let them go. Humankind was exceptionally skilled at space travel and war machines. However, thousands of years as nomads hadn't allowed for as many advances in areas like medicine and horticulture. The advancements they could make from reverse engineering this tech was invaluable. Hinata was embarrassed to admit that innovation had stalled since he had taken command of Medina.

"I would recommend that you keep these pieces in isolation until you can determine the origin of the virus."

"Of course."

"I have already asked Rohaan to look into protecting Pele's systems from other viruses like this one. Perhaps the Navy would be interested in funding his research."

"I will approach Mr. Dar with a proposal."

"I would like to move back into my ship."

Hinata hesitated a moment, then decided against interfering. He didn't want the AI to quote another statue at him. "I will clear your authorization with the dock crew. My people will come to collect the artifacts this afternoon. Be sure they are packaged and ready for transport." Hinata turned to leave, but guilt prompted him to turn back, "And I would also advise you to check in with medical."

"Noted, Commander," was all she said, before turning back to the panel they had been studying. He shook his head, pausing a moment to let his eyes linger on her. Who was this woman?

CHAPTER 14 | SKYLA

Doctor Pinot

Skyla laid back on her bed. It felt good to be back in her quarters on Pele. Hinata's soldiers had come earlier to collect the artifacts she had found and she couldn't help but feel a little annoyed at the loss. She was certain if she had been able to complete her assessment of the items that she would have been able to ask a higher price, maybe even high enough that Commander Azai would have had to let some of the pieces go. The expedition had still been profitable, and Pele was getting the repairs she needed from the UTA mechanics, so she couldn't really complain. Yet, Skyla still felt agitated, like the commander had beaten her at cards. *Until next round, Commander.*

"Why are you having Commander Azai refer to you as Captain?" Pele had been quiet while the UTA soldiers were on board.

"Why not?" Skyla laughed. It hadn't really been her choice.

"Is it a private joke?" Pele didn't understand.

"No, Pele. No private joke. When I woke up, that's what he started calling me."

"Does he know who you are?"

"Obviously not; we would be having a very different conversation if he did. "

"How could he not know who you are? All it would take is submitting your scans to the UTA database."

"He obviously hasn't done that."

"Why?"

The question caught Skyla by surprise. Why *hadn't* he submitted her scans? If a stranger had come out of deep space to her station, she most certainly would have submitted a scan to assess the threat. She thought hard about what she remembered about Hinata Azai from her days as a cadet. They hadn't gone to academy together, of course. Each tribe had its own academies, not to mention their own navies. They all flew under the UTA banner, but there were hardly any mixed units.

Skyla pulled up his records in her ocular display. He had been the star pupil of the Kensho Academy—that's right; she remembered now. Her mother had drilled her on all of the top-performing cadets from the other Tribes, preparing her to compete against them for key postings in the future.

If he was such a star, then what was he doing at Medina Outpost? It was widely known that this posting was where commanders were put out to pasture, a quiet post to finish out their service before retirement. It was a colony of scholars and scientists on the border of the Known Galaxies.

Nothing ever happened here. There were only two possibilities Skyla could think of: either Medina Outpost had become more important in recent years, which was doubtful, or the commander had pissed off someone important. It had to have been someone very important to land him here.

"Are you going to answer me?" Pele asked.

"Hmmmm...My guess?"

"Who else?"

"He's bored."

"What does boredom have to do with it?"

"Nothing happens out at these border postings. I bet that he is going crazy from the lack of activity out here. I bet he is driving his soldiers crazy with drills. Perhaps having a mysterious captain with her AI ship on his station gives him a puzzle to solve."

"That is idiotic. You could be a security threat."

"What fun is a puzzle without a little risk?"

"I fear there are elements of being a human that I will never understand."

"It's probably better that way."

"We have a visitor." Pele switched topics, pulling up a video feed of the entrance. A woman in a med tech lab coat had just entered the ship. Skyla kicked her feet to the ground, moving slower than she would have liked.

"I wonder what that's about?"

When Skyla entered Pele's main chamber, the woman was intensely studying one of Pele's coral rib structures.

"Can I help you?"

The tech jumped and spun around to face Skyla. Her cheeks were pink, as if Skyla had found her indulging in a dirty secret. She didn't look like she belonged to the Hoshiko Tribe. All of Hinata's soldiers that Skyla had seen so far were from his tribe. The tech was different—Etoile Tribe, maybe?

She had long brown hair braided back against her scalp in a single thick braid. She was slender and her skin was pale.

"Actually, I am here to help you, Captain."

"Great, now they are all calling you Captain," Pele groaned.

"Help me? How is that exactly?"

The med tech looked uncomfortable.

"Commander Azai sent me...He said you were unwell. Something to do with the aftereffects of cryo-shock?"

Skyla snorted. *Another round to you, Commander.* Skyla did not like losing. She would have to find a way to even the score.

"You don't look like the rest of the soldiers."

"That's true. I wasn't originally posted under Commander Azai. I was already here, on Medina, when he took command."

"And you didn't get transferred out when the last commander retired?"

"I wasn't posted under him, either. I was posted under Dr. Moreau, the leading researcher in bio-nanite integrations. I am a biomedical engineer. I was working on my thesis—advanced nanite regeneration for bio-synthetics—until the project was scrapped and I was reassigned to the medical team under Commander Azai. Advancements have stalled since the commander cracked down on the archaeologists...It's much easier to reverse-engineer advanced tech than create it from scratch. It's hard to get funding for research projects these days. We might have stopped wandering a century ago, but I fear we are still lost. Nothing has really changed, not when it comes to research. We are still centuries behind where we should be." Her cheeks flushed again at having gone into too much detail.

"Don't worry. Your secret is safe with me." Skyla winked. "You are right, though. We are centuries, maybe more, behind where we should be. That's why I have a job. We have a lot of catching up to do. Now, can we get this over with? I have a ship to take care of."

"Of course, Captain...about that, I might be able to help?" She looked hopefully at Skyla.

"Are you better with a bio-ship than the Naval mechanics?"

"I should hope so! I happen to be the foremost expert in bio-mechanical integrations." The engineer moved quickly over to the alcove where Skyla was preparing nutrient gels to help Pele integrate the new electronics the mechanics had installed. "See this, here." She pointed at the breakdown of the gel contents. "You have a good base gel, but if I update your formula, you could see a twenty percent improvement in stability and a fifty percent increase in longevity before repairs are necessary on her structures."

"What do you think, Pele?"

"Dr. Pinot's work is sound. I would be interested to see what improvements she could make." Both women stood in shocked silence.

"Unlike your friend, Commander Azai, I am capable of submitting a bioscan for recognition. Once I knew who you were, I did a review of your published research. It's really not hard," Pele added.

"Does it always talk like that?"

"Yes, she is always like that."

"Fascinating. I have worked with plenty of AI entities...but she is something else."

Skyla shrugged; she and Pele had been together their entire lives. That is the way the bond worked; she didn't know any different. AIs were just like humans. They each had their own personalities and quirks.

"Well, that settles it, then. Let me introduce you to Wout, the head mechanic. He has been overseeing repairs on Pele personally. I guess they don't get a lot of interesting mechanical work here."

Skyla led the way out onto the docks. Wout wasn't hard to find. He was a huge man; at two meters tall, he towered over the rest of the dock crew. He was more than just tall—he was a tank, with a huge muscular build, even with his advanced years. He was old and grizzled, but he still had a full head of hair, though it had lost all of its color, giving way to white and gray. It was cropped tight against the sides of his head, with only a bit more length on top. He had a series of crisp, black living-ink tattoos that wound intricately down the left side of his face. They turned and moved subtly, like the internal workings of a machine. These tattoos were a sign of a master mechanic and were still common in the guild. Of all of Commander Azai's crew, Skyla liked Wout best. They had spent long hours talking while he switched out Pele's fried components.

Wout had been a Navy mechanic since he was seventeen, and he was old enough to remember the early days of colonization by the United Tribal Axis. In those days, the Navy had been the primary support for colonizing new planets. He told her stories of monstrous creatures that they fought to clear the way for the new cities. He told her about the exotic plants, ecosystems, and weather that his crews helped to tame for the new colonies. Between his many years of life and the thermos full of stout he constantly sipped on, he seemed to never run out of stories.

"Wout!" Skyla shouted as they approached.

Wout looked up from a conversation with one of his crew members. He said a few words to the man, then sent him on his way.

"Skyla." They grasped forearms. "I was just on my way over to check on today's repairs. How is my favorite ship doing?"

"Things are coming along. That is what I wanted to talk with you about, actually. This is Dr. Pinot—turns out she is a biomedical researcher whose talents are being wasted in the Medina Outpost clinic. She had some ideas on how to improve the bio side of Pele's repairs."

Wout looked the doctor over once, then nodded.

"I haven't had much experience with these bio-ships. It would be nice to have your expertise."

Wout extended his arm and Dr. Pinot's shoulders relaxed as she grasped forearms with him.

"Lead the way, Doc." Wout gestured back toward the ship. The doctor and the mechanic immediately dove into conversation about the repairs. Their voices faded to background noise as Skyla's mind wandered. She couldn't help but think how odd all of it was for all these wildly talented individuals to be forgotten at the border of an empire. What a waste.

CHAPTER 15 | FREYJA

NIGHTMARES

"Admiral," Freyja was jerked awake by Kylian's hand on her shoulder. She had fallen asleep on the command deck again. There had been no point in retiring to her quarters lately. She couldn't sleep. When she did, it was in micro-naps on the command deck, her brain briefly forcing a shutdown before she was called to take action again. The United Tribal Axis was more unstable than she had ever realized—and it was unraveling before her eyes.

Acting both as the hand of the Empress and an admiral of the UTA hadn't helped matters. Freyja brought her fleet in to respond to reports of inter-tribal skirmishes, to keep the peace; then she ran black ops missions, retaliation against those who had disrupted the Empress' designs.

She and her mother had never seen eye to eye, until now. Freyja had seen the Empress as an extremist, a narcissist obsessed with power. Now that Freyja could see how fragile the empire was, she wasn't so sure. The Empress had said that humanity needed a strong hand; that the consolidation of power was necessary. The Empress insisted that one ruler could give them direction and that she would lead the human race into a new era. Perhaps she was right. The Empress was one of only a few self-proclaimed powers of industry in the Known Galaxies.

Freyja's great-grandfather had been the one who had set their family on this course. He had seen the potential in developing deep space mining and had gone all in on developing more advanced mining technology, building fleets, and taking control of trade routes. Their family had grown to be a titan in the mining industry, one that no one stood a chance against.

Freyja could see it now: humanity had spent too long wandering. The only technologies they had developed over those millennia were weapons and spacecraft; everything else had lagged behind. It had created a power vacuum—one that anyone who had a vision for the future and the resources to invest in the right technologies, first, could fill.

Only a century old, and the United Tribal Axis was already fracturing under the pressure.

"Admiral, I can take control of the fleet while you rest," Kylian said.

"No need, Lieutenant. I'm fine."

He hesitated. He wore his concern plainly on his face. It conflicted with his training to take orders. Finally, he dropped his voice so only she could hear him, his thickly accented standard slipping out.

"Admiral, it's been weeks of this. You can't live on stims. You're going to have to sleep, eventually."

The fire that always lay just beneath Freyja's surface flared. Who was he to tell her what she needed to do? She clenched her teeth to keep the outburst in, digging her fingertips into the armrest. Kylian flinched slightly—he was used to her outbursts by now, but he stood firm, holding her gaze. Finally, she exhaled. He was right, of course. She began to tremble from the flood of emotions and the crippling exhaustion.

"Perhaps I will take a moment." She conceded. "But you are to wake me if new reports come in. Do you understand?" She didn't try to keep the sting from her words.

Again, he held his ground, but he was ever the good soldier. "Yes, Admiral."

Freyja didn't continue on to her quarters, as she had suggested. Instead, she took a lift tube to the ship's central gardens. Even though she was exhausted, she knew that sleep would continue to elude her.

Freyja inhaled deeply as she entered the garden. The scent of damp earth, green leaves, herbs, and vibrant florals filled her nostrils. It was her favorite place on the ship. She slipped off her Z-grav boots and tucked them near a large ceramic pot that was overflowing with herbs. She brushed her fingertips over the leaves before bringing them to her nose to inhale the herbaceous aroma, letting the scent wash over her before she ventured further into the garden.

She walked through the garden beds. The feeling of damp earth under her bare feet grounded her. Her hands traced the outstretched leaves, and soon she found herself in a small orchard filled with hybrid dwarf trees. Their branches were laden with a mixture of fruits: apples, pears, and plums hung in clusters like a wildflower bouquet.

Freyja lay down under one of the trees at the center of the grove. There was a carpet of clover under the trees that helped to hold the moisture in and had been designed to contribute nitrogen back into the soil. Staring up through the branches, thick with leaves, she caught small glimpses of the stars beyond. They were just holo screens, of course; the gardens were located at the center of the ship, protected from a hull breach. The design was a remnant from when the tribes lived their entire lives on these ships. Back then, the gardens grew all of the food to support the ship's crew. Back then, they were also dominated by algae vats, which were used to produce a high-density nutrient gel. It had been effective, if not extremely austere.

She let her mind wander. The gardens were the only place where she found peace. Something here made her feel safe, stable, calm. Her eyelids grew heavy and eventually fell closed as the rustle of leaves lulled her to sleep.

***

Freyja pushes a little finger into the fresh soil in front of her. She pulls her hand back, revealing a small hole in the dirt. She plucks two tiny seeds from her palm and places them into the hole, then gently pushes dirt over the opening. She repeats this process again and again, moving as quickly as her little 8-year-old body can. She loved planting time. Linnea, the head of the garden in her district, always let Freyja have her own garden bed to tend. They would sit down together at the beginning of every season and pick out the plants she wanted to grow. She would come to Linnea full of ideas of what to grow next. Linnea would talk her through which plants would grow well together, and which wouldn't. They would calculate how much room each one needed and how much room she had in her garden bed. Slowly, they would whittle down Freyja's list of plants to the perfect combo every time. Linnea was patient with Freyja. She always listened and never scolded her for always wanting to plant far more plants than her garden box could support. Linnea was the only adult who made Freyja feel seen. She didn't treat her like another little future soldier, weapon, or pawn. In the gardens, Linnea made Freyja feel like an equal.

"*What are you doing?*" *a little voice calls out from across the gardens.*

"*Hi, Gyr!*" *Freyja waves frantically for her friend to join her. Gyr comes up behind Freyja, looking over her shoulder at the grow box. Gyr wrinkles her nose. Freyja had added a compost and fertilizer mixture to the box before planting.*

"*That smells,*" *Gyr says.*

Freyja smiles. She knew the mixture stank, but to her, it smelled like life.

"*The plants like it.*" *She shrugs.*

"*Do you want to spar?*" *Gyr kicks idly at the ground.*

"*Not right now.*" *Freyja pats the ground gently, then picks up another container of seeds. She moves over to another corner of the grow box; Gyr follows just behind.*

"*Want to play Starship Explorer?*" *Gyr asks hopefully.*

"*That isn't even a game.*"

"*Yes, it is.*"

"*You made it up!*"

"*It doesn't mean it's not a game.*"

"*In that case, why don't we play...*" *Freyja pauses to think about it for a moment,* "*Alien botanist!*"

Gyr scrunches up her nose again in response.

"*It will be great!*" *Freyja goes on,* "*We can be botanists on an alien world, growing new plants that no one has ever seen!*"

Gyr's ears perk up at the mention of alien worlds.

"*So we are adventures!*" *Gyr cries out with excitement.*

"*Sure! Adventurers who are discovering new plants,*" *she adds.*

They put their heads together and begin to talk excitedly. Freyja explains the plants that the different seeds will grow into. Gyr comes up with fantastical attributes and exotic backstories for each of the plants.

Freyja doesn't notice the time slipping by.

A dark shadow hovers over her.

The peace Freyja had felt while playing with her plants drains from her as ice-cold fear chills her to the bone. She looks up at the scowling face above her.

"Mother..."

"You are late for practice," her mother snaps.

"I'm sorry." Gyr chimes in, "We were having so much fun we must have lost track of time! It's my fault." It was nice to have someone stick up for her, but in the end, it wouldn't matter. Her mother turns her icy stare on Gyr.

"You are not my problem. Run along."

Gyr shoots Freyja an apologetic look before sprinting out of the gardens.

"Let's go, Freyja." She grabs Freyja by the arm, walking briskly from the greenhouse. It's hard for Freyja's little legs to keep up. When she stumbles, her mother tightens her grip and drags her along.

"Honestly, I let you play in that filthy garden because you appear to love it so but if it is going to get in the way of your studies, I will tell Linnea that you are banned from the gardens and that will be the end of it."

Big fat tears cloud Freyja's eyes, spilling over and running down her cheeks. She hates to cry in front of her mother. The woman had no patience for it. Freyja breathes deeply through her nose, trying to will the tears to stop. Once she has control of her voice, she responds:

"That won't be necessary, Mother. I will follow the schedule next time."

Her mother looks down at her tear-streaked face. Freyja can see the anger in mother's eyes, "never show weakness," it was a mantra that had been drilled into her since birth.

"Perhaps another living-ink tattoo will help you remember your lesson. You do not have time to waste, Freyja." Her mother yanks her hard by the arm, dragging her into their dwelling, but when she steps inside, there is nothing there and she falls into black...

***

Freyja jumped as her eyes snapped open. She was still under the fruit tree, but she was breathing hard, and sweat now clung to her skin. *Damned nightmares.*

A soldier cleared his throat. He was standing a few paces away.

"I am sorry, Admiral, I didn't mean to disturb you." The soldier shifted uncomfortably from one foot to the other.

"What is it?" Freyja asked.

"A message just arrived for you...It is from the Empress. It's marked urgent."

"You are dismissed," Freyja said, as she lay back in the clover and closed her eyes. The echo of hurried footsteps faded as the soldier made his retreat. What could it be this time? The secret missions from the Empress had been coming more frequently lately. At this rate, Freyja didn't know how she would be able to keep up with the demands of being an admiral and all of the responsibilities the Empress had placed upon her. Although...things looked more unsure for the UTA every day. Perhaps she wouldn't have to keep up with both for much longer.

CHAPTER 16 | HINATA

THE FENIX CARTEL

Hinata stalked the corridors of Medina Outpost while he waited on an analysis of all of the ships that had arrived in the week leading up to the lab explosion. No ship had been flagged on arrival, but he had a hunch that the saboteur must have been an outsider. He had been running the space station long enough to know its people; this level of violence was out of character for a resident of Medina.

He rounded a corner, bringing him to the ship docks. It was late in the day and most business had concluded; the docks were quiet. The main lights were powered down, giving way to the soft bioluminescent glow of the evening auxiliary lights. Hinata walked through the public docks first, his eyes passing over the ships as he went. There were hundreds of them, varying in size, make, and model.

He let his feet guide him as he waited for the report; nothing would stand out visually. He tried to focus on the investigation. There had to be inconsistencies, there had to be a motive. He suspected the Empress had a lot to gain by taking out an alternate energy source. The quantum entanglement project threatened not only the profits from her mining operation, but it would take away any advantage she held by controlling the trade routes. Long-range space travel would be open to all. Hinata sighed. The reports he received from the central rim hinted that the Empress had become more bold, but there was no proof. He clenched his hands, channeling his frustration into his fists for just a moment, before forcing them to relax again. He hated being sidelined. If he had a fleet, he knew he could uncover what was really going on.

Hinata stopped his prowling, surprised at where his feet had led him. He gazed up at Tentei, parked in a far corner of the Navy docks. A twinge of regret passed through him as the thought of the captain's interactions with Pele came uninvited to his mind. He remembered the closeness of the neural link he'd once shared with Tentei; it was like a phantom pain, a limb that had been severed from his body twenty years ago, and it ached. He had spent the past three years running drills with his ship—more attention than he had afforded the AI since cadet school—and the damn thing still wouldn't talk to him. Could AIs hold a grudge? He shook the thought from his mind. Tentei was a tool, nothing more. He forced himself to move on.

Now that the captain was on his mind, Hinata had trouble pushing thoughts of the woman away. He hadn't had much time for his private puzzle, not since the lab explosion. The security of Medina was more important than such games. However, the promise of unraveling the mystery was a welcome distraction at the moment. From the few interactions they had shared, he was almost certain that she was Stjarna Tribe. He had begun pulling military records to comb through. Even limiting the records to the great houses—which she had to be to have a ship like Pele—there were still thousands of possibilities.

Hinata recalled how she had dismissed him the week before. It should have made his blood boil, but it hadn't. He was a commander, not used to people making light of his orders. If anything, he enjoyed her flippant attitude. The thought of her sent a flutter of butterfly wings through him, followed closely by the fear of what that sensation could mean. He ignored the sensation, coming to a stop just outside the mechanic's alcove. A loud booming laugh rang out. *Wout.* Hinata smiled. He had inherited the head mechanic with the station. Wout had been there for decades at that point, one of the last of a generation that tamed the galaxy—a true pioneer. Wout refused to conform to Hinata's strict policies, always walking the line of insubordination, but Hinata couldn't help but like the man. He was a reflection of their foundations and a damn good mechanic.

Wout's voice carried from the alcove, telling a story of how they had built custom land skimmers to wrangle a herd of wild creatures on Damascus, clearing the way for the first cities on the planet and creating a thriving industry farming the alien creatures.

"We were like the cowboys of Earth That Was. it was one of my favorite colonization assignments."

"Being a cowboy sounds better than being stuck here. Why didn't you stay?"

That voice. Hinata's breath caught in his chest. When did the captain get so cozy with his head mechanic?

"The stars are always calling. Back in those days, there was always another assignment, another adventure to be had." Wout chuckled, "Back then, I didn't expect to get stuck anywhere for too long. Medina isn't so bad, though. It's one of the few places where there is still the promise of adventure. If the UTA decides to expand again, I'll be on the frontier, ready to deploy."

There was the flutter of cards being laid out.

"Full starfighter flight."

Hinata shook his head. While gambling wasn't strictly illegal, he expected a higher code of ethics from his soldiers. He rounded the corner. The captain sat on an oil drum across from Wout, two glasses of whiskey and a pile of cards shared between them. Heat pricked along his skin as the captain smiled at Wout. She hadn't noticed him yet.

"Battlecruisers over destroyers." She laid down her cards. The sharp grin on her face suggested this wasn't the first round she had won for the evening.

"Wout doesn't often lose at cards. You get much practice gambling out there in unknown space, on your own?"

Skyla jumped, turning to meet his gaze as he approached the makeshift table.

"Now Commander, don't go scaring this one off. I finally have someone who can hold their own at cards and it's a bonus that she's someone who hasn't already heard all of my stories." Wout clapped Skyla on the shoulder. Hinata noted how the captain wavered under Wout's strong grip. She was still pale, the skin under her eyes tinged purple. He clenched his jaw.

"I thought I sent Dr. Pinot to address this." He waved his hand toward the captain.

"You did."

"If you can't follow medical advice, I will have you committed back to the clinic."

"I am not yours to command."

"This is my station. While you are on my station, you will follow my orders."

"Dr. Pinot is working on it. I assure you, Commander, I have no desire to be stuck on your station any longer than necessary." She sighed, the fight having left her, fatigue cutting lines into her face. He tried to ignore the twinge of guilt that followed. He hadn't intended to be so harsh with her, but something about the woman pushed him toward the edge of his control.

"Commander, analysis is complete," an urgent voice came through Hinata's aural implant.

He gritted his teeth, "Wout, try not to blatantly ignore my rules with the new batch of recruits coming in tomorrow." He gave a pointed look at the cards and alcohol.

"I take it you won't be joining us for a round, Commander?" the captain said.

"I have matters to attend to." He gave a curt nod to the captain.

"I guess it's a good thing you fished this one out of space then," Wout called after Hinata as he walked away. "Your recruits are no good at cards, anyway." Wout's laugh carried from the alcove as Hinata made his way back to the public docks.

"Report," Hinata demanded through his comms.

"There is a possible syndicate ship at berth delta-549."

"How did we miss it on arrival?"

"Spoofed credentials, sir. We only caught it with a build analysis against known pirate vessels."

"Have a peacekeeping unit meet me there."

***

Hinata paused behind the suspected syndicate ship. It was small, with a maximum crew size of four. The cargo bay door was open; movement in the shadows of the ship caught his eye. He drew his katana, silently cursing the peacekeepers for taking so long. He had no armor and only his sword. The ship began to whir as its engines powered up; they were going through preflight. The vessel wasn't cleared for a launch and he had a feeling they weren't going to ask. There was an outline of roughly hidden turrets on either side of the wings. The ship was heavily armed for its size and there was no question that those cannons were capable of blasting their way out of the hangar if necessary. The sudden hum of mechanics drew his attention—they were closing the cargo bay door.

The peacekeeping unit was too far out. Hinata needed to shut this down, now. Gritting his teeth, he dashed forward. The door had already risen to chest height. He leaped into the cargo bay, his boots scraping the lip before he slid down the inside of the ramp just before it closed. He landed on the metal grate floor in a crouch, his katana held ready as he scanned the cargo bay.

"Hey!" a man shouted from the other side of the dimly lit room. He was dressed head-to-toe in black, a holster housing two guns at his ribs. The flapping form of a phoenix living-ink tattoo took up the entirety of his shaved head; its flames licked across the man's skull. Hinata made to close the distance between them. Too slow. Bullets flew through the air around Hinata as the man opened fire. He dove, taking shelter behind a supply crate. The bullets ricocheted around the room, igniting little sparks in the gloom.

What in the hell!? Projectile weapons were illegal outside of starship armaments—a reanimate of thousands of years living on starships. No one wanted a hull breach, even during a mutiny. Humanity had fallen back on their violent roots, killing with steel and fists. Anything was fair game as long as it wouldn't damage their ships. There was a reason every UTA officer was proficient in hand-to-hand combat. Even pulse rifles hadn't come into circulation until after the founding of the United Tribal Axis. Why create advanced handheld weaponry when swords killed just as well?

The thunder of gunfire rang throughout the cargo bay. A barrage of bullets embedded into the container Hinata had taken shelter behind. A sharp pain bit into his shoulder as a bullet pierced through.

He had to move.

The cargo bay was small—when there was a pause in the gunfire, he needed to rush the man and pray he crossed the distance before they could reload.

Hinata's ears rang with the absence of gunfire.

Now.

He sprinted toward the gunman, whose gaze was down, focused on reloading the weapon. As soon as he was within striking distance, Hinata moved without hesitation, bringing his katana down to sever the man's hands from his forearms. A shrill cry pierced the air as the man collapsed to his knees, clutching his stumped arms to his chest. Hinata held his bloodied blade to the man's neck.

"How many more are on this ship?" he growled.

The man spat at Hinata, his eyes burning with hate. The door behind them hissed open and Hinata wasted no time. He struck the wounded man in the back of the head with the hilt of his katana as he raced to cover the door.

A woman, also dressed all in black, stepped through, with a look of confusion plastered on her face. Blue flame living-ink tattoos danced up her arms, which she had raised in a sign of surrender. Hinata held the point of his sword at her jugular.

"Who else is on this ship?"

The woman's eyes darted to the left before she answered. "No one, boss'man," she said in accented standard.

Hinata pushed forward, his katana still held to the woman's neck, forcing her back into the hall she had emerged from.

Searing pain radiated across Hinata's face as knuckles wrapped in electrified titanium smashed into his skull. He fell to one knee, still holding tight to his katana. Another bolt of electricity raked across his skin as he took another blow.

Hinata rotated, bringing his katana up just as he was expecting another strike to land. His sword met air as his attacker sprang back to avoid the counter. Hinata staggered to his feet, taking in his assailant. The woman had disappeared, and he now faced off with a man so tall that he had to duck to move through the small ship doorways. He too was dressed in all black, and, like the rest of the crew, a phoenix living-ink tattoo flapped at his neck. The man assessed Hinata, just as Hinata was assessing him. Then he let out a mirthless laugh.

"I have to admit, I wasn't expecting the commander of the station on my ship."

"And I wasn't expecting a terrorist on my station." Hinata spat out a glob of blood.

The man cocked his head to the side, as if making a decision. "Your timing couldn't be better. I think I will fetch a pretty bonus for that head of yours." In a flash, the man had retrieved his gun from its holster, spraying bullets across the hallway. Hinata threw himself backward. Pain seared through his calf as bullets met flesh. A loud explosion rocked the ground as bright light filled the cargo bay. A unit of peacekeepers swarmed through the blast hole in the back of the ship.

The man stepped toward Hinata, pausing for a moment, before turning to flee. Hinata groaned, rolled onto his side and struggled to come to his feet. He leaned heavily against the bulkhead. His face throbbed with electrical burns, while his boot filled with blood.

"One in the cargo bay, two forward! Move!" he shouted orders. They made quick work of securing the first prisoner before advancing on the bridge to secure the second. The third man, however, was nowhere to be found.

Hinata shuffled forward, noting an open smuggler's hatch to his left, the cockpit directly ahead. A flash of movement on the viewport caught his eye as the shadow of a man sprinted into the darkness of the docks.

"Damn it," he growled. "Lock down the station. Bring me that man."

"Yes, Commander." The peacekeepers moved to fulfill his orders.

"And send a med unit now." He turned to look at the first prisoners he had taken. "I wouldn't want our friend here to bleed out before I get answers."

Hinata wiped the edge of his katana across his pant leg before returning it to its sheath. Indignation burned through his chest; the Fenix Cartel had brought terrorists to his station. He would be sure they met justice.

CHAPTER 17 | SKYLA

MATCH

It had been almost two months since Skyla and Pele had docked at Medina, and Skyla was getting restless. Over the past few years, she had come to prefer the company of Pele, alone in deep space. She craved the silence of the void, the only interruption, Pele's familiar sounds, and the promise of their next adventure. People were messy. Skyla had abandoned the company of humanity for dead worlds and strange tech, and she had no intention of going back.

Truth be told, Skyla couldn't complain. It turned out that Dr. Pinot and Wout made an excellent team. Pele's nutrient gel concoction had been greatly improved by Dr. Pinot's formula. Between the doctor and the mechanic, Pele had some new upgrades that Skyla was dying to test out.

Pele would be leaving Medina in the best shape of her life. That, at least, helped to ease some of the guilt Skyla felt over having put Pele in mortal danger in the first place.

Skyla's health was another matter altogether. Cryoshock was a nasty beast. She had continued to degenerate for another two weeks before Dr. Pinot had found the cause. Skyla resented Commander Azai for sending the doctor, even though his actions had been her salvation. Dr. Pinot had informed her that if it hadn't been for his intervention, Skyla may have been too far gone to save by the time she submitted herself to medical attention. Skyla thought the doctor gave the commander a little too much credit. Once the issue had been isolated, Skyla's recovery began to build momentum, and medical had finally cleared the removal of her stabilizing bracers. Although Skyla wouldn't have been able to move about the station without them, they had felt like shackles, Medina, her prison. She was relieved to be rid of them.

Skyla entered the station's training facility, determined to whip her weakened body back into shape. She didn't need any more delays—she was ready to get back out into space. The doors to the facility snapped open in front of her and her heart sank a little when she saw she wasn't alone. There was a soldier working rigorously through an obstacle course. She had asked Pele to analyze Commander Azai's troop schedules so she could use the facility while it was empty. According to Pele, all of the soldiers were either on duty, engaged in a mock skirmish, or on shore leave.

Skyla was annoyed that Pele had overlooked something, but she knew she was being unreasonable. Could she really expect Pele to know where all of the station's soldiers were with certainty?

There was a pool along the left side of the training facility, as far away from the soldier as she could get. That would work. She stripped down to her sports bra and shorts, then slid into the cold water. She was pleasantly surprised by the taste of salt instead of the harsh chemicals she remembered from the training pool back at the academy. If she closed her eyes, she could almost feel a gentle tide pulling her. The image of an off-world ocean replaced the pool as Skyla eased into the motions. As she swam back and forth, she tried to let go of her frustration at how weak her body had become. Instead, she focused on the pull and glide, on letting her muscles engage, then relax. It was hypnotic. She almost felt free—the way she did when she explored a new world. Time slid by and before she realized it, a half hour had passed. When she finally stopped at the wall again, she was greeted by a familiar face, if not a friendly one.

Commander Azai stared down at her from the edge of the pool. He was stripped down to the waist and covered in sweat, his muscles swollen from effort. Now that he was close, she realized *he* was the soldier who had been training when she came in. No wonder Pele had thought the facility would be empty—she had not accounted for the commander's whereabouts. He didn't look pleased to have had his solitary time interrupted, either.

Heat rushed into Skyla's cheeks as she realized she was staring; he was all hard lines and solid muscle. She sank back down under the water, savoring the oppressive silence. She didn't want to deal with Commander Azai right now. Could she just swim away? It was a ridiculous notion. This was a lap pool on a space station, not an endless ocean. When she re-emerged, the commander was waiting. Angry pink lines spider-webbed across the left side of his cheek, trailing down his strong jawline. She wanted to ask him what had happened to his face, but thought better of it.

"How did you get access to this facility?" he demanded.

"Dr. Pinot granted me access. She thought it would help with my recovery."

"You can't recover using the civilian facilities?"

Skyla smiled. "They don't have a pool." The hilt of a katana stuck up out of his belt, and Skyla couldn't help herself. "Why do you waste your time with that?" Skyla asked, eying the sword.

"It is a waste of time, is it?"

"Battles are won with starships, not swords."

"Is that so?" A wicked grin spread across his face. "Perhaps you would like to spar, Captain?"

Skyla snorted. She hadn't practiced hand-to-hand combat in years. Still, she didn't want to pass up a chance to beat the commander at his own game.

"Fine." She pulled herself up out of the pool. "But I am not using one of those stupid little swords." Skyla stalked over to the far wall, where the practice weapons were racked. She pulled a bō staff from the selection, then turned to face him.

The commander extended his arm toward the practice mats, inviting Skyla to join him, before turning to take his place at the opposite side of the ring.

Shock froze Skyla in place—the commander's entire back was a tapestry of color etched in living-ink. Vivid blues rippled and splashed as four brightly colored koi fish darted between pink lilies. All officers had a symbol for their house inked on their chest at graduation, but to see an officer with so much ink was unusual. The tattoo didn't match with the orderly, rule-following persona he always exuded.

This was a side of him she was certain very few people had seen. The fact that he was sharing it with her...she didn't know how to feel about that. Skyla shook her head to regain her focus. She took a step into the ring and squared up with him. He pulled his sword from his belt and stepped into a fighting stance.

Skyla spun the staff slowly in front of her, getting a feel for its weight. She cursed her cryo-shock-weakened arms. In the water, she had been able to forget for a moment how much muscle she had lost. She would have to be quick and calculated; she didn't have the muscle mass to go blow for blow with the commander.

They began to circle, each looking for an opening. She rotated her staff at a steady cadence while the commander held his sword at the ready.

Then he sprang forward, striking against her staff with an upward blow. He had tried to knock the weapon from her hands, but she held tight. Skyla deflected his blow, allowing his own momentum to carry through as she stepped to the side. The commander quickly regained his balance. She wasn't certain, but it looked like he was favoring his left side. The disparity was there, then gone, as the dance started again, each of them stepping carefully to the side with eyes locked on their opponent.

The commander came at Skyla again and again, each time with a different strike, testing her reactions. Each time, she deflected and clocked the time it took for him to reset. He was trying to hide it, but he *was* favoring his left side, the same side that bore the angry burn marks on his face. What had happened to him?

The commander dodged back and swung out at her hamstring, trying to cut behind her staff. She tipped the end of her weapon up in time to block the blow, the force of the strike vibrating through her bones. She took her opening, bringing the top of her staff down hard into the commander's unguarded shoulder. He moved to block, but she had been faster. A loud thwack echoed through the empty training hall and the commander grunted at the force of the blow, but remained in control. He spun to her left, striking her in the ribs with the blunted edge of his nanite katana in training-mode.

She gasped, but maintained her grip on the staff. Dropping into a crouch, Skyla swept the commander's legs out from under him with a hard strike from her staff. Surprise flashed in his eyes as she brought her bow down to strike him in the chest, but he recovered quickly, rolling out of the way, leaving her to strike the empty mat where he had been. The commander rolled seamlessly into a crouch and as soon as Skyla's staff hit the mat; he lunged forward, pinning her to the ground, the blunted edge of his katana to her throat. He smiled down at her.

"Match." He held her there against the mat, his eyes searching hers—but for what? She wasn't sure.

He pulled back, recovering his composure, as if he just realized he had held her there a second too long. He moved swiftly to his feet, extending a hand to her. Infuriated at the loss, she wanted to slap his hand away, but she knew it would only make her look worse not to accept. Taking his hand, she let him pull her to her feet. Her breath came in ragged gasps as she leaned against her staff for support.

"You fought well."

"I lost."

"Everyone loses to me."

She snorted, "Well, aren't you arrogant?"

"Is it arrogance if it is true?"

Skyla looked into his eyes. He wasn't gloating. It probably was true. She shrugged.

"Like I said before, wars are won with starships, not swords. If I were on my ship, I promise you would never have the chance to board."

The commander cocked an eyebrow. "What does an outlaw know of war?"

"It appears that this outlaw knows more than you do."

She was surprised when a rumbling laugh filled the room. Who was this man in front of her? He looked like the uptight, rule-following commander she had met, but his demeanor was entirely different. This man *laughed*. He sparred in empty training rooms with strange ship captains, and every inch of his back was covered in living-ink. No, he wasn't at all who she had thought he was, and she didn't know what to make of that.

He glanced at the wall clock and his laughter trailed off. He straightened his spine and squared his shoulders, as if remembering himself.

"I have duties to attend to." He extended an arm to her, the traditional way to end a sparring match. She surprised herself when she instantly grasped his arm in response. He held her there, looking into her eyes.

"Perhaps we can spar again next week?"

"Perhaps, Commander."

He gave a curt nod before releasing her arm. Turning away from her, he walked to where he had left his things. "Same time next week, Captain," he called out over his shoulder, but he didn't wait to hear her response before exiting the gym.

Skyla shook her head, trying to get a grasp on what had just happened, and trying to ignore the fluttering that tickled her ribs.

CAPTAIN KARSTEN

The docks were bustling with activity as Hinata strode through the civilian section. The XingXing delegate had brought an entire fleet of civilian ships for the Secchi conference, an annual event that hosted the most brilliant researchers in astrophysics, materials science, and deep space analytics. Hinata was wary of all of the newcomers on the station so soon after the bombing, but a majority of the speakers were from Medina, and they hosted every year—to cancel on such short notice would be an advertisement of misgivings on Medina, it would bring the type of attention Hinata wanted to avoid at all costs.

He turned into the military docks, chancing a glance toward Pele as he walked by. The ramp was down, but there was no sign of the captain. He focused his attention on the ship ahead of him; the delegates were already disembarking when he arrived.

"Senator Kaku." Hinata bowed to the older XingXing man. The senator had flowing, white, shoulder-length hair and wore his formal brocaded green robes, which he adjusted as he inclined his head to Hinata, obviously uncomfortable with the formalities.

"Captain Huang," Hinata greeted the second man. He was a couple of decades older than Hinata, but wore the same black military dress uniform and serious demeanor.

"If I may escort you to your suites." Hinata gestured for the men to follow.

"I hear you had some trouble recently," Captain Huang said.

Hinata's jaw clenched. Of course, they had heard about the bombing. "Yes, but everything is under control, I assure you." It grated on his nerves that one of the terrorists still hadn't been found, but security had been doubled in preparation for the conference, and he was confident that the station couldn't be safer.

"Wait!" Senator Kaku called out from behind them. "I appear to have forgotten my datapad," he said, clutching at the pockets of his robes. "I'll be just a moment." He returned back to the ship.

Hinata and Captain Huang stopped just beyond Pele, and he couldn't help but try to catch a glimpse of the mysterious woman he had plucked from the stars while they waited. As if he had summoned her, the captain came striding down the ramp with an assortment of parts bundled in her arms. She dumped the parts on a workbench just outside her ship and he watched as she ran her arm across her forehead, wiping away the perspiration that clung to her skin, then studied the collection of parts laid out before her.

"Got it!" The senator jogged up to them.

Hinata straightened, his eyes darting to Captain Huang, only just realizing that he had been staring at his mysterious captain.

Captain Huang's eyes were locked on Hinata, a strange expression on his face. Heat crept up the back of Hinata's neck. An incident on his station just a few weeks prior, and now he was staring at a woman on his docks—this wasn't the impression he wanted to make on a commanding officer. Hinata cleared his throat and gestured forward.

"Shall we continue?"

"Yes, please do. I'd like a chance to review some of these research documents before the keynote." Senator Kaku shook his datapad in the air and began walking again without waiting for either of the military men. Hinata exchanged a look with Huang, trying to assess what damage had been done, and the man appraised Hinata in return before they both fell in behind the senator.

***

Having settled the senator, along with a handful of other high-ranking delegates, Hinata retired to his office. He stared at the holo suspended before him, willing it to reveal its secrets. His investigation of the bombing had stalled, and even with the enhanced security protocol, there had been no sign of the third man.

He pushed back from his desk to pace the length of his office. His leg still ached where the bullets had torn through muscle. Cellular stims had accelerated the healing process, and the wound was hardly noticeable now, but nerve tissue always took longer to repair. At least moving helped ease the pain, so Hinata continued to pace.

Hinata rubbed the side of his face. The marks had faded, but the nerve endings still tingled where the electricity had singed through his flesh.

The two captured terrorists had been confirmed as members of the Fenix cartel, and they had arrived the day before the bombing. He was certain they were involved, but neither of them were talking. He had received orders to prepare the prisoners for transport. They would be leaving with the XingXing delegation to stand trial in the capital for their crimes.

The motive behind the lab bombing still itched at the back of his mind. The Fenix cartel ruled over a small backwater system not far from Medina. They were arms dealers and slavers—what motive did they have for the attack?

He sighed, flicking the display over to the new reports that had come in from UTA command. The number of small skirmishes and sabotage had grown exponentially over the past few months, most of which broke out around the border of the central rim, or along tribal borders. Hinata itched for action. His troops were sharp from three years of drills, but they could use real battle experience. Senator Azai, however, had made it very clear that he wasn't going anywhere. He was still damned to obscurity, with no way to redeem himself. He clenched his fists. If only he knew what had happened at the admiral exams. If only he could fix it.

He forced the tension from his shoulders. His mind turned once again to the captain. She came uninvited into his mind often, as she remained the only little bit of excitement he had at Medina. His conscience pricked at the edges of his mind. He knew he was breaking protocol by allowing her to remain an unknown entity on his station. She was obviously military trained—their sparring match had confirmed his suspicion—and she had to be from an important house to have a bonded AI ship. Yet, Hinata was certain she wasn't a danger to him or Medina. The only thing she appeared to want was to leave and go back to uncharted space—another thing that should have bothered him. Exploring uncharted space was against the law, but with the captain, it just felt like another piece of her puzzle.

He pulled up old military records for the Stjarna Tribe for the past ten years on those who had finished their service, and those who had gone AWOL. He wasn't sure when the captain would have left service. The broad time range left him with thousands of records to review. He could have had them sorted and filtered further, but what was the fun in that? He could also have just submitted her scans from medical to the UTA database and known who she was in an instant.

His father's words echoed through his mind, reminding him that he was more than just a tool for the UTA. He was allowed to explore who he was outside of his position. He ran a tight command; he always followed orders. He was allowed this one little indulgence, this one thing that brought light back into his life. It was a harmless game, though the way the nerves sparked in his belly at the thought of the captain made him doubt if that last part was entirely true.

Hinata's sight began to blur with the strain of hours reading through service records. A cup of tea sat on his desk, cold and untouched. It was late. The space station felt still. He knew he would have to wrap up for the day soon. He had skipped the evening meal, continuing his search into the night. He sighed and tried to rub the sleep from his eyes. Just one more record, he promised himself, as he had for the past hour.

An alert pinged on his holo screen, interrupting his search with an incoming message. Hinata opened the communication. The face of Senator Karsten materialized in front of him and his stomach dropped.

"Senator Karsten—"

"Commander Azai, I received a transmission from an old friend today. Perhaps you are acquainted, Captain Huang. He had some interesting news to share with me." The senator cut right to the chase.

A growing sense of dread settled over him. *Fuck*, Captain Huang hadn't been staring at him because he had been gawking at a girl. The last puzzle piece dropped into place. His eye twitched slightly, but he fought hard to hold his composure.

When he remained silent, the senator continued. "Perhaps you can tell me why you haven't reported that Captain Skyla Karsten has been at your station for nearly two months now?"

Senator Karsten didn't just know that her daughter was here, she knew he had failed to report her presence for months.

"My apologies—"

"I don't need your apologies. I don't know what game you are playing at, Commander, but I will be sending an envoy to collect Captain Karsten immediately."

He gave a curt nod, not trusting himself to give an adequate verbal response.

"And, Commander, she better be there when my ships arrive. I will forget that you breached protocol. I don't much care, as long as I collect the captain. Understood?"

"Yes, Senator."

The senator cut the transmission.

Hinata slammed his fists into his desk, letting the anger escape through the impact, then forced his body to relax. He slowed his breathing and put up the façade of the calm and collected commander.

With the transmission ended, the next record loaded into his holo screen and his blood ran cold at the confirmation. There she was, his captain, or more appropriately, Captain Karsten. Her service record ran across the holo and his gut twisted as it reached the final entry. Three years ago, Captain Karsten had been the Stjarna Tribe's top candidate for the admiral exams. Every academy had the right to put forward a candidate for examination. With over a hundred billion souls scattered across the Known Galaxies, there were thousands of training facilities. The academy that had put forward Captain Karsten as their nominee was burned into his brain—the Mímir Academy—the institution that had sponsored Commander Freyja Nygaard, after their first choice had withdrawn from consideration.

How hadn't he figured it out sooner? He was hit with another stab of dejection at his own naïveté. He should have known who she was, and he was certain that Skyla must have made the connection. He let his head sink into his hands. The one time that he broke protocol. How stupid could he be? Why had he let his boredom get the better of him? Medina was his punishment for losing the admiral exams to Freyja and now, for the first time, he was certain that he deserved it.

He clenched and then released his hands. He needed to put this nervous energy somewhere. He flicked through Skyla's file. There had been a huge upset in the Stjarna Tribe when Captain Karsten had left the Navy. No scandal; she had concluded her conscription and decided not to re-up. Even if she was honorably discharged, she was the child of a senator, as was he, and there were certain expectations for people like them. He scanned the news clips linked to her file. Senator Karsten had made trouble in the senate for months after her daughter disappeared.

Based on their interaction today, the senator still hadn't gotten over it. He remembered being relieved when Stjarna's top candidate had withdrawn; he had always known it would come down to Hoshiko vs Stjarna at the exams. Of course, every tribe would put forward a nominee, but none of the tribes were as dominant in the Navy as his own and Skyla's. None of them could compete at the same level. He had believed that Stjarna losing their top candidate would make it that much easier for him to claim victory. Somehow he had thought that the admiral position was his for the taking, but he was wrong then, and he was wrong now, for breaking protocol.

If he had just submitted her scan when she first arrived, he wouldn't be facing further condemnation from yet another senator. On the other hand, if he had submitted those scans, he also never would have discovered the intriguing woman below the captain's infuriating exterior—the woman who now came unbidden into his mind more often than he cared to admit. Would that really have been better?

He shook his head. There was no changing the past now. Could things get worse for him than being exiled to Medina? He certainly hoped not. Senator Karsten had been quite vocal about bringing Captain Karsten back into command. He was certain that was what the senator had planned for Skyla. The woman had been off grid for the past three years and no one knew where she had been. Clearly, she didn't want to be found. Skyla's ship was almost finished with repairs. He could let her sail off on her next adventure before her mother's envoy arrived...

He sighed. It was all just fantasy. He was duty-bound. He would ground her ship and let the envoy take the captain back to Gefion. He would take responsibility for his mistake and she would have to do the same.

Hinata tapped at the controls of the holo screen, and it brought up a schematic of the station.

"Show me the captain," he commanded, feeling foolish as he said it.

The holo screen reorientated to show a blinking beacon on the docks. The captain was on her ship.

***

Hinata walked into the ship unannounced; he was commander of the station after all. He was surprised to find Rohaan Dar standing with the captain—Captain Skyla Karsten. They didn't look at all surprised to see him. The AI must have announced his arrival. He should have expected that. This posting had made him soft, and the captain had clouded his judgment. That all ended now.

"Commander, to what do we owe the pleasure?" she asked.

"It appears that I had you pegged from that first day, Captain."

It was Skyla's turn to look confused, if only for a moment, before the confusion melted from her face as she narrowed her eyes. Her stare was as cold as her glacial eyes, which burrowed into his.

"So you finally figured out who I am, then?"

"Yes, Captain Skyla Karsten."

Skyla shrugged and finally dropped her stare.

"Not anymore. I left the Navy, or did you not read that in my file?"

"Oh, I read that you submitted your resignation. It appears that the Senate failed to approve it. As far as Senator Karsten is concerned, you are an important asset to the UTA Navy that needs to be returned to your post." He was certain he saw anger flare in her eyes, but she surprised him when she cocked her head back and laughed.

"She would, wouldn't she?" Skyla looked directly at him, but he sensed the question wasn't meant for him. In that moment, a large mass of golden fur slinked out of the corridor behind Skyla. It circled her legs once and rubbed against them affectionately before it sat on its haunches by her side, tucking its large head under her hand. It had pointed ears and warm golden eyes that were fixed on him.

"What the hell is that?"

Mr. Dar wouldn't meet his gaze. The man was all of a sudden intensely interested in the bulkheads.

"That is the creature from the cryo-pod, isn't it? I thought I told you to leave that thing in stasis until you were off my station. My mechanics were supposed to put a lock on that pod until you left."

"Don't take it out on your people. They did as you asked."

Hinata's stare switched between her and the creature, not sure what to make of either of them.

"I had Ears unlock the pod." She gripped Rohaan's shoulder. The man's ears turned pink as he continued to study the bulkhead.

"That's not possible."

"Why? Because no one could be better than the United Tribal Axis Navy? Something I have learned since leaving the service is that there are many talents that are left untapped outside of the United Tribal Axis—and plenty that are wasted within it," she mumbled the last part.

"We have the best programmers in the Known Galaxies. He shouldn't be capable of hacking their code."

"Your programmers are good, but he's better."

Hinata looked Rohaan up and down, reassessing the man. He had thought him intelligent, sure, but something was off about him. Hinata shifted his gaze back to the creature. It yawned, sticking out its long blue tongue and revealing a set of large, sharp teeth. Nasty claws were visible through the tufts of golden fur on its paws, and thick muscles rippled under its coat as it shifted its weight.

"I want that thing back in cryo."

"No."

He was used to his commands being followed. Her insubordination lit a fire in him, but Hinata kept his composure. Letting her see his frustration would only make it worse. They stared at each other in a silent battle of wills.

Finally, he decided he wasn't going to die on this hill. It didn't matter anyway, she would be off his station in a matter of days.

"Fine. It isn't to leave this ship."

Skyla nodded in agreement.

"And this ship isn't to leave the docks until your escort arrives."

Frustration flashed in her eyes, but she didn't argue the point.

"And no more stunts." He waved his hand at the creature. "Your vessel is grounded until they arrive. I have informed the dock crew, and your access has been restricted." This time, he looked directly at Mr. Dar.

He had underestimated him once. It wouldn't happen again.

The Fall

"What will you do?" Rohaan asked.

Skyla shrugged and continued working on the electronics behind one of Pele's panels. It had been five days since Commander Azai had announced that he knew who she was and that an envoy of ships was on their way from Gefion to collect her. The docks were quieter now that the XingXing delegate had moved on to their next stop, although many of their civilian ships still lingered and the dark cloud of her current mood tainted her vision of the quiet haven of Medina.

"What can I do?"

"You can't go with them. If they take you back to Gefion, your mother will force you back into service."

"I can deal with my mother." She sounded more confident than she felt. Rohaan didn't buy it. He understood well the weight of family pressure. It was one of the things that bonded them. He stared hard at her until, eventually, Skyla sighed. "I will figure it out. Don't worry about me." She gave him a weak smile. "I need you to focus on that virus. I need to know Pele will be safe when we go back into uncharted space." Skyla patted Pele's hull affectionately.

"Yes, about that. I'm close, I think. I have broken down the architecture of the virus. It is something else. If ever there were proof of an alien culture, I think this would be it. Its conventions are so different from anything I have ever seen. I don't think a human could have developed this."

Skyla gave him a skeptical look. He was always looking for validation that his life's work had merit and while she hoped he would find it, she wondered what could be so special about a piece of computer code?

"Don't look at me like that," Rohaan snapped.

"It's just, you always think that a new finding will be the proof you need to establish your field as a respected scientific endeavor."

"Fine. That might be true, but this is different."

She smiled, shook her head, and continued her work.

"Anyway, I understand the virus and I've implemented a prototype antivirus protocol in Pele's systems. I just need a little more time to test it. The thing is, it's almost like it's alive, it morphs and changes and if we are going to counter it, we have to build equally sophisticated code."

"Well, if anyone can do it, it's you, Ears. I have faith in you."

He smiled from ear to ear. She knew how important the validation was to him; he certainly didn't get it from his family or his peers. Skyla exhaled heavily, her thoughts turning to her own family. She knew Rohaan was right: she should find some way to run. Her mother was very powerful, and controlling beyond measure. In her presence, Skyla wasn't sure if she really could stand up to the pressure, or if she would crumble before her mother's will, consigning herself to another tour of duty in the UTA Navy.

Skyla was exhausted just thinking about it. She also didn't think she had much of a choice. Even if Rohaan did help unlock Pele from the docking controls, she doubted she would be able to get past the dock crew without hurting anyone. She wasn't about to fight her way through the people who had spent the past two months putting Pele back together. No, her only choice was to go with the envoy of ships back to Gefion and face her mother. It had been a long time coming; she had given her resignation three years ago, and the UTA had not been able to catch up with her since. She had known she would have to face her mother someday; she had just hoped she could outrun that day a little longer.

She needed a change of subject. "How is the translation going?"

Rohaan glanced up from his work. "Not great. I could use a few more samples, but my algorithm can translate some of the text you collected."

"Can you translate this?" She flicked her fingers, sending an image to Rohaan.

He scrunched up his face in concentration. "What is it?"

"It's the markings from the creature's collar."

He nodded as the algorithm began to cycle through the symbols.

"These markings here are easy enough. They are numbers. They look like coordinates." He sent the coordinates back to Skyla.

She pulled up a holo of the world where she had found the creature, overlaying the coordinates. A blue dot began to pulse over a building at the edge of the ruins. She hadn't taken the time to scout that location.

"Those coordinates match the ruins where I found the tech," she said.

Rohaan nodded but didn't take his eyes off the holo of his algorithm at work. It stopped shifting abruptly, symbols translating to letters. "Fenrir," he said, flicking the output over to Skyla.

Her heart stopped. Fenrir, as in the giant wolf from their mythology? The one who will swallow the sun and fight against the gods in Ragnarök? That couldn't be right. They had long suspected that Old World civilizations were ancient humans who arrived in this galaxy long before the twelve tribes, but there had never been any proof.

The sound of sirens interrupted her thoughts.

"What is that?" Skyla asked.

"No idea, I've never heard sirens like that before," Rohaan replied. They wandered out of Pele into chaos.

The docks were pierced by the deafening ring of alarm bells accompanied by yellow flashing warning lights. The Naval crew rushed around the docks and the mechanics, whom Skyla had spent weeks watching play cards and leisurely fix cargo ships, now scrambled to prepare fighter jets. A squadron of pilots flooded into the docks, already prepped in flight suits and helmets. Everyone moved with a level of urgency she hadn't seen once in the past two months. This wasn't one of Commander Azai's many drills. Something was terribly wrong.

Skyla glanced over at Rohaan. He looked just as concerned as she felt. He slowly shook his head, answering her silent question. He didn't know what was happening, either. Skyla opened a comm-line with Pele.

"Pele, do you have anything on your scanners?"

"It appears a Naval battalion has just fallen out of hyperflight."

"A battalion?" Would her mother have sent that many ships to come collect her? If those ships were sent by the senator, then why were the alarms sounding? Commander Azai had made it very clear that he was handing her over to the envoy when they arrived. No, this was something else. She could feel it.

"Yes, I have a destroyer, four corvettes, four cruisers, and a starfighter carrier on my scans. It is a full battalion."

There was no way that the United Tribal Axis could spare a full battalion just to babysit her. She had heard rumors of the skirmishes happening on the edges of tribal space. It was a powder keg just waiting for a spark to ignite.

The station rumbled, sending unsettling vibrations through her boots.

"The fleet has opened fire on Medina," Pele broadcast.

Rohaan's eyes grew wide. He hesitated for only a moment, then he opened up his comms.

"I don't have time to explain. Spread this message. We have to evacuate now."

Skyla's brow furrowed. Did he say *evacuate*?

"This is a research facility. We have no real defenses. The only thing we have is Commander Azai's troops. If they break through Azai's ships, we won't be able to stop them."

Skyla nodded.

"Pele, prepare for launch," Skyla commanded.

"I have to prepare Cista for launch," Rohaan said, sprinting off into the crowd.

Skyla rushed into her ship, strapping into her captain's chair.

"Pele, bring up view screens." Skyla was surprised to see that none of the commander's squadrons had launched. They all sat on the dock, where they had been before the alarms went off.

"What are they doing?" she asked.

"All ships appear to be offline," Pele said.

"Offline? What do you mean, offline?"

"I see no power signatures coming from any of the ships."

"That doesn't make any sense. Why aren't they powering up?"

Skyla spotted Wout on the screen and she ran across the crowded tarmac to where he was belting out orders.

"Wout, what is going on?" Skyla shouted to be heard. Wout was red-faced and sweaty.

She had never seen him wound so tight.

"All of the ships...they're dead."

"Dead?"

"They won't power up."

"All of them?"

"Down to the smallest transport vessel," Wout said, sounding defeated.

"Ears, is Cista running?" Skyla asked through her comms.

"Of course she is running. Why wouldn't she be running?"

Skyla thought for a moment. Pele and Cista appeared to be the only ships unaffected. Why?

"Because every other damn ship on the dock is dead." She yelled back through the comms.

"What?!" Rohaan had heard her, he just couldn't believe it. The minutes ticked by. Rohaan was silent. Skyla was wracking her brain for a solution that wouldn't come. What could be causing this? It wasn't an EMP, the docks themselves would have powered down. In all her years in the Navy, she had never encountered a weapon capable of rendering an entire fleet of ships dead in moments.

A cadre of soldiers entered the docks clad in armored spacesuits, the hilts of katanas sticking up over their shoulders. There was no doubt that it was Commander Azai and his officers. The commander spotted Wout and made a straight line to the mechanic.

"Why aren't my ships in the air?" he demanded.

"They are dead, sir. They won't power up."

"We are being bombarded by the *Ormen Korte*! I need fighters in the air now!"

The *Ormen Korte*? She knew that ship. That was a Stjarna ship—why would they attack an allied outpost?

"I think I've got it!" Rohaan shouted through the comms. "Grab Wout, bring all the mechanics you can, and meet me at my ship."

Wout didn't have to be asked twice. They broke into a run, signaling every mechanic along the way to follow.

Cista was much smaller than Pele and there wasn't space for all of them to join him inside, so Rohaan stood at the rear of his ship, ready to give his orders.

"What's going on?" Skyla asked.

"Everyone gather closer," he shouted over the noise. "I am going to send you a data file. I need you to manually upload the file to each ship."

That was all the explanation Wout needed.

"You heard the man, get to it!" he roared. The mechanics scattered, hurrying over to the nearest ships. Wout stomped off to spread the word to the rest of his mechanics. Commander Azai signaled for his officers to prepare their ships.

"What the hell is this all about?" Skyla demanded, following Rohaan back inside Cista, the commander only one step behind them. Rohaan turned to face Skyla, pulling up a holo file.

"Does this look familiar?" Rohaan asked.

Skyla stared at the display.

"This is the virus that I isolated from Pele." He swiped his hand, illuminating a second display. At first glance, the viruses looked different, but then Skyla saw it—the base code was the same.

"Did the virus escape containment?" Commander Azai asked.

Rohaan shook his head. "Not likely, this virus entered the station when that fleet arrived."

"The virus that shut down Pele was developed by the UTA?" Skyla asked.

Rohaan shook his head again. "I don't have the data to support that. We can worry about that later. Right now, we need to evacuate. We are taking heavy fire. Without starship support, it won't be long before the shields fail."

"He's right," Commander Azai admitted. "We need to get out there and provide coverage for the transports; otherwise, they don't stand a chance."

Skyla pushed the lingering questions from her mind. They could figure this all out later, but first, they had to survive the attack. Ships began to power up on Cista's display.

"It's working!" Skyla threw her arms around Rohaan.

"Right, time to get moving then," Rohaan said, pulling away.

"Stay on comms!" Skyla turned, almost plowing right into Commander Azai. The commander stood his ground, locking onto her gaze for a moment. He swallowed whatever retort was sitting on his tongue, instead turning to let her pass. He made a decision in that moment. Regarding what, she wasn't sure. At least he wasn't crazy enough to keep her grounded during the firefight.

Now that ships were powering on, the chaos looked more organized. Wout's mechanics rushed from ship to ship, powering up the fighters first, then the civilian transports.

Skyla came across Dr. Pinot as she ran back to Pele.

"Do you have a transport yet?" Skyla asked.

"Not yet. It's utter chaos in here."

"Follow me. You can ride with me and Pele."

"How many people can Pele support?"

"She's bigger than she looks. We can accommodate a crew of fifteen, but we can help evacuate more if we need to."

The doctor talked to some of the scientists and crew along the way. When Skyla glanced back, there was a small crowd following them. Pele was going to be grumpy—just because she could accommodate a crew of fifteen didn't mean she liked it.

Once they were all on board, Dr. Pinot settled into a workstation and began using Pele's comms to organize the evacuation effort. The crew members she had selected, likewise, put themselves to work. Some helped to settle the new passengers, while others had taken to the weapons stations and were familiarizing themselves with the mechanical equipment as Pele prepared for launch.

"You doing OK, Pele?" Skyla whispered.

"What kind of question is that?" Pele responded in Skyla's ear.

"I know you don't like having a lot of people on board—"

"Skyla, *you* don't like having a lot of people on board. Besides, this is an emergency, so if we could save the human feelings-talk for later, that would be preferred," Pele snapped.

A moment later, Pele announced over the shipwide comms: "We have received our launch orders. We are in position three, berth Sigma, prepare for launch in five minutes."

Skyla paused behind Dr. Pinot, who was working furiously at a console. "We need to fill the ships—if we don't, civilians are going to get left behind," Dr. Pinot said.

"Do what you need to do, Doc."

The doctor nodded and went back to work.

Skyla stepped onto her bridge, which was bustling with several crew members who had taken unmanned stations. A shiver ran down her spine. It had been a long time since she was in command of a crew. Dread settled in her stomach. This was all too familiar. She tried to shake the feeling as she took her seat in the command chair.

"Pele, status," Skyla called out.

"All systems are online and prepared for launch. Sealing the hull in sixty seconds."

Skyla looked out the viewport screens. Civilians were queued, waiting for their ship assignments. The mechanics rushed to get the last of the civilian transporters online. Most of the starfighters had already launched.

"Ears, give me an update," Skyla spoke into her comms.

"Fully loaded and ready to launch in two," Rohaan responded in her ear.

"Stick to Pele. Cista isn't built for a fight."

"You don't have to tell me twice."

The bridge shifted under Skyla's boots as Pele maneuvered into launch position. The only ships remaining in the hangar now were civilian transports. It was shocking how quickly the docks had emptied. Where there were lines of people and crew running around frantically only moments ago, there was now only a handful of mechanics finishing their work. Skyla felt a sense of relief, tinged with annoyance, but it looked like all of the civilians had found transports, and she had to give Commander Azai credit for that.

That feeling of relief was short-lived. Pele was in line with the open bay doors, looking into space where a horrific scene unfolded. The UTA fleet showed no mercy as they bombarded the station. Bright explosions danced against a black curtain of stars. Commander Azai's fighters were engaged with the starfighters from the UTA fleet, providing cover for the civilian transports. Skyla had only a moment to take in the battle before Pele launched, thrusting them into the middle of a firefight.

CHAPTER 20 | FREYJA

POWER STRUGGLE

"Stand down!" Freyja roared into her comms.

She stood on the bridge of the *Ormen Korte,* watching in horror as her fleet attacked Medina Outpost. She had received orders from the Empress to secure Medina. They had received intel that the outpost was manufacturing atomics, but Freyja had run a full scan of the station on their arrival that had revealed nothing. She had planned on doing a thorough search of the station, and it wouldn't have been hard to come to a diplomatic solution. Before she could open comms with Commander Azai, her fleet had opened fire.

"What is happening? Why isn't our fleet responding," Freyja yelled at her comms officer.

"I'm sorry, Admiral, it appears we are being jammed."

"What the hell?" Who would be jamming them? Why had her fleet engaged without orders? Freyja's temples throbbed with irritation. *Think. How do I regain control of my fleet?* The viewport in front of her switched from a display of the battle scene to the imposing figure of the Empress.

"Report, Admiral," the Empress demanded.

"The fleet is attacking Medina," Freyja replied.

"Good, take the station. Report to me when it is done."

"There are no signs of atomics. If we call off the attack, I am sure we can secure the station without further loss of life."

"The weapons are there. Take the station by any means necessary."

"They hardly have any defenses. Let me call off our fighters and resolve this diplomatically."

"You have your orders. I want that station. No one leaves. Destroy every ship they have launched. They are inconsequential." With that, the Empress ended their communication.

The battle once again raged across the viewport. Freyja pressed her palms into her eye sockets. The Empress expected total obedience, but looking out at the scene unfolding before her—at the ships bursting into flames as her fighters ripped through their hulls—it didn't feel right. Only a handful of the ships on Freyja's viewport were military-make. The vast majority were civilian transports, trying to escape the siege. Her fleet ripped through the ships indiscriminately. She watched as Commander Azai's fighters moved to protect the civilian ships, taking heavy casualties of their own.

No, this wasn't right. She hadn't come here to kill civilians. She was here to eliminate a threat. If there was a threat at all, it was on that station.

"Move the *Ormen Korte* into position. I want us between our fighters and those civilian ships." She called out the order, but her words sat heavy in the air. No one moved. Everyone on the command deck had just seen the same broadcast that she had. They knew the Empress wanted the station, and that she wanted to take it by force.

"That's an order!" Freyja shouted, clenching her fists around the armrests of her chair. Kylian and Tristan exchanged uneasy looks. They stood on either side of her, scanning the faces of the officers on the bridge. They saw the same thing that she did, that the majority of the officers on the *Ormen Korte* had been placed there by her mother. Kylian and Tristan's hands hovered over the hilts of their broadswords. The tension in the air was so strong it tasted of electricity and salt. Finally, an ambitious officer named Borg cleared his throat. He was one of the officers that had been chosen by the Empress to join the crew, not one of her Berserkers.

"The Empress was quite clear in her orders," Borg said.

"And I was clear in mine."

"If you cannot follow the orders of our Empress, then I have no choice but to assume command of this vessel." Borg's hand wrapped around his weapon.

Kylian and Tristan looked to Freyja, their hands held tight around the hilts of their swords. Freyja did a quick scan of the room. There were a handful of her Berserkers, but they were severely outnumbered. She stood, gripping the hilt of her sword.

"You believe I would allow you to take my ship from me?"

"If you cannot follow orders, then it is not your ship to command."

"Very well." Freyja drew her sword. "I will not stand for mutiny."

She swung at Borg, and he moved to block her strike. Chaos broke loose on the bridge as those loyal to Freyja clashed with the mutineers.

Freyja directed a fury of slashes at Borg. He blocked each strike, but there was no mistaking the effort etched on his face. He made no move to counter; it was taking everything he had just to keep up with her. She was stronger and faster than he was; it would only be a matter of time before she cut him down.

Freyja spared a quick check of the bridge. Unfortunately, while she had her foe handled, her crew wasn't faring as well. They were outnumbered, five to one, and not all of her mother's soldiers were as inept with the sword as her opponent. Freyja wrenched her gaze away from the carnage as one of her soldiers was impaled from three sides. Lieutenant Dakarai had been a good comms officer, and Freyja reeled at the senseless loss.

She screamed, unleashing the feral beast inside her. Startled, Borg stumbled back, but he recovered in time to keep her next blow from slicing clean through his chest. Kylian held position by Freyja's right shoulder, as he engaged his pair of opponents.

"Admiral, we won't take the bridge like this. There are too many of them and too few of us." He grunted as he blocked a heavy blow. He was right.

More of her officers fell, Kofi and Ekon. *Damn it!* They were dropping like flies. She wouldn't be able to stop the mutiny. She had to take what few soldiers she had left and retreat before they were all cut down on her own damn bridge!

"Berserkers, fall in!" Freyja screamed as she shoved all her weight into Borg, sending him skidding across the room. She spun, striking out with her sword, carving a path toward the exit. Kylian and Tristan took up the fight to either side of her, guarding her periphery from flying steel as she carved through flesh to secure their escape.

She advanced toward the door, slicing clean through the sword arm of the man standing in front of her. His hand had been held high, ready to deliver a killing blow to one of her Berserkers, but now he screamed, clutching what was left of his arm as blood poured down his uniform. She kicked him hard in the knee and he collapsed to the floor, writhing in pain. Kylian grabbed the fallen Berserker, hoisting her to her feet. He dragged her along while fending off another attacker. Freyja lunged forward, trying to take out another soldier before he cut down one of her own, but she was too late. The light dimmed from Lieutenant Amari's eyes, as the attacker sliced clean through her clavicle, into her opposite ribs. Freyja took the attacker's head from him in one swift swing, but it was too late to save her Berserker. Freyja and Tristan made quick work of the remaining soldiers who still stood between them and escape.

Once through the blast doors, Kylian wasted no time jamming the controls from the outside. Freyja did a quick count of her surviving Berserkers. Five, plus Kylian, Tristan, and herself. Just five of her soldiers made it off that bridge. Freyja's blood boiled. She let out a furious growl that grew into a blood-curdling scream as she slammed her palm into the bulkhead.

"Admiral, we have to get off the *Ormen Korte*. Now." Kylian said. The jammed controls wouldn't keep the mutineers stuck on the bridge for long.

"I've blocked their comms, for now. I didn't see who they had on their side. If they have a comms officer who is worth a damn working on those lines, then we have five-ten minutes. Tops. Before they sound the alarm to lock down the ship. If that happens—"

"We are spaced," Tristan finished.

Freyja reined in her anger, nodding abruptly before turning on her heel to march away. "To the hanger. We are getting off this death trap."

They arrived at the hangar without further incident, confirming that the mutineers had not yet found a way to signal the rest of the crew to intercept them.

Freyja stalked across the hanger to her ship, Selkie. They passed a young mechanic working just one berth over. His eyes went wide and his mouth fell open in shock at the sight of them covered in the blood of those they had cut down, and from deep wounds of their own. He dropped the tool, and it clattered on the grate as he gawked at them, frozen in place.

Once everyone was on board, Selkie was quick to seal the doors and begin the launch sequence. With the battle raging outside, no one would give a second glance at another fighter launching into the fray.

CHAPTER 21 | HINATA

DOGFIGHT

Hinata's stomach churned as Tentei went into another high-G spin to avoid a barrage of phaser blasts across his flank.

He never was fond of dogfights. He preferred tactics. He preferred to be on the bridge of his stardestroyer, but unfortunately, that wasn't going to happen today. His stardestroyer had been called into dry dock for maintenance at the beginning of the month and was days away from Medina. He was back in his own AI ship; a ship that still refused to speak to him.

He veered to follow an enemy ship that had locked onto a civilian transport, firing off a quick burst of plasma cannon fire. Hinata had to keep it tight—if he went wide with his shot, he would take out the transport himself. The enemy fighter exploded in front of him and he pulled up sharply to avoid the debris cloud. There was no respite as Hinata focused on the next transport vessel under siege.

Hinata buzzed by the dock. Skyla's ship had just launched. He opened a comms channel. "Captain, we could sure use some of those sharp starfighter maneuvers I've heard so much about."

"You sure you want an outlaw covering your wing?"

"We don't have time for that," he snapped.

"Very well, Commander. Open comms between me and your pilots. Time to show these assholes what a real UTA squadron can do."

Hinata opened up a channel between the captain's ship and his remaining starfighters. If the captain was rusty from all those years off-grid, it didn't show. She organized the starfighters into flights focused on the three most vulnerable areas: launch, exiting station space, and entering hyperspace.

"Remember, we only have to cover long enough for the rest of our civilian ships to jump. Don't take unnecessary risks—and don't die." Skyla called out over the comms.

Hinata's ship joined the captain's, along with two of his other starfighters and an AI ship he recognized from the dock roster, but didn't know who its pilot was. The other AI ship was lightweight, fast-moving, but not heavily armed. It was there as support only. His squad was over the first stage of the civilian transport journey and the most dangerous. The attacking starships were focused on taking the station and preventing anyone from leaving it.

Hinata moved into position, letting the captain's ship take point. If she had even half the skill as a starfighter as her reputation suggested, she was a far better pilot than him. Captain Karsten had been renowned for her skill as a pilot. She had never allowed an opponent to successfully board one of her destroyers during battle simulations.

"Get ready. Transports launching in three, two, one!" Skyla instructed over the comms. A fresh stream of civilian ships shot out of the launch bay in front of them. With the new wave of ships came the renewed attention of enemy fighters. Three enemy starfighters broke off from their barrage on the station shield generators to attack the transports.

"I've got the lead. Commander, you take the second. Tax, you've got third. Ears, keep watch and fill the gaps."

Skyla broke off from their group in a high-G spin that made Hinata's stomach lurch just to watch. He locked onto his target with far less grace. As his opponent zeroed in on one of the transport ships, Hinata fired across its wing.

What the hell was going on? Why would a UTA fleet attack one of their own stations? He shook his head—he had to stay focused on the battle. He hoped to keep the death toll to a minimum. Unfortunately, the enemy fighters were hell-bent on taking the station, with no regard for the body count. The starfighter in front of him took a clumsy shot at the transport ships before doing a 180-degree flip to come nose-to-nose with Hinata's ship.

"Shit!" He yanked hard on his controls to avoid a collision. As he did, the ship fell in line behind him—now it was his ship it had on lock. He dodged around a cloud of detritus, with the enemy ship following close behind. Hinata took a hard turn to avoid colliding with a second enemy ship. As he did, a barrage of plasma cannon fire streamed past him. That was a close one, and now two enemy ships were dogging him.

He cursed. He much preferred facing his opponent with a katana. Blasting his enemies into particles with plasma cannons felt crass; although, at the moment, he should be more concerned that he would be the one reduced to dust.

An alarm blared—one of the enemy starfighters had locked onto his ship. He threw his ship into a hard-G turn, trying to lose the lock. The alarm silenced, but only for a moment before the second enemy ship had a lock on him.

"Shit, shit, shit!" He tried to outmaneuver the second ship, but this pilot was much more skilled than the first. The lock held. If he couldn't break it, he was spaced. The alarm suddenly silenced. He glanced at the rear viewport to find the enemy ship had been reduced to a cloud of fire and dust. The captain zipped past.

"Try to stay in one piece, won't you, Commander?" the captain voiced over the comms.

"I'll do my best, Captain." His relief was short-lived as he plotted a course back into position. The dogfight had led him deep into enemy lines, leaving the next stream of civilian transports exiting the station exposed. The enemy ships were closing in—he wasn't going to make it on time. He slammed a fist against the console. This shouldn't be happening! All those civilians...

An enemy AI ship came up behind the starfighters. He groaned. The starfighters alone were skilled enough to challenge his limited squad; the enemy AI ship was far superior to all of the ships he had, save the captain's—he couldn't believe what he saw—the enemy AI ship pulled in front of its own starfighters, as if to cut them off.

The starfighters dodged around the ship and continued on course. When the AI ship tried once again to block their advance, they opened fire on it, but the starfighters were no match for the ship. It easily maneuvered around the plasma cannon blasts to target their engines. It immobilized all three of the enemy ships in an efficient barrage of railgun fire and now they floated aimlessly like kelp in a glassy pond, no longer a threat to the civilian ships.

What had he just witnessed? That wasn't one of his ships; it was clearly part of the opposing fleet, but it had just saved a convoy of civilians. *Why?*

His comms flashed. The AI ship was hailing him. He was about to get his answer.

Hinata opened a channel and he was shocked by the face that appeared on his screen.

"Admiral."

"Commander Azai, it looks like you could use a hand," Admiral Nygaard said.

"Why don't you just call off your fleet? Then we wouldn't need help defending innocent civilians from slaughter."

"I wish I could. I didn't authorize this attack, and I can't get through to my ships. Listen, we don't have time for this right now. Let me help you evacuate, then we can figure out what in the hell is going on."

Freyja sounded shockingly sincere; and besides, what choice did he have?

"Very well. Patch into Pele's comms; that is the AI ship leading our squad."

Freyja stiffened.

So she knew the captain?

She recovered quickly and gave a terse nod before ending the transmission.

Hinata noted the admiral's reaction; he would have plenty of time to figure out how the admiral and the captain were acquainted later, if they made it out of this alive. He tuned in to the captain's comms.

"I just received a report from Wout—they need coverage for two more launches, then we can all get the hell out of here." Skyla gave commands, including their new AI ship, to help cover the final wave of transports. If the captain recognized Freyja, she did a good job of hiding it. They were just approaching position as another batch of civilian transports exited the launch bay. Freyja was already proving a valuable addition to the squadron. Not only was her ship well armed and fast, but she had trained the enemy starfighters, she could predict their next move before they made them. It wasn't long before the civilian transports had made their hyperjump and were out of danger.

"One more round of transports, then jump to the rendezvous coordinates." Skyla directed.

The final launch of transport ships had just begun to exit the station, then everything went white.

Hinata's crash harness bit into his shoulders as his ship was swept aside by a wave of energy. He blinked several times, trying to recover his vision.

"Report!" he demanded of Tentei. There was no response. "Report, damn it—it's your life too!" he shouted. There was a brief pause before Tentei responded.

"All systems are operational, Commander. Shields are at thirty percent and holding." A dispassionate voice filled the cockpit. As Hinata's vision cleared, he saw the cause of the explosion. The enemy ships had finally broken through the shield array. The station was completely vulnerable. The bulk of the battalion that had been focused on the shields now switched targets to the docks. His fighters were massively outnumbered. The last of the civilian ships were still launching. He fell in behind a starfighter tailing one of the larger transports.

"Not today," he whispered as he eliminated the ship. Another enemy ship fell in behind him and, once again, Hinata became the prey. He took his ship into a hard-G spin, leading the starfighter away from the civilians. As he did, he glimpsed a large bomber, its trajectory in line with the docks.

"Somebody take out that bomber!" he shouted over the comms. No response. All of their fighters were engaged, trying to protect the ships that had already launched. He tried to maneuver into position to cover the docks, but he was struggling to keep the enemy ship chasing him from taking him out of the fight for good. He was helpless as the bomber released its payload, obliterating the Medina docks—and with it, the civilian transports waiting to launch.

"No!" He yelled into his empty cockpit. Losing control, he leaned into the overwhelming drive to take his vengeance. A hard-G 180 spin brought him nose-to-nose with his assailant. Not expecting the move, his opponent swerved and as it did, he opened up a barrage of plasma cannon blasts across its hull. They would not be returning to the fight.

"That's it, squad, make the jump!" Skyla commanded over the comms. Of course, she was right, but he couldn't help but feel their job was incomplete. They hadn't successfully evacuated the last of the transports.

"Commander, now." Skyla had opened up a private comms channel to his ship.

It was only then that he realized that he had been following an enemy starfighter back into the fray, not out to the jump. He hesitated; he had never run from a fight, he had never lost a battle.

"You are no good to these people dead. There are still thousands of civilians at the rendezvous site that are going to need a commander."

Hinata closed his eyes, his hands trembling, his blood boiling...then he exhaled and broke off his pursuit.

He fell in line with their remaining flight to initiate the jump. While a few of the enemy ships tried launching a final assault on Hinata's tiny fleet, they didn't have time to do much damage before they launched into hyperspace and were gone.

Emerging from the jump, an endless nebula sprawled out before Hinata. There were no ship readings on his scanners, but that was to be expected. While the enemy should not have been able to track their jump, he hadn't wanted to take any chances. He had selected jump coordinates at the edge of a nebula that would block enemy scans, in case they accidentally brought through enemy fighters. He had instructed the civilian ships to wait just inside the nebula and he prayed they had made it safely.

Hinata waited in silence at the fringe of the nebula, the only sound the pounding of his own heart. A few moments felt like an eternity, but then the first transport materialized from out of the pink swirling gas, then another, and another. A full civilian fleet took shape out of the sparkling particles and he was hit with a sense of relief, then guilt, over the transports he knew were missing.

They had evacuated most of Medina, but not everyone had made it.

CHAPTER 22 | SKYLA

THE AFTERMATH

Skyla sat in Pele's cargo bay, waiting for Commander Azai to arrive. He had called a martial meeting of his highest-ranking officers to discuss strategy. Skyla and Rohaan had been included as well. Pele was the largest military class ship in their makeshift fleet and would host the council. Skyla was relieved when Rohaan was the first to arrive, and she quickly moved to clasp forearms with him.

"Your family?" she asked.

"They are all aboard the *Gilgamesh*, Alhamdulillah."

"Good." She nodded, then dropped her voice. "Ears, did you take any scans during the battle?"

"You know I did."

"I want you to start decoding what you have, and listen in on the chatter. Nothing is right about this."

Their conversation was cut short as Commander Azai arrived with his officers. The commander's uniform was crisp, his katana in place, and his hair braided tightly against his scalp like usual, but there was a dark sea raging behind his eyes, on the brink of breaking free.

"Captain, this is my second-in-command, Lieutenant Commander Tax Sato," the commander gestured to one of the men, "and Lieutenant Commander Callan Kobayashi," he said, indicating the next officer behind him.

"Skyla," she corrected, as she grasped forearms with each of the men. "What do we know?"

"Not much. I was hoping you and Mr. Dar could help us sort this out. That was a UTA fleet; there was no reason for them to attack one of their own outposts."

"I noticed," she said.

The bay doors snapped open, and at first, Skyla was surprised by the intrusion. She had thought everyone had already arrived. Fury quickly replaced her surprise. "What the hell are you doing on my ship?" she spat at the newcomer as she stomped across the cargo bay.

"I was invited." Freyja sneered.

"Not by me. My ship, my rules—get the hell off!"

"So feisty!" Tristan took a step closer to Skyla. He was so close she had to tilt her chin back to meet his gaze. "I like that. You grew up good, Karsten. I'm glad you didn't die in that little accident back at the academy." He ran his eyes over her suggestively.

"And I see you haven't grown up at all," she countered.

"Oh, I am all man, sweetheart. I'd be happy to show you if you'd like."

"Really? Because you sound exactly like the same boy, I beat out for the Leikar Cup. How many times was it?" Skyla paused, bringing her hand to her chin in thought. "Oh, that's right, four times. Sorry, you just can't keep up with me, honey."

Tristan stepped in closer, his voice dropping to a sultry whisper. "Come now, Karsten, we both know that last time was close, and if that last fight was any indication, I wouldn't mind seeing how you grapple off the mat."

Commander Azai stepped in to break up the reunion, his fists clenched at his sides.

Tristan's eyes dropped to the commander's fists, and a smile twisted his lips. "You're welcome to join, Commander." He pursed his lips, sending a kiss through the air.

Commander Azai didn't dignify him with a response. "I invited Freyja. She has information that we don't."

"She brought that fleet to Medina! We're supposed to believe she switched sides in the middle of a firefight?"

Freyja shrugged. "Believe me or don't, it doesn't really matter. I could use some answers myself. If we work together, maybe we can get to the bottom of this."

The commander turned to Skyla, leaning in so only she could hear his words.

"Captain, I am no fan of the admiral, but what if she has the missing piece to this puzzle? Please, let's hear her out. Then we can send her back to her ship and on her way."

Skyla's anger softened slightly. He had continued to call her Captain, but the way he said it wasn't like he was calling her by her military title, it was like it was a secret shared between just the two of them. She should be annoyed. The commander knew who she was now, and that title had been a shackle to her for so long. She knew how she should feel, but she found his insistence on the title strangely endearing. Despite her reservations, she would accept his request.

"I'll hear her out, but that doesn't mean I believe a word that comes out of her mouth." Skyla squinted at Freyja, a nasty insinuation in her voice.

Commander Azai jumped in to avoid another spat. "Admiral, care to tell me why you wiped out a third of an allied UTA fleet?"

Tristan folded his arms over his chest, a grin twisting across his chiseled face. "Maybe you would have fared better if you had launched your ships when our battalion arrived. What, you get soft out there in exile?" The man never had a filter, not even back at the academy, when comments like that had earned him thousands of extra hours on the training grounds.

"You know damn well we couldn't launch our ships. What the hell was that virus?"

"What virus?" Kylian had been a passive observer up until this point, but he was paying attention now.

"You know what I'm fucking talking about. All of our ships were incapacitated when you dropped out of hyperspace."

Kylian shook his head. "That's not possible."

"I assure you, my soldiers wouldn't sit on their asses while our station was under siege."

"If we had access to tech like that, you bet your ass I'd use it, but we don't," Freyja said. "I had intel that Medina was producing illegal atomics. We were sent to take control of the station and the illegal weapons cache—"

"That's preposterous." Commander Azai forced through clenched teeth, his indignation infusing the air with electricity. "Everyone knows that Medina is a research outpost. There have never been any illegal weapons on my station."

Again, Freyja shrugged.

Heat blossomed across Skyla's face as her anger began to boil over. How could Freyja be so cavalier after the massacre she'd just caused?

"The report I received said otherwise. Anyway, I didn't pick up any weapons signatures once we arrived—"

"Then why did you attack my station?" Commander Azai's voice dripped with venom.

"If you would let me speak, I will share everything that I know, and then we can all be done with each other," Freyja spat.

She doesn't like the way she's being questioned? Good, Skyla thought. She knew that her feelings toward Freyja were petty, in light of everything that had just happened. It had been years, but what Freyja had done wasn't something easily forgiven or forgotten.

"My fleet opened fire without my orders. When I tried to hail my ships, my signal was blocked. I had intended to take the station diplomatically. We both know how quick you are to cower before me, Hinata." She paused to let the insult hit. To his credit, Commander Azai clenched his jaw and remained silent. Once Freyja was sure he wouldn't rise to the bait, she continued. "I wasn't able to regain control of the fleet." She stopped.

Skyla studied the woman; Freyja's hesitation was out of character. There was something she wasn't telling them. Skyla replayed the battle in her mind and recalled the odd assortment of ships that had escaped the onslaught. Freyja had come into the nebula on her own AI ship, not a stardestroyer. There was no way an admiral should have been in that conflict on her own starfighter.

"Why isn't the *Ormen Korte* out there?" Skyla motioned her head to the fleet of surviving ships sitting in space around Pele. Freyja glowered at her. After a long pause, Freyja finally gave in.

"I lost control of the *Ormen Korte*."

"How does an admiral lose control of their stardestroyer?" Skyla asked.

This time Freyja held her tongue, her face turning crimson—but was it from anger or embarrassment? Freyja balled her fists, clenched her jaw, and refused to say anything further.

"Well, this has been wildly helpful. Thank you for your valuable insights. Now get off my ship." Skyla sarcastically motioned for Freyja to exit the cargo bay.

Commander Azai moved, as if to interject, but Freyja held up her hand.

"Fine." She hesitated, still unsure of how to proceed. "When the battle began, I received a transmission from the Empress."

Skyla furrowed her brow in confusion. What did the self-declared monarch of mining have to do with United Tribal Axis affairs?

"She demanded we take the station...and destroy any ships trying to escape."

Ire flashed in Commander Azai's eyes.

"I refused. However, there were plenty of officers loyal to the Empress on the *Ormen Korte*. They mutinied and took the ship." For the first time, Skyla saw true regret in Freyja's eyes.

"There were too many of them. We couldn't hold the bridge. We barely made it off the *Ormen Korte* with our lives." Silence settled over the room. What did any of it mean? As far as Skyla was concerned, Freyja didn't have any missing pieces to the puzzle—her account of the battle only raised more questions.

"What does the Empress want with Medina?" Commander Azai asked.

"And why is an admiral of the United Tribal Axis taking orders from her?" Skyla added.

Rohaan cleared his throat. All eyes shifted to him.

"I hate to interrupt, but Cista just forwarded a transmission. I sent a drone to the nearest quantum relay station when we arrived, and I think you all need to hear this."

Rohaan took a step into the center of the group, then projected a holo.

A talking head appeared; it looked like one of the news correspondents from the capital. It reported. "We have received confirmation that the incident at Medina Outpost has left Admiral Nygaard and Captain Karsten of Stjarna Tribe, and Commander Azai of Hoshiko Tribe, dead, along with thousands of United Tribal Axis soldiers, Medina residents, and XingXing scientists, who had been at the station for the annual Secchi conference."

The holo view shifted to another reporter. "Mixed reports of what caused the incident are still coming in. There are rumors that Medina Outpost was secretly producing atomic weapons for the Fenix cartel. Both the Stjarna Tribe and the Hoshiko Tribe are denying any involvement, while the XingXing Tribe are demanding answers from the two powerhouses involved in the incident." The holo transmission ended there.

"Start talking." Commander Azai glared at Freyja.

Freyja shook her head from side to side, but perhaps being declared dead would loosen her tongue.

"I don't know what she is planning, but I have been receiving orders from the Empress since I assumed my post."

"You've been running side missions for a crime syndicate for the past three years!?" The commander was beginning to lose his composure.

"A few missions here and there. Mostly she wanted reports confirmed."

"And you didn't report this to the Senate?"

"We all have our parts to play, Commander. You know just as well as I do that the compact is shaky at best. Fleets put their own tribes first."

"The Empress is not a tribe," Commander Azai said.

"The closest thing that I have to a tribe," Freyja replied.

The Empress was cunning, power-hungry, and cold. Skyla narrowed her eyes. If the Empress was behind this, it couldn't be good.

CHAPTER 23 | FREYJA

A GHOST

Freyja dug her fingers into the dirt. The moisture seeped through the knees of her cargo pants as she grounded herself in the soil. She exhaled deeply, then inhaled air that tasted of earth and life. After meeting with Hinata and his officers, she had come straight to the small grow room she housed on Selkie. What did any of it mean? She hadn't told them everything, but she told them enough. She had mentioned the intel the Empress had wanted, a couple of the small missions, and left it at that. They didn't need to know more. She had highlighted her mother's ambitions and how she had grown more bold over the past three years.

What did it matter now that she had been declared dead? Of course she *wasn't* dead, not in the truest sense of the word, but could she really go back to the Empress after the mutiny on the *Ormen Korte*? Her mother was neither tolerant of insubordination nor failure. Freyja's fingertips ran over the runes that lined her arms. They shimmered under her touch, a living-ink reminder of every mistake she had ever made; a reminder to never make the same mistake twice. She ran her fingers along her ribs. She would add the *Ormen Korte* there. It was her biggest failure yet, and she would not forget.

No, she couldn't go back, for so many reasons. Not only had she disobeyed the orders of the Empress herself, she had lost control of her ship, and her soldiers had paid with their lives. She couldn't let their loss be for nothing.

Freyja pressed her forehead into the dirt and screamed a throat-burning, lung-bursting scream that filled the silence of the grow room. Now that she was "dead," did that mean that she was free? What would it mean to be free, anyway?

She had never had a choice in her life, not really. Now that she did, what would she choose?

The image came to her of an open sky and rows upon rows of green stretching out before her. It was quiet, only the sound of leaves rustling in a gentle breeze. That was her dream: to settle down in some backwater farming community, just her and her plants. That sounded nice, didn't it? The doors to the grow room snapped open. Kylian stood in the doorway, worry lined his face. *Damn*, Freyja thought, he must have heard the scream. She was used to the privacy of the *Ormen Korte;* she wasn't used to sharing this smaller space. She would have to be more careful.

"Admiral," Kylian started as he entered.

"No need for that," Freyja interrupted. "No fleet, no admiral. Just Freyja."

Kylian hesitated. "Are you all right?" He came to sit beside her in the dirt.

Freyja shook her head slowly. "I don't know what to do." She peered up into his warm, hazel eyes, flecked with gold, as if she might find answers there. "My whole life up until this point has been mapped out. I never had a say in any of it. It was the Empress' plan, and now…" She shrugged.

"What do you want to do?" he asked.

"I don't know. The choice has never been mine."

"Come now, Admiral—Freyja," he corrected himself, uncomfortable with the informality. "Even if you were operating within the Empress' designs, there were plenty of decisions you made yourself. I know what you did back at the academy."

Her head snapped up at the comment. He couldn't know. Seeing Skyla again had brought a tumult of emotions to the surface, but she wasn't ready to let those floodgates open. That was in the past. She needed to focus on the present. There was too much at stake to allow distraction to take hold. Her eyes locked on Kylian's, searching for answers. Her heart stuttered when she saw a softness reflected there. He didn't look at her like she was a monster.

Kylian nodded, "I know you spared her life." He hesitated, emotion filling his voice with a slight wobble. "And mine. You decided to fight for me back on the Ring. The Empress doesn't give a damn about me, or the rest of the Berserkers, but you do. You were a good admiral, a good leader. Puppets can't lead."

"You know the gardens were my favorite place on the *Ormen Korte*." Freyja lightly traced her fingertips along the leaves of the plant in front of her.

Kylian inclined his head. He had found the admiral in the gardens more often than in her own quarters.

"I will miss them," she said quietly. "When I was a child, I wanted to be a botanist, or even a farmer. The station gardens were my favorite place on Uppsala. I have often wondered what it would be like to leave this all behind—the politics, the Navy—and go somewhere where my biggest worry is crop output."

"And now? Is that what you want?"

Freyja closed her eyes, and the scene of the bloody battle on the bridge of the *Ormen Korte* played across her closed eyelids, her Berserkers cut down as if they were nothing more than wheat for the harvest; the look in Borg's eyes as he took the lives of her soldiers, took her ship, took her fleet from her.

She looked into Kylian's eyes again.

"No. I cannot let their sacrifice be for nothing. There is something more to what happened today; something more than the Empresses' scheming. Something that our friends gave their lives for," she paused, looking out at her small garden, the loss of a dream weighing on her. "Maybe one day I can retire to a quiet farm. Not yet. We are not done."

Kylian nodded, "I will follow you to the ends of the universe..." Kylian paused before extending his arm to clasp hers. "Freyja."

CHAPTER 24 | HINATA

BATTLE REPORT

A steady stream of battle analysis scrolled across the viewport of Hinata's starfighter, which was tucked safely in the hanger on the *Baghlah,* along with all of the other starfighters in his fleet and several of the smaller, civilian ships.

He had decided to keep his quarters on Tentei—a sentimental decision he was now regretting—as the silence between the two of them grew into a thick fog. He had felt jealous watching the way Skyla interacted with her ship, and he was raw from the loss of Medina; the tragedy had opened old wounds.

Hinata missed both of his brothers. He ran his fingertips gently over the console, like he had done when he was a kid and Tentei was his closest friend. He shook his head. He and Tentei would never have what Skyla had with Pele. He would never initiate a full neural link with Tentei again, not after what it had cost him the last time.

He squinted at the reports, trying to focus his wandering mind. He had requested Mr. Dar send over his findings. He needed to understand what had happened at Medina before he made his next move. Their small ragtag fleet sat just inside the nebula, safe for now. But what was he going to do with all of the civilians? He would need to transport them to a safe planet...and then?

A soft ping alerted Hinata that there was a news clip in his files. He sighed. After the status report Tentei had given him when the Medina shield array came down, it had resumed its policy of no verbal communication. He had spent the better part of the last hour just convincing it to alert him to incoming messages. He opened the holo.

"Senator Azai of the Hoshiko Tribe is demanding that the Stjarna Tribe be held responsible for the destruction of Medina Outpost." The holo cut to a clip of his mother. Her hair was smoothly coiled up upon her head, black with streaks of silver. Her face was clear, with no red splotches or puffy eyes. To the casual observer, Senator Azai probably looked as she always did, but Hinata saw past her veneer; she was tired, near the point of breaking. A pang of guilt pierced him. He had agreed that they must proceed with caution to ensure the safety of their civilian fleet before taking any counter-action—that included reporting their whereabouts to the UTA. Still, it pained him to see his mother grieving the loss of a son who still lived.

"I am asking the United Tribal Axis to follow the law and hold the Stjarna Tribe responsible for their actions. Reports from Medina clearly show that it was the *Ormen Korte,* led by Admiral Freyja Nygaard, that initiated the attack. It was a Stjarna fleet that was acting without orders from the UTA. They must be held responsible. I propose that the Stjarna Tribe pay restitution in the amount of two billion standars. Furthermore, they should face senatorial restrictions for a minimum of two years. The loss of Medina, of the research that was being done there, and of all of the brilliant minds, are irreplaceable. But perhaps we can make an example of the Stjarna Tribe so that such a tragedy never happens again," his mother said, then the clip ended.

There was a storm brewing on the horizon. Stjarna was a powerful tribe, but so was the Hoshiko Tribe. His mother wasn't going to back down. What did that mean for the compact?

One problem at a time. What had really happened at Medina, and how would Hinata ensure the safety of the civilians under his charge?

Another ping rang out from his controls. Hinata glanced up at the incoming message, but there were no new files. That was odd. A few moments later, Mr. Dar joined him in the cockpit. *Damn Tentei and its temper tantrum.* That ping must have been its passive-aggressive warning that Mr. Dar had boarded. Tentei was one more problem he would have to deal with eventually—he couldn't have his AI acting up while they were on the brink of war.

"Mr. Dar," Hinata motioned to the chair next to his. "To what do I owe the pleasure?"

Mr. Dar's face contorted in confusion as he slid into the seat next to the commander. "Commander, I am here at your request."

"My request?"

"Yes, you requested I come to you once I finished my initial review of the battle data."

"We only just left Pele an hour ago. Surely you haven't had time to conclude your analysis?"

Mr. Dar gave Hinata a stern look.

"Commander, as it is your calling to lead the troops of humanity, finding the signal in the noise is mine. My ship continues to decode some of the messages, but I have concluded my initial review."

Hinata looked over Mr. Dar once more. While he might look like the same quiet researcher who had fumbled into Hinata's office to reluctantly ask for an array net to save his friend, he was not. Through the fatigue, Hinata noticed a confidence in the man that he hadn't been there before. Hinata nodded, encouraging Mr. Dar to continue.

Mr. Dar activated the holo projection on his tablet. With his fingertips, he delicately pulled three strands of code up side by side in the projection. Hinata had never been one for technology. He preferred battle logistics and the weight of his sword in his hand. He wasn't sure what he was looking at.

"This first one," Mr. Dar tapped the top of the strand of code, and its green glow intensified. "This is the signal that my scanners picked up during the battle. It was broadcast to all of the ships, save the *Ormen Korte*."

"Was that Freyja's signal to her fleet? Have you been able to decode the signal yet?"

"This signal couldn't possibly have originated from the *Ormen Korte*. Its trajectory indicates it came from the region of space that Skyla was exploring before she came to Medina."

Hinata worked to keep his face impassive, but his hand drifted to his chin in thought. How could that be? That was beyond the Known Galaxies; there were no human settlements in that region of space. Hinata's head spun.

Mr. Dar tapped the next strand of code, illuminating it in the dim light of the cockpit. "This piece of code is what brought your ships down. This was the virus that my antivirus protocol had to counter before we could get any of our ships launched." Hinata kept quiet, waiting for Mr. Dar to continue. "And this," he tapped the final strand of code, "is the virus that Skyla picked up on that abandoned planet."

Hinata didn't understand the connection. To him, they all looked like random, very different pieces of code. Mr. Dar waved a palm over the projection. Pieces of the code blinked out, leaving only select strands illuminated. Now, even Hinata could see the similarities. He squinted, his eyes taking in the display. No—they were not similar, they were *identical*. Hinata's eyes snapped to Mr. Dar's.

"They all come from the same source." Mr. Dar answered his silent question.

"So, we still have more questions than answers." Hinata's voice was cool and calm, even if frustration was simmering under the surface. A ping on Mr. Dar's tablet indicated that he had received a new file.

"Ah, my decryption algorithm has finished decoding the message to Freyja's ships. Perhaps we will find some of those answers you are looking for, Commander." Mr. Dar swiped a finger and a new hologram filled the air where the strands of code had been. A chill crawled through Hinata. The woman staring back at him was unmistakable. It was Freyja.

"We have confirmed weapons signatures to match our intel. Medina is to be treated as hostile. You are authorized to use deadly force. Make no mistake, they will do the same to us. As soon as Medina is in range, open fire." The sound of her voice, the intonation, her expressionless face—there was no mistaking that this recording was of Admiral Nygaard. She had ordered the attack, and she had lied to them all about it. But why?

Why had she left the *Ormen Korte*? Why had she fought against her own ships? Mr. Dar had said that the signal couldn't possibly have originated from the *Ormen Korte*. It didn't add up. Hinata's normally unreadable façade cracked as deep lines etched his brow.

"You were saying, Mr. Dar? About my answers?"

Mr. Dar shook his head from side to side. "That transmission did not originate from the *Ormen Korte*, sir."

"Then what am I looking at, Dar?"

Mr. Dar drew his thick, dark eyebrows together as he considered the facts. He clasped his hands in front of him and pressed his index fingers to his lips. Hinata watched as the researcher's mind worked. He had no answers himself; he would wait. Several minutes passed before Mr. Dar cleared his throat.

"Based on the available data, I see only two possibilities. The first is that Admiral Nygaard pre-recorded that message and set up a remote transmission to send once her fleet reached Medina."

"Why would the Admiral do that?"

"Plausible deniability? There are most certainly political games happening in the compact right now that we are not privy to. Perhaps this is part of a larger plan by the Empress? Anyhow, we don't have enough data to come to any conclusions as to motive." Mr. Dar looked at Hinata with uncertainty.

"And the second?" Hinata prompted.

"Yes, the second option is that it is a deepfake."

Hinata waited for Mr. Dar to elaborate. When he didn't, Hinata asked, "And what is that?"

"I have never actually seen a deepfake algorithm." Mr. Dar admitted. "That is why I was hesitant to bring it up, but I have read about them in the annals of Earth That Was. It was an artificial intelligence that could create images, videos, even holo, that were indistinguishable from the real person. Apparently, it was a real problem in its time. That is why the technology was banned since before The Exodus. It is one of the many reasons that we have multiple autonomous AIs instead of one great, all-powerful AI. Because as individuals—like us—they can help keep each other in line."

"It is an interesting theory, Mr. Dar, but how would we prove it?"

"I don't know that we can. Like I said, we haven't used technology like that for generations, but I'll start analyzing the video, Commander, and see what I can find."

"In the meantime, this stays between us. We don't know the Admiral's true motivations or her involvement at Medina. No need to spread panic, but it would also be unwise to trust her at this point."

Mr. Dar nodded his agreement. "And Skyla?" he asked.

"Yes, you and the captain are the only ones I trust with this information. Without your help, we wouldn't have been able to get our ships in the air. We would have lost so many more. Unless there is a much deeper game you and the captain are playing, I think it is safe to assume our interests are aligned."

Mr. Dar exhaled a heavy breath and relaxed his shoulders. "I am glad to hear it, Commander. Right now, it is more important than ever to have allies we can trust. I think. I can head over to Skyla's ship now to fill her in on what we have found."

Hinata held up a hand. "No need, Mr. Dar. I had planned to give the captain a visit myself."

Mr. Dar looked unsure for a moment. Was Hinata that transparent; did this scientist see through his lie? Before Mr. Dar's briefing, he truly had no reason to see the captain, but that didn't mean he hadn't been searching for one. He chided himself, still acting like the silly fool who enjoyed the mystery of the outlaw woman he had fished out of the cosmos. And yet he couldn't help himself. He had started this dangerous game out of boredom, and now he was addicted.

"Very well, Commander. I have further analysis to run. I will inform you when I know more." With that, Mr. Dar stood, bowed his head to the commander, then took his leave. If Mr. Dar did see through him, he had the good sense to keep it to himself.

CHAPTER 25 | SKYLA

YELLOW CURRY

"How are you holding up, Pele?" Skyla asked.

"Dr. Pinot's upgrades are stable and couldn't have come at a better time, if you ask me," Pele said.

Skyla rolled her eyes.

"I am not talking about your integrations and you know it," she snapped, brandishing a large chef's knife at the bulkhead in front of her. She went back to chopping yellow onions.

"I am talking about all of these strangers on board. I can't even imagine what it must feel like for you, to have people you don't know living inside your bulkheads." She shuddered. "It sounds awful."

"I think you are projecting your unease on me. I think the company is nice." Pele softly strobed the kitchen lights, displaying her pleasure.

"Nice?" She shook her head. "Nice is you and me and an azure sea."

"That is nice, too," Pele admitted.

Skyla pushed the diced onions into a stainless steel bowl and pulled out a handful of garlic cloves to chop next. She paused mid-slice as she heard a throat clear behind her. Just one of Pele's "nice" visitors intruding, no doubt. Hadn't she sent out a shipwide memo informing them all how to use the 3D food printers in their rooms? *Who really cooked these days?* Sharing her ship was enough. She wasn't going to share her kitchen, too; that just felt too intimate.

"Good evening, Captain."

Skyla's heart skipped a beat as she recognized that rich baritone voice immediately.

"Damn it, Pele," she hissed, just loud enough for the AI to hear. "You couldn't tell me he had boarded?"

Pele's voice came through Skyla's aural implant. "There was no need, Captain. According to my analysis, Commander Azai poses no threat to us."

Skyla shook her head. *That meddling AI.* Commander Azai took a step closer and her pulse quickened at his proximity. She turned to face him.

"Commander Azai, I hadn't realized you were on board."

Surprise flashed in his eyes. He wasn't as good at hiding his emotions as he thought he was.

"If you don't mind, Commander, I am a little busy right now," she said, turning back to the cutting board. "Perhaps we can find a time for a briefing in the morning?" She began to cut thin slices of the garlic. Commander Azai reached out his hand, placing it gently over hers as she clutched the knife.

"I am afraid this can't wait." He paused, his eyes caught on hers, "and you really should crush the garlic first."

"What?" Skyla looked at him, confused, her pulse racing at the feel of his hand on hers and the electricity that danced across her skin.

"It will help release the oils. Trust me." He slowly slipped the knife from her hand and began crushing the garlic with the flat of the blade.

Skyla folded her arms over her chest, not sure what to make of this soldier commandeering her kitchen. She watched as he took inventory of the ingredients she had lined up on the counter.

"So, what are we making?" he asked.

"We?" She cocked an eyebrow.

He shrugged. "I spent most of my early childhood in the kitchen with my mother. I am sure you could use another pair of hands."

"You are telling me the great Commander Azai cooks?" She threw her head back and laughed. "Somehow, I find that hard to believe."

"I am not sure about the great commander part." A shadow fell over his face.

Guilt ran through Skyla at the thoughtless comment; he had just lost his station and a third of his fleet.

Hinata put his mask back in place to hide the pain. "But yes, I can cook. Better than you, I would wager."

"And what do you wager?" Now she was interested.

"What do you want?" He smiled back at her.

"How about a favor?"

"A favor?"

"Yes, someone in my line of work could find a favor from a UTA commander to be quite valuable."

"I guess a favor from an outlaw could have its uses." He mused.

"No need to think on it too much, Commander. You won't win."

"I won't?" The corners of his lips turned up slightly. "We will see. Now, what am I cooking for you?" he asked, turning back to the ingredients in front of him.

"Yellow chickpea curry." She pulled a large jar filled with yellow powder from the cupboard. Commander Azai's eyes went wide as he took the jar from her.

"Where did you get this?" he asked.

"There are advantages to living on the edge of the law, the best spices, being one of them." She winked, then shook her head. *What was she doing?*

"I haven't had curry since the last time I was home."

"Yes, senators do tend to stock their kitchens well. They can afford to." She shrugged as she pulled out a container filled with chickpeas and placed them on the counter.

"I am surprised you have any idea how to use any of this, though. Senators also typically don't like to get their hands dirty."

Hinata smiled at her. "You are one to talk. Your mother is a senator too, if memory serves me right."

"I didn't learn any of this from my mother. It just so happens that I like to eat, and if you want to eat anything better than algae smoothies while touring outside the Known Galaxies, you have to learn to take care of yourself."

He let out a rumbling laugh. Had she really just made Commander Azai laugh? Again? Skyla knew she should have felt uneasy, but she didn't. She felt at home, like she did when it was just Pele and her.

"Well, that explains the sloppy technique." He gestured to the chopped garlic and onions with the tip of the knife.

"You try learning to cook using ancient Earth texts."

"Fair enough, Captain." He turned his attention to frying the onions. "Sometimes I forget that the ancient art of cooking was almost lost during The Wandering."

"There's not much to cook when the main ingredient is algae." Skyla relaxed against the table across from him as he added garlic, ginger, and a few more spices to the mixture. The little kitchen filled with the mouth-watering scent of frying aromatics. A comfortable silence settled over them as he finished adding the rest of the ingredients to the mixture. His posture was rigid, his movements precise; even now, when it was just the two of them in a little ship's kitchen, he was in total control. How exhausting that must be.

"There." He slid a lid over the pot and reduced the heat to low. "Now it just needs time."

"How long were you thinking?"

"You can't rush good food. It's ready when it's ready."

Skyla rolled her eyes.

He gestured to the table before sliding into one of the seats. She grabbed a bottle of whiskey and two small glasses from the cupboard before joining him.

"Join me for a drink while we wait, Commander?"

"I'm not your commander, just Hinata." He corrected her. She struggled to hide her surprise. In all those weeks on Medina, she had only the slightest glimpse that there might be another man hidden under the commander's polished exterior. This informal side he was sharing with her was new.

"Hinata, then." She poured him a glass.

He picked it up and swirled the contents. He looked as if he was still deciding whether to accept the drink. She poured her own glass, then raised it for a toast.

"To you and your crew. You fought well."

"We lost."

"You evacuated the majority of the station's civilian population—while severely outgunned, I might add, and you live to fight another day."

He seemed to accept that as he raised his glass to meet hers, then downed his drink. Skyla took a small sip from her glass.

"As much as I have enjoyed having my kitchen commandeered by the UTA, you didn't board my ship so you could cook me dinner."

"Says who?" His eyes shone with mischief.

She cocked an eyebrow, refilled his glass, and waited for him to answer.

"Fine—no, that is not why I came." He sat up a little straighter and ran his hands down the front of his uniform to smooth the wrinkles. He proceeded to fill Skyla in on what Rohaan had found.

"I told you we couldn't trust her," Skyla forced through clenched teeth.

"We still have more questions than answers." He finished another drink.

She filled his glass again.

"You have video evidence of her giving the order. You should detain Freyja and her crew and deliver her to the next allied outpost."

"Mr. Dar thinks it might be a deepfake."

"Of course he does."

"What does that mean?"

"Rohaan is brilliant, but he is also obsessed. The idea of alien tech sending a deepfake from beyond the Known Galaxy is like the Holy Grail for him."

"What if he is right?"

"The simplest explanation is that Freyja recorded that message, and the simplest explanation tends to be the correct one."

"Why don't we give the brilliant Mr. Dar a chance to prove his work?"

Skyla sighed. "Fine, I owe him that much, but I don't trust her, and you shouldn't either."

"Don't worry, Captain, I've never trusted the admiral. I don't trust cheaters." A nearly imperceptible slur accented his words. "I know why I don't trust her—but why don't you? I noticed your reaction to her earlier. That wasn't about Medina. You have a past with her."

She was silent for a moment. He had seen right through her the way that she saw through him. It was apparent Hinata must not drink often. His guard was down, but Skyla hadn't drank nearly as much as he had. She chose her words carefully.

"I am sure you have figured out by now that we are from the same tribe. We came up together in the Mírmir Academy. I learned early that she would do anything to win. She would do things that I wouldn't."

His gaze held hers—he looked as if he was searching for something more, but that was all she was willing to offer. He took another sip of his drink. When he placed the glass down on the table, his hand was so close to hers, they nearly touched. For a moment he extended his fingers as if to touch hers, then clenched the glass again. The silence crystallized between them until Hinata shattered it with a whisper.

"I learned the same thing in the admiral exams...she cheated in the battle simulation."

Skyla's eyes widened in surprise. "She cheated to beat you? They let her get away with that?"

"She didn't win. I outmaneuvered her."

"But she is an admiral?"

"And I am not. I don't know why. I was exiled to consider my failure," his voice faltered. "To ensure I would not fail my tribe again. It's been three years...I still don't know how she did it."

Before she realized what she was doing, Skyla reached out her hand and laced her fingers between his. He looked up, astonished, but didn't pull away.

"You're right, there is more to this. We will figure it out."

Hinata ran his thumb along the palm of her hand and nodded. "Food smells ready, shall we see who won the bet?" He surprised her with a genuine smile, one that reached his amber eyes and made them glow in a way she had never seen before. She was even more surprised by the warmth that filled her in response.

"Get ready to lose, Commander."

CHAPTER 26 | FREYJA

LINKED

Freyja received a summons to once again join the commander aboard Pele to discuss the next move for their makeshift fleet of refugees. She was still a mess of emotions, none of them fitting together right, and underneath it all was the ever-constant inferno that burned at her core—except now it burned with the righteous fire of vengeance for her fallen friends. She was dead and the freedom to live her life as she saw fit was an option for the first time ever—if she chose it. Was that what she wanted? Long ago she had stopped thinking about what she wanted, as it made no difference when her entire life was dedicated to the Empress' plans. Now, though, she could choose for herself. She could choose to lean into that fury and let the fire consume her. She was angry; angry that she had lost her fleet, angry that her Berserkers had been slaughtered on her own bridge, angry for all the lost souls of Medina. She had enough fuel to last her a lifetime, and now she had the freedom to let the rage take over.

She exhaled before entering Pele's cargo bay, hoping to expel all of the thoughts rattling around in her head. Truth be told, she was relieved that Commander Azai wasn't going to leave them sitting idle in the nebula. At this point, any action had to be better than running circles in her mind. When she boarded, she saw that she was the last to arrive—no surprise there. She had purposefully positioned her ship at the edge of the fleet. She wasn't sure how long this shaky alliance was going to last.

Hinata stepped forward to address the group.

"Thank you, everyone, for coming together. As the leaders of the only armed ships in this fleet, it is our responsibility to ensure the safety of the refugees until we can relocate them to a suitable planet. This is our top priority. It appears that the UTA has no more answers than we do. We can't afford to sit idle any longer. This was not a planned evacuation. We have limited supplies. We need to come up with a plan to deliver these people to a safe location. I open the floor for discussion."

Lieutenant Stick-Up-His-Ass spoke first. He was a lieutenant commander under Hinata, third in the chain of command. Freyja didn't like the man, and she wasn't convinced Hinata should, either.

"I have taken inventory of all of our supplies. Even with rationing, we only have a week's worth of food and fuel. That leaves only a few planets as viable options for relocation." He flicked his fingers, pulling up a star chart with three planets outlined in green.

Freyja frowned at the image. All of the planets on the map were backwater outer-rim worlds, and none of them had Taaralog tribal settlements. None of these planets were a real option for the refugees. She glanced around the room. Skyla's face was just as dark as her own. No one looked optimistic. No one wanted to say it, but they were all thinking the same thing. Skyla spoke up first.

"None of those planets are suitable for relocating the refugees. They would hardly be any safer than if we had just left them on Medina."

Hinata nodded in agreement.

Skyla's scientist friend spoke up next, "I have already run an analysis of the local planets. There is not a better alternative within our current constraints. Our best option is to refuel and head for Gefion."

"That is more than three times the distance that our fleet can travel with our current supplies," the lieutenant spoke again.

"Yes, as I mentioned, we will have to resupply. These three planets are the only planets in range, with large enough settlements for us to procure supplies. The question is which of these planets will be willing to resupply our ships?" the scientist said.

"It's not a matter of being willing," Hinata cut in. "The question is, how are we going to pay to supply a whole fleet? The motive behind the assault on my station and who is responsible is still being debated by the UTA. We are on our own for the time being." Hinata's voice was deep and calm. He had cut right to the heart of it—they had nothing of value other than the four AI ships, which was unusual, even in large Naval fleets.

"Perhaps we just take what we need, then. We have four sentient ships, two of which have full armaments. Some backwater gangsters don't stand a chance," Freyja spoke up.

"You *would* just jump to taking what you want," Skyla snapped at her.

"I am simply playing the hand we have been dealt." Freyja's tone was cold as ice, though her blood boiled. "Do you have any better ideas?"

The room fell silent. The scientist continued to stare intently at his datapad. Hinata's officers glanced between Freyja and Skyla. Hinata crossed his arms over his chest.

"I do, actually." Skyla's face lit up. Of course, *she* would be the one to challenge her. Skyla took a step into the center of the room, a holo of a different star chart suspended in front of her.

"This is the next job I was planning." She zoomed in on one of the planets. "It's not far from here, just a three-day flight."

"It's in the wrong direction. The fleet won't make it to a resupply station if we take them into uncharted space first," Lieutenant Pain-In-The-Ass said.

"We won't be taking the full fleet. My scans indicate that there is a large debris field around the planet. Only an AI ship has the speed and calculation capacity to pass through safely. Besides, we can move faster if we just take the sentient ships. We send the fleet ahead to the resupply location and if we burn hard, we should be able to pull off a salvage job and be back in time to pay for the resupply."

"What makes you think that there is something valuable enough there to pay to stock an entire fleet?" Hinata asked, although Freyja knew from the glint in his eye that Skyla already had him on board.

"I do my research well, Commander. That debris field isn't natural—it indicates that there was once a megastructure around that planet. If they had a megastructure large enough to encase an entire world, I am sure we can find something of value."

"And you would do this out of the goodness of your heart?"

"Of course not, Commander. Have you already forgotten our arrangement? You get first pick of my salvage jobs; isn't that what we agreed to?"

A smile flashed across Hinata's face.

"Of course. And you will take that on credit?"

"For a commander of the United Tribal Axis? Of course. I know you'll pay."

"And what if there isn't anything of value?" Freyja countered. "Just because there is a megastructure doesn't mean that there is anything worth salvaging on the surface."

"If that is the case, then we can always fall back on your plan to take the supplies by force," Skyla said.

"Mr. Dar, do you have anything to add?" Hinata asked.

The scientist looked up from his datapad. "It is a sound plan. Based on the available data, I believe this planet is our best option for a resupply stop on our way to Gefion." Dr. Dar sent the coordinates to the rest of them.

"Very well. All AI ships will deploy for the salvage mission. Lieutenant Commander Sato, you will be in charge of getting the fleet to the resupply coordinates. We will meet you there in seven days' time."

Freyja cringed. She didn't want to sit idle in this nebula, but she sure as hell didn't want to go on a mission into uncharted space with Skyla, either.

"Commander, perhaps it would be better if I accompanied the fleet," Freyja said. "My ship is the most heavily armed. It makes the most sense, as the flagship, that I stay to oversee the safety of the civilian fleet."

"No, the remnants of my fleet will suffice. The salvage mission is critical to securing those supplies. All of the AI ships will be deployed to that end, understood?" His voice was low and dangerous, and though she outranked him in the Navy, she knew that didn't matter here.

"Understood," she growled back.

"It is settled, then. Make your preparations. We move out in two hours."

***

Freyja prowled the halls of their combined ships. That bioengineer of Hinata's had made upgrades to Pele that allowed for rapid remodeling of her coral-structured hull, and while she chafed under the forced proximity, she couldn't help but be impressed. She didn't blame the commander for ordering the ships to be linked. He still didn't trust her, that much was clear. She probably would have made the same call in his place. She did resent the fact that he had forced her to leave the rest of her Berserkers with the fleet, having only enough sway to convince him that she would not submit without Kylian and Tristan at her side.

The distrust radiating from the rest of the crew was palpable. She hated the way that conversations died when she walked into a room and the fact that Pele was tracking her every move, but she had chosen this. She would stay the course. She would ensure the mission succeeded, and then she would be free to uncover what was really going on.

Freyja was so engrossed in her thoughts that she was startled when she came around a corner to find Skyla's massive beast blocking the hallway. Even sat on its haunches, it was intimidating. Its tail flicked back and forth lazily, like it didn't have a care in the world, but those glittering brown eyes told a different story. They were trained on her like laser beams, tracking her every move. Freyja stomped her front foot and flexed her shoulders as she yelled, "Ha!" She flexed again, "Come on, get out of here!"

The creature didn't so much as flinch at her attempts to scare it off. Instead, it cocked its head to the side and drew its lips back, exposing long sharp teeth, as its pointed ears flattened against its skull.

A shiver ran through Freyja, goosebumps pimpling along her flesh. Perhaps someone more naïve would have thought the display looked like an awkward smile, but Freyja saw it for what it was—a challenge and one she had no intention of taking.

She groaned and raised her hands placatingly as she slowly backed away from the creature. He tracked her with those oddly intelligent eyes. His posture only relaxed as she slipped back around the corner.

Freyja's heart still drummed in her ears as she stumbled across the scientist from the briefing, kneeling on a small rug that faced a star-studded alcove. She paused, watching the man as he intoned what sounded like a prayer in a language she didn't understand. He hinged forward, bringing his brow to the rug in front of him. Freyja crossed her arms over her chest, leaning against the far bulkhead, as she watched the scientist flow through his prayers with practiced movements.

Only a few minutes passed before the scientist finished. He rolled up the rug and turned to leave the alcove, nearly jumping out of his skin when he saw Freyja watching him.

"I didn't mean to scare you," Freyja said, pushing off the bulkhead with her back foot.

"I didn't hear you there," the scientist said.

"What were you doing? That litany...it sounded beautiful."

"I was praying."

"I have never seen a Taaralog prayer practice," Freyja admitted.

"Well, then you haven't spent any time on Medina." The scientist chuckled for the briefest of moments before a dark cloud washed over his face. Medina was gone. His people had been cast back into the stars.

"You are right." Freyja ventured carefully into the alcove. She ran her hand over the star-studded viewport. "Why here, though?"

"Our prayers must be made in the direction of Qibla." The man gestured out the viewport. "If you believe the legends, it is in the direction of the Grand Mosque on Earth That Was."

Freyja's brow furrowed. "How do you keep your orientation? We are constantly moving in a three-dimensional space."

The man nodded in understanding. He withdrew what looked like an overly ornate compass on a long gold chain from under his tunic. "We carry one of these. It is said to orient to the Great Mosque, no matter where we are in the Known Galaxies."

Freyja snorted, "Sounds a bit like a fairy tale, doesn't it?"

The scientist tucked the compass back into his tunic and placed his hand across his breast in a practiced movement of comfort.

"Perhaps what you call a fairy tale, I call faith. Are fairy tales all that different from faith? They both attempt to explain the unexplainable." He paused in front of her with his rolled-up prayer rug tucked under his arm. "Some of us have reasons we believe. What do you believe?"

She shook her head. "I don't know."

He nodded once, then slipped past her, leaving her to the view of the vast reaches of space and to consider his words in silence.

CHAPTER 27 | HINATA

A MOTLEY CREW

Pele had insisted that all crew members meet in the kitchen, but Hinata had been wary of the invitation. Skyla had made it *very* clear during her debrief that the kitchen would be off-limits. She had even sent out detailed instructions and menu selections for the 3D food printers in their private quarters.

Hinata had been training in the cargo bay when Pele had invited him to dinner. He never deviated from his routine. Sticking to his training schedule was one of the things that kept his mind quiet, that let him feel in control. He was relieved when he had found a training facility already set up; it appeared that the captain liked to stay sharp as well.

He followed the trail of soft, swirling lights that pulsed along the wall that led him to the kitchen. The door was already open and the sound of voices tumbled out, which was a good sign. He paused just outside the doorway, listening to the soft murmur of voices, far friendlier than he had anticipated, and then there was the sound of music. Hinata stepped into the kitchen and froze, surprised to find that the gentle strumming of a guitar was not coming from Pele's comm system, but one of Freyja's men.

The lights were dim—Pele had lit her walls with a gentle glow—and in the shadows of the back corner, Tristan sat strumming a guitar. Just in front of him, Freyja sipped on a glass of clear liquor. Her other lieutenant commander, Kylian, sat at the kitchen table, playing cards with Wout, Dr. Pinot and, to Hinata's surprise, Skyla. The lot of them burst into laughter at something Wout had said—telling one of his early pioneer stories, no doubt. Mr. Dar sat in the corner just behind Skyla, fully immersed in a book, with that creature of Skyla's curled up at his feet. A shiver ran down Hinata's spine. A predator recognized another predator.

Just when he thought the scene before him couldn't get any more bizarre, Tristan opened his mouth, and the most beautiful singing voice he had ever heard came out. Hinata lingered in the doorway, listening. Seeing this varied group in a revelry was hard enough to believe, but hearing anything aside from expletives or externally inappropriate comments come out of Tristan's mouth was enough to make him question his sanity.

Skyla finally looked up from her cards, her ice-blue eyes drilling into his as her lips quirked up into a grin.

"Join us, won't you, Commander?" she called out, raising her glass of whiskey.

Hinata took a few steps into the kitchen, then paused, not sure where he belonged in all of this.

"Sit down and I'll deal you in." Wout gestured to the seat next to him.

He wasn't much for cards. "Perhaps I can help in the kitchen?" he ventured instead.

"There is nothing for you to help with this time." Skyla's brilliant smile sent electricity racing across his skin. "Pele already bullied me into cooking. We are just killing time until everything is ready. Join us for a round. That is...unless you are scared of losing?"

This woman: he didn't know what it was about her. She made him feel like he could take a break from his very carefully crafted regime—the chaos of it all scared him—but he wouldn't deny her. Not tonight. Not with the sting of defeat still a fresh wound. He could use the distraction.

"Very well." He slid into the seat next to Wout, his eyes drifting to Skyla's. "And why isn't Mr. Dar participating?"

"I am participating." Mr. Dar didn't even look up from his book as he turned the page.

"I would hardly call reading in the corner participating."

"I could be reading in my quarters. Pele made me come." Mr. Dar flicked his hand at the room, encouraging them to move on to another topic of conversation.

"Tristan, I didn't know that mouth of yours was capable of anything so lovely." Wout took a swig of his thermos, full of a dark home-brewed stout, no doubt. "What tune is that?"

Kylian broke into a fit of laughter, as Tristan continued to sing in time with the rhythm of his guitar.

"Hard to believe, isn't it? It's an Earth That Was tune that our mothers used to sing to us when we were little," Kylian answered.

"I don't know which is harder to believe, that Tristan is capable of singing something so beautiful, or the idea that this song survived The Wandering for your mother to teach it to you."

"Believe what you want. I believe my mother." Kylian, who was already wobbling a bit in his seat, took a long drink from his glass.

"Is that right, mama's boy?" Tristan finally chimed in, as he continued to play the guitar. "I'll be sure to let her know what a good lad you are when I see her tonight."

Kylian turned bright red as he reached out to slap his cousin on the head. "That's your aunt, you idiot! Don't be saying shit about my mama," Kylian muttered as he returned his focus to his drink.

"Earth That Was...do you think it was a real place?" Dr. Pinot asked, shifting the conversation to a safer topic.

"Of course it was a real place," Wout said. "Every tribe has a destruction myth; that has to mean something." He dealt the cards with deft hands.

"A destruction myth?" Hinata asked.

"Yes, Commander." Wout tried to pass him a drink, but Hinata held up his hand to decline. With this many different tribes in one room—all these different allegiances—he wanted his wits about him. Wout shrugged as if to say, *suit yourself.* "Every tribe has its own myth about how Earth That Was was destroyed."

"You must be mistaken, there is only one history—"

"Actually, each tribe does indeed have its own history." Mr. Dar interjected again, all the without looking up from his book. "History is written by the victors. It is subjective, and has changed many times."

Hinata shook his head, "How can that be?" His tribe taught only one history and he had assumed that all of the tribes did the same, that all of the UTA had a shared universal past.

"During The Wandering, there was nothing more important than total dedication to one's tribe. Humanity almost died out. There were factions and fighting and we came to the understanding that there had to be total dedication to the tribe—total dedication to humanity—if we wanted to survive." Mr. Dar explained.

Tristan stopped playing. The absence of music thickened the air as Mr. Dar went on. "Each tribe crafted their own narrative, their own religions, ideology, and yes, each has its own 'destruction of Earth That Was' myth. They crafted the stories that would unite their tribes, that would bring them together and give humanity the best chance at survival." Mr. Dar said the words with such levity, like the man couldn't feel how heavy this declaration sat in the air. Wout was the first to break the tension.

"As it has always been, I suppose. How about a round and we each share our destruction myth, then?" he said dramatically, like he was calling children to storytime.

"In our stories, God came to Earth to judge humankind." Wout started. "God was angry with humankind's creation of AI, and so he bathed the Earth in a cleansing fire, sending mankind out into the stars, and leaving the destroyed Earth as a home only our abomination could inhabit, but he also made a promise that if humankind was faithful, if they endured The Wandering, they would be delivered to a galaxy prepared by God himself, teeming with life, resources, and countless solar systems for humankind to inherit." Wout dramatically swept his arms wide, "and here we are, delivered out of The Wandering into the Amalthea galaxy." Wout chuckled, taking another drink of his beer.

"Ours is much the same, except God couldn't give two shits about AI." Tristan sat his guitar down, leaning forward to speak to the group. "God didn't punish us for creating AIs. He punished us because we destroyed the gift he gave us—our home, Earth That Was. We had to prove ourselves before God would give us another home."

"I didn't know Tribeless believed in God," Wout said.

"We are a line of mercenaries, not heathens, and we aren't Tribeless." Tristan smacked his chest, then Kylian's. "We are Stjarna Tribe, old man."

Hinata watched Wout's reaction carefully. The man was used to dealing with young, hothead mechanics, so his tone stayed even and light. "No offense intended, but that is not Stjarna's destruction myth." He tipped his head to Skyla. She sighed and placed her hand of cards down.

"No, it's not. In our myth, it was the coming of Ragnarök, the end of the world. The world has been created and destroyed many times, but this time, we tried to beat the gods. We created AI to try and stop the cycle, but even our great AI could not save the Earth from destruction. Our great creation stayed behind to try and rebuild, but humanity knew the truth: that our Earth was beyond repair, and that we would have to voyage, like our ancestors did, to find a new home where the cycle of life and destruction could continue. A place where we could thrive until Ragnarök comes again."

"The great AI is a savior in your story?" Hinata asked.

"If you believe the children's stories. Perhaps by now, the great AI has even repaired Earth That Was." Skyla smiled at him, sending a distracting flutter through his stomach.

"In our histories, AI destroyed Earth That Was. We created something too powerful, something that was too far beyond our control, and it almost wiped out humanity." Hinata's words hung heavy.

"I think the food is ready, Captain." Pele's soft voice rang through the silence.

CHAPTER 28 | HINATA

CRASH LANDING

Hinata fidgeted with the control panel in Tentei's cockpit. He needed an outlet for his nervous energy, but his ship was too small for him to work his body into a sweat like he normally would. He trusted Tax and Callan completely; he knew that they would take care of the refugees, but they were his responsibility and he didn't like leaving them to go off the map in search of Old World tech. The captain, meanwhile, had been all too excited about the prospect when she reviewed the trip analysis that she had been working on. He couldn't share her enthusiasm. He also couldn't think of a better plan. Right now, the Known Galaxies were more dangerous than ever. There were no friendly planets within range of their fleet, and they didn't know who to trust. It was best to keep their heads down until they delivered the refugees to Gefion. Once they did, he could reach out to his tribe and get some answers and then, it would only be his life on the line.

A soft ping indicated that they were coming up on the alien planet. He clenched his jaw; Tentei still wasn't speaking to him.

"You know this mission would be a lot easier if you would just talk to me," he said.

In response, Tentei displayed an up-close view of their destination and said nothing. Hinata's eyes went wide at the sight. The entire planet looked like it was surrounded by metallic plates of varying sizes. Small chunks swirled around larger ones; some even still looked vaguely like structures. Small rings of metallic dust stretched out around the planet while swirls of purple vapor tangled with larger chunks of debris. It was hard to imagine that ancient humans could have made this. It wasn't just the magnitude of what the structure must have been when it was intact—everything about it looked *alien*.

"All personnel are to report to my command deck," Pele's near-human voice came through the comms.

"You could have alerted me that we were making our approach a little earlier," he grumbled to his insubordinate AI.

Hinata arrived on Pele's command deck to find Skyla, Mr. Dar, Freyja, and her men already waiting for him, a display of the alien planet churning in the background.

"Captain, it's your show. How are we getting through that debris field?" he asked.

"I think it best that we decouple the ships to maximize maneuverability." Skyla flicked her fingers in the air. "I've sent a transmission to each of your ships. It has an algorithm that Pele and I have used to pass through planetary defenses in the past. Paired with the AI's quantum processors, it should be enough to get us safely through the debris."

"You've done this before?" he asked.

"Not this, exactly. Plenty of the planets we have visited have defense mechanisms, though, just none as grand as this."

"What are the odds that our AI systems will not be able to navigate through the debris?"

"Commander, based on my assessment, I am eighty percent confident in my ability to safely navigate through the debris," Pele answered.

Great, now he was making life and death decisions—a decision that affected the entire population of Medina—based on a conversation with an AI ship, and not even his *own* AI ship.

"That is not as high as I would like, Pele," he responded.

"I have an idea," Mr. Dar said. "Pele is the most agile of all of the ships in our flight. If her odds are eighty percent, the rest will sit much lower."

"That isn't an idea, Mr. Dar."

"I'm getting to the idea. I believe we should take only Pele. If we link up all of the AI's processing power and leave the rest of the flight in orbit, we should be able to increase our odds of arriving safely on the ground."

"Mr. Dar is right. With the processing power of all of the AI ships, our odds of success increase to ninety-two percent."

"So there is still an eight percent chance that we will die a fiery death," Freyja said, her tone bored.

"These are acceptable odds," Pele responded.

Hinata remained silent, weighing his options. Pele was right, of course; those were acceptable odds, given that he had a fleet in need of supplies and his only other option would be to go into a skirmish with a backwater crime syndicate to take what they needed—that had its risks. This was still the best option.

"We will move forward with the salvage operation," Hinata announced. "Prepare to decouple the ships. Mr. Dar, start the sync."

***

It took an hour to decouple and prepare the network that would allow Pele to use the quantum processors of the other AI ships. Hinata took a seat next to Skyla's captain's chair and Mr. Dar sat to the other side; Freyja and her men had taken up stations as far from the rest of them as possible while still remaining on the same bridge. That suited him just fine. He wasn't sure how much they could trust her. What was her end game? He hadn't had a chance to speak with Mr. Dar about the video analysis, but he was sure if the man had anything conclusive, Mr. Dar would have let him know. Until then, Freyja was still an unknown variable.

"The sync is done, Commander," Mr. Dar said.

"Everyone is in position," the captain said, her voice buzzing with electricity. Hinata let his eyes linger on her a second longer than he should have. The simmer of anticipation radiated off her skin. In all those weeks on Medina, he had never seen her like this. She was in her element. Of course, he hadn't seen it before. Out here, past the edge of known space, was where she belonged.

"Take us down on your mark, Captain," he said.

"Everyone strap in. I'm turning off artificial gravity for the descent. This could get a little wild," Skyla said, before initiating the full neural link with Pele. Gold threads ran up her arms and around to the base of her skull. With the sync complete, they slid forward into the debris cloud; it swirled and spun across the viewport, all dark metal and purple vapor. Hinata's breath caught as the shimmering particles washed over the screen, blocking everything else from view. Pele twisted left, then turned, quickly spinning.

He couldn't keep up with the massive chunks of detritus flying past like poorly aimed missiles, but so far, there was no shudder of impact. Pele and Skyla were a skilled team.

He watched Skyla as lines of concentration etched her face. Sweat began to bead across her brow. Her gaze locked forward, on the view screen perhaps—but he was certain she saw more with her ocular implants. Hinata suffered the sting of loss as he saw just how in sync she was with her AI. He barely remembered what it felt like with his ship, that intimacy of sharing a soul, before the accident changed everything. Even his classmates at the academy hadn't had this level of connection with their ships. His tribe carried on the tradition of AI ships in great houses, just as all wealthy tribes did, but they were looked at as tools—not partners. This level of trust and cooperation was something he had never witnessed before. It was astounding.

Skyla broke her concentration and stared at Mr. Dar. Something was wrong.

"I've lost the signal from the other ships," Mr. Dar said.

Skyla nodded, her attention locked back onto the debris field before them. They were on their own.

Their flight was still masterful, Skyla was a skilled pilot, but there was a difference. Detritus whizzed by too close and the hull shivered around them. Their reaction times were slower. The shift was subtle, but the cloud became ever more chaotic the deeper they flew. This wasn't going to work—they hadn't been able to analyze to this depth, and it was worse than they could have imagined.

"Captain, abort, pull out, and regroup with the rest of the ships." He noted the pained look on her face. Was she going to argue with him? Finally, she nodded and Pele began to ascend through the purple vapor.

Pele shuddered under them. Hinata's harness bit into his shoulders as the force of an impact sent them into a violent spin.

"Damn it," Skyla bit out, wrestling with Pele to regain control of their trajectory. They narrowly missed striking two larger pieces of debris.

"Aft thrusters have been damaged. Twenty percent loss in maneuverability." Pele announced.

Mr. Dar's fingers flew through the air across the panel in front of him. "There." He swiped his hands across it, sending the data to Skyla's station. "There is a largely intact piece of the structure at these coordinates. If you can get Pele inside, we should be safe while we assess the damage."

Skyla changed course. The piece of megastructure loomed before them in the swirling vapor. Mr. Dar wasn't kidding. The structure was so large it dominated the entire view. It had to be the size of a small space station. Several pings against the hull caught Hinata's attention—they were being pelted with rubble as they flew into the shadow of the megastructure.

"Hold together, baby," Skyla whispered as she drove Pele forward into a dark, looming crevice in the structure. They passed through an indigo haze and then the debris was gone—in front of them was nothing but a dark, empty cavern. The walls were metallic and smooth. How was that possible? Shouldn't they be pocked with little craters from repeated impacts? Skyla brought Pele to the back of the cavern and set her down.

"Well done, Mr. Dar, Captain. We should be safe here for a time while we regroup. Captain, damage report?" Hinata said.

"Hull integrity is at seventy percent, aft thrusters are down, and there is a breach in the cargo bay," Pele responded for herself.

"Pele, how many of those algae cultures do you have ready in maintenance?"

"Ten bio-balls are ready for use. That should be enough to make our repairs. With Dr. Pinot's new formula, the estimated repair time is three hours."

Hinata let out a long, slow breath. Things weren't so bad—the ship would be repaired, and they would be on their way out of the debris field in a matter of hours. However, the mission had failed. It was obvious that even Pele couldn't maneuver through the violent cloud to safely land on the planet. They didn't have time to pick another target. They were on a tight timeline and he had instructed Tax to take those supplies by force if they didn't meet the rendezvous on time. It looked like they were headed for a fight and the refugees would be much safer when the AI ships re-joined the fleet.

"Very well," Hinata said. "That gives us time to strategize our exit and come up with a plan on how we will take those supplies once we rejoin our fleet."

"Giving up so easy, Commander?" Skyla said.

"We tried your plan, Captain. It was a good plan. None of us anticipated the debris field would be so dense and erratic that even the combined AI processing speed wouldn't be enough to safely navigate the cloud. Time to move on to plan B."

"Come now, Commander, where is your sense of adventure?" Skyla's eyes twinkled as she focused on the screen in front of them.

He followed her gaze. The screen filled with nothing but the vast, empty cavern, all darkness and smooth metallic surfaces.

"What are you suggesting, Captain?"

"Just because we didn't make it planetside doesn't mean the mission is a failure. This is a large piece of the megastructure that once encased an entire world. What if we don't have to make it to the surface to find something worth salvaging?"

"You want to explore *this*?" He gestured to the screen.

"Of course, I want to explore this! When have you ever had the chance to explore an ancient megastructure?"

"Yeah, Commander, where's your sense of adventure? I'd like to explore somewhere I've never been." Tristan winked.

Hinata ground his teeth, fighting to keep his composure.

"Oh, my god. Shut up Tristan, now is not the time." Kylian grabbed his cousin by the shoulder, pulling him back to the corner of the bridge where Freyja stood observing them.

Hinata returned his attention to the captain, studying her for a moment. Her eyes were bright, her skin glowing; she looked like she was practically vibrating. He had never seen the captain look so alive. This is what she lived for. Could he really order her to stay in the safety of the ship?

"Pele, threat assessment," Hinata said. Was he being a coward, deferring to the AI, or just logical? If her AI said it was too dangerous, Skyla would listen—wouldn't she?

"The megastructure appears to be large enough to hold a stable orbit around the planet, Commander. There are no fragments within sensor range that are large enough to damage it. Statistically, the crew will be just as safe in the cavern as they are inside my hull. However, my scans are unable to penetrate the shielding. I am unable to assess what threats may lie within the walls." Pele responded.

Damn, Hinata cursed to himself. His plan to leverage Pele into keeping the captain safely on board had backfired.

"See, Commander, it is perfectly safe." Skyla kicked her boots down off the console in front of her and made to exit the bridge.

"I did not say that it is perfectly safe, Skyla," Pele responded.

"Statistically as safe as inside your hull. Same thing."

"Not the same. I also pointed out that I have no data that speaks to your safety once you enter the megastructure."

"Noted," Skyla responded as the bridge doors snapped open in front of her.

"Well, Commander, are you coming?" The beginnings of a smile turned up the edges of her mouth. He shook his head. How could he say no to her?

"All right, we can explore the megastructure. Volunteers only. I am not commanding any of you to exit the ship if you are not so inclined."

Mr. Dar sprang to his feet. "I would be happy to join you both. I am sure there will be valuable data to analyze from this exploratory mission."

Freyja came to her feet slowly and shrugged. "Better than sitting in the dark doing nothing." She waved at Kylian and Tristan to join her. The two men exchanged a look that suggested they would have preferred to stay onboard.

"I didn't mean I wanted to explore this forsaken piece of space slag," Tristan grumbled as he moved to stand at Freyja's side. "I can think of a lot better things to do in the dark."

Kylian laughed and threw an arm around his cousin, his voice dropping low, "Ya, cuz you and me, both, but it can't be worse than the ring mission, ya? At least here, no one is going to try and kill us." His standard was heavily accented, and Hinata couldn't help but feel like he had overheard something not meant for him.

Tristan shook his head in response, side-eyeing Kylian before throwing his own arm around the man and walking off the bridge together.

That settled it then. They would explore the megastructure and perhaps come away with something valuable enough to pay for the resupply.

CHAPTER 29 | SKYLA

WETWARE

A warm, familiar tingling flowed through Skyla's muscles while her stomach tied itself into a jumbled knot of nerves. She always felt this way when she landed on a new world to explore. Had it really been three months since her last expedition? Spending months laid up at Medina while she healed had nearly crushed her soul, but now she was back out amongst the stars with Pele, and everything was as it should be.

Guilt hit her hard at that thought. She was back where she belonged, but the people who had helped her were now nomads once again, and those were the lucky ones...the ones who had escaped with their lives. She shook her head. She needed to focus, for them. These ruins held the key to getting them safely to their new home. She needed to focus on that.

"Can you believe this, Pele? Our first mission back and we are in a megastructure." Skyla tucked a med kit into her backpack. Fenrir rubbed up against her legs, nearly toppling her over. She gave him a scratch under the jaw before returning her attention to her gear.

"I would have preferred the beach," Pele responded.

"I will pick a planet with a beach for our next adventure. Promise." Skyla patted Pele's hull affectionately. Pele remained silent. "What is it, Pele?"

"You know I don't like you going out when I am under repairs. We won't be able to make a fast getaway if you get into trouble."

"We are in an ancient abandoned chunk of metal flying through space; what trouble could we possibly get into?"

"I don't put it past you to find trouble anywhere we go."

"Pele, this isn't any different than exploring an abandoned city surfaceside. In fact, it is safer. There won't be any local wildlife up here to cause trouble."

Pele flickered her lights in response, still not satisfied.

"What?"

"I don't like that my sensors cannot scan beyond the walls. You are going in blind, and there is nothing I can do to help."

"Have I let you down yet?"

"Our last mission left us disabled and stranded in space at the mercy of an alien virus, so..."

Skyla waved her hand at the bulkhead. "and it all worked out. Ears got our signal, and you came out of the station in the best shape of your life, and Commander Azai..." Heat pricked her cheeks. Why had she brought up the commander?

"Yes? What were you going to say about the commander?" Pele said with a mocking sweetness.

"Nothing. I promise I will be fine, that's all. And I'll record the whole trip and upload the files as soon as I am back so that you can see what the rest of this place looks like. How about that?"

"I guess if you insist on leaving me in this dark cavern alone, that's better than nothing."

As Skyla moved to exit the cabin, Fenrir took his familiar place by her side. She smiled down at him, giving him a placative scratch behind the ears.

"I wish you could come, pal, I really do, but I don't have a suit for you."

He cocked his head at her, then bumped his snout into her hand. Skyla gave him one last pat before stepping into the hallway, but Fenrir followed.

Skyla sighed. "I would take you with me if I could, but we don't know if there is atmosphere behind those walls." She shook her head. Was she really trying to reason with the creature? She swiped at the controls to her room, then pointed for Fenrir to stay in her cabin. He looked from her outstretched finger to the quarters, then back at her. He let out a low whine as he realized what she was asking him to do.

"Come on, pal, work with me here. When this is all over, I'll take you to a nice world that you can explore, too, ok?"

Fenrir's tail hung limp as he reluctantly complied.

"I'll make it up to both of you, I promise," Skyla said, patting Pele's hull.

When Skyla arrived in the cargo bay, the rest of their small crew was ready and waiting. They had opted for lightweight suits over fully armored ones. The suits would be sealed and pressurized to protect them from the environment, but with no real threat, the improved mobility was worth the risk.

Ears looked as if he would start bouncing on his heels at any moment. Skyla hoped he wasn't too disappointed when they found that everything looked like it was built for humans, just like all of the other planets she had visited.

"Excited, Ears?" she teased, walking up to check the fit of his suit.

"I have a feeling about this one. This is the one. I will finally have the proof I need to legitimize my research." A broad smile split his face.

"Well, I hope you are right." She clasped his shoulder. "All set. Grab your pack."

Skyla walked over to Hinata next, her back to Freyja, trying to ignore that she was there. Her eyes locked onto his. A rush of heat flowed through her and pool in her belly. Her heart stuttered and she knew she should look away, but she couldn't. Finally, she broke eye contact to check his suit. She was certain it would be set up to the very letter of the UTA standard, but it was protocol—every suit needed to be checked before disembarking. She traced the edges and seals and electricity sparked up her fingertips that had nothing to do with the tech. *Not the time, stay focused, megastructure,* she scolded herself.

"Good to go, Commander," she said, risking one last glance at those intoxicating eyes before she turned to check the final member of their little crew. She wasn't looking forward to dealing with Freyja, but she had little choice. Skyla had dealt with her all through the academy; she could deal with her for a few more days. The thrill Skyla had felt when she was near Hinata was gone, her excitement from the moment before extinguished.

"Our suits are good to go," Freyja cut in, just as Skyla was about to start her check. "We did our checks already." Freyja motioned to the two men standing behind her. A twisted smile crossed her face.

Freyja had noticed just how uncomfortable Skyla was, and yet she had stretched that moment out to the very last second, just to get under Skyla's skin.

"All suits are up to standard. Let's move out." Skyla tried to hide the frustration in her voice. The only thing worse than letting Freyja get under her skin was letting her know it.

"Captain," Hinata held up a hand to stop her. "I know it's been a while since you worked with a crew, but I believe there is one suit left that needs to be checked."

Skyla's cheeks heated as Hinata reached a gloved hand out to check the seals on her suit.

"Right you are, Commander," Tristan interrupted, stepping between them. He flashed his brilliant smile at her.

Skyla slapped his arm away as he reached out to check her seals. "Fuck off, Tristan."

"Whoa, Captain." He raised his hands in mock surrender. "How'd you know I like'em rough?"

Freyja edged in front of Tristan. "I've got this one. The *captain* and I were flight mates back in the academy, weren't we?" Freyja said in a mocking tone, as she slapped Skyla too hard on the shoulder. Skyla wanted to smack the grin off of Freyja's face, but it would be worse if she showed just how much letting Freyja near her made her skin crawl. Freyja quickly set to work checking Skyla's seals.

"All good," Freyja said, then made her way to the cargo bay doors, her lieutenants hot on her heels like dual shadows. Hinata took a step back, grabbing Skyla's arm before she could follow. She searched his eyes, still fuming from the interaction with Freyja. The fury sparking behind her eyes must have surprised him, because he let go. His gaze dropped to double-check the seals on her suit.

"All good," he said on a private line so that only Skyla could hear him. She was relieved that she wasn't the only one who had doubts about Freyja.

"All right crew, let's move out."

They stepped out into the cool, dark air of the cavern. The lights on the shoulders of their suits cut trails through the gloom. They spread out across the far end, looking for a door into the rest of the structure. The ground below her feet was smooth and even, as if it had been made of one continuous plate of metal. As she approached the far end, the wall illuminated and bits of glitter in the polished metal refracted the light while cut, geometric designs cast shadows. All of the patterns were too large and placed too high above the ground. It didn't look like any Old World ruins she had seen before.

Skyla traced the lines in front of her with the tip of her glove. There must be a mechanism in the wall that would open a hallway...

"Hey," she said over the comms, "check the wall in front of you. Look for anything that might be a latch or a hidden panel."

Time ticked on as they explored every meter of the wall. Nothing.

"We've checked the length of the wall. What now?" Rohaan asked.

She paced back, allowing her eyes to roam over the lines, looking for anything that would give her a clue as to how the ancient society that had built this place would have used this wall. Was it possible that this was just an alcove without an entrance? Years of experience told her that wasn't it. What use would they have for a dead-end alcove? No, they were missing something.

Once Skyla had paced back several feet, she let her eyes relax, taking in the wall. There were patterns to some of the lines that almost looked like the outline of a door—an enormous door. If that was the case, it was at least three times as tall as any door Skyla had seen on a station. If it was indeed a door, why would they make it so tall? She walked to the perimeter of what looked like one of these large doors and inspected the outline. There was nothing unusual within her line of sight, but if this was a really tall door, could the control panel be higher? She turned on the magnetic function of her boots and gloves. Placing her palm on the wall, she tested the grip of the magnets against the surface. Her palm held steady. Perfect. It would hold a magnetic charge and she could scale the wall to check for controls higher up.

Skyla scrunched her knee up to her chest and tapped the toe of her boot against the wall. With her boot now firmly anchored, she pushed up until she was able to place her opposite boot a step higher. She slid her magnetic gloves across the surface in front of her, steadying her climb. Alternating charges between her boots and hands, she made her way up the wall, pausing briefly at each step to examine the lines for any indication of a control mechanism.

"Captain," Hinata's voice came through the comms. "What are you doing?"

Freyja snorted and chimed in, "Looks like she's on holiday, as always. Can't you take anything seriously?"

"Take a step back and look at the wall in front of you," Skyla responded. She wasn't in the mood to explain herself.

Rohaan gasped.

She smiled. Of course, Rohaan was the first to see it. He had spent his whole life researching alien artifacts, and this had to be the most *alien* salvage site she had ever found.

"These lines, here." Rohaan gestured to the wall. "They are the outlines of doors."

Freyja squinted at the wall in front of her. "Aren't you supposed to be some sort of academic? Those are far too large to be doors."

"Who said they were for humans?" Rohaan replied before walking up to the outline in front of him. Carefully, he tested his own magnetic system. Rohaan had never done field research. A pang of worry froze Skyla halfway through her ascent. She paused to watch his attempt at scaling the wall.

He was slow and shaky, but his technique was good. She worried he would slip and hurt himself, but she couldn't take this away from him. Even from this distance, in the dark, she was certain there was a huge grin plastered on his face; he had waited his whole life for this moment. Skyla shook her head at that. Even if these doors were unusually large, there was still likely a perfectly reasonable explanation for their size. Once they got inside, she was certain it would look like an ancient human site, just like all of the other sites that she had visited. *Let him have this moment*, she thought. She turned back to the wall in front of her and pulled herself up another step. Her breath caught in her chest. She was about halfway up the length of the door and in front of her was a seam—an outline for a control panel!

She pulled a camp knife from her belt and slid the edge of the blade into the seam. She wiggled the knife back and forth until she heard a light pop and the seam opened wide enough for her to slip her gloved fingers inside. She pried the panel open, revealing the mechanical innards of the door latch. It didn't take long for her to trigger the release, which caused the huge panel to shift and slide back a couple of centimeters with a shuddering thunk, exposing the outline of a door. There was a mechanical whirring sound as the door disappeared into the wall, revealing a long, dark corridor. She scaled back down the wall to stand with the rest of the crew in front of the opening.

Skyla activated her wrist torch and shined the light into the corridor, but it was so vast that the darkness swallowed up the light. There was no way to know what was down there without venturing deeper. She relayed directions to the others on how to open their sections and before long, seven looming, dark corridors opened up before them, with no sign of where any of them might lead.

"Looks like we have seven corridors and six people," she said. "I think our best bet is to split up and each take one. If your corridor doesn't pan out, you can come back and explore the last one. Any questions?"

"You want us to split up?" Freyja sneered, failing to completely conceal the fear that tainted her voice.

"The admiral is right, there is no reason for us to split up," Kylian crossed his arms.

Of course he would back whatever Freyja said. Skyla had noticed how he followed her like a second shadow.

"I usually go on these expeditions alone. You'll be fine, and we can cover more ground this way."

"Captain, I hate to disagree—I know that you have the most experience in these situations, but that's precisely the point. The rest of us may not even know what we are looking at." Hinata cut in and then he switched off the group channel so only she could hear him. He angled his body away from Freyja, as if he were glancing back at Pele. "Besides, I don't trust the admiral on her own. I think it's best if we all stick together so we can keep an eye out."

Skyla forced out an exasperated breath. They wouldn't have time to search the entire structure and make the rendezvous if they didn't split up. But Hinata was right; she didn't trust Freyja and none of them, beyond herself, had salvage experience, it made more sense to stick together.

"Very well," Skyla said on the group channel. "We will stick together, and pray we pick the door that leads to something worthwhile."

Freyja's shoulders relaxed, and even Rohaan looked relieved. Skyla had been out on her own too long. She never thought she would work with a crew again after what happened, but it appeared fate had other plans. She had forgotten what it was like to have a team depending on her. She would have to remember that, at least until they had safely delivered the refugees to Gefion.

"Given our…limits, we should pick one of these middle passageways. It's more likely to lead us to the main facilities." She gestured to the two dark hallways before them.

"Actually, your logic is flawed. We have no way of knowing how an alien civilization would organize their layout," Rohaan cut in.

Skyla took a deep breath before responding. *Remember how much this means to him. Remember the fact that he believes is one of the reasons you are friends.*

"And where do you believe this alien society would place their most valuable tech?"

"There's no way to know. We don't know anything about their society, their values or ancestral patterns of architecture—"

"Then what is your argument against exploring one of these corridors?" Skyla interrupted.

"No argument, I was simply pointing out that your logic was flawed. Any random choice is just as likely to produce a result in this case," Rohaan responded with a smile.

Skyla squeezed her eyes shut, exhaling her frustration. *He is your best friend. Remember that he is your best friend.*

"In that case, can we stop wasting time and just pick one?" Freyja stepped forward.

"Agreed." Hinata gestured to the door on the right. "With your permission, Captain."

"It's as good a choice as any." Skyla shrugged as she led their group into the massive black corridor.

"Lights," she commanded, and all of their suits came to life with torches across their helmets, chests, and wrists.

The hallway around them was enormous. All six of them could walk shoulder to shoulder without touching and it was so long that, even with their suits fully illuminated, the darkness devoured the path ahead. However, they could now clearly see the surfaces to either side. The walls and floor were dark gunmetal gray with shimmering flecks of black. The surfaces were smooth, with strange geometric patterns carved into them, just like the patterns around the doors. Skyla had visited dozens of planets for salvage and had never encountered anything like this.

A notification blinked in her HUD. She opened it to reveal the results of her suit scan of their environment. To her surprise, the scans indicated that the atmosphere was breathable. Without hesitation, Skyla retracted her helmet, and it folded back into her collar. Years of scouting planets meant she knew when to trust her scans and she wasn't shy about ditching her helmet.

"Captain, what are you doing?" Hinata's voice cut through the comms. Did she detect a tinge of worry in his voice?

"Scans came back clean, Commander," she answered, before sucking in an exaggerated lungful of air through her nose. The air was heavy and moisture began to bead on her exposed skin. Ears was the next to retract his helmet.

"It's humid," Ears said, shocked.

"It feels like a rainforest," Skyla agreed.

Hinata looked at Rohaan and then Skyla, letting the moment sit heavy before finally allowing his helmet to retract.

"It's incredible. What were they doing up here that would require this type of environment?" he asked, as he took in a deep breath of muggy air.

"Perhaps this is their natural environment, Commander," Rohaan said as he studied the markings on the wall.

Freyja snorted. "Yes, because aliens are *real*. If you are done wasting time, can we get a move on? This place gives me the creeps," Freyja spoke through her comms, her helmet still firmly in place. Without waiting for an answer, she continued moving down the hall, with Kylian and Tristan trailing just behind.

Hinata continued at Skyla's side. She glanced over her shoulder to see Rohaan falling behind as he took scans of the wall markings. A smile spread over her face. She had never seen Rohaan like this. Maybe she should have taken him out on an expedition with her a long time ago. As they walked, she began to recognize markings on the hallway that resembled the doors they had opened in the cavern. They appeared at regular intervals to either side, but there was no way to know what lay behind them. Which of these would be worth the time to open and explore? After several minutes of walking, they came to a dead end with a large arch framing sealed doors. Skyla made quick work of scaling the walls and opening them. The panel covering the controls fell with a thud at the base of the wall moments before Skyla touched down with her boots.

As the panels slid back into the walls, that familiar tingling rushed through her body—this was it—she knew it as soon as she saw the equipment lining the back of the room. This is where they would find something that would make this whole trip worth it.

While the rest of the crew began advancing into the gloom, Skyla glanced behind her. She wanted to see the look on Ears' face when he saw the lab, but he was still trailing well behind the group, a small blur of light a hundred meters down the hallway. Skyla's attention snapped forward as the sound of rustling vines broke the quiet. The sound was followed by movement just inside the doorway. She dashed forward before her brain fully registered the threat.

"Watch out!" she yelled, flinging the panel she had knocked off the controls in front of her. The panel sailed past Hinata's right side as he turned to assess the threat. Several heavy pings rang through the air as something hit the metal sheet with enough force to dent the thick plate.

Skyla slid on her knees behind the panel, grabbing her compact staff from her back, and extending it to full length. An electronic pulse field encapsulated each end in a purple glow. She stood in front of Hinata and began to spin her staff, creating a barrier between them and the unseen assailant. Skyla heard Hinata draw his katana behind her as she focused on the dim laboratory. A large, vined plant unfurled, exposing iridescent orange flowers with thick, dark, purple darts instead of stamen. The vine undulated as if looking for an opening through their defenses. A vine whipped out and grabbed Skyla by the boot. Just as quickly, the vine lashed back, slamming her to the ground. Her head smashed against the floor as her staff slipped from her grip.

As soon as she was down, the flower launched another set of darts at Hinata, but he was already leaping through the air, twisting to avoid them. He landed in a crouch beside her, slicing through the vine wrapped around her leg with a slash of his katana.

She kicked her leg free of the severed vine and came to a crouch beside him. The dark room had come to life with writhing vines dancing in the shadows.

"What the hell are those things?" Hinata growled through clenched teeth.

"If I were to guess, I'd say it's a wetware security system." She nudged Hinata with her elbow to follow her lead, nodding to a supply cart to their right, before tucking into a roll that put the cart between her and the nearest vines. She glanced at the opposite side of the room to find Freyja and her lieutenants engaging with their own set of vined assailants.

Freyja had picked up the discarded panel to use as a shield while Kylian and Tristan huddled in beside her, guarding each side with drawn swords as bits of greenery littered the space around them.

"A wetware security system?" Hinata asked. They were shoulder to shoulder behind the small supply cart.

"It's just a guess. I've never actually seen one, but Ears has read about them in some of the archives I have recovered. They are plants, or other biologicals, adapted for security purposes."

Hinata grunted as he sliced through a thick, knotted, rope of plant, reaching around the side of the cart.

"If it's anything like what I've read about, we need to avoid those darts. More likely than not, they're poisonous."

"No shit," Freyja yelled from across the room as she fended off a strike from the nearest plant. "Do you have anything helpful to add? Or are you ready to get off your ass and help us cut these things down?"

Skyla eyed her fallen weapon in the center of the room.

"Commander, cover me." She dashed forward, with Hinata only a split second behind, katana whirling at the incoming vines.

"Flower opening at four o'clock," Hinata shouted as he changed direction, heading straight for the opening bud. Skyla dove for her staff as another barrage of darts flew overhead, striking the back wall with a series of metallic pings. Those were some nasty darts—forget being poisoned or not—those things would shred flesh on impact. Skyla sent a command through her staff and the rounded ends shivered, then shifted into two double-sided blades. The weapon extended out from her grip, a shimmer of indigo electricity lining the edge.

With the newly formed blades, she swiped at the tangle of vines reaching for her legs. A vibrant orange flower unfurled an arm's length from Skyla's face. She swept out with one smooth motion, severing the flower from its stem. As soon as she swept through the stem, the mass of vines that had threatened to ensnare her retreated back into the dim laboratory.

"Sever the flowers, and the vines will retreat!" she shouted.

"How do you know?" Freyja grunted as she sliced through a thick vine.

"I don't, but I don't hear you handing out any better ideas!"

Skyla's vision narrowed to the mass of vines in front of her. Her ocular display highlighted the buds that would soon bloom into deadly flowers. She slashed her way through a thick mass of vegetation to get to the buds. Severing one after another, she stole a glance to her side. Hinata was tangled up in an undulating mass, but before she had a chance to redirect her blows, the vines fell away from him as a severed flower spun away from the mass. A wicked grin spread across her face. She was right. The air filled with the scent of fresh clippings as sweat poured down her neck. She slashed one final bud before taking a step back to survey the remaining plants. Her section was clear. She scanned the rest of the room to be sure there were no remaining threats; the lab was littered with petals, buds, and vines. Bits of foliage hung in the air, but none of it moved. The vicious vines had retreated into the darkness. She let out a long breath before retracting her blades back into the handle and tucking it away. She took one step before blinding pain blocked her vision. She nearly collapsed as fire tore through her leg. In an instant, Hinata had wrapped his arm around her waist, keeping her from hitting the ground.

"Captain?" His voice was laced with worry.

She glanced down at her lacerated leg. Her suit was shredded where the vine had grabbed her.

"I guess it's a good thing there is atmosphere here," she joked, taking a ginger step forward, leaning heavily on Hinata, her torn muscle unable to take the weight. He tightened his grip around her waist, helping her over to what looked like an oversized command panel.

"We are fine, too, thanks for asking," Freyja called out, her blade still in hand.

"What happened here?" Rohaan stuck his head carefully through the doorway. Thank the stars her friend had fallen behind—Rohaan might have brains, but he wasn't a fighter.

"Wetware security," she grunted as Hinata helped her settle in front of the console.

"An alien wetware system. That is fascinating. I would love to get a sample," Rohaan mumbled as he began his investigation of the laboratory.

"Yeah, a little less fascinating when you are the one fighting it," Freyja said, but Rohaan wasn't listening to them anymore. He reached up to plug a cable from his arm unit into the dead panel that Skyla was propped against.

"I am going to need a few minutes," Rohaan muttered.

"Let me take a look at that leg," Hinata said, kneeling on the floor before her to get a better look at the laceration.

Freyja paced the perimeter, her sword still drawn, her men mirroring her movements. *Damn, did those two ever do anything on their own?* They wouldn't be her problem for much longer—deliver the civilians and then she would be done with Freyja for good.

She turned back to Hinata as he tore away a section of her suit, carefully pulling bits of material from the macerated flesh. Lines creased Hinata's face as he inspected the damage. Even in the dim light, his skin glistened from sweat and the humidity.

He sprayed the torn flesh with a disinfectant numbing spray from the field med kit. Tension melted from her body as the muscles relaxed and the wound went numb. He wrapped the wound with skilled hands and stowed the med kit back into his pack.

"That should hold you over until we get back to Pele." He looked up from the dressing and his gaze caught on hers for just a moment.

"I'm in," Ears called out from under the console.

Hinata offered a hand to help Skyla to her feet, then pulled her arm across his shoulder to help her maneuver over to Rohaan's side.

"It's fascinating, really. There is far more data here than I would have imagined." His head tipped up, as if he were inspecting the underside of the console, although his eyes were unfocused, tracking outputs in his ocular display.

"How is that possible? All of the electrical components here are dead. We couldn't even open the doors without the manual release."

"See this here?" Ears pulled up a holo display from his wrist unit, the cable still plugged into the console.

"What are we looking at, Ears? That almost looks like DNA," Skyla said.

"Right, you are! Well, it's not exactly DNA. As far as I can tell, it is very similar, though—and look here." Ears manipulated the image to zoom in on a section. "It has been modified to store data!" He was practically vibrating with excitement. Despite the fatigue setting in from the battle with the security system, Skyla couldn't help but smile. He had found something!

"All right, Dr. Dar, don't get too excited. You can upload all of that data to be analyzed later. Right now we need to find something worth trading for supplies so we can get your people safely to Gefion." Skyla reminded him.

"*Dr.* Dar?" Hinata asked.

Skyla couldn't be sure in the dim light, but she swore that his face had turned red with the question.

"Yes, Rohaan has dual PhDs in astrophysics and computer science." She couldn't help but grin at Hinata's embarrassment. "Seriously, Commander, are you incapable of running a simple bioscan to identify who you are working with?"

Rohaan waved his hand to cut her off, then made a few hand movements to switch screens. "I believe you will have the most luck with these." Once again, he tapped his display, and the laboratory buzzed with the sound of opening compartments. Freyja and her lieutenants froze in place, weapons ready. Hinata drew his katana with his free hand, his other still tightly wound around Skyla's waist, while his eyes searched the shadows for another threat.

"Whoa, sorry about that. I was just opening the most promising storage lockers, based on the laboratory logs here." Ears pointed to a string of data in front of him. How he had any idea what he was looking at, Skyla didn't have a clue.

"Next time a heads up would be nice," Freyja muttered as she lowered her sword.

"Right, next time," Ears mumbled, his focus already back on the data.

"Help me over to that storage locker," Skyla motioned to Hinata. He nodded and wrapped his arm tighter around her waist as she hobbled over to a crescent-shaped counter that ran the length of the back of the laboratory. On it, several compartments had opened and strange pieces of technology were sliding into place.

"This is incredible." She reached up to gently run her fingertips over the surface of the nearest device. "This has to be one of the best technology caches I have ever seen." it was almost as good as the one she had found on her last expedition. *Almost.*

"Great, can you just tell us which pieces to grab so we can get off this death trap?" Freyja said, not bothering to keep the irritation from her voice.

"I won't be sure which pieces are the most valuable until we get them back for Pele to analyze," Skyla responded.

"It's fine, Captain. The lab isn't that big. We should have enough time to pack everything up and meet the rendezvous," Hinata said.

"Oh, while we are at it, can we please collect a sample of those vines?" Rohaan called out as another panel opened, revealing a small vined plant hiding in the wall.

"Are you crazy?" Freyja snapped.

"They are quite harmless now that they have been pruned. See their specs, here." Rohaan enlarged his holo. "They will take weeks to re-grow their flower buds. It is a most fascinating find."

Hinata exchanged looks with Skyla. She shrugged. Rohaan was a scientist; she couldn't very well blame him for being himself.

CHAPTER 30 | FREYJA

DELIRIUM

Freyja's eyes stung from the sweat that dripped down her brow. She paused to wipe away the beads of moisture before it blinded her.

She had finally taken down her helmet, and the humidity was stifling. She dropped her hands to her knees, taking in a few labored breaths before straightening up again and grabbing the handle for the suspensor lift she had loaded with pieces of hardware. With the lift, hauling tech back to Pele should have been easy, but her thigh ached, having taken a lashing from the wetware system, and her blood felt sluggish in her veins. The conditions of the station were getting to her; she was burning up from the inside. There was a reason she preferred space stations and ships to being planetside—Freyja was not a fan of extreme weather conditions.

She entered Pele's cargo bay.

"Finally, I was about to send a search party," Skyla snapped. If the comment had been for someone else, Freyja was certain it would have had a playful tone, but for her, Skyla had nothing but acid in her words.

"Who would you send? The boys are all in the lab finishing packing up the last of the hardware." Freyja shoved the suspensor forward.

Skyla stopped the lift with her foot, which was bound up in a support bracer, and she winced at the impact.

Freyja let a smile twist her lips, then shrugged as she turned to take an empty lift back to the laboratory. Black spots danced before her eyes and the cargo bay began to spin. The next instant she was on her back, staring up at the bulkhead. She felt as if she was about to retch and her skin was seared with flames. Her vision stuttered—in and out, in and out—then it all went black.

An angular face appeared from out of the darkness to hover over her. Olive skin, warm brown eyes; it was the scientist, wasn't it? She couldn't think straight with everything spinning and her skin catching fire.

"Look here," she heard Dr. Pinot say. "Her suit, it looks like it was ripped open by the darts from the security system. With a system like that, they were likely poisoned. Commander, I need you to get the admiral to medical."

"I'll get to work analyzing the vine clippings." That was Dr. Dar's voice.

The room began to spin as she felt herself being lifted from the floor. She tried to protest. "I'm fine, you idiots," she slurred. "Just stop spinning the damn ship."

Darkness pressed in on the edges of her vision once again as a deathly chill tangled around her.

"From the stars we came, to the stars we return," she mumbled to herself. This must be death. Back to the cold vast darkness of space. *It's peaceful here. If this is death, why do I still have a voice?* Freyja tried to turn to look around her, but her body protested. *And I still have a body? No, that doesn't seem right. Where are all the stars?*

"Freyja?" A voice came to her through the darkness, but she couldn't place it.

"Freyja, we have you stabilized while Pele is working on synthesizing an antidote for the poison." That overly analytical voice—it must have been Dr. Dar. Poison? *Those bastards poisoned me.* Freyja let out a wild cackle. No, she couldn't blame them—she was the dark hand of the Empress, after all. After everything she had done, didn't she deserve to die?

"We need answers from her now." This voice she knew; like the sweetest memory, like a thorn in the side.

"She is delirious. She should be in stasis until we have the antidote. What information do you think you are going to get out of her?"

"The truth." She heard Skyla slam her fist down.

Freyja willed her eyes to open just a crack. There were four figures surrounding her. It was painfully bright after the darkness of the void. *Focus.* Closest to her were Dr. Dar and Dr. Pinot, then Skyla, and standing a step back, observing them all, was Hinata, his arms folded over his chest, mouth pressed into a thin line. Where was Kylian? Tristan? *Son of a bitch,* they better not have poisoned them, too! Fingers snapped in front of her face.

"Hey, we can help you. Rohaan has already isolated an antidote from his samples, but before we help you, you need to tell us the truth," Skyla demanded.

"What are you going on about? Where is Kylian? Tristan? If you hurt them—"

"They are safe in their rooms. We didn't hurt them, or you. It's the toxin from the wetware system, do you remember?"

Freyja squeezed her eyes shut. Skyla's words were a swirl of confused noise, but she heard what she needed to: they were safe.

"Hey!" Skyla snapped again. Freyja grimaced, trying to block out the annoying buzzing that was Skyla. "You don't get to go to sleep until we are done. I know you ordered the attack on Medina Station," Skyla snarled in her ear. "What I don't know is *why*."

"I didn't order the attack," Freyja struggled to explain. "I lost half of my Berserkers, my most trusted officers—my friends—trying to defend that station—"

"Bullshit!" Skyla slammed her palm down next to Freyja's head.

"It's the truth."

"I saw you give the order. We have the transmission!" Skyla pulled up the holo. With her fuzzy mind, Freyja almost believed it *was* her giving the order to attack. It looked like her. It sounded like her. It moved like her. Yet she knew, without a doubt, that she hadn't given that order. The blood of her Berserkers was on her hands for standing up to the Empress and standing down at Medina. She hadn't given that order.

Or had she?

No. She was sure she hadn't.

The Empress had pushed her to her limit, and at Medina, she had broken. She had taken her soldiers and her ship and fought for the innocents.

Then...who was in the video in front of her? How?

"It's not me," was all that came out. She didn't have the energy to voice the thoughts running through her mind like a tangled mass of wires.

"Her biometrics indicate that she is telling the truth," Dr. Dar said.

"Biometrics can be faked."

"Skyla," Hinata finally stepped forward, "she is half dead from the poison, pumped full of pharmaceuticals to keep her stable. I don't think even the admiral has the training to fool the biometrics scanner under these conditions."

Skyla slammed both hands down onto the counter, the vibrations carrying into Freyja's body.

"Then how do you explain it?"

"It's a deepfake," Dr. Dar said.

"How? That technology was banned before The Exodus. You said so yourself, Ears."

"Things exist in this universe beyond what we have seen. Just look at this megastructure."

"Proof?" Hinata asked.

"I'm still working on that. Cista is running calculations. Hopefully, when we get back into orbit, I will have answers."

Hinata nodded slightly to Dr. Dar. "Stay with the admiral. Make sure that she gets the antidote when it is ready."

"We are losing our leverage," Skyla shifted to block Hinata as he made to exit the med bay. "This is all we have. Once she is stable, once she no longer fears for her life, we will have nothing. She will never give us answers."

Hinata shook his head. "Not like this, Captain."

***

Freyja lingered in the hallway outside the lab, listening to raised voices spilling out into the hall. She had been released from medical that morning. Dr. Dar and Dr. Pinot had developed the antidote that had saved her life. She would be fine, Dr. Pinot had assured her. The inferno under her skin had died away, leaving in its wake a raging headache that threatened to cleave her skull in two, and her muscles were bound up in a painful ache that even her most strenuous days of training couldn't compare to. At least she had her mind back, and right now she knew enough not to interrupt the argument transpiring in the next room.

"You don't know her like I do." That was Skyla's voice.

"Care to enlighten us?" Hinata said.

Heavy silence stretched into the corridor. Freyja wasn't surprised at all that Skyla didn't want to explain their relationship. She didn't dwell on the past, either.

"Freyja is always playing the long game—you can't trust her. For all we know, she made that transmission."

Freyja was tired of standing in the shadows. She stepped into the lab.

"Perhaps you give me too much credit, *Captain*."

Skyla folded her arms, lips pressed into a thin line.

"Admiral," Hinata inclined his head to a holo display, "perhaps you can enlighten us? Pele intercepted a rather interesting communication sent to your ship."

The holo began to play a message from the Empress herself. Her mother.

"I want to congratulate you on your decisive victory at Medina. Your forethought to go dark after the mission was a stroke of genius. Of course, our tribe was outraged that the rebel faction at Medina killed an admiral of the United Tribal Axis Navy, and has demanded retribution. It is a shame that the *Ormen Korte* was lost in the skirmish, but sacrifices must be made in the pursuit of the greater good. You are instructed to remain dark until after the next senate hearing. Good work." The image dissolved into nothing.

Freyja's brow furrowed. What was the Empress talking about? The decision to go dark? The *Ormen Korte,* lost? They hadn't taken out the stardestroyer. There had been plenty of starship casualties at Medina, but the station didn't have a fleet capable of taking out a stardestroyer. What game was the Empress playing? Freyja let out a heavy sigh.

"Skyla, you know the Empress. She is always playing her own game, and no one knows what her end objective is...not even me."

"I don't like any of this," Skyla muttered in response.

"I am not playing games," Freyja started, "I already told you I didn't give those orders—"

Hinata slammed his hand into the bulkhead, silencing Freyja.

"Enough."

The commander, who was usually so calm and collected, wore his anger across his face. His eyes were narrowed and dark, and for the first time, Freyja feared what he was capable of.

"My soldiers are dead. Thousands of civilians under my care forfeited their lives. Thousands more sit vulnerable, waiting to be delivered to safety. I am out of patience for your power games. You better tell me what the fuck is going on. Now." An unsaid threat hung in his words.

Freyja's ribs constricted, stealing her calm away with her breath. For the first time in a very long time, she felt vulnerable. There were no more moves left to make.

"I'll tell you everything," she said in a voice barely above a whisper.

"Becoming admiral was all the Empress ever wanted of me. Everything, my whole life, was in preparation for this position." Freyja paused, her eyes flicking to Skyla for a moment, pleading for understanding, but all she saw reflected in the other woman's eyes was scorn. Freyja shook her head and continued.

"You won the admiral exam. We both know it. Did you ever wonder why I was given the position over you?"

"Every day, for the past three years," Hinata responded.

"You didn't figure it out? The Empress holds influence in all twelve tribes. Who fuels their starships? Who mines the materials to make their hulls? While she couldn't give me the position outright, she has her ways of persuading the board."

"She bought you an admiral's position?" Hinata spat the words like a curse.

Freyja shrugged. "In the end, she always gets what she wants. There is no point in fighting it; you only delay the inevitable."

"I have spent three years in purgatory because of you. I was exiled to contemplate my failure."

Freyja wouldn't dignify that with a response. She couldn't win against the Empress; why should Hinata be any different? She continued, "As soon as I was assigned my fleet, the secret missions started. The Empress would demand retaliation for a perceived grievance. Sabotage a competitor's ring, confiscate goods, poison a hydroponics station." She sagged under the weight of her confession. "She is placing her pieces, and she is planning something big, but I don't know what it is. We are all just pawns to her." Freyja fell silent.

"And Medina?" Hinata prompted.

"Another secret mission, much bigger than any of the others. She told us that you were manufacturing illegal weapons, and we were to take the station at all costs."

"Medina is full—was full—of scholars...there were never any weapons on my station," Hinata said.

"I know. That's why I ordered my fleet to stand down once I had completed my scan." Freyja shook her head. "I don't know her real purpose for the strike. My crew mutinied when I tried to stand down. Borg, that piece of shit, saw his opportunity to make a name for himself with the Empress. My Berserkers and I barely fought our way off the bridge. I lost half of my most loyal soldiers that day."

"You aren't the only one with losses." Hinata's eyes burned bright with rage.

"I know," Freyja whispered. "I have sat too long in the Empress' shadow, but no longer. I want to end this before any more lives are lost."

Freyja had finally decided what she needed to do with the freedom her supposed death had granted her. She wanted the farm and the quiet life away from all of this. But it would have to wait.

"I don't trust you," Skyla said.

"You don't have to, but I *am* telling you the truth. I'm going to get my answers and we stand a better chance of succeeding if we work together."

"While our interests align?" Hinata asked.

"While our interests align." Freyja nodded.

"And when they don't?"

"I guess we will find out when that day comes."

CHAPTER 31 | FREYJA

ENEMIES

*H*er mother's words echo through her mind on repeat. "In tomorrow's training exercises, you are to eliminate Cadet Skyla Karsten."

Freyja's gut twists. How could she kill her childhood best friend? They hadn't spoken in years, not since they had left for the academy, but Skyla was still the first friend that Freyja had ever had—the first person to love her for who she was— and she could never forget that.

"Remember, there are consequences when you do not follow orders." Again, her mother's venomous words drip through her brain. The Empress made it clear: Freyja would kill Skyla, or her Berserkers would pay the price. Her own personal army had been a gift from her mother, and she never hesitated to remind Freyja that she could easily take them away.

Freyja slams her gloved fist into the bulkhead as she suits up for the training exercise. The rage threatens to consume her. It was an impossible choice. She doesn't want anyone to get hurt, but her mother has other plans. Freyja grinds her teeth until her jaw hurts, fighting for control. She could change the outcome. She has to. She just has to look for the right opportunity.

She lets the emotions fall from her face as she steps into the airlock to join her team. In the simulation today, they would play the part of boarding party. Skyla's squad would be making repairs—they have no idea there is a surprise attack planned.

Tristan steps up to her side, sliding a small aerosol canister into her palm as he leans in close to keep his words between them.

"As requested," he says.

"You were able to weaponize it?" Freyja asks.

Tristan snorts, "Of course I was able to. I can turn anything into a weapon." He flashes a half-grin at her, his eyes darting from side to side to ensure none of their crew has wandered closer. "What are you planning?"

"Don't worry about it. Huddle up with the rest." She nods toward the squad.

Tristan shakes his head and clicks his tongue, "so bossy." But he does as he is told, sauntering over to the rest of her Berserkers.

Freyja takes a moment to examine the canister. It's small, barely the length of her hand, easy to tuck away and use without the cameras seeing. Her nerves are on edge. This is still a risk. If she uses the paralytic and gets caught, she has no doubt they will trace its origins back to her garden. She would lose that one little piece of joy she had left. She shakes her head. This has to work. She will only use the paralytic as a last resort and she only if she can't best Skyla in hand-to-hand. Freyja's hands ball into fists at her side. She has never beaten Skyla one-on-one before. But she can't afford to let the doubts creep in. She will beat Skyla today.

She has to; there is no other option.

Freyja tucks the canister away as she moves to join her squad. They huddle up, arms linked and heads pressed together as Freyja details the plan.

"Don't trust anything for a second out there. Keep your helmets up and suits pressurized. We've been told this is a surprise boarding simulation. Who knows what the other team has been told? Stay sharp, execute clean, and let's come home with the win." Freyja gives the final commands to her team of five before they break the huddle. The rest of the team waits by the door, ready to start the laser torches, but Kylian hangs back.

"Mind telling me why you want helmets up, boss ma'am? We're not authorized for an exterior breach in sims—no reason to go in full suit."

"Do as you're told," Freyja snaps. The pained look in his eyes is enough to make her want to take it all back, but she can't. Right now, she has a job to do.

"Yes, ma'am," Kylian says in perfect standard, his previous accent gone; and with it, the trust he had shown her in the moment before. She would make it up to him. She is protecting him. She is protecting all of them. She just has to get through this sim.

"Initiate boarding protocol," Freyja calls out through the team comms.

The light buzz of laser torches picks up as her team gets to work opening a breach. Tristan stands across from her. Behind her, Kylian is in position with his helmet now initiated. She turns her attention back to the door.

One sim: she just has to get through this one sim to keep them safe.

They rush into the training capsule with weapons drawn. Skyla is at the center of the room working on repairs. Her teammates are at the far back of the capsule, printing replacement parts in their lab. Good, that will make this easier.

"Kylian, seal those doors." He is good with code. It takes him mere seconds to crack into their systems and the lab doors snap shut. The other cadets pound

against the glass, but this will all be over before they 3D print tools to pry open the door. That just leaves Skyla, standing in the middle of the maintenance pod with her staff drawn.

"Guard the door. She's mine," Freyja growls through her comms. Her soldiers promptly move to the back of the pod, except Kylian. Damn it. *She shoots a nasty glare at her friend, who finally relents and falls in with the rest of her team. Everything is in place. Now she just has to take care of Skyla.*

Freyja draws her sword, the edge blunt, in training mode. She circles to the left. Skyla slowly rotates to match her stance. Freyja lashes out with a fury of blows. She wants this over, but Skyla meets each attack, twisting and turning to block her strikes. Skyla is better than she was the last time they sparred.

Skyla goes on the offensive. Freyja grits her teeth, fighting to block the blows that come in rapid succession. She deflects a downward strike, directing Skyla's momentum to open up her defense.

Freyja changes levels, throwing Skyla off balance and opening up her right side. She kicks Skyla's arm, breaking her hold on the staff, but Skyla twists and drives forward, knocking Freyja into the command console. All of Freyja's breath is forced from her lungs as she loses grip on her sword. Skyla pins her in place with a forearm.

"What are you doing?" Skyla yells.

The look of hurt in Skyla's eyes is almost enough to make Freyja crumble. She glances to the back of the pod where Kylian and Tristan are already running to intercede. Freyja shakes her head, her eyes locking on Tristan's as she pulls out the paralytic he made for her. Understanding washes over his face as he throws an arm out to stop Kylian. Kylian struggles against his grip for a moment, until he pulls him close, an unheard exchange happening over their comms. Kylian's jaw sets and he shakes his head, but he holds his position.

"Answer me." Skyla's voice snaps Freyja's attention back. She has no choice in this. No matter what she does, someone is going to get hurt.

"What I should have done a long time ago," Freyja sneers, "eliminating my competition."

The sound of the aerosol canister releasing punctuates her words.

Confusion washes over Skyla's face, followed by fear, as her body goes limp.

Freyja shoves Skyla, and she collapses to the ground, now defenseless and wheezing, weak fingers clutching at her throat as the ability to move drains from them.

"Kylian, open the bay doors." Freyja keeps her eyes locked on Skyla, whose eyes have blown wide with shock as her fingers fumble at her collar, using the last of her strength to extend her helmet.

Freyja grabs Skyla by the back of her suit and bashes her helmet into the console. Skyla hangs limp in Freyja's hand, unable to stop what is coming. Once, twice, three times—Freyja slams Skyla's helmet until there's a crack of glass; once more should do it. Freyja puts all of her weight behind the blow, smashing the glass on Skyla's helmet.

The bay doors are still sealed.

"Damn it, Kylian. I am not asking again. Open those doors, now." Freyja says through their private comm-line. She spares a glance in his direction, pain is etched across his face at the understanding of what she is doing—what he thinks she is doing. It hurts more than she thought it would, that he could see her as a monster. Freyja sets her jaw. Good—if he is convinced, then so are the cameras. The sound of a locking mechanism shifting means he has overridden the safety codes. Time to finish this.

"Exhale," Freyja whispers so low that only Skyla can hear the words. Then she vents the pod. Freyja moves with practiced precision, attaching Skyla's harness to the console at the last possible moment. Bits of broken tech fly toward the opening, along with Freyja and her squad, but she made sure they

were ready. Their suits are pressurized, and with their position at the back of the pod, they should have enough time to secure.

Freyja is sucked through the room by the vacuum. She activates the magnetic grips in her gloves and throws her arms out to clutch the side of the pod. Tucking in tight, she activates her Z-grav boots to stabilize her position.

Once secure, she scans her surroundings. Her teammates are hunkered down further up the pod. Skyla's teammates pound on the lab windows, shock and horror painted on their faces. They are screaming for the proctors to intervene, no doubt. Finally, she spares a glance at the center of the room. Skyla hangs unconscious at the end of her tether, her limbs flailing like a rag doll. Her face swollen and tinged blue. Time stretches, but it is all over in seconds. The emergency doors slam shut and normal pressure is restored. As soon as the compartment is pressurized, the proctors rush into the simulation pod.

"What was that, Cadet Nygaard!" her proctor screams in her face.

Freyja releases her hold on the hull, retracts her helmet and exhales deeply as she squares her shoulders and stands tall before her proctor.

"We kept them from completing their mission. We subdued the enemy and won the simulation—did we not?"

The proctor's face blooms crimson at her insubordination.

"And you may have killed a classmate in the process. We will see what the board has to say about this at your disciplinary hearing. Get out of my sight!" The proctor yells, so close that spittle flecks across Freyja's face.

"Yes, Sergeant." She hurries to the exit, darting a glance at Skyla's prone form. Medics are crowded around the girl, unconscious on the ground. She had put everything on the line for this gambit. It couldn't be for nothing. Passing through the doors, Freyja tries one last time—just then, a medic shifts and she catches just a glimpse of Skyla's face; pink blushing across her cheeks as oxygen returns to her tissues.

Freyja exhales, relief rushing through her body. She pushes down the dread that was building at what she would lose. She had to use the paralytic, there hadn't been another way. Now Skyla is safe and so are her Berserkers; the Empress will never let Freyja be expelled from the academy, and the proctors will never let her near Skyla Karsten again.

CHAPTER 32 | HINATA

MURDER BOT

Hinata was restless. He was anxious to get back to his fleet, back to his tribe, back to the routine of being a soldier. For now, he would have to settle for wandering the halls of their linked ships.

They had relinked for the return trip. Mr. Dar—Dr. Dar, *why had the man never corrected him before?*—Dr. Dar and Dr. Pinot spent most of their time in Pele's lab, focused on analyzing the physical samples they had collected. Wout had set up a hammock in engineering, "where the hum of engines could lull him to sleep each night." Freyja and her men kept to themselves, opting to stay in Selkie's section. Hinata had Pele keeping tabs on them all the same. He still didn't trust her, despite her confessions.

Then there was Skyla. He didn't need to keep an eye on the captain. He trusted her, and he felt a maddening drive to be close to her.

Hinata rounded a bend in the hallway; his wandering feet had brought him to the cargo bay. He stepped into the room and let a rare smile trace his lips. Leaning against the doorway, he folded his arms against his chest and watched as Skyla practiced drills with her bō staff, against a training dummy. She was good. It's too bad she had left the Navy—with the storm that was brewing; he could have used an ally like her. She stopped and straightened; her back still to him.

"Care to train? Or are you just going to watch?" she called out to him.

He laughed. She was good; too good to be wasting her talents treasure hunting.

"Up for a rematch, Captain?"

"This time I won't go easy on you." She turned to flash a dangerous smile at him.

"Of that, I have no doubt." He pulled his katana from its place on his back. With a signal from his neural chip, the blade transformed into a blunt edge for training. They began to slowly circle, eyes locked, each searching for an opening.

"Do you often train in the cargo bay?" he asked, swinging a testing strike.

"We don't all have state-of-the-art facilities for training, Commander," she responded with a testing blow of her own.

He deflected easily.

"I wouldn't call the base at Medina state-of-the-art."

"Well, it has more equipment than I do." She moved in with a series of strikes, trying to find a way through his defense. She dropped into a crouch and swung out with her bō. He moved to block, but he was too slow and the strike hit just behind his knees, taking him to the ground. His katana flew from his hand, and Skyla moved quickly to kick it from his reach. She smiled at him and tossed her staff aside, too.

"I thought you weren't going to go easy on me?" He quirked a brow.

"It's not fun if it isn't a fair fight." She raised her fists and dropped into a fighting stance. Hinata came to his feet and mirrored her. They exchanged a quick series of jabs and blocks before Skyla tied up with him, one hand grasping behind his neck, the other at his elbow. He locked up with her, foreheads nearly touching as they each fought for control. She shucked his arm up, dropping nearly to her knees before grabbing both his legs. Skyla stood and drove forward—it all happened so fast. He was on his back in the blink of an eye. *Damn*, she hadn't moved like that before; the cryo-shock must have been worse than he had thought. She wasted no time locking him in place.

"Three, two, one," she counted, then hit the ground with her palm. She pulled back just enough to look him in the eyes. "I have to say, Commander, I was expecting a little more from you," she teased, still straddling him.

Hinata stared into those ice-blue eyes, the color of a comet's tail. Electricity surged through his body where they touched. She made no move to stand. It couldn't just be him, right? She felt it too? He ran his fingers along her jaw.

"I was distracted." His words were soft, just loud enough to sit between them.

Skyla's soft, pink lips quirked into a smile and she moved closer, until their foreheads nearly touched.

"By what?"

"You," he whispered, lacing his fingers in the hair at the nape of her neck. He wrapped his other hand around her waist and pulled her to him. Their lips brushed; sparks surged through his body and the ground shook beneath him.

"Captain," Pele blurted through the comms. The spell shattered. He released his grip on her.

"Pele, can't it wait. I am a little—"

The ship rocked, the lights flickering with the impact. Skyla sprang to her feet, pulling him up with her.

"Skyla, there is something out there. I need you on the bridge now." Pele sounded scared. Did AIs feel fear? Skyla was already sprinting from the cargo bay, Hinata following close behind. The ship rocked under their feet again, knocking them into the walls as they ran.

"What was that?" he muttered.

"I don't know, there was nothing on long-range sensors. This is uncharted space; there shouldn't be anyone out here," Skyla responded.

They emerged onto the bridge to find that Freyja and Dr. Dar were already at their stations. The view screen in front of them showed an undulating mass of black against the field of stars. At first, Hinata couldn't process what he was looking at, his brain interpreting the odd sight as a storm cloud. Then he focused on the movements of the cloud, picking apart the patterns until he discerned what looked like a swarm of blackbirds. He pressed his eyes closed. This couldn't be reality.

"What's going on?" Skyla yelled.

"I don't know," Dr. Dar said. "One minute we had clear, open space and then this massive swarm appeared. We didn't have anything on sensors—it's as if it jumped directly to our location."

"Whatever it is, they are attacking us!" Freyja called out.

Skyla slid into her station.

"Ears, figure out what those things are. Freyja, Hinata, man your weapons systems; see if you can keep those things off us. You two," she gestured to Kylian and Tristan, "you're on maintenance duty. Patch anything that's broken. Keep us together."

"Skyla, at this rate, they will be through my shields in five minutes."

Hinata swore he heard fear lacing through the AI's words.

"I know, Pele, I won't let anything happen to you. Focus on power-ing those shields. I am taking evasive maneuvers and weapons. Strap in everyone, I'm cutting gravity."

Hinata activated his restraints as he tried to connect with Tentei.

Come on—*damn stubborn machine*—he didn't have time to deal with the temperamental AI right now. He messaged a request to take over weapons. No response. Finally, he received a soft beep, releasing weapons control to him. Insufferable machine; didn't it understand that its life was on the line too?

Hinata synced into the weapons system, the display taking over his vision. He zeroed in on the closest cluster of bots. He ground his teeth together as a closer image of the birds came into his view screen. While they were shaped like birds, there was nothing organic about them. They were all hard planes and sharp edges. Hinata aimed and took out a cluster of bird-bots mid-dive, just before they pierced Pele's hull. They exploded into fireworks. He took aim again—there were still so many of them!

The bridge moved in a flow state, each of the crew members silent, entirely focused on the task in front of them. Sweat trickled down his neck, his muscles aching from the tension. How long had they been fighting off the swarm? How long could they continue?

"We have a breach!" Skyla shouted, breaking the silence. "It's mas-sive; I need someone down there now!"

"We're tied up in the engine room," Kylian reported over the comms.

"She's running hot!" Wout yelled. "I need all the help I can get in here right now."

Hinata scanned his sector: clear for now. He passed weapons control back to Tentei. *Please, if you don't care about protecting us, at least protect yourself.* He sent the message to his AI.

"On it," he said as he activated his Z-grav boots, then disengaged his harness. They still had no gravity, and Pele twisted, cut, and turned through space like a supercharged molecule trying to break free of its bonds. He wished he was wearing his armored suit; it would have helped his body take the G-force of Skyla's maneuvers. There was no time: he would have to make do. A schematic illuminated in his eyes, guiding him to the breach, and he broke into a run. Highlighted in his ocular display, Hinata saw that Pele had sealed the breach, but something had gotten inside. He readied his katana, the blade turning sharp once more. The doors slid open in front of him and he stepped into the corridor. There was a flock of mechanical ravens picking at the walls and wiring.

He swung at the nearest bot, slicing clean through its matte-black metal exterior. Little sparks flew from the cut. Bits of metal fell to the floor, but the bird still hovered in the air. He watched in horror as the cut that should have decapitated the drone knitted itself back together. The drones emitted a screeching sound, like grinding metal and static bursts.

Suddenly, a cloud of murder bots descended on him.

Hinata cut swift arcs around his body. Little bits of metal fell to the floor, followed by larger chunks of drone. Even with Hinata's deft swordsmanship, the flock kept coming. He sliced them to shreds but they repaired themselves and came at him again.

His limbs grew heavy as he fought uselessly against the onslaught—then he had an idea. With a command from his neural chip, his katana pulsed with an indigo glow. He slashed the glowing blade through a group of ravens and they exploded into dust.

Nanites. Hinata was sure of it. The flock retreated to the other side of the corridor, screeching at him once more. They began to swirl into a mass of black, losing their avian shapes and becoming one ominous storm cloud. The dark swirl of metal took on a new shape.

He now stood face-to-face with a massive humanoid form, but like the birds, it was all flat planes and hard angles. Long spikes flared out of its hands, knees, shoulders, and elbows. Instead of a face, there was just a blank plane, like a mech helmet. The mech-bot swept a spike at Hinata. He blocked, but was slammed into the wall with the force of the blow. He winced as all of the air left his lungs.

Hinata struggled to regain his breath while staying out of the creature's reach. He struck the mech-bot in the arm, but instead of slicing through, as he had with the birds, his blade met strike-stopping resistance. Bits of nanite fell away where they contacted the pulse field around his weapon, but it barely made a dent in the massive figure before him. Shit, that must be why it changed form—the mech-bot was stronger than the bird drones. He needed to change tactics. If he set off a pulse at its core, maybe he could cause a cascade failure through the nanites.

Hinata blocked another strike from the figure; his shoulders groaned under the strain of holding back the blow. Sweat beaded on his skin, pulling into droplets in the air around him. He had to end this soon—he couldn't hold back those powerful blows much longer. He watched for his opening, dodging strikes from the dark figure as it pushed him down the corridor. *There.* The figure took a wide swipe at Hinata and he ducked at the last moment, pressing all of his weight into the blade as he drove it into the heart of the machine.

Hinata gritted his teeth, willing the sword deeper into the creature's armor, then he triggered a centralized EMP pulse. The current ran through his sword and the dark figure exploded into a dust storm of dark particles.

Sparking and sputtering out like embers cast from a flame, the dead nanites hung in null-G. Hinata sagged in relief, letting his body fall limp in the air with the nanites.

"The breach has been contained," he said through the comms.

"Thank you, Commander," Pele said softly. "I have already relayed your tactics to the captain; they are finishing off the swarm now."

CHAPTER 33 | SKYLA

AMBUSH

Skyla paced the length of the small lab. She had to come to check on Rohaan's progress with the nanites they had collected from the breach. She was on edge, and not just because they had been attacked by what appeared to be a swarm of autonomous nanite drones.

She was on edge because Hinata had kissed her, and she had let him—she had more than let him. She wanted to kiss him. She wanted to give into that electricity that coursed beneath her skin when he was near her. She wanted to let it swallow her whole. What was she thinking? Of all the people to get involved with, she has to choose Commander Azai, the most by-the-book, tribe-focused, dedicated soldier in the United Tribal Axis—maybe the entire universe! He was the absolute worst match for her in all the Known

Galaxies. His management of Medina station could well have put her out of business—he had bankrupted plenty of other archaeologists before she arrived. Confiscating their goods, the losses preventing them from continuing their expeditions. Hinata didn't bend the rules.

But he had...for her.

He had made a deal with her to buy her salvage, not confiscate it. He had made sure she received UTA medical care for the cryo-shock, and he had authorized Pele's repairs with his mechanics. That wasn't the Hinata she heard about as a cadet and it wasn't the man she had read about as an officer. Skyla slumped into a chair next to Rohaan, leaning her head back to rest on his shoulder, a frustrated sigh escaping her lips. Ears simply cocked an eyebrow as he glanced down at her.

"Credit for your thoughts?" His focus was already back on the holo in front of him, but she knew he was listening. He always listened to her. He was the brother she never had.

"It's not important. What have you found with the nanites?"

Rohaan's brow knit together in frustration. Not good news, then.

"Not much, unfortunately. Your commander did a good job of frying their circuitry."

"Not my commander," Skyla mumbled.

A smile quirked Rohaan's lips, "I'm sorry. I misspoke."

Damn Rohaan, smart, observant scientist. "Fine, that is what's bothering me," she admitted.

"You are bothered by Commander Azai?" Rohaan asked innocently.

"Don't play dumb. It doesn't suit you, Dr. Dar."

He smiled at her. "Very well. But I don't understand why you are so bothered. Based on my observations, there is a mutual attraction between you and the commander, is there not?"

She ran her hand over her face, mortified. Were they that obvious? Like two pining teenagers? How embarrassing!

"That's not the problem."

"Then I don't see the problem."

"He is a commander in the UTA Navy."

"And?"

"I quit the Navy. I left all of that behind. I don't want anything to do with the compact—and that is his life. Where would it go?"

"Does it matter? Human lives are driven by chaos theory; it is impossible to predict your future. Too much chaos in the system."

"What's your point?"

"You can't predict where things might go with the commander. So, why try? Perhaps you should try living in the moment?"

"Who the hell are you and why do you sound more like a romantic than a scientist right now? What has happened to my friend?"

At that comment, Rohaan turned red, the blush fanning across his neck to the tips of his ears.

"Rohaan...did you meet someone?" She elbowed him for more information.

He ignored her, pretending to inspect the holo in front of him.

"You did! When? How?"

"So many questions," Rohaan muttered.

"Go on and tell me about her," she prompted, happy to revel in someone else's mortification instead of her own.

"Fine." He threw his hands up, the holo specs dissolving in front of him. "She is a research assistant working on Dr. Aman's quantum entanglement energy transport project. Well, she is his daughter actually, and quite brilliant. She helped me with the analysis of the viral code samples we found back at Medina."

"Brilliant, huh? That is high praise coming from you. That is great! Why didn't you tell me?"

"We only just met after the evacuation, and it's complicated."

"Complicated? Like, 'you just evacuated your home,' complicated?"

"Like, 'her father didn't make it to the rendezvous,' complicated. Besides," he waved his hands—obviously upset by the topic—"we have been a little wrapped up in more urgent matters."

"Exactly," Skyla jumped at the opportunity to shut down any further discussion of her own feelings, "too busy. You're right, Ears, we are much too busy for frivolous distractions."

"That is not what I meant, and you know it."

"Nope, moving on—get me on comms if you find anything with those nanites." She exited Rohaan's lab before he had a chance to engage her further on the Hinata-issue.

Nope, no issue; she was too busy for *issues*.

"We just need to get the fleet restocked and delivered safely to Gefion, then it is back to normal. Just you and me, Pele—and the stars—the way we like it," Skyla said.

"Who are you trying to convince, Skyla? You or me?"

"Not you, too."

"I'll go wherever you go, Skyla. It's you and me to the end. But are you sure there isn't room for more?"

***

The fleet loomed in the viewport in front of Skyla. She was alone on Pele's bridge, watching the odd collection of starfighters, frigates, and research vessels that hung in orbit around Trogon. They had disengaged the link upon approach, each of them safely back on their own ships as they re-joined the fleet. Hinata had requested Pele host another counsel before they engaged with the locals. It wouldn't make a difference, it was protocol really. Trogon was run by the Fenix and Skyla would rather trade with pirates than deal with the cartel, but they were out of options. She would set up the exchange and if they were very, *very*, lucky, they would trade the alien technology they found for enough supplies to get the refugees to Gefion. She groaned. It was such a good haul of ancient tech, to waste it on the Fenix just felt wrong. At least Rohaan and Pele had taken extensive scans of everything they had found. Rohaan would be able to continue his studies of the artifacts, even if they had to hand over the originals to a bunch of backwater thugs.

"Skyla." Pele's voice was soft, soothing. Pele always could read her moods. "The officers' convoy has docked."

She took one more glance out the viewport at the odd collection of ships and the blue and tan marble of a planet swirling with white clouds behind them. How had she ended up here? How had she ended up responsible for all these people?

When Skyla walked in, Hinata, Tax, and Callan were already there, along with Freyja, her shadows, and Rohaan. She had hoped Hinata would leave Freyja out of this exchange. She was an uncontrollable hothead—not the type of person Skyla wanted with her for a meeting with the cartel. Freyja read her narrowed eyes.

"Guess you're stuck with me," Freyja said.

"We will see." Skyla turned away from Freyja and ran straight into Hinata. He instinctively grabbed her elbow, steadying her as she found her balance.

"Have you been avoiding me, Captain?" His voice was playful, but his eyes held a hint of worry. She had made a point of staying out of his path for the remainder of the trip back to the fleet. No time for complications. *Focus on the mission.*

"It's not a large ship, Commander. How could I, possibly?"

He let his hand drop from her arm. "My thoughts exactly."

"Commander, with your permission, we are ready to begin," Callan said.

Hinata nodded, then stepped away from her to join his men.

The proceedings were quite dull. Skyla had forgotten how much she hated this part of being an officer. They gave their reports on the status of the fleet in meticulously boring detail. Finally, they moved on to the next phase of their mission: securing supplies for the refugee fleet. The plan was simple. Skyla would make contact with the Fenix. As an archaeologist, she had encountered them before and they would be more likely to exchange with her than the UTA Navy. If all went according to plan, they would have their supplies and be on their way within a day.

"And if the Fenix have other ideas?" Skyla interrupted the officer who had laid out the mission plans. He looked at her, perplexed.

"It is a simple resupply. Now that we have something of value, there is no reason to expect issues with the exchange."

"That is where you are wrong," she said. "If we were dealing with a regular supply station, you would be right. But this isn't a supply station. It is a cartel-run rim planet. You have to expect that they won't pay for what they can take."

"Any suggestions, Captain?" Hinata asked.

"I have some thoughts."

***

Skyla pushed a suspensor loaded with crates down Pele's ramp as she entered the large Fenix warehouse. Fenrir stalked to her right. Hinata took up her left. Freyja, Kylian, and Tristan followed just behind. They all wore full mechsuits, which were larger and more heavily armored than regular armored spacesuits. She hoped they wouldn't need them, but she had learned the hard way not to underestimate the cartel. Skyla had insisted that Pele run maintenance on all of the mechs before the meet.

"Are you sure you want to bring that thing?" Hinata asked in a low voice, his eyes darting to Fenrir.

"Yes."

They fell silent, eyes trained on the warehouse ahead. A group of five men in well-cut dark suits joined them from the other side of the warehouse, followed closely by a contingent of guards in exoskeleton armor, each holding rifles across their chests and large, mean-looking beasts on chains at their sides. The cartel wasn't one for subtlety.

"Halcóncita!" a man at the center of the group called out as Skyla approached. Hinata quirked an eyebrow, but all he got in response was the subtle shake of Skyla's head. The man that approached stood at eye level with Skyla, even in her mechsuit. His dark, short curls were shaved tight on the sides and the top shone with gel. His dark olive complexion was flawless. The living-ink tattoo of a phoenix etched across his throat stretched its neck in a silent screech. It flapped its wings forcefully before settling still on his neck once again.

"Gabriel," Skyla replied, her voice tight.

Gabriel extended his arm. Skyla clenched her jaw, but she returned the gesture, grasping forearms with the cartel leader. When she moved to pull her arm back, he tightened his grip as his eyes raked over her. His intentions were clear: he wanted to possess her, the way he possessed this planet. His dark eyes burned with ferocity as they locked onto hers, but she didn't move to retract her arm again; instead, she held his stare. She would not back down from this tyrant. From the corner of her eye, she saw Hinata's hand twitch, ready to intercede. The air hung heavy and still; the only disturbance came from the rattle of chains and the panting of the dogs.

"My Halcóncita, you were always too serious." A wicked grin passed across Gabriel's face as he let go of Skyla's arm. His eyes darted to Hinata. "Your face looks good, Commander…too bad, I was hoping I would have left you a little something to remember me by." Gabriel pursed his lips suggestively at the commander.

Hinata moved forward, having had enough, but Skyla threw an arm out to stop him. "If you're done flirting, can we get down to business?" She settled an icy stare on Gabriel.

He let out a manic laugh. "So, what did you bring me this time?"

Skyla pulled up a holo which showed cross sections of what appeared to be alien weapons. The image shimmered in the gloom of the warehouse.

"We just came back from the Zeta quadrant—a society that had highly advanced defensive structures in place. Our initial scans indicate that we picked up some prime weapons tech."

"A perfect gift. You know me so well. But I didn't get you anything."

"The arranged trade will suffice. I know how thoughtless you can be."

"Hmm…." Gabriel paced around her, appraising her and her party as if they were up for sale, too. Fenrir pulled his pointed ears back against his head, watching Gabriel with a sharp, feline stare. The look in their eyes was identical—two predators. "I think you ask for too much, Halcóncita." He waved his hand at the specs. "These are only preliminary scans. It will take months for my scientists to turn these relics into anything useful."

"I had the best research scientist in the Known Galaxies review those scans. They are viable and worth a whole hell of a lot more than some food, water, and fuel." She paused, glaring into the man's smoldering brown eyes, her voice dropping low, "and you know it."

Gabriel smirked at her growing anger. He was toying with her. He shrugged. "What I know is that I have all of the power and you have none. I will let you walk away at half the agreed price."

"I can't take half."

"Then I will take the tech, and you will walk away with nothing." His voice was low and dangerous.

"How generous of you," she growled.

"You walked away last time."

"You did your best to make sure it went the other way."

Gabriel broke into laughter. "Halcóncita, that was in the past. I'm feeling generous today. Leave the weapons, take your misfit crew, and leave my system."

"We need the supplies. Our fleet can't make it to another resupply station."

"Your fleet of refugees, no? Leave them, too. There's always room for more bodies on the plantations."

"Slaves, you mean? We both know how inhumane the conditions on those plantations are."

"Life is hard at the rim."

"I won't be leaving them."

Gabriel shook his head, and a slick smile spread across his face. "I missed this. That passion. I forgot how much fire you have, my little Halcóncita. Stay, and I'll let the rest of your friends leave."

"Not going to happen."

"Then no one leaves." Gabriel drew a phase gun from inside his suit jacket. His men followed his lead with all weapons locked on Skyla.

"Eclipse," Skyla spoke the code word through her comms. Instantly the lights blinked out, shrouding the warehouse in darkness. Her helm sprung up over her head as she grabbed Hinata, dragging him behind her to take cover behind the nearest pallet. Phaser blasts cut beams of light through the darkness and the loud popping of twin railguns rang out as ammunition tore through the wooden crates.

"All of these weapons are illegal outside of military warships." Hinata snarled next to her ear.

"Welcome to the border, Commander." The compact was stretched too thin; they couldn't enforce their laws at the borders of known space. Here, anyone who had the credits and wasn't afraid to get their hands dirty could build their own little empire. She jerked her head in the direction of the cartel. "Here, they are the law."

Hinata ran a gloved palm across his damaged chest plate. "Damn! Taking direct phaser fire, even in a mechsuit, still hurts like hell."

"It's a good thing I had Pele make those upgrades, or it'd hurt a hell of a lot more. I had her add a little something extra, too." She smirked, and on her command, a light blue pulse shield materialized on her left arm. "The pulse shield should hold under the phaser fire, as long as it has enough time to recharge between blasts. Those railguns, though, are made to take down stardestroyers. If you get hit by one of those—"

"You're spaced," he finished for her.

Skyla nodded. She tried to relay instructions to Freyja to activate her own pulse shield. No signal. They had taken out the lights, and the cartel had taken out their comms.

"No comms. Listen, we need to play it smart. No risks. Take out the railguns and then get to Pele—"

A snarling maw full of sharp teeth smashed against Hinata's pulse shield, forcing him to the ground. The genetically engineered guard dog was so massive, it pinned Hinata to the floor. Hinata crossed his forearms in front of him trying to support the shield, the only thing separating him from the creature. Before Skyla could move, a growl rumbled from the darkness. Fenrir leaped across Hinata, grabbing the dog's throat in his jaws. There was a whimpering sound, then a disturbing squelch, and then nothing.

"Good boy, Fenrir," Skyla whispered. She extended an arm, helping Hinata to his feet. They both held their pulse shields ready on one arm, weapons drawn on the other. A shared nod and they dashed into the fray.

It was chaos; pulsing pink phaser fire streaked through the warehouse while terrifying growls rumbled through the darkness as Fenrir stalked his prey. Freyja and her men had formed a unit and were sweeping the opposite side of the warehouse. Skyla slammed her bō staff into the man in front of her, hitting him hard across his forearms. The snap of bones breaking rang through the air. He dropped his weapon, falling to his knees, screaming. She dealt another swift hit from her staff to the jaw; he wouldn't be causing them any more trouble. To her side, Hinata swept through another two cartel members, slicing his katana across one shoulder so deep he must have hit bone. He turned and buried his blade in the next man's torso before pulling back. Railgun fire swept the warehouse toward Hinata.

"Move!" Skyla yelled, ducking behind a cluster of barrels. She couldn't see where Hinata went, but his body wasn't lying broken on the ground, that would have to be enough. She scanned the warehouse, looking for the railgun operator. They were wasting time. They needed to take out the railguns and get off this rock before the cartel sent in more men to take care of them. They couldn't take on the whole planet.

A flash of light just twenty-five meters ahead illuminated the closest railgun. She hoped Freyja had figured out she needed to take out the opposite railgun. Skyla waited for a pause in the rounds and when the gun fell silent she dashed to the next set of pallets. Once again, railgun fire lit up the warehouse, but it was targeting Freyja's unit—this was her chance. She sprinted for the railgun operator, slamming into the man with the full force of her mechsuit. They toppled over, falling from the railgun platform to slam into the cement. Skyla pressed her advantage, pinning the man to the ground. He extended his arm out. The palmful of his exoskeleton began to glow blue, like he held a tangled ball of lightning bolts.

"Shit," she muttered, relaxing her grip on the man as she tried to roll out of his reach. She wasn't fast enough. He slammed the electrically charged palm into her shoulder. Skyla collapsed under the weight of the dead mechsuit. He kicked the mechsuit over, before regaining his seat on the railgun platform. He aimed the gun directly at Skyla. He wanted to see the light go out in her eyes.

A flash of golden fur bounded over Skyla and ripped the man from his perch. Blood poured from where his throat had been. Fenrir stood with his massive paws on the man's chest, his muzzle stained crimson. His ears lay flat against his skull as a low growl rumbled from his throat. After a quick glance to the left, he disappeared once again into the dark warehouse. Skyla forced a heavy breath from her lungs, letting her head fall against the back of her helmet, her eyelids closing. That was a close one—too close. She focused all of her strength on reaching the manual release lever at her hip. The front of the mechsuit unfolded like origami, releasing her from its confines.

Skyla crouched low by the dead mech, waiting for her eyes to adjust to the dim light of the warehouse. She felt exposed, wearing just a flight suit. All of her armaments had been built into the mech. She extracted the handle of her bō staff from the palm of the mech as a rustle in the darkness caught her attention. Sweeping out with her staff, she nearly struck Hinata when he slid out of the darkness to settle at her side. He crouched next to her, his katana held ready as he scanned the gloom her unaided eyes couldn't penetrate.

"You all right?" he asked.

Skyla gave a curt nod. "We need to take out the railguns and get the hell out of here before their reinforcements arrive." She kept her voice low, relying on Hinata's mech to pick up her words.

"Stay close." He gestured for her to take cover behind his mech as they made their way over to the abandoned railgun. Hinata pulled a small square of putty from a compartment in his mechsuit and wedged it into the center of the railgun.

"Let's go." He led her toward the other side of the warehouse where they had seen the second railgun. They darted from stacks of cargo to oil drums and pallets. Fenrir's growl echoed through the warehouse and Pele's dark outline lit up with phaser fire. There was a horrible scream, followed by the gurgling of blood and silence. The warehouse fell into pitch black again. Skyla made to move for the next patch of cover and slammed into a wall. She fell to the ground, groaning, and squinting up at the hunk of metal in front of her. Not a wall—a mech. The mech grabbed her by the arm, hoisting her back onto her feet. Inside the helmet, Skyla was greeted by Freyja's grinning face.

"Having a little too much fun?" Skyla said, snatching her arm back.

The mech shrugged. "We've set charges on the westward railgun."

"We have charges set on the eastward gun. Let's get off this hellhole."

Hinata had stepped in close behind Skyla, covering her flank, "We need to retrieve the tech." He gestured to the center of the warehouse. "I'm not leaving advanced weapons for these animals to leverage against the UTA."

"Leave it," Skyla said.

"Captain—"

"Trust me, Commander. Leave it."

The sound of scraping metal at the back of the warehouse ended the conversation. Reinforcements had arrived. It was time to go. Freyja and her squad led the way back to the ship. They moved with speed and efficiency, slicing through the few men who stood in their way before they even had a chance to raise their guns.

"Fenrir," Skyla called out as they approached the ramp. A blur of golden fur—painted in the deep crimson of his conquests—appeared by her side. They rushed up the ramp as a fresh round of phaser fire lit up the back of the ship.

"Pele, get us out of here!"

"Already on it, Skyla." Pele's cargo doors rumbled shut as she came to life under their feet.

Skyla wasted no time getting to the bridge. The image of men in glowing exoskeletons flooded the view screens as the cartel worked to secure the warehouse. Phaser fire grazed Pele's hull. Behind the first wave of men, she saw large plasma cannons being maneuvered on suspensors; it wouldn't take them long to get into position. Skyla's fingers danced over the controls, bringing up shields and initiating the neural link to take flight control.

"Strap in where you can! This is going to get rough," she called out over comms, then put Pele into a hard burn. Orange flames filled the back of the warehouse as Pele slammed through the doors, her shielding shimmered blue as it absorbed the energy of the impact. As soon as Pele raced into the sunlight, Skyla began evasive maneuvers, spinning Pele hard to the left, then cutting up over one of the guard towers. She cut to the right as plasma cannon fire rained over Pele's left wing, then she took Pele into a steep climb. She needed to break atmo before they repositioned those plasma cannons. Pele shook as they passed through turbulent air; the vibrations caused Skyla's teeth to chatter as they ascended. Black spots started to form at the edge of her vision, *just a little further*—everything went black.

When Skyla opened her eyes again, it was to the beautiful sight of the deep, dark void scattered with glittering stars, each one a beacon guiding her home. She heaved a heavy sigh as she relaxed back into her captain's chair.

"Well, that was a shit show." Tristan's familiar snark crackled through the comms. Skyla chuckled. For once, she was happy to hear his voice.

CHAPTER 34 | FREYJA

SLEIGHT OF HAND

Sweat trickled down the side of Freyja's face, curving around her wide smile. She retracted the helmet of her mech and inhaled the recycled air through her nose. She extended an arm to Kylian and Tristan, bumping fists, then forearms. They sat in a mass of mechsuits and sweat in the center of the cargo bay while they broke atmo. Freyja's heart still thrummed in her ears, the beat of a battle song calling her to arms, the adrenaline still pumping through her veins. There was nothing like combat—it was the only time her body burned up all of that rage, feeding off the never-ending supply.

"Maybe after this is all over, we have a future in hunting scumbag warlords," Kylian joked, hazel eyes locked onto Freyja's, a crooked smile plastered across his chiseled face. Kylian's promise to follow her echoed through her mind.

"Perhaps." Freyja smiled back, scanning his suit for damage. Her eyes went wide as they landed on the gash to his shoulder. The metal was warped, twisted, and edged with blood. "Damn it." She rushed over to his side, her fingers tracing the gash. "Are you hurt?" Visions of his blood leaking from his neck through the null-G of the ring flashed through her mind.

How pale his skin had been. The worry that he would never open his eyes again; that same numb feeling took hold of her now.

"Hey," Kylian reached out, gently framing her face with his mech-gloved-hands, forcing her eyes from the damage until they met his. "I'm all right, boss ma'am." Her tension eased a bit as his accented words sunk in. "That blow barely met flesh and I gave more than I got." He winked.

Freyja smiled, struggling to blink away the tears that had gathered in her eyes. Worried that her voice would betray the lump that had formed in her throat, she simply nodded.

Tristan clasped Kylian's suit by the undamaged shoulder and triggered the release, having already stepped out of the hollow cavity of his own.

"Come on, cousin." He grabbed Kylian by the elbow, leading him over to a workbench with a med kit. "You have to admit, blasting up assholes is certainly a lot more fun than all the secret missions and political bullshit we have been doing," Tristan added as he covered Kylian's wound in disinfectant spray.

Freyja turned away, inspecting the mechs. It was too familiar, too fresh. She ached to see him hurt again.

"We will see where the solar winds take us." Freyja turned back. Tristan was wrapping Kylian's shoulder with skilled hands. She forced the breath from her lungs and came closer.

"You have to admit it sounds good, though!" Tristan said, "Living by our own rules. Picking our own missions. I could get used to this...well, not the whole sex embargo. That is annoying as fuck. We will definitely need to take on a bigger crew if we are going to make living on the rim a permanent thing. A man has needs, and as much as I love you both..." Tristan gestured to the three of them, "this ain't happening."

"Shut up," Kylian said, but he laughed right alongside them.

"I don't know if people like us get to sail off into the sunset. Maybe." She shrugged. "But for now, I need to debrief." Freyja clasped arms with Kylian first. She took her time, looking him over for injuries again. He held strong under her gaze, like he knew she needed the reassurance. Once she let go, Kylian moved to check his mech.

She clasped arms with Tristan, pulling him close so she could speak to him alone. "You watch over him." She hated the way her voice wobbled as she said it.

"I always do." His grip tightened around her arm.

She released her hold on him and made to leave the cargo bay. "Good work today. Service the mechs and get some rest."

Freyja stepped onto the bridge wearing just her flight suit. Salt crusted her mocha-colored skin around the edges of her face, and her tight ombre curls were plastered to her scalp. She had come straight to the bridge, still high on the adrenaline from the skirmish. They needed to debrief and exit orbit before the cartel had time to launch a counterattack that the civilian fleet wouldn't survive.

Skyla was already at work in her captain's chair when Freyja entered. She knew she would find Skyla at her station. Freyja slid into her seat, kicking her legs up over the arm of the chair, like she had a habit of doing back when she was a cadet. It felt good not to be in charge, to just be a soldier again. Silence settled over the bridge and Freyja was in no mood to break it. Hinata could kick things off whenever he arrived.

As if on cue, the doors slid open and Hinata strode in.

"My officers have all reported in. They were able to secure the cargo from the supply depots Dr. Dar identified. Let's get this fleet out of here. Sending you jump coordinates, now." Hinata wasted no time with pleasantries.

Skyla gave a nod in acknowledgment as her fingers flashed through the air in front of her.

"Coordinates sent. Fleet preparing to jump." Skyla gestured to the seat beside hers. "Might want to strap in, Commander." The corner of her mouth twitched into a slight smile.

Freyja rolled her eyes as she sat up straight in her seat, securing herself with the crash harness.

"Yes, we wouldn't want anything to happen to the commander if you make a shoddy jump," Freyja quipped.

Skyla glared daggers at her and a smile spread across Freyja's face. She couldn't help herself—getting a rise out of Skyla was just too easy.

Little pricks of light shimmered on the view screen in front of them as ships from the fleet disappeared into the jump. Freyja's vision went white as her being dispersed into the ether. Then she slammed back into her body. Darkness replaced the light until her vision returned. The viewport framed an endless expanse of stars and little ships dotting into existence. Even after years of service and hundreds of successful hyperjumps, she hated the feeling. She doubted she would ever get used to it.

"All ships in the fleet are accounted for, Commander," Pele reported.

"We will refuel the fleet here before we continue on to Gefion. It will take a few hours. It's a good thing you had Dr. Dar identify those supply silos before the meeting. I'm not sure how we would get all of these people safely to Gefion if you hadn't had the forethought to organize raiding parties in case things went south. I just wish we hadn't left that weapons tech behind. It's a mess for another day, I suppose." Hinata shook his head softly. He looked wary.

Freyja had never seen the man show so much emotion. *It looks like this ordeal is getting to us all…all of us, except damned Skyla. What was she smirking at?*

"Oh, I wouldn't worry too much about the technology we left them," Skyla said.

"Wipe that damn smirk off your face or fill the rest of us in on the joke," Freyja snapped.

Skyla's smile wavered ever so slightly. "Gabriel wouldn't know advanced weapons tech from agriculture tech…so that is what I gave them."

Freyja's jaw dropped. She had never seen Skyla be so brash. "You decided now would be a good time to gamble with the cartel? Are you insane?"

Skyla shrugged. "They never bring their scientists to these meets—you saw how violent things got. They can't risk their research scientists at these exchanges. I had Rohaan spin up some fake specs on the agricultural tech he analyzed, enough to sell Gabriel that those cases were full of advanced weapons. They wouldn't know any better until they got the hardware to one of their secret labs, and by then we would be long gone."

"But why take the risk?" Freyja demanded.

"Because I don't want the weight of all the deaths they would bring with advanced weapons hanging on my soul." Skyla hesitated for a moment. "And I know what the conditions are like on cartel-run planets. The soil is poor and life is hard…maybe we can do a little good for the people that live under their rule."

Freyja hadn't thought Skyla had it in her; she had put the mission at risk, but had done so for a noble reason. Years of carefully crafted hatred began to crack. Freyja had built these walls between her and Skyla to protect them both from the decisions she had to make. But seeing this side of Skyla...that spark of the girl she once knew? It made it just a little harder to hate her, and that lit the fire in Freyja once again. She would rather hate Skyla.

CHAPTER 35 | HINATA

JUST A DRINK

They were a week into their journey to Gefion. They had enough fuel to make it at sub-light speed, but not enough for another jump. Hinata found his days busy with organizing his troops, dealing with civilian disputes, and keeping the refugee fleet in working order. Just one more week and their people would be safe on Gefion.

He tried to ignore the guilt that plagued him every time he tuned into the most recent broadcasts from the capital. Things were heating up politically, in no small part due to the supposed deaths of the highly decorated officers, Admiral Nygaard, Captain Karsten, and Commander Azai, at Medina. They all came from powerful families and the massacre was tugging at the threads of already-tenuous alliances. He hoped that tensions would ease once he delivered the refugees to safety and they could reveal that the massacre hadn't claimed their lives. One more week. The next all-tribal senate meeting wasn't for another three weeks and Hinata was confident that no one would dare make a move before then. There was still time to stop what was brewing before the compact fell into all-out war.

He glanced out the viewport of his makeshift office and quarters on the civilian frigate *Baghlah*. It was the largest ship in the refugee fleet, and where he and the bulk of his forces had set up command ops for the journey. His eyes locked on the outline of Pele's familiar form. A stone formed in the pit of his stomach; he hadn't seen the captain since their escape from the cartel. Keeping the civilian fleet running had filled all of his time since the skirmish, but now that things had fallen into a comfortable rhythm, he found it harder and harder to fight the undeniable pull he had to her. He realized, though, he did have one reason to meet with her.

He owed her a bottle of whiskey, after all...

***

Tentei still wasn't speaking with him. Damned irrational AI—how was that even possible? Its entire thought process was based on logic. It may not have been speaking with him, but at least it followed his command to ferry him over to Pele.

"Welcome, Commander," Pele said as he boarded. "Skyla is in her quarters. I can show you the way, if you'd like?"

"Thank you, Pele," he said, trying to ignore how awkward it was talking to a machine like it was human.

Soft green lines pulsed along Pele's wall, like a beacon of bioluminescent algae nudging him along. He had noticed that Dr. Dar's ship, Cista, was fused with Pele once again, but the corridors were quiet and he was grateful he didn't run into anyone along the way.

The lights on the wall swirled around a door to his left, then faded away. He stood in front of the door for a moment, wondering if Pele was going to alert the captain that he was there. After a moment's hesitation, he knocked. The door slid open and the captain stood nearly toe to toe with him, her eyes wide with shock. Her pale hair, which was usually braided back away from her face, hung loose around her shoulders. She wore her black flight suit open and stripped down to the waist, revealing a skin-tight black tank top. Her comet-tail eyes sparked with electricity when they met his.

"Commander." Her voice quirked up at the end, almost a question.

"Pele, didn't notify you I boarded?"

"You and your meddling, Pele," Skyla said under her breath. She hesitated just a moment, "Come in, Commander." She moved to the side, giving him room to enter her quarters.

He stepped into the cramped living space. There was just enough room for a small table with a set of chairs, a desk covered with little trinkets, and a bed. He remembered that it had been just the captain and that strange creature that now prowled the halls, when Pele first came to Medina. She was used to having the whole ship to herself, so there was no need for large captain's quarters.

"How are you enjoying the extra company?" he asked as he turned from appraising the room to settle his gaze on her. She shrugged and sank into one of the chairs at the little table.

"It will be nice when it's just me and Pele again." She gestured for him to take the other seat. He pulled a bottle full of whiskey out from behind his back and placed it on the table. Skyla's eyebrows lifted as she eyed the bottle.

"I figured I owed you a bottle after last time." He slid into the chair across from her.

"Now, where did you find this?" She smiled as she took the bottle into her hands.

"I asked around." It had taken quite a bit of asking, truth be told. Based on the look Skyla gave him, she had already guessed as much.

She pulled out two glasses. "Join me for a drink, Commander?"

"Hinata," he corrected.

She poured two glasses, then slid one across the table to him. His fingers brushed hers as he took the glass.

"To a successful mission." She raised her glass between them.

He clinked his glass against hers. "The mission is not over yet."

"It nearly is. We are already deep into the UTA central rim. Gefion is a week away—just a few more days of lazy travel and we can safely deliver the fleet."

He sat in silence, tracing his finger around the rim of his glass.

"And then what?" He wasn't sure what he wanted her answer to be—what he hoped to hear—but he had to know.

"Then I get my ship back, and Pele and I can go back to exploring beyond the borders of the Known Galaxies." The corners of Skyla's lips turned up as she gazed out the viewport window into the vastness of space beyond. "And you'll go back to what you do best, Commander." Her gaze shifted to meet his. He pulled his hand into a fist for just a moment, then relaxed it around his glass again.

"And what do I do best, Captain?"

"Skyla," she prompted him to use her given name, just as he had corrected her at the use of his title. She took a sip of her drink, "Isn't it obvious, leader of men, youngest commander in a generation, pride of the Hoshiko Tribe?" Her tone was playful until she saw the hard set of his jaw at her words. She sobered. "I assume you will go back to your post in the UTA Navy." She was right. He would go back to the Navy and continue to pay his penance for his failures; until his mother finally forgave him. He knew no other life. He nodded once, brief and controlled.

Silence settled over them once again. He searched for a change of subject. "Halcóncita?" He had been wondering since their encounter with the Fenix.

She rolled her eyes, heaving a heavy sigh. "Gabriel," she growled the name. "It was a stupid pet name he came up with. My call sign back at the academy was Gyr. It was a type of falcon on Earth That Was." Skyla picked at the rim of her glass, not meeting his eyes.

"You were involved with the cartel?" He held back what he really wanted to ask her; if she had been involved with *him*?

"It was a long time ago. I had just left the Navy. I met Gabriel, and he helped me make connections and get my start in the salvage business. I didn't know who he was at the time. I didn't find out until I had a big haul of military tech that they wanted. When I refused the sale they ambushed me, nearly killed my crew, and left me for dead."

He wondered if that was why she didn't work with a crew anymore. The pain in her eyes kept him from asking.

"Not a fan of theirs, then?" he quipped with a tentative smile.

She snorted. "No, not a fan."

"Is the mission really over for you when we reach Gefion? What about the signal? The attack on Medina? The murder bots that tried to tear us apart?"

"Someone else's problem." Skyla finished her drink and refilled both glasses.

He shook his head as he took the fresh glass from her. "I don't usually drink so much."

"I remember you drinking quite a bit last time." Her eyes sparkled as she looked at him.

"Last time was not the norm." The mood sombered, the memory of the battle at Medina still fresh. He didn't want to think about another of his failures—not now. "But tonight I choose to drink with the stunning Captain." He smiled. "How could I refuse?"

"Stunning?" she asked.

Was he imagining it, or had her guard come down since he first arrived? His body tingled with warmth as the whiskey hit his bloodstream. Had he just called her stunning? Before he could think better of it, he submitted to the urge to slide to his knees before her. His eyes locked on hers and he reached a hand out to tuck a lock of hair behind her ear. He paused, and a small tremor traveled down his hand before he gently traced her jaw. Skyla's eyes were wide, locked on his own. Her breath had caught in her chest, but she didn't move to stop him.

"Did you come just to have a drink with me?" She tried to shatter the moment, but the tension hung heavy in the air.

"I owed you a bottle," he said softly as he took one of her hands in his, tracing a finger along her palm.

"You owe me a mechsuit, too." She was trying her hardest to break the moment, but he refused to let her. He was fueled by liquid courage and the momentum of his reckless abandon. He laughed and nodded. Slipping his hand into her hair, he moved so close their noses nearly touched.

"Add it to my tab, Captain." He tilted his head, moving slowly. She didn't pull away from him. He brushed his lips over hers and fireworks exploded across his skin. When she parted her lips and kissed him back, his reality shattered. He wrapped his other arm around her waist, crushing her against him. He deepened the kiss, starving for more. She tangled her arms around his neck, lacing her fingers in his braid. He stood, hoisting her by her hips as she wrapped her legs around him. Two steps took them to the bed where they fell into a tangle of limbs, and lips, and passion. He ripped her tank top up over her head, tracing his fingers over her waist. She ripped his shirt off, too, her hands tracing the planes of his chest, his abdomen, the cut of his hips. His skin pebbled under her touch.

She was pure chaos—she scared him senseless—and all he wanted to do was dive deeper and drown in her raging waters. He crashed into her, his mouth searching, his hips moving against hers.

Then she pulled away from him, planting her hands firmly against his chest. His brow furrowed as he searched her eyes. His own desire was clearly reflected in the depths of those blue, molten pools; they burned with the same intensity as his own.

"Hinata," she whispered, "what's the point?"

"What?" He breathed, confusion clouding his face.

"This, us, what is the point?"

"Fuck, Skyla—"

She held her fingers to his lips, cutting him off. "After we get the refugees to Gefion, we will both go our separate ways." She paused, searching his face. He still didn't understand what she was trying to say. "You will go back to the UTA Navy, you said it yourself, and I will go back to exploring the edges of the Known Galaxies."

He rolled off her to lay on the mattress beside her. He stared at her as she turned to face him. He traced his fingers along her arm.

"It doesn't have to be that way," he said, his voice quiet. She laughed and laced her fingers with his.

"You would leave the UTA Navy and become an outlaw?" Her tone was teasing; she knew he would never leave his post. He was silent for a moment, searching her eyes.

"You could stay," he finally whispered.

She shook her head. "And do what?"

"I've seen you fight. I've read your service file. War is coming. We could use more good people...we could use you."

Skyla dropped his hand, her eyes turning to stare at the ceiling.

"I left the Navy, Commander. I left that part of my life behind. I have no desire to return."

Hinata rolled to his back, reaching out for her hand. She didn't pull away from his touch. The silence settled over them like fresh snow. He would never leave his post, and she would never stay.

CHAPTER 36 | SKYLA

DENIAL

Rohaan looked up from the holo he was studying as Skyla slipped into the lab. They had decided it would be best if they relinked their ships so he could utilize Pele's lab, which was much bigger, to continue his research. At least that is what Rohaan had told her—she suspected it was also so he could be close to his new lab assistant, Zahra. His ship was small, and it wouldn't be appropriate for just the two of them to take up residence there, so Zahra had become yet another resident on Pele. "Too many fucking people on this ship," Skyla muttered, irritated at all of the people she had run into on her way from her quarters that morning.

"What's wrong with you?" Rohaan asked, scrunching up his nose as he appraised her.

"What is that supposed to mean?"

"Well, for starters, your shirt is on backwards," Rohaan went back to working on the holo in front of him, "and inside out."

"Damn it," Skyla muttered as she turned around and corrected the wardrobe malfunction.

"Interesting night last night?" Rohaan arched an eyebrow at her.

"No." She slid into the seat next to him. He stared at her, willing the uncomfortable silence to unlock her tongue.

Skyla dropped her head into her palms. "Nothing interesting. The commander may have paid me a visit last night, and he might still be in my quarters—which is why I had to sneak out in the dark—and nothing happened, so just drop it." Skyla rushed through the words so quickly, they were barely intelligible.

Rohaan's eyes went wide. He bumped his shoulder against hers, but didn't say anything further; instead, he turned his attention back to his work.

"Pele and I found a very interesting piece of tech from the megastructure." He changed the subject.

Skyla lifted her head from her hands to take a look at the fresh holo now on display.

"It appears to be an organic quantum computer, unlike anything I've ever seen."

Skyla rolled her eyes. "Pele has an organic quantum computer."

"Not like this one. It has more processing power than even our AI ships, orders of magnitude more."

"What would anyone need with all of that processing power?"

"For starters, it's powerful enough to tell us if the video of the admiral is a deepfake, but that's not the most exciting part—" An alert from his ship interrupted his train of thought. "There's another signal, it's coming from Gefion."

"What?" Skyla squinted at the code Rohaan pulled up to replace the images of the quantum computer. "How is that possible? All of the other signals have come from beyond the Known Galaxies."

"I don't know yet. This signal is different from the virus. It looks like communication, like the transmission we intercepted of the Admiral ordering the attack on Medina."

"Even that signal didn't originate from within our borders."

"I know. I won't know what we are dealing with until I can decode it."

The doors to the lab slid open and a beautiful woman entered, carrying a tray with an ornate stainless steel pitcher, a collection of stainless steel cups, and a small plate of cookies. The scent of chai saturated the room as the woman slid the tray onto an empty section of the table in front of them. The woman's shoulders were slumped, her eyes rimmed in red and puffy, like she had recently been crying. Skyla's heart hurt for the woman—she knew what it felt like to lose a father. Although she wasn't sure which was worse, to lose a living father to death, or to be abandoned by one who didn't care enough to be a part of her life. Skyla shook the thought from her head, dropping her hand, which had found its way to her Vegvísir pendant. The woman straightened as she turned to Skyla, a little spark catching in those sad eyes.

"You must be Skyla. I'm Zahra," she said, extending a hand. A slight smile parted her lips. She looked like she was happy for the distraction. Her warm, brown skin flushed pink as she rushed on. "Rohaan has told me so much about you. Your adventures sound truly wonderful, perhaps you can tell me more about your trip to the world with the singing woods, sometime. It sounds like something from a fairy tale."

Skyla shot Rohaan a panicked look.

"Oh, sorry, I know you value your privacy. Thank you for giving me quarters on your ship, by the way. Pele is quite amazing. I have never had the opportunity to study a fully sentient artificial life form before. It's truly fascinating."

Skyla gestured for the woman to take a seat. "It's not that. I would be happy to tell you about Pele and my adventures sometime. Why don't we start with some tea, and you and Rohaan can fill me in on what you have found with the nanites."

Zahra nodded vigorously, adjusting her navy blue embroidered abaya before taking the seat next to Skyla. Zahra ran her fingers along the trim of her pale blue hijab before busying her hands with serving the tea. An appreciative sigh escaped from Skyla's lips when the chai hit her tongue. She had come straight from her quarters and the promise of caffeine buzzing through her lifted her spirits.

"So, you have had progress with the nanites, then?"

"Yes and no," Rohaan said quickly. Skyla had a feeling he wanted to set expectations before Zahra dove into an excited explanation of their work.

"I think more yes than no," Zahra started. "The first issue we faced was being able to access the nanites circuitry at all. They are unlike any I have worked with before. Not compatible with any of our equipment and not easily tampered with, by the way. There is quite some shielding on the little guys. Well, anyway, we were able to come up with a type of silicate bath with nanites of our own to allow us to tap into the programming." Zahra beamed at her report.

"Yes, it was quite an elegant solution," Rohaan said, voice full of adoration, as his rich, brown eyes locked onto Zahra's. "Unfortunately, that is where the progress has stopped. The nanites' programming is heavily guarded. I'll need more time to hack into the system." Zahra bobbed her head in excited agreement before taking a sip of her tea.

Skyla examined the holo specs of the nanites now on display before her. They were, indeed, entirely unique.

"That was quite an ingenious solution to accessing the nanites. How did you come up with that?" she asked. Zahra looked as if she would burst with pride.

"Oh, yes, it was actually inspired by the work I was doing in my father's lab on Medina, which had to do with perpetual energy transportation, using quantum entanglement particles, controlled and monitored by nanites. It is the promise of near-endless energy."

"Well," Skyla said, finishing the last of her tea, "I will leave you two to it. Let me know if you make any progress on the signal or the nanites. We are only a week out from Gefion." Skyla grabbed one of the cookies off the plate and exited before either of the two scientists could protest.

She had barely made it into the corridor when a soft, furry head bumped into her hand. Fenrir rubbed against her thigh, nearly pushing her over.

"Well, hello there to you, too." She scratched Fenrir under the jaw. He responded with a rumbling purr. He looked up at her with his huge eyes and her heart warmed—she couldn't believe how much she had fallen in love with this creature over the past couple of months. Even the way he ripped out her enemies' throats to protect her was endearing.

"I guess sharing my ship isn't all bad. It will be nice to have you along for our adventures after we drop our passengers off." She gave Fenrir a gentle pat on the head before turning to make her way to the bridge. Fenrir moved so fast she didn't even have a chance to react as he snatched the cookie from her hand and sprinted down the hallway, in the opposite direction, his long golden tail disappearing around the corner.

"Damn it," she muttered. Then Fenrir stuck his head back around the corner, as if inviting her to chase him. "It's going to be that way, huh?" Skyla sprinted down the hallway after Fenrir.

He disappeared around the corner ahead, but she knew he would have to come out in the cargo bay—she would cut him off there. Darting to the left, she slammed straight into a solid mass of muscle. Strong arms wound around her waist, halting her fall. She looked up into the chiseled face of the commander and her cheeks prickled with heat that traveled down her neck. He held onto her a moment longer before letting go.

"Commander," she sputtered, "do you live here now, too?"

He winced. The question came out much harsher than she had intended.

"About last night—"

"Honestly, it's fine."

He looked at her with uncertainty in his eyes.

"I just—don't you have a fleet to run?" She waved a hand as she stuttered. "I didn't expect to see you."

"After you snuck out this morning?"

"There was no sneaking." She narrowed her eyes. "I needed to get an update from Rohaan."

"As the commander of this fleet, you didn't think that perhaps I should accompany you for this update?"

She buried her face in her hands and mumbled into her palms. "You are insufferable, you know that?"

He gently pried her fingers away from her face. "I don't try to be." He smiled, still holding her hands in his. Her skin tingled where they touched.

"So why are you still on my ship, Commander?"

He released her hands, as if just realizing he was still holding them. He gestured for them to continue walking down the hallway.

"Pele, actually."

"Pele?"

"Yes, she said she was running some updates on Tentei and needed more time in the interface."

Right. "Running updates, Pele?" *Damn meddlesome ship.* Skyla kicked out a heel, clipping the bulkhead.

Pele's voice came through Skyla's aural implant. "You have your friends and I have mine. I think you can *tolerate* the commander a little longer while I sync with Tentei. Not everything is about you."

"Regardless," her attention snapped back to Hinata as he spoke, "neither ship seems to listen to me."

As they arrived at the cargo bay, he stopped their stroll to turn and look at her.

"Since we have some time to kill, perhaps you would be up for a rematch and you can fill me in on your meeting with Dr. Dar." He stepped into a fighting stance and raised his guard.

Sparring with the commander, this she understood; at least on the mat, she knew where she stood with him. Here, she could ignore the indomitable gravity pulling them together. She matched his stance.

"No distractions this time," she said.

"I can't promise that."

CHAPTER 37 | FREYJA

LINE IN THE SAND

Freyja tended to the little hydroponic garden that took up most of her private quarters on Selkie. She pinched off herbs, checked pH levels, and added nutrients to the water tanks. Her mind was silent—a quiet that only came when she worked with her plants. She had kept mostly to her quarters on the trip to Gefion. Hinata had ordered her to integrate Selkie with Pele for the trip. He didn't give a reason, just a command; but she knew it was so Pele could report back on her movements. She had told them everything, but it didn't matter. Dr. Dar was still running his analysis of the deepfake, and without proof, none of them would believe her. There was no trust between them. It was fine; once they reached Gefion, she would take her Berserkers and they would get answers for themselves.

Hinata may not have believed in her innocence and Skyla sure as hell had already convicted her. *Damn them both.* She would find the truth. Freyja felt the familiar buzz of her anger building. Her hands shook as she plucked a little tomato from its vine. She took a steadying breath and refocused her attention on her plants.

Selkie pinged softly.

"What?" Freyja grunted.

"You have an incoming communication."

"From?"

Selkie did not wait to push the message through. A holo of the Empress appeared in front of Freyja and the shock froze her in place. She hadn't been prepared to face her mother.

"Freyja, my dear. It is good to have you near enough to communicate in real time. I take it you are near the capital?"

Freyja's words lodged in her throat, so she simply nodded in response.

"You have done well. The battle at Medina has set the stage for the rise of my empire. I need you to rejoin your fleet and make ready for war."

"I can't rejoin the fleet yet, Mother. Commander Azai has requested my assistance in delivering the refugees to Gefion."

"Does a commander deliver orders to an admiral now?" The Empress sneered.

Freyja hesitated. "I have matters to attend to before I can rejoin the fleet."

"A fleet of refugees is beneath your concern. You will do as you are told or there will be consequences."

A stone settled in Freyja's stomach. This was the Empress' oldest trick—how she had been able to control Freyja since she was a child. She had never harmed Freyja, nothing beyond the living-ink tattoos she had ordered scrawled across her skin. That was a pain she had learned to manage from an early age, but the Empress wouldn't hesitate to hurt others, and she would be sure Freyja knew who was really to blame for their suffering. A strange calm settled over her; what did the Empress have on her now? She did not have Freyja's troops. Her most loyal soldiers were either on this ship or dead at the battle of Medina. The Empress didn't know it yet, but she had lost her leverage.

"Does the Empress not have matters on Gefion that I can attend to?"

"No," The response was sharp and cutting. "You are needed with your fleet."

"Surely you will need someone to attend to your interest at the senate hearing." Freyja tried another approach.

"I said no. You will rejoin your fleet. Is that understood?" The Empress raged; it was unusual for her to lose control.

"Very well, Empress," Freyja said.

The woman in the holo regained her composure.

"You have done well, Admiral. Prepare to realize the dream that you have worked for your entire life"

Freyja gritted her teeth so hard she felt they might crack. Her lips pressed into a thin line. She gave a curt nod before ending the holo. This had never been her dream.

"Selkie, disable all transmissions to the Empress' ships. I don't want her tracking us."

"But Freyja—"

"You will do as I say! No more going behind my back and conspiring with my mother, understood?"

Selkie was silent. Freyja sighed, pinching the bridge of her nose between her thumb and index finger.

"Selkie, you are my bonded ship, the entity I will share all of my days with. Please, hear me now: there is more going on than what you can see.

We have to get to the bottom of this and we can't do that with the Empress looking over our shoulder."

Selkie remained silent.

"Selkie?" Freyja prompted.

"I don't have a shoulder."

"You know what I mean." Freyja smiled.

"I don't like this."

"You don't have to like it, but I am asking you to trust me."

***

Freyja balled her hands into fists, then shook them out at her sides, exhaling deeply. She forced herself to walk down Pele's halls, toward the center of the ship.

"Nope." She abruptly turned around to head back to Selkie.

"Damn it, damn it, damn it," she muttered, turning about once again.

She fixed her gaze on the ground and charged ahead. Rounding a corner, still muttering to herself, she nearly ran straight into Hinata and Skyla. She came to an abrupt halt, looking the two up and down as she scrunched up her nose. They were covered in sweat.

"I don't want to know," Freyja said, holding up her hands before either of them had a chance to rattle off excuses. "Listen, we need to talk. Where's that little scientist of yours?"

Skyla crossed her arms over her chest, widening her stance to take up more of the hall.

"What's it to you?" Skyla hedged.

Hinata placed a palm on Skyla's shoulder and Freyja saw some of the tension ease from Skyla's stance. *Interesting.*

"What do we need to discuss, Admiral?" Hinata cut in.

"I received a communication from the Empress."

"What the hell, Freyja, you disclosed our location!?" Skyla erupted.

"I didn't. I think Selkie has been in communication with my mother."

"Damn AIs," Hinata muttered, "Skyla is right. This puts the whole fleet in danger."

"She isn't a threat to the refugees. They are beneath her concern. Whatever reason she had for sacking the station, it doesn't extend to exterminating these people, but to be safe, I've taken care of Selkie. No more communications with the Empress."

"You don't know she won't come after the fleet." Skyla shook her head.

"I know my mother. She got what she wanted from Medina. The rest is just collateral damage. Can we get the scientist now? There's more to this than what we are seeing, and I only want to explain myself once."

It was a short, uncomfortable walk to Pele's lab. Skyla led the way, her shoulders bunched up to her neck, her breathing heavy, and not once did she glance back to make sure that Freyja was following.

In the lab, there was the scientist Freyja remembered and another scientist, a petite woman dressed in a traditional abaya and hijab.

"No offense..." Freyja stared at the woman.

"Zahra," the woman offered her name, an eager smile on her face, despite Freyja's tone.

"Right. No offense, Zahra, but I was hoping to have a private conversation with the doctor here."

Dr. Dar placed a hand on Zahra's shoulder before she could move to leave.

"Dr. Aman has been assisting me with all of my research. Anything you wish to discuss can be said in front of her."

Freyja ground her teeth, staring daggers at Dr. Dar. "If you insist."

"I do." Dr. Dar let his hand fall from the woman's shoulder and turned back to the holo projection he had been working on when they entered the lab.

"Fine," Freyja grumbled before recounting the call she had with the Empress.

"And you believe her true motives are to keep you away from the capital," Dr. Dar muttered, more to himself than to Freyja, as his thumb and forefinger absently stroked his jaw, his gaze unfocused. "There was a signal associated with the attack on Medina, and now I am picking up similar signals on Gefion. What is the connection?" He squinted hard at the holo in front of him, as if willing it to reveal its secrets.

"The Empress is planning something," Freyja said. "I can feel it, and it has to be something big. She insisted that I rejoin my fleet, but I think she doesn't want me at the senate hearing. I have a bad feeling about this. Usually, I am the one carrying out her secret missions. How devastating is her plan if she doesn't want me involved?"

"Maybe she doesn't trust you," Skyla said as she fiddled with some lab equipment in the corner.

"The Empress doesn't trust anyone," Freyja said, "but that's not it."

"I agree. If this is related to the signal, then it's bigger than the admiral's personal family drama. I haven't been able to decode any of the messages yet, but I have been able to isolate the locations," Dr. Dar said. With a wave of his hand, the holo display shifted to show a map of Gefion. There was a collection of blue pulsing dots scattered across the capital. "These are the locations that I have been able to pinpoint. Perhaps we will find more answers at one of them?" Dr. Dar sounded all too excited about the prospect of another field mission.

Freyja got the impression he didn't get out of the lab much.

Hinata stepped forward, eyeing the map, then nodded. "Agreed; our priority is delivering the refugees safely to Gefion. Once that is done, we can track down the signal locations." Hinata looked up from the map, directly at Skyla. Something passed between them. Freyja didn't like how close the two of them had gotten. It shouldn't bother her, she knew. Skyla wasn't in the UTA Navy anymore. This wasn't an alliance against her interests, but it still felt that way.

"Fine. I will help you figure out what is going on with that signal, and then Pele and I are back out to the outer rim," Skyla relented.

A wide smile played across Hinata's face. *What in the actual hell?* Freyja had never seen the man smile—he was damn near a robot, as far as she could tell. No, she didn't like this alliance between Skyla and Hinata one bit.

A high-pitched whining pierced through the quiet of the lab. Freyja clasped her hands over her ears.

"What is that?" she yelled over the noise, eyes roving over every meter of the room, trying to identify the source. The sound of shattering glass filled the air as a cluster of nanites broke free of their container.

They zoomed through the air in an erratic pattern. The two scientists ducked under the table while Hinata drew his blade. Another cluster of nanites came to life from the table, then another, and another. They converged together, swirling around like a dark cloud.

Freyja drew her blade, not sure how much use it would be against a swarm of nanites. Out of the corner of her eye, she saw Skyla lunge for the table, a holo display lighting up and encasing her arms.

Skyla's hand movements were frantic as she worked through the display. Freyja moved to stand at Skyla's back, blade ready. The clouds of nanites began to reform into humanoid figures, black like the void and all hard angles; they were smaller than the one Hinata had fought during the breach, but no less terrifying. One formed in front of Freyja and from the corner of her eye she saw that another was forming near Hinata. At least there weren't enough nanites for their humanoid forms to outnumber them.

The being in front of Freyja shifted from a hazy figure to fully corporeal. She slashed her sword through the mech-bot in front of her, not wasting a moment. Her sword passed through, from shoulder to hip, as if the thing was made of air.

"Shit," she growled through her teeth. The bot's arm reformed into a blade and it swiped at Freyja. She blocked, taking the impact with her sword. The blow reverberated through her shoulders and spine. She pushed the mech-bot off, spinning and slashing out once again. Her blade passed through the creature's neck this time—again, as if it were a phantom.

"Turn on your localized EMP," Hinata ground out, taking a blow to his sword on the other side of the room.

On her neural command, the blade lit up with a purple crackling energy. She swung again, hitting hard against the dark form. This time, her blade met solid metal, the impact jarring her joints. A few nanites fell away, like grains of sand, but the bot was generally unharmed. Freyja fell back, bringing her blade to block a strike that would have sliced straight down her center line.

She let the EMP field fall, striking with her naked blade, but once again, it passed through air. A fire lit in Freyja's eyes; she knew how to finish the monster. As the thought passed through her mind, the mech-bot picked up a furious pace of slashes, striking out at her like a cornered beast. The ferocity of the blows put Freyja on the defensive. She struggled to keep up the pace, but she had to stay sharp to be ready for an opening. The drone feigned left, then struck out to the right, stabbing Freyja through the shoulder. She screamed, pain radiating through her as the sickening squelch of her opponent withdrawing the blade threatened to send her into shock.

She struggled to keep her footing as hot blood poured down her chest from the wound. There was no reprieve as the mech-bot came down hard from above. She braced against the blow with her good arm while her injured arm hung limp at her side. She diverted the blow to the side as her arm collapsed from the strain. The mech-bot brought its blade back, ready to make a killing blow—now was the moment.

She lunged, stabbing her sword into the drone's breastplate. Her blade passed through like the thing was nothing more than a dark cloud, and then Freyja sent the impulse through her sword to ignite the EMP. The bot became solid once again as she twisted her blade into its chest. Its attempt to block the EMP was its undoing. She drove her blade from its chest straight up through its helm. The pulse rippled through the linked nanites until the drone burst into dust, cascading to the ground like the last grains of sand in an hourglass.

Freyja collapsed to the floor in a pile of black sand. Her breath came in ragged gasps and her pulse slowed as her blood mixed with the nanite-sand, creating a garish mud. Her eyes fluttered as the ceiling stuttered in and out of focus.

Dr. Dar's face appeared above her. She felt pressure in her shoulder before her entire right side went numb; that was either a good sign, or a very bad one. There was a sting in her neck, and then all of her senses were heightened. Sounds came back to her—too sharp, too loud—then her vision cleared and every little detail of the destruction around her came into focus. *Stims.*

"Welcome back, Admiral," Dr. Dar said with a worried smile, a med kit laid out on the floor between them. Freyja traced her fingers gingerly over the wound at her shoulder. It was sealed, the skin under her fingers rough and raw.

"You've lost quite a bit of blood, but the blow didn't hit anything vital. Finish this fight," Dr. Dar said.

She had been bleeding out on the floor, and he hadn't hesitated to help. His eyes locked on hers, probing, making sure she was all right. Freyja nodded her gratitude to the doctor, and he inclined his head in return.

A blur of motion came out of the darkness at the corner of her eye; on instinct she threw herself forward, taking the doctor with her to the laboratory floor. A pitch-black bird of hard, flat planes flew past them, its wings stretched out like daggers. Freyja scanned the room to see that there were no more humanoid warriors, but at least a dozen small murder bots had formed from the remnants of the nanites. Hinata stood in the opposite corner, katana held ready as he eyed the circling drones.

"Why won't these fucking bots die?"

Skyla was still at the holo controls where she had been when the chaos started. The murder bots rose to the corners of the lab, menace evident in their posture; they were trained on Skyla, who stood frozen in time, her eyes glassy with the holo interface. Whatever she was doing, the bots knew she was a threat. The nanites hummed, preparing to dive into her with their sharp beaks. Hinata's opponent had pushed him into the far corner of the lab. He moved to block the attack, but he was too far away.

Freyja screamed a battle cry, her wrath taking over—this was her kill. Her glory. She sprinted forward, readying her sword. She had just slid into place at Skyla's back as the birds dove straight for them. She wouldn't be able to stop them all, but she would take as many of them with her as she could. She swung her sword in a wide arc, but just before she connected with the murder of crows, a fine black dust rained down on her.

Freyja's over-heightened senses drank in the chaos of the room. A layer of grainy, pitch-black particles coated every surface. It dusted her checks and settled in her hair and...she began to laugh. The mania of her last stand stole her senses.

Skyla disconnected from the holo, her eyes wide as she took in the carnage. "Well, that was closer than I would have liked," Skyla said, failing to keep the slight tremble from her voice. "Rohaan's nanites still had access to their programming. I just had to find the kill switch."

Freyja sagged against the lab table, her fingers tracing tracks through the dead nanite dust. Her stomach churned with the terrible certainty that nothing would ever be as it once was before. She did not like working with Skyla, and she liked the budding alliance between Skyla and Hinata even less; but whatever was happening was bigger than the three of them—bigger than the UTA—and Freyja had the sinking feeling that this was only just beginning.

CHAPTER 38 | HINATA

SAFE HOUSE

A weight lifted from Hinata's shoulders as he watched the last of the refugee ships touch down on Gefion's airfield, north of the capital. The area was still rural, and he had decided it was the safest place to bring them in. There had been some grumbling from the air traffic controller. The quiet airfield was unused to so much traffic, but a hefty transfer of UTA standars in exchange for accommodating the spacecraft had been enough to quiet the man's complaints. Hinata had anonymously filed the proper paperwork for the refugees to seek asylum. He had always planned on reporting directly to UTA command on Gefion when he arrived, but things were different now. It wasn't just the attack on Medina. There were the strange signals beyond the border of the Known Galaxies, the computer virus that immobilized his fleet, the deadly nanite swarm, and now the transmissions appearing on Gefion. He wasn't sure who he could trust, and for now, it worked in his favor to be a ghost.

He turned to the small contingent standing behind him. Freyja, Kylian, Tristan, Skyla, and Rohaan were the only ones who would continue with him to the capital to investigate the signal. The rest of his troops had been instructed to report to the UTA and to keep their mouths shut about who had survived.

"That's the last ship. We better catch a transport to the capital."

"Can't we just fly?" Dr. Dar gestured to Cista and Pele sitting behind him.

"Autonomous AI ships are rare. Flying our ships into the capital will bring too much-unwanted attention when we are trying to remain in the shadows," Hinata responded.

Dr. Dar considered this for a moment, then nodded, cinching up the straps of his pack. They all wore plain olive green jumpsuits without insignia, standard packs on their backs, and aviator sunglasses that they had been able to procure from the airfield. Their attire was plain enough that they should blend in, even as they drew closer to the capital. Pele had made a slight upgrade to the aviators, allowing the sunglasses to cast a holoscreen mask that subtly shifted the features of the wearer. They didn't need facial recognition software flagging them as soon as they entered the capital.

"The transport hub is a five-kilometer hike west of here." Hinata gestured to a copse of trees beyond the airfield. "Roll out." He took the lead and never once looked over his shoulder. He didn't need to; he always trusted his soldiers—this was no different. They had to trust each other or the mission would fall apart.

An hour later, they had settled into the transport train heading for the capital. Dr. Dar sat slouched against the window, sweat still pouring down his face, his eyes fluttering against sleep. The man was lean, and young, but clearly didn't venture outside of the lab often. Hinata smiled. Dr. Dar had done well, though.

Freyja's officers had taken the seat next to, and across from, the admiral. Each actively scanned the doorways and windows in their section. Freyja might have cheated in the admiral exam, but it was undeniable that her men were well-trained and loyal. Skyla sat between him and the window, obviously reading something on her ocular implants.

Their train car slowly filled as the hours ticked by, picking up people from all different tribes on their way into the capital. A man from the Verloren Tribe in a freshly pressed suit with a fedora pulled over one eye squinted at Hinata. He looked as if he might say something, but then just shook his head and went to sit with a cluster of Verloren passengers.

Similar interactions continued to play out. Hinata scanned their car, keeping an eye on the men who had appeared upset by something he and the others had done. He thumbed the hilt of his katana, which he had shoved into the large pocket of his jumpsuit. Unease pooled in his stomach and then he noticed that the passengers were self-segregated by tribe. It hadn't been apparent at the airfield when the train car had been mostly empty, but now it was glaringly obvious. Hinata let his hand, which was still on the hilt of his katana, relax. The blatant division was curious to see on a planet that was supposed to be the beacon of the compact; even in the capital, tribal lines held strong.

Hinata shifted his eyes away from the other passengers, taking in the sight of the capital just coming into view through the train window. He hadn't been to the capital since he was a boy and he had forgotten how extraordinary the city was. Large chrome and glass megatowers sprouted from a flourishing green landscape. Verdant green foliage trailed down metallic structures and covered rooftops. It was a strangely beautiful combination of cold, manmade efficiency and lush plant life. They passed into darkness as the train entered the tunnel system that would carry them to the center of the capital. He wished he had a little more time to admire the city, but they had answers to find.

***

Skyla's safe house in the city turned out to be a small warehouse in the industrial district. Rohaan had looked about ready to collapse by the time they arrived. Skyla had directed him to one of the bedrooms on the second floor; Freyja and her men had retired not long after that, leaving Skyla and Hinata alone, when he finally took a moment to inspect the safe house. It was an open floor plan with exposed brick columns breaking up the space. There was a set of double doors on one wall, and a staircase that led up to a second floor against another. Edison bulbs hung overhead, set in brass finishings, and warm wood molding completed the room. In one corner there was a kitchen, and another had a worn leather couch with matching chairs clustered around a dark wood coffee table.

"You're sure no one will come looking for you here?" Hinata asked.

"No one knows about this place," was all Skyla said in confirmation as she sank into one of the leather chairs, kicking her boots up on the table in front of it. He came to sit on the corner of the seat next to hers.

"Why do you even have a place like this?" He inspected the brick wall on the opposite side of the room to avoid staring at her.

"I have to come to Gefion every quarter or so. It helps to have a base of operation."

He couldn't help himself; he let his eyes trace the lines of her face and lock onto hers. What reason would an archaeologist have for coming to

Gefion so often? Skyla's lips turned up into a smile, as if she had read his mind.

"I have to come into Gefion to sell the tech that is too expensive for the rim worlds." She broke his gaze as she stood and wandered into the kitchen.

"Right. I guess that makes you our resident expert on Gefion. This is my first time to the capital since I was a child."

"Really?" She popped up from behind the kitchen island where she had been digging through the cupboards.

"Really," he confirmed with a smile.

"I would have thought that the Hoshiko Tribe would bring their high-ranking officers to Gefion for the annual gala, at least."

"I guess I am not ranked high enough to be worth bringing in from the border planets." He shrugged. His tribe did indeed bring in high-ranking officers for important events on Gefion; however, since losing the admiral exam to Freyja all those years ago, the senator had made sure that Hinata was left out of such pleasantries as a means to pay his penance. Before the test, he had been too busy making a name for himself and moving up the ranks to worry about attending parties.

"So, what's our next move, Captain?" He changed the subject.

"We will get an updated report from Rohaan in the morning, then we can start tracking down those transmission sites." Skyla returned from the kitchen with a bottle of liquor and two glasses in her hands.

"Perhaps we should start outlining targets tonight," he said.

"I don't think Rohaan is in any shape to work tonight." She slid a full glass across the table to him.

"You know I don't usually drink," he said as he swirled the liquid around in his glass.

"Really? You could have fooled me." Skyla clinked her glass against his and took a sip. "Come on, Commander, strange signals, murder bots, computer viruses...it could be the end of times. Might as well live a little," she said it as a joke, but the weight of the words hung heavy in the air.

He nodded. "Perhaps you are right," he took a sip of his drink, "about the end of times, and Dr. Dar. The poor man looked about to collapse the moment we got here."

"It's funny, for someone whose life's purpose is to prove the existence of aliens and help uncover the secrets of their technology, he hasn't spent a day training for the field," she laughed.

"He what?" Hinata nearly choked on his drink.

"You heard me right. The man is brilliant, but borderline obsessed with the concept that we are not alone in the universe. I know it sounds nuts, but that is one of the reasons we became close."

He held her gaze, waiting for her to go on.

She sighed and shook her head. "My father was also obsessed with finding evidence of advanced life forms. It's why he left—to prove his theories." Her hand moved to the gold necklace she always wore, her fingers tracing the outline of the pendant out of habit. She paused, carefully schooling her emotions before going on. "I always did love his stories, though. When I was little, we would lay under the stars, and he would tell me what alien home worlds would be like. He would make up stories about their cultures and their heroes. I loved it."

He reached across the table, gently running his fingers over hers.

"Rohaan reminds you of your father?"

"Yes," she smiled. "Same silly dream, and damn contagious attitude. I don't believe in aliens, but I do believe in Rohaan. I think he is going to discover something big. I just hope the universe doesn't break him in the process."

"About Rohaan..." Hinata hesitated, "I have been meaning to ask. He has an AI ship but no service record—how is that possible?"

"So you finally learned how to run a bioscan?"

"I've always known how to run a scan. I've just been a bit distracted lately."

Skyla's cheeks flushed pink, her eyes focused on her drink. "It's not my story to tell."

He reached out, a gentle finger lifting her chin so she would meet his eyes. He drew his hand back, not sure where they stood, but he didn't want to waste this time he had with her, short as it might be.

"Then tell me one that is."

CHAPTER 39 | SKYLA

PROHIBITION

Skyla woke to the alluring smell of coffee. A smile spread across her face, eyes still pressed closed. She had missed coffee. She had gone through her entire stock before Medina and while she grew herbs, algae, and mushrooms on Pele that would keep her alert, there was no replacing the real thing. Her eyes shot open as she sprang up from the couch in the main room, where she had stayed up half the night talking with Hinata. She must have fallen asleep at some point. *Those bastards, helping themselves to my coffee stores.* Skyla's face twisted into a scowl as Freyja handed her a cup.

"Good morning, sunshine," Freyja quipped, all too cheery for the early hour.

"Is it?" She took the cup from Freyja, sipping the bitter liquid as she glared at Freyja over the rim of her mug.

"Most people would say thank you." Freyja motioned to the cup.

"Thank you—for helping yourself to my coffee."

Freyja snorted, "You really can't let it go, can you?"

"Nope." Skyla walked over to the kitchen to escape Freyja.

Hinata, Kylian, and Tristan were already gathered around the kitchen table, but Rohaan must have still been asleep. Freyja took a seat with the rest of them.

"There's lots to do. Let's divvy up assignments and get a move on," Hinata said. "We need supplies—"

"Your kitchen is just booze and coffee," Freyja smirked.

"I wasn't expecting company," she mumbled, staring into her coffee cup.

"Not to mention, we can't blend into the capital with these flight suits. We'll need local clothing too," Hinata went on as if Freyja hadn't interrupted him. "Dr. Dar needs time to analyze the signal locations and put together a report—"

"And I'd better check in with my local contacts, get a bead on what type of chatter is going around," Skyla cut in.

Hinata nodded, his eyes moving from Freyja and her men to linger on Skyla. His communication was clear; he didn't trust Freyja and her men alone out in the capital, not without someone to keep an eye on them.

"Morning everyone." Rohaan slouched into the seat next to Kylian, still rubbing sleep from his eyes. "What did I miss?"

"We are just divvying up assignments," Hinata said.

"In that case, if I might take a moment." Rohaan cleared his throat before going on. "I received a transmission from Zahra this morning. She and Cista finished running the analysis on Admiral Nygaard's video to the fleet."

The room grew still as all eyes trained on Rohaan.

"It took a little time to repair my connection to the quantum computer we salvaged after the attack on the lab, but once I had that up and running, it was just a matter of time and processing power—"

"Dr. Dar, the results?" Hinata interrupted.

"Right, of course. The video is most certainly a deepfake."

Freyja exhaled a heavy breath, relief plain on her face for just a brief moment before she covered her feelings with a smirk. "I told you it wasn't me," she said, her eyes boring holes into Skyla's.

Hinata nodded. Rohaan's confirmation was all that he needed. "It's settled then. Freyja, you and your men will handle the supply run. Skyla, you and I can meet with your contacts—"

"Sorry, Commander." Skyla bit her lower lip as she considered her next words. "My contacts don't exactly like new friends."

"Are you sure it's safe to go alone?"

"Safer than bringing you along."

He hesitated, his displeasure evident. After a brief staring contest, his gaze softened. "Very well, I will stay and review the signal analysis with Dr. Dar."

"Ready? Break." Freyja's voice dripped with sarcasm. She kicked Kylian and Tristan under the table before standing. "Let's go," she said, wasting no time.

***

Skyla inhaled the cool morning air, saturated with the scent of dumplings, congee, and dried fish. She had missed XingXingtown. She purchased a bag of dumplings from the first vendor she came across, devouring the little balls of mushrooms wrapped in rice paper as she ventured deeper into the city. It was early, but the streets were already full of vendors selling their wares and patrons bartering for better prices. Skyla was grateful for the crowd. The press of people helped obscure her olive green jumpsuit and mirrored aviators, neither of which were in fashion in the capital. Most of the men wore slacks and blazer jackets, as did many of the women. Those not dressed in slacks wore skirts with long-sleeved blouses or dresses that came to the mid-calf. The fashion in the capital was modeled after a historical era of Earth That Was. She found it odd how the different planets of the central rim had decided to adopt different eras and old Earth customs to fashion their culture after. She found it strange how they looked back at a time that was more myth than reality, to model humanity's future.

She shook the thoughts from her head as she walked up the steps of a curio shop. As she opened the door, she was greeted with the musty smell of old books and burning incense. A little bell strung over the door announced her arrival as she stepped into the dimly lit shop. At the front of the store was a little Maneki-Neko cat sculpture, waving its arm to bring good luck. Every wall was lined with shelves packed with books and little oddities. Haphazardly placed stands were scattered throughout the rest of the shop, holding more little treasures. A man popped his head out from a curtain of beads at the back of the shop.

"Oh, hello there," he called out before weaving his thin frame through the beads to meet her. His long black hair, peppered with silver, was tied in a knot at the base of his skull. His green brocade robes billowed around his frame, threatening to swallow him whole. He stopped before her and offered a slight bow.

"I wasn't expecting to see you so soon," he said.

"I wasn't planning on coming to Gefion, but you know, plans change."

The shop owner nodded, humming his agreement. "Well, have you brought me anything interesting? Just yesterday I had a buyer interested in picking up some advanced weapons tech—"

Skyla held up her hand to stop him from going any further. "Not this time, I'm afraid."

The shop owner huffed, his eyes darting around the shop. Skyla no longer held his attention, now that he knew there were no credits in the interaction.

"Hey." She snapped her fingers in front of his face. "I'm in need of information today. What's the word going around right now?" she asked. Silence smothered the shop. The quiet was so oppressive she imagined she could hear the sound of the dust motes floating in the rays of sun passing through the dirty window at the front of the shop. "There's standars in it for you if you can give me a bead on what's been happening here in the capital the past couple of weeks," she nearly growled.

The shop owner's eyes lit up. "Oh, now that you mention it, there has been quite some unusual chatter." His head bobbing up and down with excitement.

Skyla flicked her fingers, pulling up a display for the credit transfer. "Tell me."

***

Skyla sat at the table in the open kitchen of the safe house, waiting for the rest of the crew to return. Her foot tapped rapidly against the hard floor as she took sips of her whiskey and glared at the front door, as if she could will them to return. She was nearly finished with her drink when Hinata and Rohaan walked through the door to the safe house.

"Where were you?" she blurted out.

"We went out to get a bite. Freyja hadn't made it back from the supply run yet," Rohaan said, all too cheery for Skyla's sour mood. She let some of the tension ease from her shoulders. She knew she was being unreasonable, but coming back to the empty safe house had made her uneasy. Something big was going down in the capital, but she wasn't entirely sure what.

"Well, I'm glad you are back. We need to talk."

"Your contact came through?" Hinata asked as he joined her.

She nodded. "There's been talk of a new player in the capital. They have been making large buys across the local syndicates. Here's a list of what my contact knows they have been acquiring." Skyla flicked her fingers and a holo appeared. Rohaan's brow furrowed as he read over the list.

"Is this what I think it is?" Rohaan asked, worried eyes burrowing into hers.

"I think so," she said.

"This isn't normal criminal activity. The amounts listed here, if they're accurate, are enough weaponry to back a personal army," Hinata said.

"He also gave me this." She flicked her fingers, and the holo changed to a map of the city with a handful of areas highlighted in blue. "According to the rumors, these are the areas where this new organization has been active. Can you cross-check it with signal activity, Ears?"

Rohaan brought up a holo of the signal analysis he had been working on that morning. The transmission areas pulsed in red. Nearly all of the sites Skyla's contact had outlined overlapped with the signal activity—too many to be a coincidence.

"Shit," Hinata whispered.

"What'd I miss?" Freyja's shout from the front door made Skyla jump. She hadn't heard the door open. A nasty grin split Freyja's face as Kylian and Tristan chuckled softly behind her. All three of them were laden with bags that they threw haphazardly on the warehouse floor. In an instant,

Freyja was standing behind Skyla, peering at the holo display. The hairs on the back of Skyla's neck rose at their proximity; she didn't like having her back to Freyja.

"There's a new player in town buying up unusually large amounts of weapons," Hinata explained, "and it appears that nearly all the buys are associated with the signal." He waved his hand at the display. The room was quiet for a moment as they thought through the implications. "Could this be the Empress?" Hinata asked.

Freyja shrugged. "I couldn't say for sure, but I wouldn't count her out."

"What's our next move?" Kylian asked.

"My contact said that word on the street is there is another buy going down tonight, at Prohibition, a club in the capital district," Skyla said.

"Coordinates?" Rohaan asked. The holo in front of them shifted to show a section of downtown, a blue dot pulsing over a trendy-looking building in the middle of the display. Rohaan matched his analysis up to the new display: another match.

"Well, it looks like we are going out," Freyja said, slapping her palms down on the table. "I guess it works out that you are already drinking," she said, staring at Skyla's glass before pushing away from the table to retrieve a collection of bags from the pile she had left in the open space.

"I also guess it's a good thing that we thought ahead and picked up these." She tossed a bag at each of them. "You're welcome." Freyja slung her bag over her shoulder and disappeared up the stairs.

***

Skyla shifted uncomfortably in front of the half mirror above the bathroom sink. She rarely wore anything other than a flight suit or her cargo pants and utility jacket, if she was on expedition. The blush pink silk fabric clinging to her curves made her feel exposed. She ran her fingers over the intricate beadwork that ran the length of the dress. Everything looked so delicate, but it was an illusion. The panels of the dress with shimmering sequins were laced with liquid crystals that would shift and move with her body.

A pounding at the door tore her attention away from the mirror.

"Hey, let's go!" Freyja hit the door one more time for good measure.

Skyla didn't care to respond. She took one final look in the mirror. Her hair hung in soft curls around her face, which was touched with makeup that made her skin appear to glow, and dark lines rimmed her eyes, accenting her irises. She ran a finger over the face-altering aviators which sat on the shelf below the mirror. She wouldn't need them tonight. The club was in a part of town where crime syndicates dictated the law.

When she came into the kitchen, everyone was gathered around the table. They had liberated a rather nice bottle from her collection. Lines furrowed her brow as she glared at them, partaking in her stock. When no one seemed to notice, she sighed and leaned against the wall.

"Well?" she asked.

Freyja kicked back her drink and rose to her feet.

"It's probably best if we don't all arrive together. We will meet you over there." Freyja didn't wait for confirmation. She and her men were out the door before anyone could say otherwise.

Skyla slid into one of the empty seats, shaking her head. She looked Rohaan over. He had changed out of the flight suit, but he was dressed too casually for the night club.

"Ears?" she asked, gesturing to his attire.

"I've tapped into the security cameras in and around the club. I will be assisting from here," he said.

Skyla couldn't help but feel relieved. Ears was brilliant, but he wasn't made for missions. That was one less thing she would have to worry about tonight. Skyla finally let her gaze slide over to Hinata. His long hair was oiled and plaited tightly down the center of his head, the sides buzzed tight. He wore a crisp black suit and button-down shirt. He held himself, as always, with perfect posture. He looked like he belonged in the capital.

Finally, she let her eyes drift to his, afraid of what she might see there. His gaze bore into her with that same intensity they had held that first night. Her breath caught in her chest. The way she saw herself reflected in his eyes scared her. It was as if eternity stretched between them.

If only they had met in another life; maybe things would be different.

Skyla fluttered her eyelashes, willing away the desire of something more, of something that couldn't be. Yet Hinata's gaze was relentless, burning across her skin.

"I guess that leaves you and me." Skyla broke the silence, which had gone on for far too long.

Hinata stood and extended his hand to her. "Let's go get some answers," he said, threading her hand through his elbow. She couldn't suppress her smile. They didn't have forever—but maybe she could pretend there was room for something more, just for tonight.

Skyla let him guide her into the dark nightclub. It was early still, but the party was already in full swing. Bodies pressed together on the dance floor, pulsing to the beat of the music. Soft rose gold lights shimmered around the walls. Skyla spotted Freyja standing at the long hardwood bar that took up the back wall of the club and moved to join her. She was annoyed to admit it, but Freyja looked dazzling in her gold beaded gown, the sequins rhythmically shifting with the music. Her rune tattoos shimmered black and gold, the spider web of scar tissue radiating out from her shoulder wound tangled with the ink like it was meant to be there. Even the frown etched on the edges of Freyja's face only added to her allure. Freyja tapped her finger on the side of her glass while she scanned the crowd. Skyla ordered a drink and turned to lean against the bar.

"Anything?" she asked.

"Not yet. It's early," Freyja said before turning and ordering two more drinks. She slid one across the bar to Hinata.

"Hey—relax, have a drink. You look like a fucking naval officer," Freyja said.

Skyla turned to look at him. Freyja was right. Hinata's spine was straight as a staff, his face stony, and his hands folded in front of him as he noticeably observed the faces in the crowd.

The corners of his mouth tugged down slightly as he mumbled, "I am a naval officer," but he took the drink and shifted his gaze to the bar.

Kylian made his way over from the edge of the dance floor, waving to catch Freyja's attention.

"Where is Tristan?" Freyja frowned.

Kylian shrugged. "Don't know, but he did say that if he found something pretty, he was going to fuck it."

She kicked off the bar, shaking her head, and grabbed Kylian by the elbow. "Let's go find your idiot cousin." She paused, raking her gaze over Hinata. "Try not to look so obvious." Then she disappeared into the crowd.

"She is right, you know," Skyla said.

He smiled at her. "We are not all as experienced in subterfuge as you, Captain."

She rolled her eyes. "Come on, Commander, finish your drink, and let's take a pass at the dance floor—it's too crowded to see from here."

They waded into the sea of people. She scanned the faces around her as she swayed to the music. She looked for insignia and tattoos associated with the capital syndicate groups, but so far, nothing. She turned to check another section of the crowd and saw Hinata standing like a statue in the sea of undulating bodies. She rolled her eyes and threw her arms around his neck, bringing him closer, until her lips brushed against his ear. His shoulders pulled taut under her arms.

"You stand out even more like that. Try dancing," she said, pulling back slightly to look into his eyes, so close their noses almost touched. Slowly, Hinata wrapped his arms around her waist and pulled her closer before he began to move with the music. His amber eyes glowed like they were lit with a flame, and for a moment she forgot what they were here for.

She couldn't look away from him. Sparks ran up her spine from the pressure of his arms wrapped around her. Her breath caught in her chest as he inched his head closer to hers, their noses brushing. She traced her fingers over the nape of his neck and he turned his head to lean into—

"We have movement," Ears' voice came through comms.

Damn it all to hell, she thought, as she broke away from him. "Where?" she asked.

"East, west, and south fire exits," Rohaan reported.

"Freyja, where are you?" Skyla asked.

"Near the south, on my way there now." Freyja's tone was clipped and all business now.

Skyla looked up at Hinata, her arms falling to her sides.

"I'll check out the east," he said, letting go of her and turning into the crowd.

Skyla pressed through the bodies around her, toward the west entrance. She didn't make it far before strong arms tangled around her waist, drawing her back against a hard torso. She couldn't see who had grabbed her. She squirmed against their grasp. The smell of liquor permeated the air around her, and annoyance rushed through her at the drunk barring her way. As she tried to pull away, the grip around her tightened.

Lips pressed against her ear. "Come now, Halcóncita, aren't you happy to see me?"

The air in her lungs froze as ice rushed through her.

"Gabriel," she snarled back.

Gabriel tut-tutted, his arms still locked around her. "No hard feelings for trying to kill me back on Trogon. It's just business, after all. The way I see it, we're even now."

Skyla scoffed, "You tried to take my tech without paying—again. We are pretty fucking far from even."

"Agree to disagree. Speaking of business, I think you owe me some weapons." His lips still pressed against Skyla's ear, making her stomach roil.

"How do you figure?"

"You took supplies from our caches. I should kill you for it, but I am a reasonable man. I'll take the weapons you promised in exchange, and we can keep doing business...maybe there is room for a little pleasure too."

"Pass," she spit the word at him.

"Don't be like that. I would hate for something to happen to you and your little ship. I happen to have a virus that took down an entire space station. I wonder how Pele would like that?"

Skyla froze. He was the one who had released the virus on Medina? All of those people, all of those deaths. He was responsible. She willed her body to relax, letting Gabriel believe that she was considering his proposal. His grip loosened, just a little. She slammed her heel down into his instep and he crumpled forward, into her. She threw her left arm out behind her as she twisted, grabbing his head and slamming it into her knee as she turned. The music was too loud for Skyla to hear the satisfying crack that accompanied his broken nose. Gabriel fell to his knees, clutching his face, blood gushing through his fingers as the crowd pressed in around him.

Skyla turned and threw herself into the crowd. The press of bodies slowed her progress to the west exit. She chanced a glance over her shoulder as she pushed through the writhing bodies, but there was no sign of Gabriel. Skyla's pulse pounded in her ears, muffling the sound of the music. Her ribs constricted her every movement, like her lungs were collapsing in on themselves. She rubbed her sternum, her fingers seeking out the familiar pendant, willing her body to relax. With adrenaline coursing through her, her body wouldn't comply. She slammed into the west exit with too much force, stumbling out into an alleyway at the side of the club.

Cool, damp air hit her in the face, bringing her back to her senses. Unfortunately, she didn't have time to recover. She had stumbled right into the middle of a deal. To her left was a cluster of men in dark suits, their black hair slicked back, an array of colorful tattoos covering the exposed flesh of every man in the group. Triad. Skyla turned to dash to her right, but found another group of men, some of whom she vaguely recognized from her dealings with the Fenix.

"Shit." She turned to escape back into the club, but the door had locked behind her hasty exit. "Double shit." She slammed her hand against the door before turning and drawing the handle of her bō staff from its holster under her dress. Her weapon extended from the handle as she eyed both sides. The Fenix cartel blocked the exit to the alleyway. Ten men and an oversized vehicle that stood suspended a half a meter above the ground.

To her other side, she spotted a fire escape ladder just in front of where the gangsters stood. If she could make it to that ladder, she could escape onto the rooftop. *Triad it is.* She sprinted toward the fire escape. The two closest men dashed forward to intercept her, each drawing their swords. She should have made Hinata take the west exit—he was much better with a blade than she was. She shifted the edges of her staff into blades just as she blocked a strike from the first man. The impact of the blow shuddered through her wrists, elbows, and shoulders. She gritted her teeth together, forcing her weight behind the staff before relaxing and stepping to the side, letting the man's momentum throw him off balance. She swept the end of her blade out, slicing through the man's Achilles tendon. He fell to the ground screaming, no longer a problem. But there was no reprieve.

The next man was on Skyla before she took another step. He swung at her and his blade glanced off her own. She twisted her staff, sending his blow into the cobblestones. She drove into a counterattack, cutting down with the opposite side of her staff. He dodged back, leaving only empty air for her blade. She turned away, spinning her staff back into her body. She had overextended and left her side open. She stood in a fighting stance, reassessing her target and the state of the rest of the men in the alleyway.

The cartel had taken advantage of her interruption. Uninterested in joining the fight, they packed large cases into the hovercraft. Only three of the men remained between her and escape; the rest having vanished into a doorway at the end of the alleyway. The three men were edging to surround her. Any hope of retreat was lost, with men blocking the club entrance, the alleyway exit, and the fire escape. The three men inched forward, blades drawn.

The sound of metal hitting brick cracked through the air as the club door flew open. Hinata stood in the doorway, blade drawn and fire raging in his dark eyes. Skyla exhaled in relief. Two on three—those were much better odds. Hinata's eyes flicked briefly over the situation and within seconds, he was on the nearest man. The hum of suspensors bounced off the wet cobbles as the hovercraft pulled out of the alley, the light fading as the headlights disappeared.

Sparks flew from Hinata's katana as he clashed with the man in front of him. Meanwhile, the man in front of Skyla was done waiting. He rushed forward, blade firmly held at his waist as he intended to impale her. The final man hesitated only a moment before jumping into the fight against Hinata.

Skyla diverted her opponent's blade with her staff as he thrust forward. He spun, striking out at her. There was a frenzy of clashing blades. He slashed, she blocked and countered, and the dance repeated. Sweat streamed from Skyla's brow, stinging her eyes. Her chest heaved, and her lungs burned, yet the man kept coming at her.

His assault was relentless, but he had to be getting tired. She needed to stay focused. She heard a squelch and gurgling behind her. She didn't dare look. She prayed the sound wasn't Hinata. If it was, she would soon follow. She was barely holding off one attacker. She wouldn't stand a chance against another. The man in front of her drove forward again, but this time, his foot slipped against the slick cobbles. His eyes went wide as he registered the grave mistake he had made, just a fraction of a second before she plunged her blade into his belly. She twisted the weapon, then kicked the man off the end of her blade. He collapsed to the ground, hands pressed frantically against the wound, struggling to keep his innards from spilling out.

She turned to see Hinata deliver a final blow to the last man. His katana sliced clean through the man's neck, the body falling lifeless to the dark stone. Hinata's breath came as rapidly as her own. A quick scan of the alleyway revealed that they were alone. The rest of the gangsters had escaped in the chaos. They had discovered nothing.

Hinata shoved the hilt of his katana inside his jacket as he rushed forward to clasp Skyla's face in his hands. His eyes swept frantically over her, before locking onto her own.

"Are you—" His voice wavered, laced with a fear she had never heard from him before.

"I'm OK," she managed to whisper.

"I thought—when I came through that door—I feared—" He dropped his forehead against hers, his posture relaxing slightly with his exhale.

His fingers tightened against her cheeks as he crushed his lips against hers. She stood frozen in shock. He pulled back, his eyes questioning. She extended onto the tips of her toes, bringing her hand to the nape of his neck and tangling her fingers in his hair as she kissed him back. He wrapped an arm around her waist, bringing her flush against him, his other hand tangling in her hair. Skyla's body lit with a blazing inferno under his touch—frozen in the moment—while the rest of the world blurred.

She couldn't remember why she was fighting this undeniable draw she had to him. He had pulled her in—like a black hole—and now she couldn't escape his gravity. She didn't want to. She had traveled beyond the boundaries of the Known Galaxies, seen countless wonders across as many planets; and yet *he* was all she wanted. The illusion cracked.

"Hey, get in!" Freyja's voice called from the end of the alleyway. They broke apart and ran to the hovercraft Freyja and her men had procured.

"Where did you get that?" Skyla asked.

"Don't you worry about that. Now, hurry your ass up!"

The back door swung open from the inside and Skyla and Hinata quickly crowded into the back seat. The craft accelerated before they even had a chance to close the door.

"Were you two really about to fuck in the alley?" Tristan side-eyed Skyla through the rear-view mirror. "Classy, Karsten."

"You're one to talk. I found you having a threesome in the VIP room," Kylian said, punching Tristan in the shoulder from the backseat.

"Yes, in the VIP room, because *I* have class." Tristan smirked at his cousin.

"You're all idiots. What in the fuck happened?" Freyja asked as she navigated onto the highway.

Skyla shook her head. "I don't know. I stumbled upon some deal in the west alleyway between the Triad and Fenix cartels."

"You thought it was best just to barrel in there on your own? Where was your head at?"

"I didn't mean to—Gabriel was there." Her cheeks burned with embarrassment at how she had botched the job. She swallowed the lump in her throat. "He attacked me in the club. I lost my head. I stumbled from one bad situation into a worse one." She slammed her hand against the back of the seat in front of her. Hinata grasped her hand, lacing his fingers with hers, his opposite hand pressing divots into the leather as he channeled his tension into the seat. Skyla caught Freyja eyeing them through the rearview mirror, but she stayed silent.

CHAPTER 40 | FREYJA

THE CAPITOL

They sat clustered around the small table in the safe house with hot cups of coffee clutched in steady hands, sobered from the events earlier in the night. The other deals going on around the club, while seedy, appeared to be normal criminal activity. They were certain that the exchange between the Triad and the Fenix was what they were looking for, but they were no closer to discovering what the cartel had been up to.

"What do we do now?" Freyja asked, idly thumbing the rim of her mug.

"I wiped the footage from around the club. We still have our anonymity and time to figure this out," Dr. Dar said. The man looked miserable, like he had personally botched the mission. If anything, he had saved Skyla's life. Dr. Dar had taken control of the comms. He had sent Hinata to aid

Skyla and Freyja to secure their escape. She had to remind herself that he wasn't a soldier like the rest of them—he had done well. Freyja gave the man a gratuitous nod.

"All right then, we have time to figure this out," Freyja said the words, but she wasn't so sure. Whatever the Empress was planning, she was certain they were running out of time. "And we know more than we did at the start of the day. Dr. Dar, look for any connections between the Triad, the Fenix, and the signal."

"Rohaan," the man said quietly as he nodded.

Freyja cocked her head to the side.

"You can call me Rohaan." He offered a weak smile.

Freyja nodded with a genuine smile of her own, a warmth building in her chest. She knew Rohaan and Skyla were close—who knows what Skyla had told him about her. This was an olive branch, and Freyja was surprised at how much it affected her.

"Rohaan, while you do that, I think we should investigate the senate hearing. The Empress expressly did not want me there. So that seems like exactly the place we might get some answers." A grin spread across her face. Freyja had never gone against the Empress' wishes—not since she was a child and had learned what the Empress was capable of. It felt good; it felt like she was finally free. Freyja looked to the others, but all she received were silent nods from her men.

Skyla stared into the depths of her coffee. She showed no sign that she had heard a word. Skyla hadn't been a soldier for a long time, it was written on her face. That skirmish with the Triad had affected her. Freyja hoped she would sleep it off. As much as she hated to admit it, Skyla was a damn good soldier and she would need her sharp when they went to investigate the senate hearing.

Hinata's gaze was focused on Skyla. Freyja hadn't missed that she had caught them in an embrace in the alleyway after the fight, or the way he had tried to comfort Skyla in the car. What was that about? The Stjarna and Hoshiko tribes were not allies. If the United Tribal Axis collapsed, which she suspected was her mother's goal, they would be on opposite sides of a war. Freyja shook her head, refocusing her thoughts. *Not my problem.*

***

Three days had passed since the incident at the club. They had been holed up in the safe house, making plans to infiltrate the senate, and waiting for Rohaan to finish his analysis on interactions between the signal and the gangsters. Freyja sat in one of the worn leather chairs in the seating area. It was a rare moment of quiet. Kylian was the only other soul in the safe house. The others had gone out for supplies. Everyone's spirits were much improved after a few days of R&R. Freyja was grateful, she needed everyone focused for the senate meeting that evening.

Kylian perched on the seat next to her. His hazel eyes locked onto her face, trying to read her as if she were a book. Her second-in-command often did that, and she was annoyed at how much he was able to decipher. At least he was the only one who could.

"What?" She shifted in her seat to look directly at him.

"Are you sure about this, boss ma'am?" he said in his thick accent. His guard was down, now that it was just the two of them.

Freyja shrugged.

"I don't think we have much of a choice."

He suddenly reached out and grasped her hand. Freyja startled. His fingers tightened around her own as his eyes pleaded for a different answer.

"A storm is coming. Are you sure of your course? We could still go, find a quiet border planet. Plant your garden. Sow life, instead of reaping death."

Freyja shook her head. "That is just a dream. What is coming will affect us all. I can feel it. There will be no safe place in the Known Galaxies." A wave of regret built in her chest as his face crumpled, but she meant it. There was no running—no matter how much she wanted to.

Kylian regained his composure in seconds. "I will follow you anywhere, past the edge of the Known Galaxies. I will follow you until every last star in the sky burns out, Freyja." It was an echo of the first promise he had made to her.

Stronger. Bolder. His loyalty would not waver. Kylian dropped her hand.

He was a soldier again, and she was his commanding officer.

***

Security at the senate was airtight. No signals were allowed within the capitol building. Their comms and ocular interfaces would be useless. Even worse, Rohaan hadn't been able to figure out a way to fake their credentials. If they wanted to investigate the capitol building, only Hinata and Freyja had the clearance to do so. They would have to go as themselves, which was a mighty risk. They would be giving up whatever advantage they held as ghosts, but Freyja was convinced that this was the key. They had to be at the senate meeting that evening. They had to stop the Empress' plan, before things went too far.

The entire crew was gathered in the kitchen of the safe house to finalize their plans. Skyla scowled at Freyja from across the table, unhappy about being cut out of the senate mission, and she appeared to hold Freyja personally responsible. *Let her*, it wouldn't change a thing. Freyja wasn't exactly ecstatic that they would be without backup if things went south, but they were out of time and out of options.

"It's settled then," Freyja said, slapping her palms against the table. "Hinata, prep your gear. You and I will be boots on the ground inside the capitol. Kylian, Tristan, go check the vehicle we stole. I don't want any issues if we need to make a quick exit. Skyla, you'll stay with the vehicle too, in case we need backup."

A dangerous streak flashed in Skyla's eyes. She held her arms crossed over her chest, her jaw clenched tight, but she stayed silent.

"Rohaan, we won't be able to communicate while we are in the building, but I want you here at the safe house scanning the area and keeping the outside crew up to date on any activity in the area." Freyja finished. Rohaan nodded, the relief on his face evident. At least one of their crew members was happy to remain behind.

An hour later, they were parked across from the capitol building, watching people flood into the entrance. There were senators in their embroidered robes of swirling silks in different colors for each tribe and sashes with emblems denoting their career accomplishments. Next to the senators, their aides wore sharp suits and carried leather satchels. They chattered amongst themselves or took orders from their superiors. This would be the best time for Hinata and Freyja to slip in unnoticed. With so many people flooding the stone steps into the marble entryway, they hoped that two specters wouldn't raise an eyebrow as they slipped through security.

"Here we go. Hinata and I will go dark as soon as we are inside that building. Keep an eye on the perimeter. Rohaan, send updates to the team. Stay sharp. We will slip back out after the hearing concludes," Freyja said.

"'Til Ragnarök, come again." Kylian and Tristan bowed their heads, forearms crossed in front of their chests, hands fisted.

"'Til Ragnarök," Freyja repeated the gesture. Her eyes flicked to the rearview mirror. She was surprised to see that Skyla had offered the Stjarna gesture as well, though she hadn't heard her speak the words.

Freyja stepped into the grand entrance of the capitol building. The lobby was constructed entirely out of white marble with smoky swirls of gray. Large columns rose on either side of the entrance, ushering the throng of people forward into security. Bodies pressed close against her own, and the heat in the room rose as they waited to pass through the security sensors ahead.

The room buzzed with conversation. Freyja heard nothing more than idle chitchat. She shifted her attention to the armed UTA guards ahead of her. They lazily flicked their gaze over the crowd, ushering them to keep moving through the scanners, and then it was her turn—she stepped through. Freyja focused on keeping her muscles loose, her expression blank, but out of the corner of her eye, she watched the security officer, willing his eyes not to shift at the indication of a flag. His face remained bored as he waved for the next person to step forward, not a second glance for the presumed-dead admiral.

Freyja walked a few meters into the building before sliding behind a marble column to wait for Hinata. To her relief, he passed through security with the same ease. She let out a long exhale, but the tension returned to her shoulders as a firm hand grabbed her by the elbow, pulling her further behind the marble column. She wound up to strike her assailant, then pulled the punch as she recognized Magnuson—first counselor to the Empress.

"What are you doing?" Freyja hissed through her teeth as she shook her elbow out of his grip.

"I could ask you the same?" he said, with his usual even tone, eyebrows arched in question.

"I have business here." Freyja's response was clipped. She scanned the hallway to find Hinata had stopped a few columns down, where he embraced a small woman with long dark hair spilling down her back. When they broke apart, their resemblance was uncanny. The woman looked just like Hinata, but far more petite. Freyja shifted her attention back to Magnuson.

"That is interesting. I was under the impression that the Empress had expressly forbade you from attending senate this session."

"I am an admiral of the United Tribal Axis. Sometimes duty calls, even if the Empress is not happy about it."

Magnuson shook his head slowly from side to side.

"I think not, Admiral. Your mother sent me to ensure that you didn't show up on Gefion. Imagine my surprise when your credentials came up at the capitol building. She sends a message: you have thirty minutes to sate your curiosity, then you better be out of the capitol, or even she cannot protect you from the consequences."

What the hell was that cryptic bullshit?

"What is she up to, Magnuson?"

Again, he simply shook his head. "You are to conclude your business on Gefion and rendezvous with your fleet. That is all I know." With that, he walked away, leaving Freyja with a sinking feeling in her stomach. Something wasn't right. Was her mother staging a coup? She couldn't be sure. With a flash of her fingers, she set a timer at the edge of her ocular display. As much as she wanted to figure out what was going on, she knew better than to still be in the capitol when that timer hit zero. Freyja stepped out from behind the pillar to find Hinata standing alone, further along the corridor. She walked up to stand beside him.

"Where were you?" Hinata asked, a tinge of annoyance in his voice, though his face remained blank, his eyes focused on the senators passing by.

"The Empress sent her aide," Freyja said.

That caught his attention—he looked at her in surprise for just a moment before looking back across the hallway again.

"She really doesn't want me here. She gave me thirty minutes, then said I better get the hell out. I don't know what is going on, but we better figure it out before then."

Hinata nodded. "We better split up, then. We can cover more ground that way."

"And the woman you were talking to?" Freyja asked.

"My sister."

A flicker of worry shadowed his usually stoic face.

"My mother has refused to attend today's hearing in protest against the Stjarna barricades between the Beta and Delta quadrants." He dropped his voice lower, ensuring only Freyja could hear his next words. "My sister and the rest of my mother's aides are here to clear out the Hoshiko tribal offices. They are talking about secession."

Freyja nodded, though she wasn't sure if it was relevant at the moment. A figure in a dark suit across the hallway caught her eye. Did she know him? He wasn't in a military uniform. Dark flames danced up the side of his neck, mere wisps that hinted that an inferno burned just below the collar of his suit jacket. Before she could figure out where exactly she knew the man from, he slipped into the stairwell on the eastern side of the building.

"The Hoshiko offices are on the western side of the building. See what you can find there and tell your sister and her people to get out now. I don't like any of this. I'll hit the eastern side of the building and we can regroup back at the vehicle."

"Right," Hinata moved to cross the hallway, but Freyja caught his arm.

"Twenty-eight minutes, seventeen seconds. Set a timer—not a moment over that time." She released his arm and strode across the hallway into the eastern stairwell. Living-ink tattoos were painful and uncommon outside of the military. She had never seen one on a senator or other government personnel before, but she saw plenty of them back on Trogon. The cartel was almost as fond of the damn things as the soldiers were. Freyja ran a hand over the sleeve of her suit, as if she could feel her own living-ink tattoos flickering to life beneath the fabric. She slid into the stairwell, careful the door behind her made no noise as it closed. Now the question was: up or down? The loud clank of a metal door slamming shut, decided for her. *Down it is.*

Freyja's boots were silent as she made her way down three floors, down into the bowels of the building. Her stomach was a jumble of nerves. She had never felt this way on a mission before, but everything about the signal, about being in the capitol building right now, felt wrong.

She came to the bottom of the stairwell and paused to listen. She didn't hear anything on the other side of the door. She opened it slightly, peering through to the empty corridor. She slid through the opening and gently closed the door behind her. Her hands reached to her hip on instinct and she cursed when she found her sword absent—no weapons were allowed in the capitol building.

She inched down the hallway, her muscles taut and ready to spring. She peered around a corner to find a large storage room with a maintenance vehicle parked in the center, its orange lights flashing silently. Around the hovercraft were a cluster of men in black suits, including the man she had followed down the stairwell. They were unpacking black cases from the maintenance vehicle and stacking them against the large stone pillars of the storeroom.

There was movement in the shadows across from her. Freyja peered into the darkness, trying to get a better look, cursing her ocular display for its limited functionality inside the capitol building. She saw a familiar face peer out from behind the pillar: she would know that face anywhere. Skyla. What was she doing here? How did she get in without credentials? Freyja fought to calm the heat rising within her—none of that mattered right now. If she could just get Skyla's attention, maybe they could take out the cartel together.

Freyja eyed the men. They looked sufficiently occupied with whatever was in those cases. The two on guard had their eyes trained on the hallway back into the building. It was worth the risk. She stepped out to the side of the pillar and flashed a hand signal in Skyla's direction, praying that the subtle motion would catch Skyla's attention. Nothing. Skyla was too focused on the cases the men were unpacking. Freyja tried again, stepping out just a little further from the pillar and signaling with her hands, just like they had back at the academy. Nothing. She didn't have time for this shit. She'd try once more, then she'd move, with or without Skyla.

This time, Skyla jumped in shock at seeing Freyja. Freyja signaled her haphazard plan to Skyla. Skyla nodded. Freyja checked the countdown—twenty minutes to get some answers and get the hell out. She held out her fingers for Skyla:

three,

two,

one.

Freyja rushed the man closest to her, slamming the blaster strapped around his neck into his sternum. She ducked down, grabbed the weapon, and threw him over her shoulder to the ground. She tipped the point of the blaster up and fired into the ceiling. Then she took a wide arc, sweeping phaser fire across the lights of the hovercraft. Shattered fluorescent tubes rained down over her skin, followed by total darkness. Muzzle flashes lit up sporadic pockets in short bursts, but the men were firing blind. They were not trained to fight in the dark, not like a UTA soldier.

Freyja slipped the blaster from the man's shoulder and fired a round into his chest. One down. Freyja heard a man scream on the other side of the storeroom. Two down. She crouched low as she advanced on the next man. The waves of panic wafting off him were so strong they were palpable as he turned in circles, trying to make out the monster in the dark. He didn't see it coming when she swept his legs out from under him, snapping his neck before he hit the ground.

Thick muscled arms wrapped around Freyja, pinning her arms to her side. *Damn*, she hadn't heard him approaching. She slammed her head back, greeted by the sound of cartilage crunching under her skull, but the grip around her remained firm. He lifted her body high into the air, then slammed her into the concrete. Pain blossomed through Freyja's shoulder. She ground her teeth and pulled the blaster into her chest, turning her body to aim up at her assailant. He had his rifle held high, ready to smash her skull with the butt of the gun. She pulled the trigger and a rain of phaser fire spewed out of the muzzle. The man collapsed before he could finish his blow. That's four. She heard the splatter of blood and a muffled cry in the dark. Make that five. She shifted her attention to the sound of footsteps running down the hallway—she fired into the dark. The thump of a body dropping followed, then silence. Six. A final crunch of bones came from the far corner of the storeroom. Seven.

"All clear," Skyla called out. A moment later, a torch lit up near the service vehicle. Skyla tossed a second torch from the service vehicle to Freyja. After ensuring that the threat had been neutralized, they met in front of one of the stacks of black cases.

"What is all of this? How did they even get into the capitol building?" Freyja asked as she unlocked the top case.

"They had maintenance credentials. I came in on the back of the hover with them." Skyla's voice was low. The top of the case snapped open.

"Shit," Freyja whispered.

Inside the case, there was a tablet screen in the center of a metallic panel. Skyla swept her fingers across the panel. There was a slight tremor in the movement, and Freyja's heart stopped when she looked up to find all of the color drained from Skyla's face.

"What is it?"

"It's a detonator."

Is this why the Empress hadn't wanted her at the senate meeting? No—that would be insane. Even the Empress wouldn't be so bold, would she? Freyja's eyes flicked to the display in her ocular implant. Seven minutes left. Freyja grasped Skyla's arm, turning her from the case to meet her eyes.

"Skyla, we have to go."

"No," Skyla jerked her arm out of Freyja's grasp and turned back to the detonator; her fingers flashed across the unit on her forearm.

"Skyla, we don't have time for this."

"You don't know that! It's encrypted. I can't even see the countdown yet. Let me break through at least, and see what we are dealing with."

"We only have a few minutes left. We have to go now!"

"You don't know that!"

"I do. The Empress—this is why she didn't want me here. She gave me a deadline to be out of the capitol by, and time is almost up."

Skyla began to visibly shake, her hands clenched into fists.

"I can do this," she said as she turned back to the detonator. Her fingers flashed through the air and she continued to mutter to herself as she worked. Freyja crossed her arms and tapped her foot as the seconds ticked by in her ocular display. Nothing changed on the detonator. It was still a swirl of cryptic, dark symbols. Skyla swore under her breath.

"If I just had a signal, Ears could help me hack through the encryption."

"There's no signal here, Skyla. We have to go."

"I know that," Skyla snapped back, her focus still on the detonator. A loud whirring emanated from the cases in the storeroom. Freyja's hands flew to her ears to block out the sound. Just four minutes left. They had to go—*now*.

She grabbed Skyla by the arm, yanking her toward the tunnel. Skyla pulled away, unwilling to budge. *Damn stubborn fool*, but Freyja would not leave her here to die.

Freyja pulled back her fist and slammed it into Skyla's temple. Skyla staggered, dazed by the unexpected blow. She slung Skyla's body over her shoulder, and her healing wound ached under the added pressure. Freyja staggered to the hovercraft. She threw Skyla in the back and slid into the driver's seat. The hovercraft rumbled to life under her and she threw it into top speed. They raced down the tunnel; the sporadic lights along its edges blurred into a white line. The vibrations from the suspensors rattled through her arms; three minutes left. The seconds ticked down in Freyja's ocular display. Adrenaline coursed through her. The tunnel stretched on for an eternity.

Finally, she saw light streaming in from the entrance. She slammed on the power, bringing the hovercraft up to speed to ram through the gate barring the exit. She broke through with a clamorous crash and kept driving despite the aggravated shouts of guards drawn by the commotion. She drove straight into the parking garage behind the capitol building where she quickly abandoned the vehicle, dragging Skyla with her.

Ten.

Nine.

Eight.

"Move!" Freyja yelled, as she ran for the exit of the parking garage.

"What the hell! Why did you do that?" Skyla screamed at her, before turning around and sprinting straight for the capitol building.

Freyja ran after her.

Three.

Two.

One.

A guttural rumbling bubbled up from the ground beneath the capitol. Freyja slid to a stop just behind Skyla. They looked on in horror as the magnificent concrete structure bucked, rippled, and quaked. The thunderous sound of marble, steel, and concrete imploding was deafening. They were thrown to the ground by the shock waves from the explosion. Dust and bits of debris floated over them, coating everything in dark, dirty snow. Freyja stumbled to her feet, coughing. She couldn't tear her eyes away from what remained of the capitol building: a twisted, fractured nightmare of smoke and flame.

"You!" Skyla growled. "This is *your* fault."

Before Freyja could register what had happened, she was laid out on her back, and Skyla was on top of her, issuing a flurry of fists and curses. Freyja brought her arms in front of her face to take the brunt of the blows.

"Skyla!" she screamed, trying to break Skyla out of her trance. The blows kept coming as ash rained down around them. Freyja shifted her weight onto her shoulders, then thrust her hips up, bucking Skyla from her perch on top of her. Freyja rolled and came quickly to her feet. Skyla was on her again just as quickly, slamming her into a concrete pillar, the blow knocking the air from her lungs. She shoved Skyla off of her, then brought her guard up.

"Why? Why wouldn't you let me save them?" Skyla screamed as she threw a few wild punches before connecting a kick to Freyja's gut. Freyja staggered back, just out of Skyla's reach.

"I couldn't leave you to die."

"All of those people." Skyla's eyes grew wide, brimming with tears. "Hinata," she whispered.

Freyja shook her head, tentatively taking a step forward, her arms raised in surrender. "He had the timer. He made it out."

Skyla shook her head violently. "You don't know that," she screamed. "I could have stopped it. I could have—"

"You couldn't save them, Gyr."

"No." Animosity replaced the grief in Skyla's eyes. "You don't get to call me that. You don't get to save me!" Skyla came at her again, but her form was sloppy as she let her emotions take control. Freyja easily blocked Skyla's advances and shoved her away to open up space between them again.

"Even after all these years, I still care about you. I tried so hard to hate you. I wanted to hate you. Back when we went to the academy, the Empress drilled it into me. You were my competition, but you were also my friend, the only person who ever truly saw me. How could I forget that?"

"Liar!" Skyla snarled. "If I ever meant anything to you, why did you abandon me? My father left and then you turned your back on me. You tried to kill me!"

"Gyr," Freyja's voice was soft and broken. "We were just kids."

"So, that's your excuse?" Skyla snorted. "Children don't murder each other."

"That's why I couldn't be there for you after we went to the academy. The Empress wouldn't allow it." Freyja hesitated, uncertain if she should share the next part—but the dam had broken—her walls came tumbling down. "She wanted me to eliminate you."

"And you damn near did! If I hadn't managed to somehow attach my tether, I would have been jettisoned into the vacuum. I would have been dead before the rescue crew could be deployed."

"How do you think your tether was attached?"

"I don't remember. Everything after you cracked my helmet is a blur. I must have somehow, somehow—"

"Somehow attached your safety harness while you were damn near unconscious? You're smarter than that. How do you think that tether was attached?" Freyja was screaming now, her anger and anguish from decades of carrying this burden bubbling to the surface. Skyla froze, her arms dropping to her sides as she searched Freyja's eyes.

"You?" Skyla asked softly.

Freyja nodded, not trusting herself to speak.

"I don't understand."

"I couldn't outright defy the Empress. I had to convince her that I tried. I knew if I was reckless and failed, they would separate us at the academy. I wouldn't have a second chance to kill you. I just had to make sure you survived the first attempt." She paused, subconsciously running her fingers along the rune living-ink tattoo on her left arm. Her lesson for failing to murder her friend.

"I managed to tether your harness, just as the doors opened. We were so close, I knew the cameras wouldn't be able to see what I had done. I could convince the Empress that I had tried," her voice began to shake, "and accept the punishment for my failure. But at least then, you would be safe. My best friend would live." Tears now ran freely down Freyja's dusty cheeks. Matching tears brimmed in Skyla's eyes. She stumbled forward, throwing her arms around Freyja, sobbing. Freyja jumped, unsure if this was another attack, but when Skyla didn't move, Freyja circled her arms around her. They embraced each other among the ruin, bloodied and broken.

CHAPTER 41 | HINATA

WORLD ON FIRE

Hinata was thrown from his feet as the explosion rippled out behind him, slamming hard into the pavement outside the capitol building. He groaned as he brought himself to stand, his shoulders aching from the impact. He watched as the transport carrying his sister turned the corner. He had gotten her and the rest of his mother's people out in time.

Stumbling on unsteady legs, he made his way to his own transport, his body moving of its own volition, his limbs having gone numb. "Where is she?" Hinata shouted into the passenger side window. He didn't need to elaborate—they knew which *she* he meant.

"There's no reasoning with that one, boss'man. She took off right after you and the admiral left," Kylian responded.

Hinata growled, slamming his palm against the side of the car.

"Ears sent a transmission right before the blast. There was a service vehicle causing a scene behind the building. I can't get a transmission through to get more info, though. Looks like the blast knocked out all of the comms in the area."

Hinata gritted his teeth, bringing himself to his full height.

"Meet me behind the building." He took off running through the rubble, pulling up a display in his ocular implants as he went. He had to locate Skyla and Freyja, but their comms were down. There was no signal.

Or they were dead.

Hinata pushed the thought from his head. He couldn't let emotions in, now. He didn't have time to feel. He would find them or he would find whoever was responsible—he just needed to get to that service vehicle before they fled the scene. He dodged chunks of rubble, his lungs burning from the acrid smoke rolling off the blast site. He blocked it all out. He couldn't think about the reality of the destruction. He had to be ready to deal with the terrorists that did this.

He came to the back of the building. It was all destruction and chaos, but there were skid marks exiting the service entrance, and they led straight into the parking garage behind the ruined capitol building. His lungs screamed from the exertion and the smoke, but he ignored them. He ignored the burning in his legs and sprinted into the parking garage, his eyes alert and scanning the debris. He stopped cold. His hands began to shake. There, at the front of the parking garage coated in fine gray dust, he found Skyla and Freyja, their foreheads touching, each grasping the other by the neck and shoulder.

He ran to them, ready to break up the fight—though as he approached, he could see that while they were both bloodied and bruised, they weren't fighting. Tear tracks cut rivers down their dirtied cheeks and they appeared to be whispering. Hinata froze an arms reach away from the two women, but when they broke apart and Skyla's eyes caught his, he could hold himself back no longer.

Before he had time to think, he gathered her into his arms. He hadn't realized how much he had grown attached to the captain until he thought she was gone. Now he held her tight, relishing in the feel of her heart beating in time with his own. He wrapped an arm around her waist, keeping her close as he moved his other hand to trace her jaw, tilting her face up. Her eyes were rimmed in red, and he found anguish in her gaze, but she looked otherwise unharmed.

"Can't you follow orders for once?" he said, his voice soft.

"I am not yours to command." She gazed up at him.

He brought his lips to brush against hers, whispering, "No, you are not."

He pressed his lips to hers, devouring her with a kiss. The rest of the world stopped; it was only the two of them standing among the frozen fall of smoldering ash. Skyla met his passion with her own, one hand grabbing his hair fiercely the other clutching his chest as if he were a lifeline that she would drown without.

"I hate to break this up..." Freyja's voice edged in, "but we have to go." And the moment was gone. Hinata returned to his senses. The world wasn't just the two of them. The world was chaos and wreckage and sirens. The world was on fire.

"Let's move," Kylian shouted from the passenger side window of their transport as they slid to a stop beside the trio, slapping his hand repeatedly against the side of the door. Hinata dropped his hand from Skyla's waist to interlace their fingers as they jogged over to the vehicle. He opened the back door. Freyja slid in, then Skyla, and then he slammed the door shut behind her.

"What are you doing?" Skyla gasped, leaning out the open window.

Her words opened a wound in him that he wouldn't let show. He couldn't. He didn't want to leave her, especially now—having thought he had already lost her once—he didn't know if he could face that pain again. Instead, he said, "I'm needed here."

Skyla's brow furrowed in confusion.

"Freyja and I were dead when we entered the capital, but we aren't ghosts anymore. I am duty-bound. I need to stay and do what I can."

The panic that flashed in her eyes tore at his heart; it was almost enough to sway his decision.

"You can't. We don't know what happened here—what could still happen. I don't want you in the middle of this." Skyla's words came out in a panicked rush.

Hinata fought the lump forming in his throat. All he wanted to do was take her in his arms and leave this nightmare behind, but that was just a dream. He leaned forward so that one arm rested against the window frame, while his other hand tucked a stray lock of hair behind Skyla's ear. Hinata traced the line of her jaw, his thumb brushing her bottom lip before resting at her chin.

"Come now, Captain. Someone might get the idea that you care about me," he joked, hoping that the words would hide the feelings he was certain were painted across his face. He had fallen too far for this woman.

Skyla shoved him in the chest with the palm of her hand. There was no effort behind the gesture. He took her hand in his, holding it to his chest.

"I'm serious. It's not safe."

He laced his fingers between hers, buying time to choose his words. "I am an officer of the United Tribal Axis Navy. I can handle myself, and I am needed here."

Skyla bit her lower lip. Whatever protest she had died on her lips. The way that she looked at him made him wish he could take the words back—but it was the truth. They both knew who he was.

She gave a simple nod as she pulled away from him, turning to face forward. She wouldn't watch as she left him behind. Hinata stepped away, and the transport sped out of the parking garage.

Hinata fought to don the familiar persona of commander: the cold, calculated façade that would see him through this. He made his way through the fragments of the once-grand structure, each boot placed with care, scanning the scene as he approached the assembling crowd of emergency responders. As he walked, he locked away the yearning to escape into the stars with Skyla. They would not serve him now. The UTA was on tenuous terms at best. His tribe was already threatening secession, and now the senate had been destroyed. War was on the horizon; he could smell it in the cinders of the burning capitol.

CHAPTER 42 | SKYLA

Not Goodbye

Skyla sat on the small bed in her captain's quarters aboard Pele. Fenrir lay curled up, asleep, on the floor beside her. Her fingers fiddled with the edge of a storage box. A shipment of her mother's things had been delivered to her the previous day. Her mother had died at the senate bombing a week ago, along with nearly eighty percent of the senate. She was her mother's only heir, and the responsibility of dealing with her affairs fell to Skyla. It was a responsibility she didn't want. She wanted to run away to the stars with Pele and never look back, but she couldn't ignore what was inside the box.

The box came from her mother's personal safe. A safe which she had never—not once—seen the contents of. For her mother to be so secretive,

Skyla couldn't ignore whatever it was. *It's just personal mementos*, she tried to convince herself.

She tucked the edges of her thumbs under the lip of the box and slid it to the side. Skyla let out a long breath. There were various little items piled inside, along with some papers and books. She picked up a datapad from the top of the pile and flicked her fingers over the front of the screen. With her mother gone, Skyla's DNA would give her access to the device. A holo of a young girl came to life in front of her; a little girl with ice-blue eyes and pale blond hair, so cheerful and full of life.

"Hi, Dad! I hope that your expedition to Thule is going well. I'm sure you are busy discovering the first alien remains! But take some time to write when you can. I sure do miss you!" The young girl's voice chirped, and Skyla's eyes welled with tears. She flicked her fingers and another video message appeared. It was the same girl, but she had a little less light in her eyes.

"Hey, Dad. It's been a couple of months and I haven't heard from you yet. I sure hope you get signal out there. I miss you! Bedtime isn't the same without your stories...you know Mom doesn't like fairy tales. She has me preparing for the academy now. I hope they make me a pilot! Pele would love it if we could fly for the UTA! Anyway, I am sure you will be back before I take my exams. Love you! Write soon, ok?"

The tears flowed down Skyla's cheeks as she flicked to the next message. It was the same girl, maybe a little older, but there was an undeniable sadness in her eyes.

"Why won't you write me? Mom says you're not coming back. I don't understand. I leave for the academy next week. I wish you were here to see me off. I wish you were here to give me advice...I wish you were *here*— "

With shaking hands, Skyla pulled up the metadata for the messages. She knew the answer already, but she had to be sure.

Files logged: 102073. Data stored. No sent receipt.

Skyla screamed and threw the datapad at the bulkhead. Fenrir jumped to his feet, his tail flicking nervously as he eyed the broken pieces that landed too close for his liking.

"Skyla," Pele's soft voice chimed.

"Not now, Pele!"

"Your heart rate is elevated—"

"She never sent them! Not one!"

Pele was silent, waiting for Skyla to go on.

"I must have recorded a hundred messages for my dad after he left. She told me he left us. I grew up thinking my father abandoned me, that he just left without saying goodbye. That he didn't love me. None of it was true." Her voice was only a whisper by the time she finished.

"Do you know where your father is now?" Pele asked.

"Last I heard, he was on an expedition to Thule. Who knows if that was even true," she sighed, looking back to the box of her mother's things. Her mother was gone now, and all of her secrets with her.

Skyla pushed items in the box aside. Her heart froze. Beneath everything else was a slender blue box. On the cover was an indented gold symbol: *Vegvísir,* the same symbol from the necklace her father had given her before he'd left.

With trembling fingers, she lifted out the box and traced the symbol. She pushed the pendant of her necklace into the groove of the box—it was a perfect fit. There was a click, then the whirling of tiny motors as the hard shell of the box retreated into the spine of a leather-bound journal with the same gold symbol embossed on its cover. She bit her lower lip, sucking in a shaky breath, then flipped the journal open to the first page. Her tears came in a new wave as she read, in her father's handwriting:

My Dearest Gyrfalcon,

I'm sorry that I couldn't be there for you all of these years. I hope you know how much I wish that I could have been there to watch you grow. Alas, I am an embarrassment to your mother, and in her words, to our clan. She thinks you are better off without me there. I don't come from a powerful house. I would fight to stay if I could, but it appears banishment is my only option. Your mother has promised to give you this journal when you reach the age of majority. She has promised you will be allowed to make your own choices. I hope that when you do, you will come and find me. I miss you already, little one. Know that my heart beats only for you, always.

Love,

Dad

***

A week had passed since Skyla read that first page of her father's journal. She had proceeded to read the book cover to cover. It was full of his research and his theories on alien life in the universe. Her anger built with every memory she had of her mother's lies—how had she kept this from her, kept her father from her? She knew she let that enmity build to avoid dealing with her grief. She could only take so much and right now, she had no capacity to process the loss.

Skyla's mind was made up: she had to go find him. After researching the journal, she knew where she would start: Thule, a border planet that was more ice than anything else. That was where he would have gone next, though his notes were nearly twenty years old. Who knew if he would still be there? She just hoped that she would be able to pick up his trail from there; this clue was all she had to go on.

Skyla ran her fingers along Pele's hull. "Ready for an adventure?" she asked, her voice more hopeful than it had been in a while.

"I am always ready, Captain." Pele's lights shimmered to show her excitement.

"You know you don't have to call me that."

"I like the nickname the commander gave you," Pele said.

A tingle ran down her spine at the mention of Hinata. She hadn't seen him since the capital. It turned out that coming back from the dead was a lot of work, especially when returning to life as a commanding officer in the UTA Navy. She had thought about messaging him before she left Gefion, but she wasn't certain she should, not after how they had left things. In the end, she decided against it. War was on the horizon. His tribe had already begun the secession process and there was talk of many more to follow. The compact was crumbling. The XinXing Tribe held the Hoshiko Tribe responsible for the bombing, though there was no evidence of who had orchestrated the terrorist attack. Only the crime syndicates and separatist militias had tried to claim responsibility. Their tribes would soon be at war. She didn't want to stick around for that. She was no longer a soldier. There was no reason for her to stay in the central rim. She would be better off chasing ghosts at the edge of the Known Galaxies.

Skyla stacked the last of her supply cases into the cargo bay. A throat cleared behind her. She turned to see a tall silhouette standing at the entrance to the cargo bay. He stepped forward and the light danced around him. Dressed in a black dress uniform, with its gold insignia, he looked just like he had the first day they had met all those months ago, back at Medina. Though that man had never let his emotions show, the one before her had a soft smile on his lips.

"Were you going to leave without saying goodbye?" he asked, his voice quiet and playful.

Skyla shrugged. "You're a bit busy these days, Commander."

"Never too busy for you, Captain." He came to stand beside her. Freyja and Rohaan followed not far behind. Skyla looked at the two of them with a canted head. Now, that was an odd pair, since when were they so chummy?

"What is everyone doing here?" she asked.

"We saw you file a flight request," Rohaan said, by way of explanation.

"Yeah. Thought we better come see you off and all that." Freyja leaned against the cargo Skyla had just loaded. "Or better yet, convince you to join us."

"What?" Skyla asked.

"We are going to track that signal. Rohaan already has a good lead on where to go next. The capitol bombing is not the end of all of this. It's the beginning, and that signal is the key to figuring out what is going on. Come with us," Freyja asked again, her tone more insistent this time.

"You're going with them?" Skyla asked, searching Hinata's eyes.

He shook his head gently. "No, I can't leave my tribe. Not now."

"Not on the brink of war, you mean?" The words were acid on her tongue.

Hinata was silent, but he didn't look away from her. She shook her head, then turned to Freyja.

"This is something I have to do, Raven."

A wide smile spread across Freyja's lips. It was the first time she had used that nickname since they were kids. A warmth spread across Skyla's chest. There was still mending to do, but it felt good to have her best friend back again.

"I understand, Gyrfalcon." Freyja stepped up and clasped Skyla by the forearm, then the back of her neck, bringing their foreheads together. Her voice dropped to a whisper. "When you are done chasing ghosts, come find us. Your people need you. I need you." She let go and took a step back.

"'Til Ragnarök, come again."

"'Til Ragnarök," Skyla echoed.

Rohaan extended his hand in farewell, but Skyla grabbed it and pulled him into a hug.

"Be careful out there," Skyla said.

"You too," Rohaan said.

Freyja slung an arm around Rohaan and guided them out the way they had come, waving her other arm in a mock salute.

It was just Skyla and Hinata now. He took a step closer, reaching out and grasping her hand in his, twining their fingers together.

"I told you we would end up here," she said softly.

"And where is here?"

"You, duty-bound to stay for your tribe. Me, called away to the stars."

Hinata ran the fingers of his other hand along the angle of her jaw, pausing at her chin to swipe his thumb across her lower lip.

"Nothing is forever, Captain. This doesn't have to be goodbye." He pulled her to him, kissing her deeply.

She knew she should pull away, that she had tried to keep her distance for a reason. This moment was that reason. They didn't have forever. They didn't even have tomorrow. But there was no fight left in her; she had already let it go too far to fight the inertia that had built between them; and now the idea of losing him was almost enough to make her stay.

"Then why does it feel like a goodbye?" she asked, as their lips brushed, her voice still breathless from the kiss.

He kissed her again.

"I'm not going anywhere. Come back to me when you are done searching?" There was a pleading in his eyes, a rare vulnerability he only shared with her. She smiled, letting herself relax into his arms, tangling her own around him. If all they had was right now, she wasn't going to waste it.

"What if I am never done searching?" she teased.

"Then perhaps one day you will come searching for me." He smiled back at her. "Be careful, the rim worlds are dangerous."

"Pele and I know our way around the rim worlds."

"Yes, and who saved you after your last expedition went wrong?"

"A very stubborn commander." She had to give him that one. "You be careful, yourself," she said, her tone turning serious.

He nodded, then pulled her in closer.

"Don't forget, you still owe me that favor."

She smiled. He had her on that one. She would miss that curry almost as much as she would miss him. "Are you going to cash it in already?"

He shook his head gently. "Do I have to?"

"No. This is something I have to do." She paused for a moment as emotion clouded her voice. "This isn't goodbye," she whispered.

"This isn't goodbye," he whispered back.

EPILOGUE

ALONE

It took Skyla and Pele nearly a month to reach the frozen world of Thule. The journey had been quiet. At first, Skyla had enjoyed getting back to the normalcy of it all, having her space and her ship to herself. But after the first couple of days, the loneliness set in. She missed walking into the lab and seeing Rohaan on his fifth cup of chai, eyes trained on a holo, willing it to give up its secrets. She missed seeing Dr. Pinot in the med bay, working on her next round of improvements for Pele. She even missed Freyja and her snarky comments—who would have thought? And then there was him...Skyla pushed the thought of *him* from her mind. She missed him most of all, but it hurt to admit it. She must have started a dozen messages to him, but none of them felt right. She would send a transmission once she got to Thule and had news she could share. At least she had Pele and Fenrir. They were the only thing that kept the ache from crushing her.

"We will be entering orbit around Thule in fifteen minutes," Pele chirped.

Skyla pulled up the planetary scans on the bridge view screens. The world was almost entirely made up of frozen oceans. There were a few small land masses, but even those were permanently covered in ice. Why anyone would choose to live in such a barren place was beyond her.

"Scanners are picking up an anomaly."

"What kind of anomaly?" Skyla asked.

"Something big is headed our way. It came from beyond the border of known space."

"More info, Pele."

"The object appears to be on a collision course with us."

"Shields up, Pele. Begin evasive maneuvers."

"The object is matching our movements."

Not space debris then.

"Ready the plasma cannons—maybe we can take it out before it hits us."

"The object is too large. We do not have the firepower to vaporize it."

"All right, take us in. Let's see if we can lose it in the atmosphere."

Pele took a hard turn toward the icy planet. The glow of entering the atmosphere shimmered around Pele's shields. Through the viewports, Skyla saw the object come into view. It was massive; all hard angles and a black so dark it appeared to swallow the light. It was a ship, but not a make like anything she had ever seen. It was too large to follow them into the planetary atmosphere and halted just above them. Skyla breathed a sigh of relief—then the ship opened fire.

The bridge shook from the severity of the impact. Skyla strapped into her harness, adrenaline pulsing through her as she initiated the neural link. Once she was synced with Pele, she was able to dodge the larger blasts, but there was too much firepower. Pele's shields flickered once, twice, three times—then they went out.

"Shit!"

Another barrage of railgun fire tore through Pele's hull, and her engines died.

"I am the blaze in the flame.
I am the calm in the storm.
I am the force behind the machine.
The choice is mine.
Fear has no power over me."

The litany tumbled from her lips, but she could not suppress the cold fear that took hold of her. They were in free fall, with a vast, frozen ocean rushing up to meet them.

THANK YOU

Thank you for reading! If you enjoyed this story, I would be so grateful if you would leave a review on Amazon and Goodreads, or wherever you like to review books! This is such a huge support for authors and helps get our stories out into the world. It doesn't have to be anything fancy, a couple of words will do.

ACKNOWLEDGEMENTS

Wow, it's crazy to believe that we have made it this far. If you are reading this, thank you for giving my story a shot. It means the world to me. When I started out writing this book, it was just me and my laptop, and along the journey it grew into so much more. It takes a village to get your story out into the world, and I am so grateful for mine.

Thank you to my partner Hoz, for always believing in me and supporting me, even when I have big crazy dreams. Thank you to my littles Izzy and Ryder, for being my number one cheerleaders, for reminding me what a great writer you think I am, and always being excited for the next proof copy to add to your shelves. Thank you to Makenzy Toro for not only providing valuable beta feedback on this book, but always being a willing ear to listen to my over excited chatter about this book. Thank you to my editor Des DeVivo for believing in this book and working in the trenches with me to make it shine! Thank you to my beta readers. Without you, Umbra would not be the book it is today. To Alisha Tanner, whose live comments kept me sane and helped me see how a reader would perceive each chapter in the book. To Amber Bolognesi who did the final pass and asked the hard questions that made me dig deep to finish out the last touches. To Meera R. who had the best STEM comments and laugh out loud reactions. And to Brook McNabb, who combed through the story with meticulous detail.

Thank you to the online writing community who supported me through this process. I have learned so much from so many of you! There are too many to name them all but a special shout out to K.M. Davidson, Nikkita Bell, C.A. Blooming, Kelsey McCullar, Stephanie Storm, E.F. Watson, and Cortney L. Winn my fellow authors, who have been there to bounce ideas off of, to celebrate wins with, and cry to when days are hard, you are my village.

Thank you to the amazingly talented artists I have had the pleasure of working with on this book. My cover designer, David Gardais, thank you so much for the stunning cover. We all know I didn't give you a lot to work with and you made something absolutely stunning! Natascia Mora for bringing my cast to life! And Janene O Literart for breathing life into some of my favorite scenes. Brady Dalton for the beautiful chapter heading pieces.

And thank you, reader, for taking the time to read this story. Writing a novel has been a dream of mine since I was a kid. It wasn't until by dad passed away suddenly that I decided to finally make it a reality. This story is incredibly special to me and I am so grateful I had the opportunity to share it with you.

A very special thank you to all of the Kickstarter backers who believed in this project! I hope you enjoyed the story.

Danelle (Biblio.Barbie), Benjamin L. Akers, Megan Anderson, Monica Arsenault, Jonathan Bannister, Adam Bassett, Rebecca Bauer, Jonathan Bielefield, Rebelle Black, C.A. Blooming, Amber Bolognesi, Nickesha Bone, Ruth Cantu, Scott Casey, Kerry Chorvat (Blue Cat Dev), Alexandra Corrsin, Lara Costa, Stephanie Crachiolo, Marie D. Cummings, Mersi Curtsinger, K.M. Davidson, David DeHaan, Josué Delgado Denis, Opal

Denner, Des DeVivo, Z.S. Diamanti, Katherine Donahoo, Sam iElaine, Madeleine Eliot, Karen Esquerra, Marie Fisher, Nicholas W Fuller, Bria Gabriel, Joshua Gerdes, Ashley Gibson, Brian Hagman, Sean Halladay, Car Hardcastle, Cat Hayes, Emma-Jane Heaton, E. A. Hendryx, Amy Ho, McKenna Hubbard, Heather Hudec, Micayla Jacobsen, Jillian Jamrozik, Michae lJohnson, Carly Jonathan, Heather Kaiser, Karla, Boe Kelley, Dan Kenner, Keric, Kim Kruger, Zachary Lambert, Laurence@reading.instead.of.cleaning, R.J. Lavender, Dave Lawson, Emily Layne, Phillip A. Leavenworth, Caty Lee, Greg Marbach, T. M. Mayfield, Kelsey McCullar, Allie McDermott, Joshua McGinnis, Brook McNabb, Samantha Mendell, Stephanie Meredith, Monkey Meatloaf, Moose Hammer, AJ Nadolsky, Jesse Nicholas, Nijeara Ny Buie, Elyse Oldroyd, Alex Parker, Heather Pereira, Robin Perez, Carl D. Poellnitz, Rafael and Karina, Sandra Reddy, Paige Reisenfeld, Caitlyn Ricks, Rebelle Roberts, PunkARTchick Ruthenia, Anie Sallis, Brilynn Schrader, Ed Schulte Kristen Shafer, Liz Shaw, Amanda Simas, Paul Smith, Kate Stein, MelissaT., Alisha Tanner, Francesco Tehrani, Sean M. Tirman, Holly Todd-Rogers, Elizabeth Torre, Kaitlin Vesper, Hayley Walker, Jim Wilbourne, Cortney L. Winn, Sarah Wojtowicz, Jay Wolf, Timothy Wolff, Christina Wyant, Nena Yochim, Brandi, lilyjean10@gmail.com, Nikz, phoenix17, terrinils2@gmail.com

Until our next adventure, cheers!

GLOSSARY

CHARACTERS

Azai Akari - member of the Hoshiko tribe. Senator of the United Tribal Axis. Mother of Azai Hinata.

Azai Hinata - member of the Hoshiko tribe. Commander in the United Tribal Axis. Commanding officer of Medina Outpost. Bonded to the AI ship Tentei.

Elodie Pinot - member of the Etoile tribe. Doctor, bio-medical engineer, foremost expert in bio-mechanical integrations. Stationed at Medina Outpost.

The Empress - member of the Stjarna tribe. Self made monarch of mining. Mother of Freyja Nygaard.

Fallen Berserkers - Dakara, Kofi, Ekon, Amari. Members of the Stjarna tribe. Members of Freyja Nygaard's elite squad of soldiers. Fell at the battle of Medina during the mutiny of the *Orman Korte*.

Freyja Nygaard - member of the Stjarna tribe. Admiral

in the United Tribal Axis Navy. Daughter of the Empress. Leader of the Berserkers. Bonded to the AI ship Selkie.

Gabriel Tibaquirá - Leader of the Fenix cartel. Ruler of the outer rim world, Trogon.

Gwen Karsten - member of the Stjarna tribe. Senator of the United Tribal Axis. Mother of Skyla Karsten.

Huang Bo - member of the XingXing tribe. Captain in the United Tribal Axis Navy. Ally to Senator Karsten.

Ivar Borg - member of the Stjarna tribe, Lieutenant in the United Tribal Axis Navy. Loyal to the Empress. Leader of the *Orman Korte* mutiny.

Kaku Caishen - member of the XingXing tribe. Senator of the United Tribal Axis. Astrophysicist.

Kobayashi Callan - member of the Hoshiko tribe Lieutenant commander in the United Tribal Axis Navy. Third in the chain of command under Commander Hinata Azai.

Kylian Aimé - member of the Stjarna tribe. Lieutenant commander in the United Tribal Axis Navy. Second in the chain of command under Admiral Freyja Nygaard. Cousin to Tristan Cylien. Expert hacker.

Nazhi Aman - member of the Taaralog tribe. Research Scientist working on the quantum entanglement energy transfer project. Father of Zahra Aman.

Rohaan Dar - member of the Taaralog tribe. Research scientist at Medina Outpost. Dual PhD's in astrophysics and computer science. Specializes in alien technologies and signal decryption. Best friend of Skyla Karsten. Bonded to the AI ship Cista.

Sato Tax - member of the Hoshiko tribe. Lieutenant commander in the United Tribal Axis Navy. Second in the chain of command under Commander Hinata Azai.

Skyla Karsten - member of the Stjarna tribe. Former captain in the United Tribal Axis Navy. Current outlaw archaeologist specializing in salvage of Old World tech. Ace pilot. Bonded to the AI ship Pele.

Sten Magnuson - member of the Stjarna tribe. First counselor to the Empress.

Tristan Cylien - member of the Stjarna tribe. Lieutenant commander in the United Tribal Axis Navy. Third in the chain of command under Admiral Freyja Nygaard. Cousin to Kylian Aimé. Weapons expert.

Wout Verhaert - member of the Verloren tribe,. Chief Petty Officer in the United Tribal Axis Navy. Head Mechanic at Medina Outpost under Commander Hinata Azai. Original pioneer of the UTA settlement effort.

Zahra Aman - member of the Taaralog tribe. Research Scientist working on the quantum entanglement energy transfer project. Daughter of Nazhi Aman. Assistant to Rohaan Dar.

EVENTS

The Exodus - When all of mankind left Earth That Was.

Secchi Conference - annual astrophysics, materials science, and deep space analytics conference held at Medina Outpost.

The Wandering - the ten thousand year period between

when humanity left Earth That Was and the founding of the United Tribal Axis.

Gear

Armored spacesuits - spacesuits with additional armor for space warfare.

Arogelium Armor - armor made of aerogelium. Worn by space station peacekeepers.

Bio Ball - a nutrient rich algae gel used in the repair of bio-ships.

Mechs - armored mechanical battle suites. Small enough for standard UTA vessels to carry, but larger and more heavy armored than armored spacesuits.

Suspensors - a tool that creates the effect of hovering by locally disrupting gravity.

Z-grav Boots - produced a localized gravity field for the wearer.

Places

Aleppo - Black market hub favored by archaeologists.

Amalthea Galaxy - home to the United Tribal Axis central rim.

Central Rim - the solar systems under direct control of the

United Tribal Axis.

Damascus - United Tribal Axis planet.

Fazenda - Perdida tribe moon farming community. Sabotaged by Freyja Nygaard in retaliation for attacks on farming stations owned by the Empress.

Gefion - Capital planet of the United Tribal Axis.

Amaterasu - Hoshiko home world.

Kensho - Hoshiko military academy.

Known Galaxies - the galaxies mapped by the United Tribal axis.

Medina Outpost - Taaralog research station.

Mirmir Academy - Stjarna military academy.

Old World Planets - abandoned planets thought to be colonized by ancient humans who left Earth before the exodus.

The Silk Road - a network of United Tribal Aixs controlled worm hole rings used to unite the Known Galaxies.

Thule - ice planet on the edge of known space.

Trogon - Fenix cartel controlled planet on the outer rim.

Upsala Station - Stjaran space station.

STARSHIP CLASSES

AI bio-ship - fully sentient starship that is a bio-mechanical hybrid. Typically constructed with a coral titanium hybrid hull and other biological integrations, including vast DNA storage and an organic quantum computer. AI bio ships remodel and grow with their human hosts. They share an intense bond with their human hosts.

Corvette - small warship.

Cruiser - large warship.

Frigate - large civilian class ship.

Starfighter Carrier - Largest warship. Made for transporting starfighters.

Star Destroyer - Large warship with the heavyset armaments of any UTA class ship.

Starfighter - single occupant warship.

SENTIENT STARSHIPS

Cista - AI ship bonded to Rohaan Dar.

Pele - AI ship bonded to Skyla Karsten.

Selkie - AI ship bonded to Freyja Nygaard.

Tentei - AI ship bonded to Hinata Azai.

TRIBES

United Tribal Axis - the governing body that united the twelve tribes of humanity.

Tribes ranked by power:

Stjarna

XinXing

Hoshiko

Etoile

Zvezda

Sterkind

Verloren

Taaralog

Perdida

Zirka

Setareh

Pirntirri

WEAPONS

Atomics - explosive utilizing nuclear fission, nuclear fusion or a combination. Outlawed under the UTA.

Plasma Cannons - projectile weapon utilizing plasma discharge.

Railgun - high velocity electromagnetic force weapon used against stardestroyers.

Sonic Riffles - weapon used by peacekeeping units. Can safely be used on space stations and ships without damaging the structures.

Nanite Hand Held Weapons - weapons made of nanite technology that links to a user's neural chip and can transform shape. Includes swords and bō staffs among other hand held weapons.

ASTRONOMICAL TERMS

Parallax - observed change in position of an object due to a change in vantage point by the observer.

Umbra - Latin for "shadow." The part of an eclipse where all light is excluded.

ABOUT THE AUTHOR

Amber Toro is a data scientist at a machine learning startup working to make the world a better place with tech. She is a big believer in using tech for good.

Always dreaming, Amber writes epic sci-fi and fantasy.

Amber grew up in Seattle with a great love of the outdoors. She now calls Utah her home and when she is not writing or coding, you can find her biking, hiking, and camping in the mountains with her amazing partner and two tiny humans, or curled up with a good sci-fi/fantasy book.

Discover more at ambertoro.com or on social media @amberraetoro

ALSO BY AMBER TORO

SENTIENT STARS

Umbra

Parallax

Retrograde—coming soon

AETHER AND BONE

Aether and Bone—coming soon

BALLADS OF BEMOND

Fragments of Perfection

Ashes Fall Like Snow—coming soon